The Island of the Dead

The first she heard was the ripping noise. Violent. Dangerous. Terrifying, because it was a noise she'd never heard before. Not here, not in this place, where people's voices were quiet and deferential and you never heard anything sudden or unregulated. She spun round. In a split second she registered the man wasn't sitting on the bench any more. Christ, he was over there by the wall. And he was transformed. Transformed from a quiet sad old man into a wild beast, twisting and turning like a maniac, arms flailing and stabbing, gouging into something. Gouging into canvas. Ripping into a picture. That picture. The one which had been hanging opposite him. The picture which he'd been staring at all that time. The picture called *The Island of the Dead*.

The Island of the Dead

Philip Hook

CORONET BOOKS
Hodder and Stoughton

British Library Cataloguing in Publication Data

Hook, Philip
Island of the Dead. – New ed
I. Title
823.914 [F]

ISBN 0 340 63532 0

Typeset by Palimpsest Book Production Limited,
Polmont, Stirlingshire
Printed and bound in Great Britain by
Cox and Wyman Ltd, Reading, Berkshire

Hodder and Stoughton
A division of Hodder Headline PLC
338 Euston Road
London NW1 3BH

To Sabine and Louis

1

She hated the uniform. Bloody detested it. The clothes did nothing for her, nothing at all, and it was a shame really, because she still had a good figure and it was a pity to hide it. If you've got it, flaunt it, that was her motto. Always had been ever since she'd first felt the lads' eyes on her as a girl. The skirt just didn't hang right. Poorly cut of course, and made of a cheap green serge that enveloped her hips and thighs like some shapeless sack. She'd still got a waist even after two children but you couldn't have told, not in this uniform. And the light green blouse, that was cheaply put together as well, nylon or some such material. Irritated the skin, didn't it? She wouldn't have been surprised if the blouses weren't the reason why she was getting those flushes more often these days, too. Typical of this mob to dish out such poor quality clothing to the staff. Sodding penny-pinchers.

She sat on the chair and stretched her legs, peering down at her shoes. There had been a lot of trouble over those shoes. She had taken one look at the horrible black lace-ups that had also come as part of the deal and said it out straight, 'You must be joking if you think I'm going to put those things on, I'm not joining the bleeding army.' 'Come on, Maureen, they're regulation, they are,' the supervisor had told her. Brian was a small, balding, worried-looking man who sweated a lot. Fancied her, she could tell from the way he sometimes glanced at her breasts when she left an extra button of her blouse undone, not that she was going to allow him any liberties, not with a beer belly like that on him. She was very particular about the way her men friends looked, and she'd always been able to pick and choose. But equally she wasn't going to be seen dead in those shoes. 'No way, José,' she'd told him. 'Look, this is a security firm not a fashion house,' he'd said, but there had been a nervousness in his tone, an uncertainty. So she'd smiled very sweetly at him and told him that she'd got some black slip-ons of her own which she didn't mind wearing, but she wasn't putting on the lace-ups. He'd gone red and said he'd have to refer it to higher management, but nothing had ever come of it until one day Mr Maggs had come down from head office and said to her, 'Corns better, love?' and she'd realised that was how Brian had swung it for her. Bastard.

She ran her eyes down her black stockinged calves, admiring their shape, then yawned and glanced mechanically round the room. Christ, this job was dull, it was sheer bloody murder. Sometimes she didn't know how she got through the day, she really didn't. Given half the chance she'd jack it all in. But jobs weren't easy to find these days, and you didn't let one go, not even one as boring as this, unless you'd got something definite to take its place. Which she hadn't. And when all was said and done she had completed the training, two weeks out of her life that had been, the company insisted on it, so it would be a pity to see all that time and effort go to waste. Not that it had meant very much. There'd been a course of demonstrations of what they called Techniques of Restraint in which the instructor had executed a series of unlikely looking arm-locks intended to 'incapacitate with a minimum of force with the object of averting danger to persons and property'. Some bloke in spectacles had rabbited on about alarm systems. Another prat had drawn a load of diagrams on a board to illustrate the quickest way to clear a building in an emergency. There had been a lot of arrows pointing in different directions and no one had understood a blinking word of it. Then there had been a bit of First Aid. She'd quite enjoyed that, the First Aid. It had been the best part, really. But none of it seemed particularly relevant to what she'd ended up doing, because what she'd ended up doing was sitting in a bloody room all day just looking at people. Just looking at people looking at pictures.

Security, that was it. She was security. You had to laugh, didn't you? When they'd told her she was going to work in the gallery, her first reaction had been what, the shooting gallery? Then they'd explained. Pictures. Oil paintings. Rembrandt and that. She was to guard them. She was to be part of a group drafted in from the private security firm she worked for to augment the resident team of keepers during the summer season. Some of these bits of old paint and canvas were priceless, weren't they? Insured for millions, and thousands of people a week trooped past to look at them. They needed extra protection, and her company had got the contract to provide that extra protection. 'Crack force, aren't we, love?' Brian had told her. 'We're the professionals, see?' She'd looked at him to check if he was serious. He had been. The daft sod saw himself as some sort of cross between Arnold Schwarzenegger and the SAS. It would have been funny if it hadn't been so pathetic.

She could have told him that the reason they'd got the contract to do this job wasn't because they were so bleeding professional. It was because they were cheap. If the contract had been put out to tender, you could bet their mob would have undercut the competition. It stood to reason, didn't it, when you knew what they paid their staff. With those rates they could afford to set their prices lower than anyone else's. The wages were diabolical, everyone said so. Even Brian. Just so long as he was out of earshot of anyone in authority. He could grouse with the best of them, could Brian. You should have heard him in the canteen for their regulation twenty-minute break at eleven, when they gathered round the Formica-topped table, dragging on the fags they'd been gasping for all morning and muttering into their tea. There'd be Brian, and her, and Robbie, the thin one with the spectacles who never said much. Brian would hold forth about the Common Market and legally enforceable minimum wages and forums for airing legitimate grievances. But it was all talk with him. The moment he was up against Maggs he'd crumple. Yes, sir. No, sir. Pardon me for breathing, sir.

Well, she'd gone into all this art lark with an open mind. She'd heard of Rembrandt when she started, but if anyone had asked her to name the most famous artist in the world she'd have probably said Rolf Harris. Everyone knew him, didn't they? At first she'd been curious about these multi-million-pound pictures, wondered what they'd look like to be worth so much money. Mostly she'd been disappointed. The people in them looked weird. Unreal. Ridiculous. Overweight, some of the women were, particularly the ones you saw dancing about in their birthday suits. Enormous rolls of flesh wobbled all over them, it was disgusting. Horrible great big pink breasts and bums. No man could find those women sexy, could they? Not the men she knew, anyway. Some Saturday nights down the rougher pubs in her area there'd be strippers. Some pretty dodgy women were getting away with baring all under cover of some pretty dodgy lighting, or so she'd heard, but imagine the reaction if the overweight cows from these pictures had come on parading their wares. They'd have been jeered off the stage. They wouldn't have stood a chance, not even at last orders on a good night. Serve 'em right, too.

No, the only paintings that had made an impression on her had been the ones she'd seen that first week in the Dutch seventeenth-century gallery. Now they had been something. Bloody miraculous they were, as good as photographs. You felt you could reach out and touch the satin in some of those dresses, they were that real. Those were true artists, the ones that had done that, she couldn't imagine anything better. But then again, you could only look at them so long, couldn't you? After a while you found you could take them or leave them. Every so often, to break the monotony, she'd get up from her chair and amble slowly round the gallery, jiggling the bunch of keys attached to the belt on her skirt, running her eye yet once more over the pictures. After a few days they got to depress her. She knew them too well. The goofy man standing behind the smug woman in the old Dutch room; the grinning fat bloke in the plumed hat playing a strange-looking guitar. By the end of the second week she never wanted to set eyes on them again, she was that sick of them.

The fourth week she'd been moved into the early Italian room. What's all this? she'd asked Brian. Rotas, he'd told her, we're all on rotas. Keeps the mind fresh, changing environments, you can't afford to get stale in this business. He'd obviously been quoting from some manual, the berk. Can't afford to get stale? That was a joke. From the word go the minutes had seemed like hours. After a day surrounded by the Italian madonnas and children, she'd been screaming to get out. It wasn't just that they were boring. There was also something about them that unsettled her, made her uneasy. She didn't like them, all those ugly babies and simpering saints. They belonged in a church, these pictures. She'd always felt edgy in churches. It was creepy, wasn't it, she'd said to Robbie one morning in the canteen. He'd blinked at her, then shaken his head very slowly and said no, they were very beautiful objects and it was a privilege to work so close to them. He was a bit weird at times, old Robbie.

The only diversion in all this was the public. The punters. The men, women and children who flowed through the rooms every day like a river. At times, lunchtime for instance, there was a surge. Then again in the middle of the afternoon it could slow to a trickle. She'd never realised there were that many foreigners in London. Bleeding tourists, weren't they? Americans in funny-coloured trousers. Earnest Germans with their earphones. Slit-eyed Japanese, hundreds of them in groups, blindly following their tour leaders. What she couldn't get over was what Brian had told her one day, that entrance to this place was free. That seemed all wrong. It stood to reason that these people should be made to pay, coming over here from their own countries and taking advantage, getting to see all this stuff for nothing. It wouldn't make much difference to them, they'd hardly notice it, but think of the amount that would roll in if each of them was made to cough up a couple of quid. Maybe then she'd get to be paid a bit more, too.

Then there were the children, dragged round the galleries by their parents. Why did they do it, for crying out loud? None of them seemed to enjoy it. All the kids wanted to do was get back out into the sunshine and have an ice-cream. There they were, pulling on their mums' and dads' arms, running about, shouting and screaming. Quiet, Emma. No, Alexander, I want you to come over here and look at these Venetian masters. And we haven't seen the Impressionists yet. Toffee-nosed gits. That was one thing she'd never inflicted on her Tina and Lynn, a visit to this place. They wouldn't have thanked her for it. They were nineteen and seventeen now, her two girls, and no angels, in fact they could be a bleeding nightmare to live with. But bringing them here when they'd been young wouldn't have made any difference to the way they'd turned out, she was quite sure of that. Anyone who tried to tell her different was off their trolley.

There was another thing about the public here. They looked past you. As if you weren't there, as if you were part of the furniture, one of the fitments like the fire-extinguisher attached to the wall. She felt affronted by the way none of them seemed to see her. Demeaned, second class. She was still an attractive woman, she knew that. It was the uniform, wasn't it? The uniform was why they didn't look at her. But then she found that normally she didn't notice them, not individually. That was her revenge. Just occasionally one of them spoke to her, asking directions mostly, but sometimes wanting information about the pictures. 'Could you tell me where I could find the Titians?' That was the signal for her to let her features glaze over into an expressionless mask. 'You'll have to ask at the information desk. We're security.' She took pleasure in perplexing them. 'Say, I seem to be lost, where are the Canalettos?' 'We're security. Information desk is at the entrance. Where you came in.'

Robbie, now he was different. She'd noticed an elderly American woman coming up to him once. She'd thought nothing of it, but a couple of minutes later she'd looked back and been amazed to find the two of them still deep in conversation. 'Bellini,' she'd heard him saying, 'the early Venetian master. Yes, you'll find two exceptional examples of his work through in the adjoining room. But my personal favourite is the Carpaccio. You should have a look at that one too.' Dangerous, she called it. As security, you weren't there to have opinions. Showing off, that's what it was. That sort of thing could land you in trouble. But despite herself she'd been impressed. He was a bit of a deep one, that Robbie. Read books and that. Be seeing him on Mastermind next, she shouldn't wonder.

The elderly man pulled the front door closed behind him and blinked distractedly in the sunlight. If he noticed the warmth of the day, it was as an irritant rather than a source of pleasure. He stumbled forward through the front garden to the pavement, and stood for a moment, as if disorientated by the riot of suburban foliage that spilled over the adjoining fences, as if deafened by the drone of the bees buzzing in the flowers. Were these the same lobelias and acanthus bushes that had struck him as so picturesque when he had first set eyes upon them four short days ago? You English, he'd declared, I knew you were a nation of gardeners, but this is extraordinary. Do you all have green fingers? Everyone had laughed, flattered and delighted.

But that was then. He was separated from that time by a gulf so vast as to be incomprehensible. That was before he had sustained the utterly unexpected blow which had precipitated a horrific shock of recognition. Before he'd been reminded of the things he'd hoped he'd never have to confront again.

He turned left, dragging his feet with a laboriousness that spoke less of old age than of an immense preoccupation. After all, he was a fit man for his sixty-nine years. People who knew him at home often complimented him on his spryness. But now he was confused and fearful. And angry, too. He had forgotten what it was like to have the past weigh down so heavily on the present. Forgotten how it felt to be striving to suppress memories rather than to revive them. He was aware that his suit was crumpled, and that he was not wearing a tie. He was aware that he had not shaved that morning. But these omissions were no longer significant. With a gathering certainty, he knew that only one thing counted now. That nothing else mattered. Not so long as he could thrust his perspiring hand into the inside pocket of his jacket and feel the reassurance of the cold steel he found there.

He walked a little faster, then slowed down again. Dear God, what was the hurry? He recognised clearly enough what he had got to do, but that didn't mean he relished it. There were some imperatives you obeyed without alacrity. Things you were driven rather than drawn to. But as it happened there was a bus already there at the bus stop, as if it had been appointed to wait for him. He did not have to break stride to board it, and the conductor set it in motion just as soon as he had lowered himself meditatively into an upstairs seat. He knew this was the bus that would take him where he had to go. He knew it because the whole sequence of the day, since that moment when he had awoken sweating from a tortured sleep, had elapsed with the certain inevitability of a well-worn newsreel. He could no more have extricated himself from the events that were unfolding now than he could have rewritten history.

He was dully aware of a figure looming over him. A figure in a uniform. Suddenly he felt the instinctive fear of officialdom that he thought he'd long since banished from his emotional repertoire. 'Where to, mate?' demanded a voice. It was not unkind, that voice. Impatient, perhaps, but not menacing. He fumbled in his pocket for money, and murmured, 'Please, to the Royal Gallery.' The ticket was issued wordlessly and the conductor clattered back down the stairs. The man settled back. He was discomposed, but not surprised by the encounter. For the past twenty-four hours his life had been a succession of sickening exposures to newly exhumed memories.

In an attempt to control the roller-coaster ride through the past into which he found himself propelled, he cast his mind back to the buses he had taken as a boy. They had not been buses like this one, chugging fitfully through the early afternoon traffic, negotiating the illegally parked Volvos and delivery vans in Putney High Street. They had been trams, clattering over points, ringing their bells in warning as they lurched round corners. He remembered the anticipation of the ending of a long wait as you heard those bells in the distance. He remembered how choked with passengers they became, so that the more intrepid made their journeys clinging precipitously to the footplates outside. He remembered the guilty adrenalin of dodging the ticket inspector when he hadn't paid the fare.

Now there was another sort of adrenalin flowing through his veins. An anxiety. And a determination, too. He was travelling on an unfamiliar bus through the suburbs of an alien city. But here in this strange and sprawling London, as the serried ranks of red-brick terraced houses guided him into its heart, here it had come to him, the realisation that at last his destiny had caught up with him. This was the moment when you shut your ears to the rational, civilised arguments which had hitherto informed your life. This was the moment when you went with your instinct and although it led you into an alien and unfamiliar land, you did what had to be done. His hand sought the inside jacket pocket and his fingers closed around the comforting coldness of what he felt there.

There was no elation. Only a deep, deep sadness.

In the gallery, Maureen glanced at her watch: 2.45. Another half an hour before she was due her afternoon break. She'd never have guessed it, but that cramped and smelly little staff canteen could seem like a bleeding eldorado when you were stuck out here on a two-hour stint. She stretched and yawned, preparing to summon the energy for the inevitable next circuit of the room. She'd moved on from the Italian rooms, thank God. She'd then spent two weeks in French eighteenth century, staring interminably at large portraits of powdered and pampered-looking women. The rich cows had driven her half-mad, they'd looked that pleased with themselves. Beauties? Not in Maureen's opinion, not in a million years.

Now that rota had come to an end, and she was in German nineteenth century. An odd bunch of pictures here. She'd been in amongst them for three days, and still wasn't quite sure what to make of them. She stood up slowly, smoothing the horrible skirt over her thighs, and ambled off to give them the old once-over.

There were two big pictures to start with. Big landscapes with foreigners in fancy costumes dancing in the foreground. According to the labels, they were painted by Germans with daft names, and the paintings were nothing to get excited about. She sighed and looked about her. It was hot outside, 25 degrees people said, and although the gallery was air-conditioned and its humidity carefully controlled, you sensed heat. You could see it on the faces of the visitors. Some of them were sweating: their foreheads glistened in the artificial light. There was an airlessness today. A lethargy.

She dragged her feet on round the room. The soles of her shoes squeaked softly on the polished wooden floor, a familiar and irritating sensation. She paused again, this time in front of a weird little painting of a man on a wintery hill. You could see trees with sharp little branches set against the skyline, and in the distance there was a church with lights coming from it. God only knew what it all meant. She certainly didn't. She looked on the label for the artist's name and found it was by Caspar David Friedrich. Whoever Caspar David Friedrich was when he was at home.

She turned the corner and on the next wall she faced something even weirder. It had an atmosphere, this picture, you had to admit that. It was an odd, upright shape, about thirty inches high. First of all you saw a rocky cliff, where mysterious dark cypresses grew. At the foot of that cliff lapped an inky-black sea. On the shore, steps were cut into the rock, leading up to a darkened doorway. What lay beyond that nightmarish entrance? Was it a prison? Or a tomb? It made the hairs on the back of your neck stand up to peer into it. But when you looked into the foreground, where the mysterious black waves lapped against the edge of the island, you saw something worse. You saw a boat gliding soundlessly round the corner of the cliff, disappearing into the night, rowed by an ancient oarsman. Further down the boat, his passenger stood upright, swathed in white. Like a corpse. The corpse was twisting his head to look back at you. It was then that you realised that his head was only a skull, and he was staring back at you with an eyeless glint of triumph. She shivered. She'd never been much of a one for horror films.

The painter's name was Arnold Böcklin. *The Island of the Dead*, the label said, second version. If that's the second version, then spare us the first, she thought to herself as she slumped back down on her chair. Christ, she felt like a fag.

The closer to the centre of the city the bus penetrated, the slower became its progress. It moved like an unwieldy piece of red flotsam on a sluggish stream, constantly held in eddies where it would lie interminably ensnared before breaking free for a ponderous surge until the next obstruction. The man sat motionless at the window, looking but not seeing. He ran his eye over a succession of little incidents in the street as he passed – a woman walking two large Alsatians, men arguing outside a betting shop, tourists buying ice-cream – but none registered.

He was entranced, utterly absorbed by the importance of the enterprise he was undertaking. He was moving in a different dimension from the people outside. He bore no meaningful relation to them. The sun beat down, bathing them in unreality. He was in another place, far removed from what was going on about him. He was in a place where no one here could touch him. He was in the past.

He hoisted himself leadenly to his feet, and almost like a sleepwalker negotiated the stairs down to the boarding deck. The bus lurched and came to a halt and he stepped gingerly out on to the pavement. He swayed slightly, momentarily disorientated, and he heard the conductor's voice calling, 'All right, mate?' He raised a silent hand to reassure him, and the bus was away again. Yes, he had been a decent man, that conductor. No need to worry about him.

Of course, now he knew where he was. Yesterday he'd made this journey too. Its details returned to him with miraculous clarity. He remembered exactly the three-minute route he must now walk to bring him to the steps of the gallery. Yesterday. As he'd wandered down this road then, idly peering into the shop windows, comparing them with the shop windows back home, he'd been a different man. There had been a lightness to his step, an optimism. Now things were changed. They could never be the same, not after what had happened yesterday afternoon. Without warning, when he'd least been expecting it, the sleeping enemy had been unleashed upon him, attacked him with a ferocity he was quite unprepared for. The enemy had been his memories. He'd fought them, but it had been no good. They had been too strong for him. And so it had come about that he had been taken prisoner by his past.

But he'd thought about it long and hard. All last night he'd moved in a land of shadows and ghosts. And by the morning it had come to him. The ransom that was demanded of him to gain release was suddenly clear.

And he was off to pay it now.

It had been quiet this afternoon. Very quiet. As she looked

about, she could see only two people in the gallery. One was an old woman with a stick, shuffling up to the pictures and balancing precarious spectacles on her nose to read the labels. Batty old crow. The other was a young man in a T-shirt and jeans with close-cropped blond hair. Now he couldn't be English, not looking like that. Probably Scandinavian. Or maybe a Kraut. There seemed to be a lot of Krauts about this summer. Seventeen minutes to go.

As she watched a third figure emerged through the far archway. She glanced at him, looked away, then glanced back. There was something familiar about him. He was in his sixties, with silvery grey hair. He had thin, gaunt features and wore a grey suit over a shirt with a frayed white collar. That was it, now she could place him. He'd been in yesterday. He'd spent quarter of an hour in this room. She'd noticed him then. But why had she noticed him? It was difficult to say exactly. She didn't usually notice people. There must have been something unusual about him. Yes, she could recall it now. It was the way he had looked at the pictures. There was a bench in the centre of the gallery. He'd sat on that and stared at the wall opposite. Really stared at it. Like he didn't want to let it out of his sight. Most people used that bench to rest on, take the weight off their feet. But he'd sat there bolt upright and looked with such concentration that she had wondered for a moment if he was all right. And then, yes that was it, he'd left very suddenly. He'd almost run out of the room, as if he'd just that instant remembered he was late for something very important.

And now he was back. Funny. He looked less spruce than he had done yesterday. More bedraggled. His suit was crumpled and he wasn't wearing a tie as he had been then, although his collar was still buttoned across. Always made a man look strange, that. Incomplete. He walked very slowly to the centre of the almost deserted room. He swayed slightly, then sat down on the central bench. Closer to, she could see he needed a shave. And he was sweating. Sweating like a pig.

The blond boy was bending forward to peer at some detail in the big landscapes. Further on, the old crow was shuffling out now, her spectacles hanging from a chain about her neck, her stick wobbling in her hand. Outside the sun beat down on Trafalgar Square. In the entrance hall, people milled about the information desk, buying postcards from the bookstall. In the staff canteen the kettle was boiling. It was a very airless afternoon.

It was like a car crash when it happened. It was that sudden.

She knew, she'd been in one eight years ago, and it all came back fresh to her. With a car crash you only realise you've been in one afterwards. You don't register anything at the point of impact, you haven't got the time. One minute you're being driven along, day-dreaming like, wondering what you're going to give the kids for their tea. And the next minute it's happened. It only sinks in a moment or two later, in amongst the twisted metal and the broken glass. Then all you can feel is the shock. Empty, sickening shock.

The first she heard was the ripping noise. Violent. Dangerous. Terrifying, because it was a noise she'd never heard before. Not here, not in this place, where people's voices were quiet and deferential and you never heard anything sudden or unregulated. She spun round. In a split second she registered the man wasn't sitting on the bench any more. Christ, he was over there by the wall. And he was transformed. Transformed from a quiet sad old man into a wild beast, twisting and turning like a maniac, arms flailing and stabbing, gouging into something. Gouging into canvas. Ripping into a picture. That picture. The one which had been hanging opposite him. The picture which he'd been staring at all that time. The picture called *The Island of the Dead*.

'Oh my God!' she said.

And then all at once it was over. He let it go. Still half held in its frame the painting disengaged itself from the chain supporting it and fell to the floor, strips of canvas flapping free from its stretcher.

He stood there, breathless, the eight-inch kitchen knife clutched in his hand. Then that too eased out of his grasp and fell to the floor. He made no move to pick it up. He couldn't now. He couldn't because he was crying, and the effort of crying absorbed all his energy, great wracking spasms engulfing his whole body.

An old man like that crying. In his crumpled grey suit and his buttoned-up shirt with the frayed collar. It was the most horrible thing she'd ever seen.

'Oh, my God!' she repeated. And then at last, almost as an afterthought, she reached for the panic button.

In a moment they were all there. Brian. Robbie. Two of the regular keepers.

'Blimey, Maureen, what's been going on here for fuck's sake?' Brian was sweating. Blustering. On the edge of panic.

She couldn't speak. She just gestured towards the wall, where the chain that had been supporting the picture hung loose, still swinging gently. On the ground below lay the debris. The battered frame and the ravaged canvas, lying there. Like a corpse.

'Oh, my Christ, Maureen, what bastard done that?'

Again she couldn't speak. She just nodded in the direction of the old man. At that moment she hated Brian because she knew that all he cared about was whether he was going to get the blame, how he could save his own skin, how it was going to look on his record. All that didn't matter any more, not now. Not by comparison with the pathetic figure standing there weeping with his buttoned-up collar and the eight-inch knife at his feet.

It was Robbie who went up to him. Robbie put an arm round him. Gently. She was grateful to Robbie for doing that. He guided the shaking form down on to the bench and sat next to him for a moment. He didn't say anything. Just sat there, almost protective like. They'd cordoned off the room now, and other keepers were redirecting the public away. Two men released the doors at either end of the room and shut them abruptly, denying any further view to the curious passers-by pausing to peer through into the gallery. The incident was now isolated. Sealed.

'There'll be trouble about this,' said Brian, shaking his head. 'Big trouble. You'll have to make statements, I shouldn't wonder. You'd better get your story together, my girl, and get it together good. Maggs'll be down, too. Maggs'll want to know the score.'

But she wasn't listening to him.

She was watching, aghast. She couldn't take her eyes off the scene: the old boy on the bench, leaning forward with his head in his hands, with Robbie next to him. The hideous tangled mess of canvas and wood and frame on the floor. That knife, still lying there, all alone on the bare polished boards. Her mind was trying to connect them. To make sense of it all.

Another man had come in now. A plump, bespectacled, self-important figure in a pin-striped suit and poncey tie. She recognised him as one of the curators, one of the airy-fairy mob from upstairs. She watched as he adjusted the creases of his trousers and squatted gingerly next to the debris of the picture, peering at it, probing it, nervously nudging a strand of canvas back into place. He positioned himself deliberately with his back to the old man on the bench. It was as if he couldn't bear to let his eyes rest on him, couldn't bear to acknowledge that he even existed. As if he felt that by blocking him out he might magically heal the hideous damage to the picture. Then, when the curator glanced up for a moment, she saw the shock on his face. He was deathly pale, almost like he was going to throw up.

Then two police constables arrived, in shirt-sleeves and peaked caps with radios in their breast pockets. They moved purposefully, striding swiftly over to where the man sat, next to Robbie. Robbie got up awkwardly and edged away. The policemen pushed past him and took the man by either arm. He dragged his feet as they led him towards the door, but they didn't slacken their pace. They handled him less gently than Robbie had. A lot less gently.

'Christ, Maureen,' said Brian later when they were back in the canteen. 'Talk about a nutter. You've been lucky, girl. Lucky he dropped that bloody knife. I can tell you, I wouldn't have fancied disarming a bloke like that myself, and I've done courses in self-defence. Reached advanced level in it, I have.'

She found she couldn't really take in what Brian was saying to her because she was shaking too much. She sat at the familiar Formica-topped table and stared at its surface, trying to compose herself. Trying not to think about it all. In the end it was Robbie who brought her a cup of tea. She drank it gratefully and reached for a cigarette.

'I don't think he was a nutter,' said Robbie carefully.

'Oh, don't you?' countered Brian. 'And what would you know about it, then?' There was a belligerence about him now. He'd been badly scared and he wanted to reassert himself. Wanted someone to pick a fight with him.

But Robbie was not to be drawn. He just shook his head and wandered off to read a paper.

'You take my word for it,' continued Brian. 'That bloke had lost his marbles. Anything could have happened out there. I mean, did you see his face?'

Maureen drew on her cigarette and said nothing. The truth was, she had seen his face. That was what was bothering her most. They had led him out of the door only a couple of feet away from her, the two young coppers hoisting the old man along, almost lifting him off the ground. She watched his face as he went by, couldn't take her eyes off it. She'd never seen such unhappiness. Bleak. Haggard. Muttering strangely. And yet resigned, too. As if what he was suffering now was an ordeal he'd been through before, a nightmare, but a nightmare whose sequence was familiar and had to be borne in silence because experience had taught him that there was no evading it. Some instinct told her that at some other time, in some far-distant place, he'd been led away before. God knew where, God knew by whom. But she knew he was no stranger to incarceration.

2

That afternoon, not much more than quarter of a mile away from the gallery where Maureen had charge of *The Island of the Dead*, Dominic Maitland was attending a memorial service. He had taken his place in church in a mood of obscure dread. Churches were restrictive, uneasy places. He tried to avoid them, except for the very occasional wedding, and weddings in their own way made him uncomfortable too. Churches conjured up grim memories of his schooldays, where chapel had been the constant element in a bleakly undistinguished education. Once every weekday, twice every Sunday. The same lugubrious hymns, the same miserable exhortations to the pursuit of a crabbed and blinkered way of life as at odds with real experience as the school's rural setting in the Somerset hills was remote from the thrilling metropolitanism of London. Nothing could rival for sheer mediocrity the humdrum ordinariness of an English minor public school. And the minor public school to which his despairing mother had consigned him at a tender age had been very ordinary indeed. It was something he'd been trying to distance himself from ever since he'd bid it a grateful farewell some fifteen years before.

His dread had been compounded by a vague apprehension that the memorial service would resemble a funeral. The only funeral he had ever before attended had been a dark and miserable ceremony in the tawdry chapel of a suburban crematorium, where tinny music sped the coffin towards an oddly unmoving combustion and oblivion. But he was wrong. This was different from that other, bitterly cold occasion. Here in the packed church, the atmosphere was oppressive with glamour. There was a curious mixture of perspiration and expensive scent in the air, testimony to the fashionableness of the gathering and the heat of the day. And just a hint of alcohol, too, wafting off those who had recently fortified themselves for the coming ordeal over lunch at White's or Brooks' or Wilton's. There were women in hats and expensive jewellery and men in pin-striped suits and the sort of discreetly garish shirts whose ready availability in nearby Jermyn Street proves that even the best-bred, most traditional Englishman is something of a closet peacock. There was a sleekness, too, about these people. Heads of beautifully brushed hair gleamed along the pews. Well-manicured hands fingered service sheets; signet rings flashed in the sunlight.

As he looked about him, he identified the gathering he had stumbled into, and in giving it a name he tamed it, gained some measure of control over it. This was the English establishment. The English establishment in all its glory. But it was possible to be more precise than that: what one saw here was the English establishment at one of its most intriguing interstices, at that nexus with Bohemia which is the West End art world. A world of odd contrasts, where flamboyance mixes with discretion, and snobbery with connoisseurship; where old taste meets new money, and old money meets new taste. Already the phrases were flapping about his head like loose battens, battens to be positioned and pinned down later with the help of the word processor. Writing about something gave him power over it. That was one of the pleasures of being a journalist.

So. Here was the flower of the London art world. The flower of the London art world gathered to mourn one of its own.

Dominic Maitland, known as Minto to his closer friends, viewed the scene with a mixture of wariness and fascination. He was thirty-two years old, tall and fair-haired. He was not wearing a pin-striped suit. He wasn't even wearing a suit at all. He wore a light summer jacket over a dark blue shirt and, as a concession to the occasion, a tie, but a tie that had certainly not come from Jermyn Street. He felt like an explorer in an exotic jungle, an anthropologist amongst a tribe from an alien culture. What was he doing here at the memorial service of a man he'd never met?

He was here because of Ridley, that was the immediate

reason. Ridley was standing next to him now, wheezing slightly. Ridley was wearing a suit, but it had seen better days and his cuffs were worn as he curled nicotine-stained fingers round the knob on the end of the pew to keep himself upright. Ridley was a hack of the old school. He'd been on the paper twenty-five years, and frankly his days were likely to be numbered. Minto wouldn't have bet on him lasting the year out in his present employment, not with the new management in place now. But for the time being his job was – what was it? – saleroom correspondent. And occasional restaurant reviewer. It was Ridley who'd rung him earlier that morning.

'You still doing that piece on Courtney, old boy?'

Minto had agreed he was. He'd been relieved at the relatively friendly tone of the enquiry. When he'd first broached the matter of the article on Courtney with Ridley, he'd sensed resentment, resentment that a general arts feature writer like Minto was trespassing on Ridley's own specialist territory. But Minto was on the rise, wasn't he? Not stuck in the mud like Ridley, wallowing in an alcoholic haze of missed deadlines and constantly recycled material. And Minto wasn't entirely unversed in the ways of the art world, either. He'd done that interview with Hockney six months ago, that piece that everyone had said was wonderful. Not that Minto had needed telling. He knew it had been good. It was just that Minto was a writer first and an art expert some way lower down the line, so he needed Ridley's help.

'Well, then, you might care to mosey down to St James's Piccadilly with me this afternoon,' Ridley had suggested.

'What's happening there?'

'Small matter of your subject's memorial service. They'll all be present. All the great and good of Bond Street and St James's, all venturing forth from their galleries and salerooms to pay their last respects. Maybe even Lady Thatcher herself. It might give you some background.'

Background. That was what he was after. Here he was, marvelling at the congregation in all its variegated forms of wealth and influence, speculating as to the assets of the most opulent-looking men, undressing with his eyes the more alluring women. He wasn't sure if the former prime minister

was there; but Ridley had pointed out to him the chairmen of
both Sotheby's and Christie's, both standing tall and erect in
rows near the front, as if market share for the year depended
on who held himself with the more military bearing for the full
duration of the service. Then there was the director of the Tate,
the surveyor of the Queen's pictures; even a representative of
the Louvre who had flown over for the occasion, and directors
of the Met and the Getty who were already over in London for
the sales.

'Christ,' muttered Ridley out of the corner of his mouth,
swaying in Minto's direction, 'if a bomb fell on this place now
it would mean the end of the art market.'

Minto laughed. He was thinking about Courtney, wondering.
Seeing all these people gathered together had brought it home
to him. What the man had been. What the power of his myth
was, at least.

The most important art dealer of modern times, people
had said. The man who made the present-day art market
what it is. Shaped it. Minto had been intrigued. Powerful
men were generally interesting subjects, made good copy.
So Minto had decided to probe a bit. He sensed a good piece
waiting to come out of this. Now the guy was dead, people
would talk more freely about him perhaps. The cuttings file
had thrown up a mountain of blandly uncritical material, a
triumph for the PR men. If you believed what you read there,
Courtney had been a cross between a financial genius and a
saint, single-handedly saving pictures for the nation when he
wasn't reporting prodigious profits for his business. Minto
intended to dig deeper. To get to the truth.

He glanced about him again. What was it Frankie had said?
'There's something sexy about money. There's something
even sexier about art. Put the two together and you've got
the ultimate mixture.' Clever girl, Frankie. Maybe a bit too
clever for her own good.

'Courtney's certainly achieved an impressive turn-out,' he
said quietly.

'You know why?' murmured Ridley. His breath was hot
and fetid and Minto suddenly wished he wasn't standing
so close.

'No?'

'They were all frightened of him.'

'Frightened of him?'

Ridley nodded. He had red, flaky skin and bags under his eyes.

'Why were they frightened of him?'

Their whispered conversation was interrupted by the swelling organ chords announcing an imminent hymn.

'Shit,' said Ridley, extracting a none-too-clean handkerchief from his pocket. 'Bloody Jerusalem. Always makes me cry.'

The English certainly sing on these occasions, thought Minto. They really join in. It's the way the upper classes pay their ecclesiastical dues, how they appease their guilt. They know they should have set a better example, been to church more often. Now they're redressing the balance by singing very loudly. Showing they know the words and aren't afraid to declare themselves. Paying easy and ostentatious tribute to Courtney, too, perhaps. The tribute of sheer volume. To the man who'd frightened them.

Five hundred voices had demanded that they be brought bows of burning gold and furnished with arrows of desire. Five hundred voices had assured the world with surging conviction that they would not rest until they had built a new Jerusalem in England's green and pleasant land. And now five hundred sharply suited and highly coutured hindquarters were lowered triumphantly back on to pews in anticipation of the address. A tall thin, balding man ambled with studied languor up the aisle and turned to face the congregation. He placed a pair of gold-rimmed spectacles on his nose, took a page of notes from his pocket, and asked the question which Minto Maitland almost beyond anyone present was anxious to have answered.

'Who was Alexander Courtney?'

Who indeed?

'Alexander Courtney was a loyal friend, a considerate husband and a loving father. He was a businessman of genius, and a connoisseur without peer. But above all, he was quite simply the leading art dealer of his generation.'

Feet shuffled. Somebody coughed. But no one disputed the assertion.

Many times afterwards Minto would reflect on these words, weighing them in the balance, estimating their justness. And, as he discovered new information about his subject, adding other words. Words of his own. Words which might not have been suitable for a memorial service address. But words which would get nearer to the truth about Alexander Courtney.

'Who's this guy?' whispered Minto.

Ridley raised a surprised eyebrow. 'Edward Purchas. Financier. Trustee of all sorts of public galleries. Fully paid-up member of the League of Great and Good. Courtney's oldest friend.'

'Alexander Courtney was born in Austria in 1925,' Purchas was continuing. He had an assured, confident, slightly drawling voice. The sort of voice that was accustomed to addressing shareholders' meetings, to announcing record profits. 'He arrived in this country with his mother as an eleven-year-old in 1936, an exile, a refugee from a land of suffering and of turmoil. But it was always Alex's great strength never to look back unnecessarily, never to dwell in the past, always to go forward positively, and from the moment that he set foot on English soil he grasped the opportunities which this country has always offered to the brave and the talented, whatever their background.'

Minto glanced round at the sea of privileged faces, faces nodding in self-congratulatory agreement with this estimate of their society's tradition of fair-minded tolerance. But what was the truth of it? Perhaps coming to England had indeed been a relief if you were escaping from the Austria of 1936, particularly if you were Jewish. Was Courtney Jewish? Presumably. That was generally the reason why people fled from Austria and Germany at that time. But would Britain during the war years have proved so welcoming, so tolerant, to a German-speaking teenager? Wouldn't there have been ill-informed persecution? Or deep suspicion, at the very least, of both mother and son? Hadn't some aliens been interned for part of the war? At what point had they changed their names, for instance, for surely Alexander had not been born Courtney? Nor indeed Alexander, if it came to that?

These were the hidden questions, the ones on which Purchas

shed no light. The rapidity with which his narrative glided on to the 1950s was significant. Significant of paucity of information, perhaps. And significant not least of the consuming desire for total assimilation as an Englishman of the late Alexander Courtney, Minto wouldn't mind betting.

'In 1957, Alexander lost his mother. In later years he rarely spoke of her, but I know that she was a profound influence on him and that he felt her loss keenly. But, as I have said already, Alexander was never the man to dwell vainly on events that could not be undone. Instead he would seize on them, improvise, use them as catalysts to beneficial change in his own life. Long afterwards he once told me that his mother's death had been a watershed. Once she had gone he decided to branch out, to expand, to give full expression to his business genius. In that way he turned her loss into something from which great good derived.

'Alexander had always been interested in pictures. He used to maintain that he had bought and sold them for as long as he could remember. He once declared in a moment of self-revelation: "Pictures are like a drug to me. But a drug with no unpleasant side-effects." And in 1958 he opened his first gallery in London, specialising in Impressionist pictures and the works of the modern masters. Very soon his consummate taste and his acute business acumen ensured that no collector visiting these shores, be they from New York, from Los Angeles, from Paris, from Zurich, could afford to miss out on his stock. Quite simply, he had an unerring eye for quality. He always bought the best.'

Like a drug. An addiction. Addicted people are weakened people, but there was no evidence of weakness in what he knew so far of the life of Alexander Courtney. It was a curious phrase to use, thought Minto.

'I myself became Alexander's client very early on. Although in those days I had little financial resource –' Purchas paused here to give a little half-laugh at the very notion that he could ever have been short of money – 'I speedily came to realise that saving up to buy one painting a year from Alexander was infinitely better an investment than frittering money away on several cheaper items from other dealers. Others too learned this lesson. There can be few of the world's great collectors or museums who have not benefited from buying from Courtney over the past thirty years.

'In 1959 another important event in Alexander's life took place. He married Cecilia Barrymore, the woman whose love and rock-like support meant so much to him, and was taken so tragically from him when she died, too young, six years ago. In 1960 his son Maximilian was born; and two years later his daughter Isabella. Despite his propensity for working sixteen hours a day, Alexander proved an excellent husband and father. It was a source of deep satisfaction to him when his son followed him into the business which he had so successfully nurtured.'

Minto was six foot two inches. He sat up very straight to try to catch a glimpse of the Courtney children. Maximilian and Isabella. Surely they must be up there, in the front row somewhere. Tight-lipped. Frightened of showing too much emotion. Or too little. Which ones were they? He could not be sure, as he ran his eye along the line of heads inclined towards the speaker. What were they like? Had Maximilian his father's strength and resolve? Sons of successful fathers often found them difficult to come to terms with. What about the daughter? Was she in the business too? And what sort of a woman had their mother Cecilia been? He knew a little about her, because he'd checked with Ridley on their way over.

'Cecilia Courtney? She came from an absolutely top-drawer family and all that,' Ridley had assured him. 'Courtney made a pretty good deal for himself when he married into the Barrymores. Opened a few doors for him, if you know what I mean.'

He thought suddenly of what Frankie had told him last week. 'There you are, Minto. If you want to get on, you should marry a rich wife. Find a nice Sloane Ranger for yourself, get some dogs, settle down in the country.' She'd annoyed him when she'd said that. That might have been Courtney's way forward, but it certainly wasn't his own. Of course she'd been teasing him. But there had also been a half-concealed wistfulness in her tone when she talked about settling down, a wistfulness that had disturbed him. Why couldn't she learn to give him space?

Purchas's address was rolling on. 'During the 1960s Courtney's business continued to expand. He moved into his Bond Street gallery in 1964 and then in 1969 he opened his Manhattan gallery on 57th Street. By the early 1970s he had also developed the old master arm of his operation. This diversity was an illustration of the versatility of his own connoisseurship. More distinguished authorities than I confessed themselves amazed by the way Alexander could move so effortlessly from evaluating the commercial potential of a Monet to distinguishing between a Poussin and Sébastien Bourdon. His range was staggering. Allied to his natural energy and business acumen, the result was irresistible.

'And make no mistake: Alex was a financial genius. Had he gone into the City he would have risen straight to the top, of that I'm quite sure. He had an extraordinary instinct, an ability to position himself in advance of bad times so as to take maximum advantage of the conditions which he saw coming. Without wishing an address such as this to partake in any degree of controversy, I sometimes wonder if Alex had gone into politics whether he wouldn't have made a rather more outstanding Chancellor of the Exchequer than one or two recent occupants of the post.'

There was a polite titter. Was a church the right place for this sort of eulogy, wondered Minto suddenly? This was *Financial Times* stuff, surely. Hadn't Christ thrown the moneymen out of the temple? But Purchas was on again, expounding the relentless catalogue of Courtney success:

'In the eighties Alexander extended his empire to Paris, where he opened a further gallery on the Rue St Honoré, and even to Tokyo, where he started up in 1983. The Courtney name is synonymous worldwide with pictures of the highest quality. That was the measure of his extraordinary achievement, to build up a reputation of ageless supremacy in little more than thirty years. As one other dealer said to me recently, it is hard to remember a time when Courtney wasn't the dominant name in the British art market. It seems as though he's always been there.

'Most of us here who had the privilege of knowing Alexander personally will remember the extraordinary forcefulness of his character. He never suffered fools gladly. One had to be on one's mettle in dealing with him, and people were occasionally upset by his directness. But his conversation was always stimulating, and he could be the most charming of companions. And his tremendous work on behalf of the National Arts Collection Fund was beyond the call of any duty. Through his uniquely energetic fund-raising efforts four major treasures in the past two decades have been saved for the nation. This was one among many reasons why his knighthood in 1985 was so richly deserved, both as a tribute to his personal qualities and his enormous professional achievement.'

He'd reached his apogee in the eighties, of course. He was the archetypal success of the Thatcher years, servicing all the newly made money of the boom times. How apposite that he should have been made Sir Alexander at that juncture. Sir Alexander and Lady Courtney. No doubt the Barrymores had been impressed. The Austrian refugee had finally become English. This wasn't just a study in entrepreneurial success. This was a story about the English class system too.

And they were all frightened of him.

Another hymn followed, 'The Day Thou Gavest, Lord is Ended'. As the last verse rose to a crescendo, Minto relived an endless sequence of Sunday evening chapels, glimpsed an infinity of melancholy. Ridley fumbled with his handkerchief and blew his nose loudly. The priest gave the blessing then melted into his vestry. The tribute was over. For a moment everyone stood in a state of indecision, a suspended animation that lasted for no more than a second. Then, like a dam breaking, the congregation began to surge out into the sunshine of Jermyn Street, gathering in knots of discreet conviviality which caused the flow of other people to eddy and swirl about them down the aisles, through the porch and on to the pavement. The organ rang out in honour of Sir Alexander Courtney. A Bach cantata. Beautiful; but music of a curiously dispassionate beauty, ultimately unrevealing about the man whose life its playing was to celebrate.

Then again, what could one expect to gather about a human

being one had never met simply by attending his memorial service? Minto felt a sudden sense of exclusion. It was like listening to the meaningless hilarities of people reminiscing about a party to which you hadn't been invited.

Minto stood for a moment in the open air, curious but oddly dissatisfied. And in the distance he caught the faint sound of a police car's siren. A police car's siren crying like a wounded animal as it accelerated down a crowded shopping street.

'What now?' said Minto.

'Must get back to the office,' muttered Ridley, blinking bloodshot eyes in the bright sunshine. 'Got a few telephone calls to make.'

'But isn't there some sort of do afterwards? Don't we all go on somewhere for a little hospitality?'

'Some may.' Ridley frowned doubtfully. He had long, unkempt grey hair brushed back from his collar. And dandruff. He looked like an unsuccessful bookmaker.

'Well, let's follow on then. This could be interesting. I can tell you, I feel like a drink.'

Ridley's ears pricked up. 'I suppose we could just take a quick one off them. It's probably at Courtney's, in the gallery. It's as big as the Albert Hall in there.'

As they followed the elegant assembly which straggled towards the tented, commissionaired doorway of Courtney's, Minto said: 'So who knows where the bodies are buried?'

'Come again, old boy?'

'Where the bodies are buried. Where's the dirt on this man? Look, I realise I haven't got your many years' experience of covering the salerooms, but I know one thing: you don't get to Courtney's eminence in a field like the art market without getting your hands dirty somewhere along the line.'

Ridley shot a glance at him. Just fleetingly Minto saw in it something more than the embarrassment of taking an uninvited drink from a rich and powerful man. He saw fear. 'I can't help you there,' said Ridley quietly.

'Yes, but who can?'

Ridley didn't answer. Whether it was because he didn't wish to or because he was preoccupied by gaining entrance to Courtney's wasn't clear. By the time they were standing in the main gallery clutching glasses of champagne it was difficult to raise the matter again.

Minto looked about him. It was a very large room indeed, and the walls were hung with an elegant red brocade as a backdrop to various expensive-looking pictures. Was that a Degas pastel over there? Even in this large gallery there was a crush. The volume of sound had increased too. If you stood still and listened the voices were like a gathering wind in the branches of a forest, or the swell of the sea; the noise surged and lulled with a separate life of its own. The memorial service congregation of ten minutes ago was in the process of converting itself into a cocktail party.

He noticed her, standing alone and disconsolate with her back to the wall next to a long grey landscape. He watched her for a while, and concluded that her solitariness was of her own choosing. People came up to her, even exchanged kisses with her, then drifted on apparently discouraged by her aloofness. She was dressed in elegant black, with a simple white silk blouse. Her hair was cut short, and she had a high-bred, at first sight almost equine face with strongly flared nostrils. It was her arrogance which caught his interest. This was a spoilt bitch, thought Minto, who liked to classify people, and enjoyed stereotypes. This is the original rich, spoilt woman. After a minute or two, in default of anything more diverting, he decided to go and look at the landscape.

It was by Corot. There was a lake, framed by trees, enveloped in a milky light. It was a dull picture, impossible to rest your eyes on for long. Finally he looked across at her and said, as he'd heard others saying, 'A beautiful service, wasn't it?'

She shrugged. 'I suppose so. If you like Bach.' She said it with a very clear, very English diction, but she looked away from him as she spoke. It was hard to catch her eyes because they did not meet his. All he was aware of was long-lashed lids. Was she very shy? Or very bored?

'Don't you like Bach?'

'Not particularly. I've had a surfeit of Bach in my time.'

'Why?'

'I suppose because Bach and my husband enjoy rather a special relationship.' She gave a wintery little laugh as if recounting a particularly sordid infidelity, committed by someone barely known to her.

'In what way special?'

'Bach's his favourite composer.'

'So is your husband a musician?'

'He's a concert pianist.'

'How fascinating.'

Now she looked at him properly for the first time. Looked at him scornfully, pausing long enough for the vacuousness of his reply to sink in. 'Do you think so?'

He laughed to cover his confusion. 'Well, I take the view that it's probably more interesting to be a concert pianist than an investment analyst.'

'And what about being married to a concert pianist?'

'The same would apply, all things being equal.'

'Who said anything about all things being equal?' She spat the words out with an unexpected bitterness.

Minto paused, uncertain how to go on. He was taken aback by her abruptness and yet at the same time intrigued by her.

'Where is your husband now?' he said at last.

'He's touring. Prague, Brussels, I don't know.'

'I suppose he travels a lot.'

'The whole time.'

'And are you a musician yourself?'

A new emotion crossed her eyes. Fleetingly. Perhaps it was impatience. Or perhaps it was something else. Something more like envy. 'I like music, if that's what you mean. But I'm no good at it. I don't play an instrument.'

'No, nor do I.'

But she wasn't looking in his direction any more. She had the capacity to turn off her interest like a tap. It was disconcerting. No, thought Minto, it was more than that. It was rude.

'I'm sorry,' he said, trying once again, 'we haven't been introduced. I'm Dominic Maitland.'

'How do you do.'

He asked casually, 'And were you an old friend of Alexander Courtney?'

She gave a little laugh. 'I suppose you could say I knew him quite well. At one point.'

It was a statement which simultaneously invited and prohibited further questioning. Minto watched her, playing with her ring as she spoke, then fingering the buttons on her sleeve.

'And Maximilian, his son, who's taken over the business? I've never actually met him. Which one is he?'

'Max?' She wheeled round, searching distant faces. 'He's somewhere around, I saw him just now. Yes, there he is. Over by the Renoir in the corner.'

Minto followed her gaze to the stocky, dark figure she indicated. He seemed to be upset about something. He was talking sharply to another man, beating his fist into his palm to emphasise his displeasure. Even at this distance, Minto could sense the aggression emanating from him, the exploding frustration. The other man was older and taller, with a greying head. He leant forward solicitously as he listened to Max's furious effusions. Only now did you realise that he was a counsellor rather than the object of Max's fury, an ally rather than an enemy. He reached across and laid a restraining arm on Max's shoulder. A thin smile played about his lips as he did so, a smile directed not at Max, but seemingly prompted by some private memory, some suddenly perceived irony. Max immediately went quiet and scowled. It was an oddly charged vignette, one that stayed with Minto as he tried to fathom its significance.

'Poor Max,' said the woman unexpectedly.

'Why do you say that?'

'I suppose because he inherited the worst of his father's temper and not the least vestige of his charm.' And she smiled at Minto for the first time, as if the statement represented the solution to a problem which had long been bothering her.

Minto nodded. He was trying to think what it was about the exchange he had just witnessed at a distance that he found disquieting. In his anger Max was unprepossessing, did not inspire sympathy or trust. But perhaps it was the other man who was the more disturbing. Max might be a blusterer and a bully, but there was something furtive, something calculating, something more dangerous about his companion. It was the way he had silenced Max with a gesture simultaneously insinuating and authoritative. You're the boss, it seemed to say; but I'm the one that really wields the power. Minto asked, 'Who's that Max is talking to?'

'That's Winter, of course.'

'Winter?'

'You don't know Winter? He was the right-hand man of . . . of Alexander Courtney.'

'What, he works here in the gallery?'

'That's right.' She looked at him, suddenly suspicious of his ignorance. 'I thought everyone knew Winter. He's supposed to be very clever.'

Winter. Minto filed him away for future reference. Now he decided to change tack. 'What about the daughter?' he asked.

'Isabella?' The woman paused. 'What about her?'

'Which one is she?'

She made a casual circuit of the room with her eyes. 'I can't see her.' She shrugged again. 'She must be here somewhere.'

'But she was in church?'

'Of course she was in church.' For a moment there was an edge to her voice. 'It was her own father's memorial service, for God's sake.'

Minto decided to put his cards on the table. Conversation with this woman was so erratic and unpredictable anyway that it would not make things any worse to tell her the truth about his presence there. And it might just help a little. 'You see, I've been commissioned to write an article about Alexander Courtney,' he said carefully. 'I am trying to get as much background as possible on him. Do you have any ideas about who I should talk to?'

She looked at him for a moment with eyebrows raised, as if he might be joking. Finally she said, with barely enough levity to prevent the remark being insulting, 'I make it a rule never to talk to journalists, I'm afraid.' Then she smiled briefly at him and drifted away.

Stupid cow, thought Minto with a sudden violence. Stupid, posturing cow. Spoiled silly, blowing hot and cold. He could do without women like that.

* * *

A little later Minto tired of wandering between the braying groups of guests. Perhaps he could have stayed among them and ingratiated himself with one or two more of the expensive-looking women, made his number with the cosy coterie of men of power and influence gathered here together. But he felt disinclined to expend the energy, depressed by his encounter with the woman in black, the concert pianist's wife. These people annoyed him. They annoyed him because, since they did not know him, they took him therefore to be of no account. They were hermetically sealed in their rarefied little world, and assumed it to be the centre of the universe. He wanted to tell them they were an absurd irrelevance, with their titles and their old master pictures and their ridiculous pretensions, that the real world was out there on the streets. That he was much more real than any of them.

But then again, it wasn't just that, was it? It was the question of Courtney, too. Courtney was perplexing him. He wanted to get beneath the surface of things, scrape away the gilt on these immaculate-looking frames and reach the woodworm. His curiosity was aroused: now he was here on the premises, at the heart of the man's empire, he wanted to probe further. He sensed an opportunity that might not present itself again. So when he noticed a door in the corner of the cavernous gallery, a door which opened as he turned the handle, he pushed through it and closed it gently behind him. If anyone stopped him, he could always say he was looking for the lavatory.

He was in a darker passage hung with more pictures. He passed two that looked familiar. Were they by Vuillard? Or perhaps by Bonnard? They were good, anyway. It was quieter here, and the noise of partying was dimmed behind him. He came to another door, ajar this time, and he ducked quickly through it into a silent room with a heavily draped window and three beautiful eighteenth-century chairs drawn up facing an easel. Presumably this was a private viewing room. The sort of discreet, sequestered enclave where Alexander Courtney once performed his most effective sales pitch. The atmosphere here was half-way between an enormously tasteful bordello and an interrogation chamber. Minto paused for a moment, wondering what it had been like to be sold a picture by Alexander

Courtney. Would it have been an irresistible experience? As you wrote out your cheque for tens of thousands of pounds to acquire the consummate little Matisse drawing you hadn't up till now realised you couldn't live without, did you feel bullied or ravished, exploited or exalted?

His vague intimations of unease in these surroundings gradually crystallised into a more specific sensation. A sensation that he was being watched. He turned round and suddenly caught sight of what was disturbing him. On a table against the wall stood a single silver-framed photograph. A photograph of extraordinary power. It showed a middle-aged man with a fine head of light-coloured hair and a hard, intelligent, confident face. He had unforgettable eyes: relentlessly penetrating, and ultimately unyielding.

Minto took the photograph into his hands and recognised beyond doubt that he was staring at the late Alexander Courtney. The man who built an empire and shaped the modern art market. The man who frightened people.

And then he was aware of someone at his side, and a woman's voice was saying, 'So you've found him, have you?'

'Hello, again,' said Minto. She looked different, now she was on her own away from the mêlée in the gallery, no longer leaning disconsolately against the wall next to the Corot. You still noticed the flare of her nostrils and the smoothness of her skin. But she was more vivid here, momentarily more accessible. Minto suddenly realised how beautiful she was.

'Do you generally walk into other people's private offices and poke around with their things?' she demanded.

Minto was about to trot out his story of the elusive lavatory but changed his mind. Instead he said, 'No more than you do.'

'That's where you're wrong.' She spoke softly, but there was a note of triumph in her voice. As if he had just fallen into a very carefully laid trap.

'Why is it not OK for me to wander into this room and look at this photograph, but perfectly acceptable for you to?'

'Because that photograph happens to be of my father.'

Because it was an unfamiliar emotion, the embarrassment

almost overwhelmed him. For a moment he couldn't speak, then he swallowed. 'Christ! You. You're Isabella.'

'Isabella Maurbach. Née Courtney.' She spoke the names with a sort of mirthless irony.

'But why didn't you say?'

She considered him carefully, weighing her words. Finally she said, 'Maybe because I like to travel incognito. And maybe because I enjoy playing games.'

And maybe, he thought suddenly to himself, because there's something in her past about her connection with her father that she wishes to deny.

For a moment he registered the intimacy of their situation, was aware of an almost intolerable closeness. Two people alone in a room. In a dangerous seclusion. Two people peering at the same photograph, joined by the same activity. Perhaps she sensed it too, because as he laid down the photograph on the table, she took a step backwards from him.

'OK,' he said, partially recovering and needing to reassert himself, 'I'm glad you've enjoyed your game. If it gives you any satisfaction, you won it hands down. I never suspected for a moment who you were, you deceived me completely. But perhaps now we've got this far you can help me. Perhaps you can tell me just a little bit about your father. For my article.'

She was growing distant again. He could feel her retreating from him. 'You should ask my brother about that,' she said. 'He's the one who's worked with him. He's the one who knows the business.' Was there a hint of bitterness as she spoke, a suggestion of resentment?

'I will ask him, of course.' He thought back to the stocky, black-haired figure, florid with anger, and he felt discouraged, so he went on: 'But I think there are some things I may learn better from you. Some things he can't tell me.'

'And why should I tell you what you want to know?'

'Because after what happened this afternoon, perhaps you owe it to me?' He knew as he was speaking that it was the wrong answer, that he'd struck the wrong note.

She snapped back, 'I owe nothing to anyone.' The tap had been switched off again. Abruptly. Mercilessly.

Minto was no more used to apologising than he was to

embarrassment, but he did so now. 'I'm sorry,' he said. 'I expressed myself badly. Of course you don't owe me anything.'

She was silent for a moment, then looked up at him. Suddenly she looked very tired. 'I'm sorry, too,' she said. 'Forget it. Maybe I'm just a little emotional after the service.'

'Of course.'

She stood, anxiously fingering the buttons on the cuff of her sleeve. She hadn't finished yet. For a moment he thought, my God, part of her really does want to tell me something, to give me some help. He wondered why; but he wasn't entirely surprised when he heard her say, 'I suppose I shouldn't tell you this, but if you want to know more about my father's early years as a dealer, there is one person you could look up.'

'Who's that?'

'Do you know a man called Theo Denton?'

Minto shook his head. 'Who's he?'

'My father's partner for a year or two in the sixties and early seventies.'

'I didn't know he had a partner then.'

'Not many people remember it. I certainly don't, it was before my time. But the two of them worked together for a while. Why don't you go and see Theo Denton? Only for God's sake don't say I sent you.' For a moment she was unexpectedly submissive. She gave him a little forlorn smile, as if to say, there, see what I've done for you. See what you've wormed out of me. Minto remembered the look. Remembered it on Frankie's face, the first time he'd made love to her, three months ago. Look what you've persuaded me into, it said. Quite touching, really. Or it would have been, if it wasn't for the lingering suspicion of some sort of calculation behind it all. Some sort of ulterior motive.

'I must go now,' she said, looking at her watch. 'I've got to catch a plane.'

'Where are you going?'

'Back to Munich.'

She held her hand out to him and he shook it, distracted, disturbed by something he couldn't at once define. 'Munich: is that where you live?'

She nodded.

For a moment he didn't want her to go. He did not want to be separated from her, for all her anger and her rudeness. Or perhaps because of it.

'When can I see you again? For help, I mean, if I need it. On the article.'

'I've no plans to come back to London,' she told him. 'I've had enough of this place.'

'Have you a number in Munich where I can ring you, at least?'

She looked at him dubiously, then relented and handed him a card from her bag. 'But I'm away a lot,' she added, as a final gesture of defiance.

And then she left him. Left him, standing in the inner sanctum of Alexander Courtney's London headquarters, with the easel and the chairs and the photograph. Left him there wondering.

Minto re-emerged into the throng in the gallery. A few yards away, he noticed Ridley, who had clearly drunk more than was good for him, recounting a story involving condoms and a quarter pound of humbugs to a bemused and uneasy audience of very grand ladies. His rat-like face was suffused with colour and he was perspiring freely. Minto edged round them unnoticed and made for the door.

As he stepped back out into the sunlight, he heard a police siren again, coming from the direction of the Royal Gallery. But at the time he thought nothing of it. Nothing of it at all.

3

It was beautiful, that light which filtered into the bare cell from high above his head. It was beautiful light because it was natural light. It came from the sun. It was his lifeline. Thomas Donat felt a surge of gratitude for the window, up close to the ceiling and heavily barred across, no more than a grille really, but retaining for him that all-important visible contact with the outside world. He lay on the bed and contemplated it, really concentrating his attention on it. This was an old technique, but miraculously it was coming back to him again now that he needed it, the technique of turning your back on the chasm of horror that threatened you by isolating one small positive feature in your immediate surroundings and working it up into such a mountain of significance that it obliterated everything else. He had sunlight. That was all he needed to know.

There had been other cells, far, far worse places than this one, places that he shuddered to remember, where the only light had been artificial, where the single bulb had glared down on you incessantly in the tiny space to which you were confined, twenty-four hours a day, so that you no longer knew what the time was, whether it was noon or midnight, Tuesday or Sunday, March or September. Everything was lost in that appalling continuum, all contact with reality; you were thrown in so totally upon yourself that even the sense of your own identity was threatened. Madness stared at you; you needed not just strength of mind but a constant spirit of mental invention to survive. That's where he'd acquired them, these techniques. These ways of coping. These ways of dealing with things too horrible to negotiate head-on.

Somewhere, beyond, lay the horrors. Somewhere not so far away, perhaps. But the important thing was that he had cut them off now, confined them to a carefully restricted area of his mind, achieved for them a temporary oblivion. He knew that something very terrible had happened to him not long ago. There had been a kitchen knife that he had held in his hand in a picture gallery, a kitchen knife with which he had committed an act of violence, resulting in his personal restraint and imprisonment in this cell. But he knew he could survive so long as he did not dwell on those matters, did not try to account for them, did not try to connect them with the events of the past and risk another reawakening of the things he thought he had forgotten. So long as he lay here and looked at the sunlight, he was going to be all right.

He felt sleepy now. That was a good sign. He let his mind drift a little. Not too far, but a little. He ran a hand across his throat, and felt the collar of his shirt. The button eased under the pressure of his finger and thumb, then he let his hand drop back to his side. He had no tie on. No tie.

She had said it once, long ago. He was called Tamás then. Another name, another place, and therefore another person. At least so he had assumed. Until yesterday, when something had happened to rejoin him to Tamás. To re-enter his previous life.

'Tamás, you are not wearing a tie.' She wasn't shy normally, quite the reverse, but now she was smiling up at him a little diffidently. 'I have never seen you before without your tie.'

It was hot, extraordinarily hot that day. He remembered it all with a sudden burning immediacy, in far greater clarity than he could recall the events even of last week. There was a special sort of Middle European heat in summer, something to do with the land mass, all that vast expanse of baking terrain that separated you in every direction from the sea. It built up, after a succession of warm days, turning the city into an oven, an unending passage of sweltering pavements and melting tarmac, a network of heat-conducting tramlines, from which you yearned to escape in order to breathe fresh air. And now that escape had come. It was Sunday. They had met at ten, at the quayside, and boarded the pleasure steamer for the trip up the river. To be surrounded by the water of the river as the craft chugged its lazy progress towards the

Danube Bend, to be cut off from the parched dry land, was a relief both mentally and physically, an emancipation. He felt elated, relaxed.

'It's because I'm free,' he said. 'It's a symbol. No tie, no shackles.' He plucked at the loose, short-sleeved shirt he was wearing open at the neck to show her what he meant.

'And when I see you in your jacket and tie, then you are shackled?'

'More than I am now, yes. But look, the sky is blue, the world is beautiful, I have a lovely companion for my river trip. Let's not talk about shackles.'

'No,' she said, suddenly thoughtful again. 'Let's not talk about shackles.'

At once he wished he hadn't said it, hadn't drawn attention to the word. He hardly knew her, of course, and it was always a delicate matter to strike the right note at this early stage with a woman. Particularly with her, when their relationship was so ambiguous. What were they doing here together, he asked himself? How had he dared to invite her? By what miracle had she agreed to come? It was still a mystery, tantalising, pregnant with possibilities. He looked across at her, sitting opposite him on the seats next to the rail. She was peering down at the wash of the water along the side of the boat. Her blonde hair was drawn back from her forehead; in profile he was aware of the elegant line of her neck, and of the smoothness of her skin. She wore a simple cotton dress which hugged her waist and clung in suddenly sensuous undulations about the curves of her body as it was caught by the gentle breeze out here on deck. There was a gap between her two front teeth which he found almost irresistible.

It had been tactless of him to talk about shackles. Ill-judged, considering she was another man's wife. He had unwittingly forced them both to confront an issue that would have been better glossed over at this stage. For a moment he was tongue-tied, uncertain how to proceed, fearful that he had done irreparable damage to something very fragile. They sat in silence watching the little houses pass by on the far bank. The boat chugged lazily by a ramshackle landing stage from which children were bathing, splashing and shouting excitedly. A little further on a line of fishermen, immobile in the heat, sat in almost religious meditation.

Finally she spoke again: 'You have never told me really what you do. What is your job, Tamás?'

'Me? I do several things.'

'Such as?'

'I like to think of myself as a writer.'

'Yes, you have told me that already, but what do you write?'

'I am a writer in different ways,' he said. 'Sometimes I'm a writer for newspapers and magazines. I write for the *Szabad Nép*. Reviews of theatres, and of books, that sort of stuff. And then I try to write other more private things, things for myself. Poetry, for instance.'

She nodded. 'That is good, Tamás,' she said. 'A writer. A poet. You are lucky.'

Thomas paused. He knew he was lucky. He was lucky because as a writer he had power. Power to influence people, to change people's minds. To tell them the truth. But first he must establish exactly what that truth was. That was the question preoccupying him at the moment. Did he want to tell her all this now? 'Why do you say I'm lucky?' he asked.

'Because if you are a writer you must have a romantic spirit.'

'And that is good?'

'Wonderful,' she giggled, rolling her eyes in mock admiration.

He looked at her and wondered. Am I too serious for her? Have I her lightness of touch? On the surface of the water he watched a dragonfly dart back and forth in the glinting sun. That was her. By comparison he moved like some lugubrious fish, whose natural habitat was the shadowy depths.

'Maybe,' he laughed.

'And what else do you do?' she persisted.

'Well, I am a teacher too. A teacher of literature in the arts faculty at Budapest University.'

'A teacher,' she repeated. The idea seemed to amuse her. 'So you can teach me things.'

'It depends, what do you want to learn?'

'I want to learn everything you have to teach me.'

In some ways she's a child, he thought. She was twenty-five, she had told him, five years younger than he was. But then again, in other ways she seemed older, more experienced. Capable of dominating him by her sheer vivacity. He asked her, 'Was that why you agreed to come with me today?'

'Perhaps.' She looked away for a moment.

'I was worried that you wouldn't turn up. That you'd think better of it. I felt I had been too forward in suggesting it.'

After all, how many times had they met before today? Not more than three. And each time he'd gathered strength to be a degree more forward than the last. The first occasion had been only ten days ago, when he'd encountered her by chance in the bar of the Astoria Hotel. It was an old-fashioned place, that bar, full of dark wooden panelling and red velvet curtains. He liked the atmosphere there, perhaps because he had always had a dangerous preoccupation with the past. He was fond of going there in the early evening, after lecturing, or if he knew he had an article to do. It unwound him, or set him in the right spirit for writing. The place was unusually crowded that day, and the only spare seat was at a table occupied by two young women. They had politely indicated their willingness to allow him to sit down, then continued their conversation. He'd watched her surreptitiously, admiring her looks, her blonde hair and her tanned skin. And the gap in her fine white teeth. Her friend, nondescript by comparison, had left in a hurry soon after, and she had made to follow in a more leisurely fashion, reaching down to gather up her bag from the floor. Perhaps it had been the sight of her graceful, long brown arms extending from her thin white blouse that had captivated him. He'd said it then, almost surprising himself with his daring: 'Won't you let me buy you one drink before you go? It would be a crime to sit opposite the most beautiful woman in all Budapest and not to offer her that one small tribute.' She sat up again, surprised to hear herself addressed at all, let alone in such flowery and old-fashioned language, then smiled back at him, taking his compliment as a bit of foolery: 'Since you ask so nicely, then why not?'

'Permit me to introduce myself: Tamás Donat.'

'Greta Kassák.' Greta. So that name had entered into his consciousness. Passed into the mythology of his imagination.

They'd talked, inconsequentially, of the heat, of the pleasures of the Astoria, of a film she'd been to see that previous week. Talked, on that tantalising edge of flirtation that can mean anything or nothing. After little more than quarter of an hour she had got up and said she had to go. 'My husband will expect his dinner. He is not happy to be kept waiting.' She'd paused, perhaps reading the disappointment in his face, then asked teasingly, 'Won't you be going back to your wife's cooking too?'

'No. Not back to a wife. I regret that I am a member of a dying and unhappy breed.'

'What breed is that?'

'A threatened species. The bachelor.'

She'd laughed. 'Not such an unhappy species, I think.' And she had gone.

What had it all amounted to? Depressingly little, he'd supposed at the time. It had been a pleasantly meaningless way for a housewife to pass a spare fifteen minutes on her way home. But, God in heaven, she'd been beautiful. And almost unconsciously his routine had changed that week, so that he found himself haunting the Astoria bar between six and seven o'clock in the evenings after work, at exactly the time he had originally met her, in the faint and ridiculous hope that he could repeat the encounter. And on the Monday, five days later, he had succeeded. He'd been sitting there, at a table for two, nursing his beer and wondering whether to indulge in the extravagance of another drink or to give up for the day when she'd come in again, on her own. She'd looked about her uncertainly; he half rose and waved to her; then she caught his eye, and smiled her unforgettable smile, the one that revealed the gap between her two front teeth. She'd come over and joined him.

'You again?' she'd said. 'This is a surprise.' But some instinct within him told him that it wasn't, not really. That what he'd seen on her face when she'd recognised him had been not amazement but relief.

This time she'd stayed for half an hour before making to leave.

'Your husband's dinner time?' he'd enquired.

She'd nodded with mock solemnity, as if to indicate a heavy sense of duty.

As she went he said, 'It would be wonderful to see you again, you know. One evening later in the week, perhaps? I can be here any time from six.'

He'd waited in an agony of uncertainty as to her reaction. But she had murmured quietly, in little more than a whisper, 'Shall we say Thursday?'

And then on Thursday when she had appeared once more, he'd made this assignation. Of course he would never have suggested it if she had not casually mentioned that her husband, who worked for the government, had to go away for a few days to visit officials in the town of Győr. But then the idea had come to him irresistibly. The weather was set fair, would only get hotter. What could be more marvellous than to take a trip with her up the Danube, to get out of this airless city for a day on the river? But even then he'd found it difficult to make the final move, to articulate the invitation. He'd sensed that what he was proposing represented an immeasurably bolder step than their occasional apparently innocent half-hours in the Astoria bar. It would take their relationship on to a different plane, setting out together to a joint destination, arranging to spend a whole day in each other's company. And yet he suddenly realised that he had never wanted anything so much in his life, that he had to ask her, that he might die if he didn't, and so there in the Astoria he had suggested it to her, and she, momentarily nervous, even blushing, had looked away from him as if embarrassed by her own shamelessness and agreed.

Now, here on the deck of the steamer on this boiling morning when the heat shimmered off the water in the distance, she said, 'Yes, you were forward. But only because I let you be.'

The boat was crowded and he felt constrained by the proximity of other people. Awkward, self-conscious, anxious to be free of them. At last they tied up at Szentendre, where many of the passengers disembarked, giggling, shouting and whistling as they spilled into the streets of the ancient town, milling round the café and jostling for tables. Thomas watched them go with a sense of elation. Szentendre was a beauty spot, decked out to attract the tripper. It had lost its innocence. It wasn't what he wanted.

'Shall we get off here?' she asked him.

'No, wait. It is better further on.'

'Where are you taking me?' There was a note of mock apprehension in her tone which suddenly made him very excited.

'The next stop is a much smaller place. Only a village. It will be much more peaceful there, I promise you.'

'How do you know these things?'

'My father brought me here, when I was a boy. We came here three or four times. It was before the war, it must be seventeen, eighteen years ago.'

Only a handful of other people got off with them, a group of determined hikers with floppy hats shielding their heads from the glare of the sun. They strode off into the wooded hinterland, leaving Thomas and Greta alone in the somnolent heat. She blinked, looking about her at the low-slung village houses, at the window-boxes, as if trying to make sense of her surroundings, to adjust herself to unknown territory. He paused and held out his hand to her. What am I doing, he asked himself again? What am I doing luring this beautiful creature of the city into such an unfamiliar world? Perhaps she doesn't understand these country things. Perhaps she's only really at home in the bar of the Astoria.

She took his hand and held it for a moment. 'So you have happy memories of this place?' she asked.

'Yes,' he said, 'yes, I do. I always loved it here. It was always so pretty. Let's go and find the inn.'

He led her round the corner into the sleepy square where he remembered stopping as a boy to drink from the pump. And then he halted, distressed. Disorientated, for a moment uncertain if he had even come to the right place.

The pump had gone. In its place stood a massive, harshly outlined construction of blackened granite. An alien abomination in the midst of these gentle village houses whose contours melded into those of the landscape itself. Moving closer, he recognised what it was. A monument. A military memorial to the fallen Soviet soldiers who had 'freed' Hungary in 1945. Erected by the liberators rather than the liberated.

He stood for a moment, horrified by its incongruity. Remembering how the village had looked the last time he'd seen it. Recalling its innocence. And his own innocence, too. Before all this.

'What are you thinking?' she asked him.

'I am sorry, but I am thinking that this object is a total monstrosity.' He was angry. 'I wish you could have seen this square before.'

'Before what?' She moved closer to him and took his arm. In sympathy, or restraint?

For a moment he could not decide how candidly he should answer her. Then he looked at the blue of the sky, at the blondeness of her hair, at the smoothness of her skin and replied slowly, with great deliberation: 'Before the party came to power. Before we began to live our lives in strait-jackets. When our country was free of outside domination.'

There. He'd done it now. Exposed himself to her. He'd said the things that it was dangerous to say too soon.

But then again, everything was dangerous. It was dangerous to be walking through the sunlight holding the hand of a woman he had only met ten days before, the hand of a woman who was married to another man. It was a dangerous seclusion to which he was enticing her in this deserted village. The very beauty of the day, the loveliness of the landscape, they were dangerous too. And then there were the other, more perilous things, the things he was telling her now, the things you couldn't say before you could be sure of the person to whom you were saying them. They were the most dangerous, because this was Hungary. And this was the summer of 1955.

For a moment he held his breath, wondering how she would react, regretting the indulgence of his self-revelation. Finally she said: 'I don't think my husband would be very pleased to hear you express such ideas.' She paused, then added with a venom that made Thomas's heart sing, 'But

I hate Peter. He's a bastard. I don't care what he thinks any more.'

Her cheeks were flushed with wine, and as she turned away from the table, dropping her napkin into the debris of their meal, she half missed her footing. 'Look at me,' she laughed, 'I'm disgraceful. It's gone straight to my head.'

He reached out and caught her arm to steady her. He held her elbow, then moved his grasp upwards so that he was squeezing the flesh of her bicep between his fingers, savouring the solidity of it, the smoothness of her skin to his touch, its very bareness. In those anxious first encounters in the Astoria bar, the chance brushing of a knee against a thigh beneath the table had been the occasion for immediate and self-conscious realignment. At that time physical contact had been inadmissible not so much through any constraint of decency but more because of the breathtaking horizons that it opened up, vistas by unspoken mutual consent too vertiginous to be negotiated in the confines of the place within which they found themselves. But now it was different. Now they had crossed a threshold. This was the first time he had intentionally touched any part of her body apart from her hand.

A kind of awe descended on him, freezing him in a moment's exquisite paralysis. Here she stood, alone with him. Here she stood with her blonde hair, drawn back from her temples, from which wisps had broken free to dance about her ears. Here she stood in her thin blue cotton dress, sleeveless, with its open collar, a covering seemingly too flimsy for her body. He sensed her physical proximity. And at the same time he sensed something else, something more elusive: he sensed her vulnerability. She was a woman who had broken free of the restraint of her husband. But she was removed from his protection, too. She was exposed. Adrift. Dangerous to others and herself.

'That was nice,' she said. 'What now?'

'What would you like to do?'

'I don't know. Anything. Nothing. But I don't feel like walking too far.'

'I think we deserve a rest. For the digestion. Let's go and find somewhere to sit for a while.'

The village was strangely deserted in the early afternoon sun. As they walked away even the inn was closing up its shutters, grateful to shut its eyes to further custom and sink into a lazy somnolence. They left the grotesque Soviet memorial behind them: he took her hand and led her along the path that he remembered from his boyhood, into the field with the line of trees and the barn. They sat on the grass, shaded by the wall, then lay on their backs, staring up at the blue sky. High above them Thomas watched a tiny bird, its wings barely moving, supported it seemed by nothing more than the heat of the air below it.

'This they cannot control,' he said slowly.

'What can't they control?'

'This. The blueness of the sky. The way one feels after a bottle of wine.'

'You think they would want to control it?'

He considered her question, uncertain how far to go in his answer. 'I think so, don't you? If they could?'

'Who are 'they', Tamás?'

'Oh, I don't know. The party. The AVOs, those cretinous secret policemen. That bald git Rákosi. The men in Moscow who pull the strings that make him dance like a puppet. All those bastards who want to limit our freedom.'

She frowned. She too was lying on her back, staring at the sky. Suddenly it seemed terribly important to get through to her, to explain how his mind worked, to let her into his thinking. Their intimacy must be underpinned by sympathy, or it was meaningless. She must understand him and what he wanted out of life. He felt a profound need to reveal himself to her, here in this enchanted meadow, away from Budapest, away from the ears that were constantly primed to detect the faintest whisper of unorthodoxy.

'Look,' he continued, 'things are changing. Gradually. We got a glimpse of what freedom might be like in those eighteen months when Nagy was in power. Nagy set some changes in motion that nothing can stop, even though that bastard Rákosi's been reimposed on us since January and he's doing his best to turn back the clock. But the seeds have been sown, and more changes will come, one way or another. I think we'll get Nagy back in the end.'

She stretched in the sun and asked slowly, 'What things are changing?' Maybe she was an innocent, thought Thomas. A beautiful innocent. What had she said on the boat? You can teach me things. I want to learn everything you have to teach me.

'Well, going to the cinema's more interesting now, isn't it?' he declared. 'I mean, two or three years ago you had no choice: every bloody cinema was showing a Soviet film. Now it's different. Now you can see French and Italian films too. That's something Nagy changed and Rákosi can't undo.'

She pondered for a moment, then asked: 'What do you really want, Tamás? I mean, really?'

I want you, he thought. Lying there in that thin cotton dress with your cheeks flushed with wine. I want you more than anything else in the world. But he had to get it clear, so he said: 'I want our country to be free.'

'Yes, but how exactly?'

'Free of Russians for a start.' When she didn't say anything, he suddenly wanted to promote a reaction from her so he added: 'I suppose your husband wouldn't approve of an idea like that.'

'You know something?' She was animated now and propped herself up on her arm to look at him as she spoke. 'I never talked much about these things with Peter, but he told me once that Hungary's only hope of progress was under the Soviet Union. Then I made him really angry. I wanted to, you see. You know what I told him? I said, Peter, I'm thinking that if a bloody Russian farted you'd thank him for cleansing the atmosphere.'

Thomas giggled. Then she began to laugh. It suddenly seemed the funniest thing he'd ever heard. He laughed out loud, and soon the two of them were rolling about like a couple of children.

But Thomas was also laughing because he was happy. He was happy because she had finally exposed herself to him, offered herself into his hands. What was more exciting, the disloyalty to her husband or the disloyalty to his beliefs? He reached across and entwined his fingers through hers, wiping the tears from his eyes with his other hand and still shaking with the occasional spasm of mirth.

'There's another thing they have no power over,' he said at last.

'What's that, Tamás?'

'They cannot control the way I feel about you.'

There was a silence, then she said softly, 'How do you feel about me?'

'When I first met you – do you remember? – I told you that you were the most beautiful woman in Budapest.'

'And you can judge that, can you? You have met them all, these beautiful women of Budapest?' She was teasing him, but there was an edge to her question. An anger. Or an insecurity.

'Every one of them,' he told her firmly. 'None can touch you.'

'You flatterer.' But he sensed her pleasure.

He raised himself up on his elbow and watched her. She lay with her eyes closed, her lips slightly parted in silent amusement.

'Greta,' he said. He was almost pleading. As he spoke he felt his throat contracting, as though his tongue was suddenly too big for speech and he could barely get her name out. 'Greta.'

She opened her eyes and he kissed her. At once her mouth opened to him and he was running his tongue along her teeth and finding that gap between the two front ones which was such a compelling constituent of her beauty. He felt her arms fold themselves about the back of his neck, then her fingers in his hair, drawing him further on top of her.

With his mouth locked on hers, he began to unbutton the front of her dress. Gradually it opened up and fell away off her shoulders. He reached for her breast, taking it in his palm, then he traced a line with his tongue from her mouth to her nipple. 'Tamás,' she whispered, 'take your things off. I want to feel your skin next to mine. I want you to be close to me.'

As they made love, there in the warm grass, with the

insects below them and the birds drifting high above, he caught a glimpse of her blonde hair falling free over her burning cheek, then cascading away down her long naked back; and in that glimpse he recognised the vertigo which they had first sensed then instantly suppressed in the bar of the Astoria Hotel.

It was dark now, and as he lay back and stared up at the grille, he missed the reassurance of the sunlight. How could he go on without sunlight? How could he be sure that it would return in the morning, that they wouldn't have blocked it off from him by the time dawn broke? He couldn't be sure, he told himself brutally. He'd learned that when you rely on something, or someone, too much, that is your moment of greatest vulnerability. That is when they can hit you hardest, strike their most telling blows. No, you could never be sure, should never count on anything. He sensed a surge of panic, welling up within him, threatening to engulf him in a torrent of hideous memories; but he faced it down. Got on top of it. Contained it.

Somewhere out there beyond his grille lay London, shrouded in a warm summer night. Out there were people, living in houses and flats, driving along in cars, going to cafés and cinemas, doing the things people do at night-time. He knew there were people out there because he could hear in the distance the low drone of traffic, an occasional blaring police car or ambulance. These were the sounds of the city; but the city of the 1990s, not the 1950s.

And beyond he could hear something else. Something very faint but very wonderful. Someone playing on a piano, through a window open to the hot night air. He could just catch the notes wafting across unknown tenements. It was someone playing jazz.

'Greta,' he had said, 'will you tell me something? Do you like jazz?'

He had lit them each a cigarette, and they lay there in the field after their love-making, watching the smoke curl up into the limitless blue sky. He felt very close to her now. The constrictions between them had been blown away. He had a sense of glorious emancipation, a desire to tell her everything about himself, things he had hitherto shared with no one.

She didn't open her eyes, but she answered dreamily, 'Jazz music? I like it, yes . . . it's kind of crazy.'

'It's my passion. My parents used to play jazz before . . . before the war. I remember it from those days, to me it's my childhood. Now I have a friend called Tibor. He knew someone in the American legation who gave him many gramophone records. My God, you should hear that music: Dizzy Gillespie, Louis Armstrong. You should come and meet Tibor sometime and listen to it.'

'I don't think I want to meet Tibor.'

'Why on earth not?'

'I'm already jealous of him, because you spend time with him.'

He looked across to see if she was serious. How could she be jealous of Tibor? Tibor, who had survived two harrowing years in one of Rákosi's jails on a trumped-up charge of crimes against the state? If it came to that, it was Thomas who should be jealous of her and that ridiculous husband of hers. She opened one eye, and laughed. Sex had made her voice husky. 'Don't worry, I'm not really that possessive. I'd like to hear the records, anyway.'

'It's the rhythm of jazz, you see,' went on Thomas, reassured. 'It doesn't conform, doesn't take things for granted. It's different, and unpredictable, and just a little bit cynical, too. And it's more than that: it's actually come to symbolise something beyond itself. I think of it as a sort of secret cult now, listening to jazz. When you turn the dial on the radio and you find one of those stations playing jazz, part of the excitement is that you are doing something forbidden. And that you know there are thousands of other people across Budapest doing exactly the same. It's exciting, that.'

'Ah, Tamás,' she whispered, stretching languorously, 'I love all this forbidden stuff.'

All this forbidden stuff. Don't think about it, Thomas, don't analyse it too much. Just enjoy it. The more you push against the limits, the more the limits will yield, and then the more you will make possible in the future. That's what Tibor had taught him. Tibor, who'd had two long years in jail to work it out for himself. Just do it. Believe in yourself. Ride your own luck. The more people start acting as individuals, the more freedom will flourish.

And for a moment it all suddenly seemed to fit in, to be part of a beautiful and inevitable plan, a new scheme of things that he was helping to put into place. If conditions aren't right, you go out and change them. If you want to listen to jazz, you seek out the forbidden station on the dial. If you want to write an article that questions the party line, you sit down and write it.

If you want another man's wife, you go out and take her.

He lay there thinking. About Tibor. How Tibor had opened his eyes. Tibor had once been a journalist on the *Szabad Nép*, the party newspaper, and he'd dared to·question the correctness of the party's judgement, woken up to their idiocies and inconsistencies long before the rest of them. And he had been imprisoned for his pains. When Thomas had seen what the state had done to Tibor, he'd known that he couldn't go on toeing the party line unthinkingly himself. He had to develop an independent point of view, it wasn't intellectually defensible to be constricted by those party goons any longer.

So here I am, he told himself, better late than never. Tamás Donat, seeker after truth and freedom.

Lying next to somebody else's wife in somebody else's field.

A little later he heard her voice murmuring, 'What are you doing, Tamás?'

'I am thinking.'

She gave a little laugh. 'You know something? You think too much. You are being too energetic, up here in your brain.' She rolled over towards him and took his head in her hands, running her fingers sinuously through his hair as if to massage away the unnecessary mental activity.

'Too energetic?'

'Yes, too energetic. You're getting too excited up there.'

'Am I?'

'My professor,' she giggled. 'I don't want you excited up there, it's not important. I want you excited down here instead.'

Her hand travelled urgently down him and he turned to reach for her again.

Afterwards they lay still once more in the grass flattened by the warmth of their bodies. And then he said, because he was curious, because he had the sudden urge to know everything about her, too: 'Have you ever done this before?'

She leant across and slapped his face very hard indeed. 'Of course not,' she said angrily.

Thinking about it afterwards, he concluded it was the greatest compliment she could have paid him.

He could still feel that smack on his cheek the next morning. He put his fingers up to his face again, here in the half-light of the cell. Here, nearly forty years later, he sensed the burning glow it had left, the stinging suffusion of surprise, embarrassment and desire. It was as if she had just hit him again, as if he was lying once more breathless in the grass next to her. His cheek was for ever impregnated with the mark of her hand. Like stigmata.

He heard a noise outside the room and he was instantly up in a sitting position, hugging himself, trying to control the fear. It was the door. His door. They were unlocking it. They were coming for him. He braced himself. No, Thomas, no. He was Thomas again now, Thomas Donat, and telling himself not to be so foolish. They will not hurt you. Not these people. Not here, not now. Not all these years afterwards, in a different country, in a different world. Not in England. He knew that what he told himself was true, but he was still trembling slightly as the door swung open.

How could he not be trembling? A network of shafts into the submerged depths of the past had suddenly and inexplicably opened up for him, with an unexpected and horrific clarity. So many different shafts, taking him back into the places he thought he had sealed for ever from his memory. Re-establishing the connection between Thomas and Tamás. The connection that he thought he had severed. Very well, then. The shaft he must keep his eyes fixed down was the one that led him to Greta, the safe one that led him to Greta in the field on that miraculous summer's day. The other shafts were unspeakable. He must be constantly on his guard never to venture near them again. Never, not on any account. These were the things that you didn't contemplate. Not if you wanted to survive. One glimpse, that was all it had taken. One glimpse of horror, and an irresistible sequence of events had been set in motion. A knife in his hands. An urge to destroy, an urge as unfamiliar as it was momentarily ungovernable. The illusion that he could thereby pay the ransom on his past, expunge it, scrub it from the books. The unutterable sadness once it had been done.

And now this. Another cell. Another set of footsteps in the corridor outside. Another sick sensation as the key turned in the lock.

Two men came into the room. He recognised one of them. One of them was a policeman, in uniform; the same sergeant who had guided his unsteady steps last night into this cell, after the bewildering journey here in the police van, and the perplexing battery of questions they'd asked him when he'd first arrived. Thomas was a connoisseur of policemen. In a brief moment of lucidity he remembered this one as a type. Not a bright man, but protected by his own lack of imagination. This was the man who had brought Leila to him, late last night, who'd stood around expressionless while they were together, as if he was supervising a pair of animals at the zoo rather than intruding on the privacy of two human beings.

In the short time allowed them, Thomas's niece had talked to him, comforted him, told him everything was going to be all right. She was a good girl, Leila. A very good girl. She conjured up images of the lobelias and acanthus bushes which surrounded her front door, brought with her the delicious scents of her own garden. But of course she didn't know, not about all this. Couldn't know. So her words meant nothing and he'd smiled bleakly back at her when she'd been with him in the cell, trying wordlessly to communicate his regret for the trouble he'd caused her and his gratitude for the good intentions behind her attempted consolations.

So now the sergeant was back, with another man. A man he'd never seen before. The policeman was addressing him: 'This is Dr Hodges, Donat. Dr Hodges has come to check you over, and have a little chat. He's the police doctor.'

Thomas nodded blindly in the direction of the voice, but he couldn't speak. He was too busy concentrating.

He heard the sergeant say to Hodges, 'OK, sir? I'll be just outside if you need me.'

Hodges replied, 'That's fine, sergeant,' and drew up a chair. Thomas was vaguely aware of a grey-suited figure crouching forward, opening a file. But he couldn't register what he looked like. Not yet. That would have been too much of a distraction, too much extra data to absorb when all his attention was given over to controlling the other perils.

'So you are Donat? Thomas Donat?'

Thomas nodded weakly.

'Good.' He rose from his seat and took Thomas's wrist. 'Right, I'm going to give you a quick examination.' They exchanged no more conversation, as Hodges set to work testing pulse, blood pressure, chest, reflexes, all with a dispassionate efficiency. Thomas still could not bring himself to look at him. Even when the doctor sat down again and took the file into his hands once more, still Thomas stared away with half-closed eyes fighting his silent battle.

'That seems to be in order,' murmured Hodges. 'Now, I want to ask you about yesterday afternoon.' He paused. 'Do you remember yesterday afternoon?' The voice was thin and reedy. And neutral. It asked questions unemotionally, as if they were statements unpunctuated by interrogation marks.

Thomas swallowed, then braced himself. Braced himself to look quickly up at Hodges's eyes. They were neutral, too. So. This man he could deal with. This man need present no threat. This man was only doing his job. Like the bus conductor yesterday. Thomas said slowly, 'I am sorry.'

'You are sorry. Can you tell me what exactly you are sorry about?'

Thomas could only gesture helplessly with his hands. Words. Words were dangerous. They must be used sparingly, if at all.

'What are you sorry about? Are you sorry that you can't remember?'

Thomas shook his head slowly.

'Are you sorry about what happened yesterday afternoon?'

'I'm sorry,' Thomas repeated.

'You know what you did yesterday afternoon, in the Royal Gallery. You know you destroyed a very valuable picture. You attacked it with a knife. Can you tell me what was going through your mind when you did that?'

This was it. This was the moment he must be strong. This was the moment he must lower into place the protective cover just below the surface. To allow no glimpses down the shafts. Then he must activate that surface, to distract attention from what was beneath, to camouflage his defences. No one must guess. No one must have access to those shafts. It could be done, because it must be done. These were the ways of coping. He had revived the spirit of invention which had saved his mind nearly forty years ago, and found it still serviceable. For that he felt an obscure gratitude.

Hodges said it again: 'Can you tell me what was going through your mind when you attacked the picture?'

'I cannot.' He spoke in little more than a whisper. There was regret in his voice, as if he were declining a kind offer of hospitality.

'Were you angry about something?'

'Not angry.'

'Or were you angry with another person?'

'Sorry. So sorry.' The words came out very slowly, painfully slowly. The effort of keeping the shield over the shafts in place was consuming him.

'Can you remember other times when you have been violent?'

Again the wordless denial, expressed by a helpless little inclination of the head.

'Do you sometimes feel that you want to do violence to things in order to get rid of feelings of frustration?'

He strained every nerve, every sinew, into an intense effort of concentration. 'Never, sir.'

'Do you find you sometimes want to hit people when they have annoyed you?'

He recoiled. No. She had hit him. There in the field where the grass had been flattened by their warm bodies, there she had hit him. Whatever had happened later, he had deserved to be hit then, because he had spoken thoughtlessly. That was the only violence he was prepared to admit to. A violence of love. He put his fingers up to the side of his face. Then he shook his head again.

'Can you explain to me why you suddenly felt you had to do violence to this picture?'

His throat was dry. 'No, sir.'

'But you would acknowledge it as an uncharacteristic action in yourself. Something that surprised you when it happened.'

He closed his eyes and mouthed a silent agreement. Heartfelt, grateful agreement. He had never been a violent man, not by nature. Not even then, all those years ago, when there had been so much violence going on about him, so many brutal, senseless acts. He wanted to explain to this gentleman, look, even when I had the gun in my hand, and I was facing the person I detested most in the world, even then I wasn't able to pull the trigger. And what was it she had said to him once, back in the apartment? 'I'm worried about you, Tamás,' she had told him. 'Maybe you're not hard enough to survive.' Not hard enough to survive.

But she'd been wrong. He'd survived, in his fashion.

Here was Hodges again, probing: 'Are you shocked to find yourself in this place, in a cell. Having mutilated private property?' It was the same even tone, the same lack of inflexion.

Thomas nodded once more. Very deliberately. With consummate care.

The neutral voice continued, but a little softer this time: 'Was there something about the picture itself that upset you?'

Now. Hold hard. Every shaft is capped. Don't dislodge anything, don't jeopardise the system. Don't even think about the question. Let it dissolve into the air as if it had never been asked, let it float away. Surely he might be permitted to disregard just one of this learned gentleman's enquiries. And if he was to be allowed to shirk one, then this must be it. He turned sad, regretful eyes towards the man in the grey suit, envisaging the way Hodges's words were wafting away into nothingness, uncoupling from each other, disjointed signals drifting into oblivion. He made a motion with his hand to ease them on their way, a gesture of unconscious gentleness.

'I understand that you are a visitor here in London. You're from Canada, aren't you?'

'Yes, Canada.' He was on surer ground now.

'Are you married?'

He shook his head. He put his hand up to his cheek once more. That was where she had hit him. In the sweltering meadow, near the village with the horrible Soviet war memorial, before they took the dusty road that led back down to the Danube.

'So you are on holiday in London. Staying with your niece, I believe?'

'Yes.'

'How is your relationship with your niece? Does she treat you well?'

He was perplexed that the question needed to be asked. 'She is a good woman,' he said finally. It was his longest sentence of their interview.

Hodges cleared his throat and continued in the same light unemotional voice: 'So I would be right in saying that you cannot at this moment account for what you did yesterday.'

Not much longer, he sensed. Hang on here. He resorted to his first, instinctive formula: 'So sorry.'

The other man was getting up, and Thomas tried to rise too but felt suddenly dizzy.

'No, no. Stay where you are. Get some rest.' After the safety of the neutrality, Thomas sensed danger in the kindness of the tone. He was immediately on his guard. Beware of the lulling, the illusion of concern. When your defences were down, that was when they hit you hardest.

*   *   *

They walked back down the road to the village to rejoin the pleasure steamer. Suddenly she was concerned, and began to run on ahead. 'Hurry, Tamás,' she said, 'if we miss the boat back we will be in trouble.'

He quickened his pace to catch up with her. It was still hot and the road was dusty. He didn't want to run, because he sensed that this was the end of something miraculous. That things would never be like this again. That running would be precipitating the end of their idyll. He resented her worrying about missing the boat back, after what they had just been through together. Why hadn't they just stayed where they were, lying in that field; then as the shadows lengthened, sought refuge in one of the little houses in the village, gone to live together for ever? Away from it all. In one of the little cottages with window-boxes.

In the shadow of the war memorial.

He laughed, in a way that he hadn't laughed before that afternoon, with an edge of bitterness.

'I'm very much afraid,' he called after her, 'that sooner or later we'll be in trouble anyway, you and I.'

4

'OK, Minto, this week's piece is going to be a winner, I can feel it in my bones. So let's talk about it.'

He looked back at her across the desk. It was conspicuously neat. Everything on it was placed, calculated, down to the angle of the p.c. screen, the position of the bottle of mineral water, the jar of sharpened pencils and coloured pens set out like a flower arrangement. He had observed her style developing since her arrival as features editor three months ago. Her desk summed it up: an arch combination of dynamism and femininity. A combination that amused him and yet made him wary. How far could you trust a woman like this?

Not that you could fault her. She did her job well enough, her calculations were generally correct; but nothing was spontaneous, everything was contrived. She'd called him Minto from their second meeting onwards. That had mildly annoyed him. It was clearly an act of strategy rather than of intimacy. Only his friends and his closest colleagues called him Minto, a nickname emanating from too deep in his childhood for him to recall instantly its precise origin. Dominic Maitland, that was the name he wrote under and answered to. Many people never went beyond that. To them he remained Dominic. He felt she hadn't done enough to warrant 'Minto' so soon. But here they were, three months on. Elaine and Minto, features editor and journalist at a leading Sunday newspaper, sitting in her office discussing this week's article.

Elaine McBride hailed from Glasgow but she now inhabited a phoney mid-Atlantic world informed by New York business-speak, Americanisms grafted on to her native Scottishness like meaningless high-tech architectural embellishments on to a simple granite façade. Presumably she had decided that this resonance of the States added to her professional lustre, carried persuasive suggestions of power and dynamism. It was almost as though she had deliberately reconstructed herself in a Manhattan image in premonition of the paper's new American ownership. In that respect she had shown some foresight, or, as she would probably have expressed it, been ahead of the game. When the take-over had happened last year there had been people who had complained loudly about transatlantic cultural imperialism; and maybe Elaine was a symptom of that imperialism. Ridley, for instance, had held forth extensively at his favourite watering hole to the world at large on the subject of 'bloody Yanks'. But as for Minto, he'd been prepared to accept a degree of colonisation if it brought with it financial stability and left him free to write what he wanted to write.

But there remained something vaguely threatening about Elaine. It was difficult to define. It wasn't that she was attractive. Maybe she was, in a heavily groomed sort of way, but she wasn't his type, not with her coiffured blonde hair and expensive clothes. That sort of perfection deadened rather than stimulated him. No, he could handle the way she looked, too.

What he couldn't come to terms with was her ultimate impenetrability, the lack of a real reaction from her. Last week's piece was sensational, Minto, magic stuff. How did you get all those great quotes out of Hockney? Hey, but listen: only nine hundred words this time, OK? Pressure of space, huh, we got those two extra reviews to fit in. What did she really mean? It was all smooth, all surface. He couldn't read her, couldn't come to grips with her at all. He didn't really trust her. Not with hair like that. And not with a desk as tidy as hers either.

'Yes, this week's piece, I've been thinking about that,' he said cautiously, leaning back in his chair and surveying the view from the window. It was pretty good, that view. You could see over the rooftops to the Thames, watch the river snaking back to Westminster. Even from his own office on the tenth floor, the panorama was breathtaking. But right up here on the fourteenth floor, he could see how it might even give you an illusion of power. 'I suppose it could be some new angle on the Braque show, or alternatively isn't Saul Bellow in town? Perhaps I could fix up an interview with him.' He had to admit neither choice really captured his imagination. But equally he wasn't having her dictating to him. As a matter of principle. So he watched her warily when she said:

'Listen to me, Minto. I'd like something a bit different this time round.'

'Different?' On his guard, he swung round from the window to meet her eyes. Sudden direct eye contact sometimes put you at an advantage. He'd used the tactic to good effect in interviews from time to time. Starting off quiet, almost diffident, not looking up much from his notebook, fiddling with the casette. Gentle, unobtrusive questions about childhood or something equally uncontroversial, nothing abrasive, nothing remotely threatening. And then, without warning, the sudden strike, the penetrating verbal thrust accompanied by the candid, uncompromising stare. The unexpected glimpse of steel. The simultaneous revelation of very deep blue eyes. It could knock your subject off their balance. But not now. Elaine McBride wasn't fazed. She smiled back at him, that smile that came a bit too easily for comfort.

'Let me run this idea past you, see what you think.'

'Mind if I smoke?'

'Sure, go ahead.' She flipped a small ashtray in his direction, then leant back to click the air-conditioning up a notch. The windows, of course, did not open. A momentary expression of distaste was quickly suppressed. But it had been there. He'd got through to her.

He flicked his lighter to the cigarette he hadn't really wanted and said, 'So what's this new idea?'

'Listen, Minto. Don't get me wrong. Let me explain where I'm coming from here. I like your range. I like the way you can deal with the director of the Louvre one week and the chairman of the Booker Prize jury the next, and still sound like you know what you're talking about. Hey, you're good, you know that?'

Minto made a non-committal gesture, as if to say, so? There was something sickening about Elaine McBride being nice, turning on the soft soap. It was unnatural, a bit like

Genghis Khan doing a television commercial. What was she after?

'By the way,' she digressed, 'how's your big piece coming along, the one on that dealer guy?'

'Courtney? That's progressing.'

'That's for the review section, isn't it, five thousand words, big picture spreads. How much longer do you need for that?'

'Another month or so.' Minto paused, uncertain how much to tell her at this stage. He disliked being quizzed on work in progress. But for a moment he felt a need to put his thoughts in order. 'He's an interesting subject, Courtney: just about the most powerful art dealer of his generation. But a difficult man to pin down.'

'That old soak Ridley been any help?'

'Very much so, as it happens.' Loyalty to Ridley did not come high on Minto's list of priorities. But Minto's private estimate of the man and what it was permissible for a woman like Elaine McBride to insinuate now suddenly seemed two very different things. 'He took me to Courtney's memorial service yesterday afternoon.'

'Anyone interesting there?'

He paused for a moment, remembering. Remembering the smooth urbanities of Edward Purchas. The exploding aggression of Max Courtney. The unyielding stare in the portrait of his father Alexander. And then recalling Isabella. Isabella, the spoilt bitch. The beautiful spoilt bitch.

All Minto said now was, 'Only the great and good of Bond Street and St James's.'

'So did you pick up a lot of material?'

'A bit.'

'Am I right, the art market's not an easy world to infiltrate?'

Minto laughed. 'I get the impression that it's paranoiacally secretive.'

'Why's that, do you think?' He sensed her calculation in the way she leant forward over her desk. Sympathetically probing. Getting to know her writers; understanding their problems. It was an act, wasn't it? Phase two in the Elaine McBride manual for handling key personnel. For Getting the Best out of Them.

'Money's one reason,' he suggested carefully. 'There's a lot of money involved in the art market now. But it's money being handled in a very discreet way. Then there are the people operating at the top end, the auctioneers and the leading dealers: they're an extraordinary bunch. How can I describe them? An unlikely mixture of the establishment and the maverick. It's still a very snobby, introverted world.'

'What was Courtney? Establishment or maverick?'

'A bit of both, I suppose. Maverick under cover of the establishment, perhaps. And also something else which I can't quite put my finger on yet.'

'Do you like what you hear of him? Is he sympathetic?'

'I'm intrigued by him, put it that way. I'm intrigued by the way he made his money. What you have to realise is that people like Courtney are trading in material that has no demonstrable objective value. So they have to create it. Essentially they're dealing in fantasy.'

'Hype, you mean.'

'That's only one aspect of it. The more obvious side. Hype's the stock-in-trade of the PR machines of the big auction houses. They pump it out at you as a journalist and you have to be careful not to end up just being their mouthpiece.'

She nodded, absorbing what he was saying. Why did he get the uneasy feeling it was being stored away, to be dusted down and used in evidence against him in some other context, at some future date? He stubbed his cigarette out abruptly. 'So what's your new idea for this week?' he asked again.

'Just a one-off. An instinct. Something I think you might do rather well.'

He stiffened. 'What's that?'

'Did you catch this news item? About what happened in the Royal Gallery yesterday?' She pushed over a piece of paper in his direction. He noticed the perfect manicure of her hands.

He glanced at the cutting from today's *Independent*, head-lined 'Picture Vandalised'. 'I vaguely registered it having happened, yes.'

'Read it. Some guy comes in out of the blue and lays into this picture with a knife. Causes serious damage, apparently, they don't know whether restoration is going to be possible at this stage.'

He ran his eye over the brief item. How an unidentified man in his sixties had walked into the German nineteenth-century room at one of London's leading public galleries at 3.15 yesterday afternoon and savagely attacked a picture by Arnold Böcklin entitled *The Island of the Dead*. How he was due to appear in Marlborough Street magistrates' court today. How museum staff were still evaluating the extent of the damage. 'So?' he said.

'So, what's your take on it?'

'Not a lot.'

'I want you to find out about this guy. Find out why he did it.'

'Why he did it?' He repeated the words slowly, for a moment glimpsing the labyrinthine horror of another man's madness. He looked back at her and added quietly, 'God knows the answer to that.'

'I want you to find out. I think it would make a good piece.'

He was suddenly angry. Angry with her for her presumption in dictating to him what he should write. Angry because of the arrangement of pencils on her desk. Angry because it was another hot day. 'For Christ's sake, Elaine, he's probably just some nutter.'

'I don't care if he's a nutter, from where I'm sitting it's still a heck of a good story. Find out what kind of a nutter he is. Find out why he chose an art gallery. Find out why he chose that particular picture.'

'You don't need me for that. You need the medical correspondent.'

'I don't think so. I think I need you. I think you're going to do it better than anyone.'

'I'm not so sure.'

'You're good with people. You get things out of them. I've got a feeling there's a lot below the surface here, waiting for someone to dig it up.'

'That remains to be seen.'

'Come on, when you think about it this story's got everything going for it. Art and violence: it's a great combination.

No, wait a minute. When you consider the value of the picture concerned, it's got money, too. Art and violence and money. It's unbeatable. It'll be a hell of a lot more readable than yet another review of the Braque show, or even an interview with Saul Bellow that everyone's done before.'

'OK.' He leaned back in his chair and stretched. She was amazing, Elaine, a joke really, a caricature. But then again, something about the idea roused his curiosity. 'So it's role-reversal time: you want me to become your mental illness correspondent. And I suppose the Braque piece can be put together by the sports desk this week. Mine not to reason why. If that's what you want, I'll give it a go.'

'Ataboy!' she exclaimed. But she was blasé: these victories came too easily to her. She was already leaning forward to check her next appointment.

He helped himself to a cup of coffee from the machine and took the lift back to his desk four floors below. Elaine McBride. He couldn't quite decide what she was up to here. But she needed watching. Even now, he wasn't entirely sure whether the best way to get back at her would be to write something parodyingly routine or make it extravagantly good. On the whole he was inclined to the latter. It was a busy week now. This piece would take quite a bit of research if it was going to amount to anything. And there was Courtney, he had to keep going on him, too. Bloody Courtney. Bloody mystery man.

When he sat down he found a note on his desk telling him Frankie had rung. He sat for a moment contemplating it. Wondering what to do. Wondering why hearing from her now depressed and unsettled him. Remembering, specifically, how happy he'd been waking up that morning.

He'd woken up feeling good because Frankie wasn't there. It was as simple as that. He had room to breathe, he had space. It was a relief to wake up untrammelled in his bed, unconstricted by a partner. Unshackled. It wasn't exactly that he wanted to kick her out. He'd miss her if he never saw her again. But he needed their relationship to change down a gear, to relax its intensity. How long had they been going out? It must be three or four months now.

She'd been sensational at the beginning. He'd thought about her the whole time, hadn't been able to concentrate on anything else. He'd first met her at that private view in March in some pretentious photographers' gallery in Covent Garden. He hadn't been able to take his eyes off her. They'd immediately been absorbed by each other, oblivious to the rest of the room milling around them. They had gone on to dinner together. That night had been unforgettable. The first night always was, of course. The anticipation as the evening unfolded. That delicious speculation as to what her body was going to be like. The thrill of the unfamiliar. The compulsion of new flesh to be explored.

After the first week there was always a tailing off, as you got to know the body's secrets too well. That was it, wasn't it? Finding something to keep it all going after the sex had become routine. Not that she didn't have anything to offer beyond her body, far from it. She was an actress, a promising one, maybe on the verge of big things. She was amusing and intelligent. Everyone who met her said she was great. Like Charles Benson, his friend on the business section, whom he'd introduced to her a few weeks ago. 'Hey, Minto, where did you find her? Wow! She's really funny, isn't she? Great sense of humour. Clever girl, too. Can't understand what she sees in you, though.' For a moment Minto wondered if he was only sticking with her out of a sense of possession of something widely coveted.

Now he lifted the telephone and made three calls in quick succession.

The first was to the news desk. They told him that the accused in the Royal Gallery vandalism case was appearing at Marlborough Street magistrates' court at two that afternoon. The second was to the Royal Gallery press office. They were persuaded to arrange an appointment for him to meet Michael Thornton-Bass, curator of German pictures, at midday. And finally he rang Frankie and left a message on her answerphone that he couldn't see her that evening because he had to go up to Birmingham for research on an article and would probably be staying overnight.

He wasn't quite clear why he had said Birmingham. He wasn't quite clear why he had told the lie at all.

Unless it was because the moment he laid down the receiver he found himself thinking of Isabella Maurbach.

A sweltering taxi ride later, Minto was being led by a uniformed keeper through the public halls of the Royal Gallery to the curators' offices. He tried to imagine this place, through which people wandered speaking in subdued and reverential voices, as the setting for yesterday's act of violence. The combination was incongruous, like a fight in a cathedral. He shivered, despite the heat. It was strange, he reflected, that part of him never really felt at ease in museums. He disliked their shadowy didacticism, the implicit threat of a lecture. His spirit rebelled against the dead hand of institutionalism, the sense of art ensnared by civil service bureaucracy. What artist ever painted a picture to hang in a museum, for God's sake? Pictures were painted for lived-in rooms, or maybe in the past for worshipped-in ones. Not for rooms whose sole *raison d'être* was as a venue for looking at pictures. Who was it who'd said that museums were mausoleums?

'It really is the most desperate business.' Michael Thornton-Bass removed his spectacles and produced an extravagant crimson handkerchief from his jacket pocket. He polished them, staring distractedly out of the tiny window of his book-lined office. Minto took the opportunity to observe the room, noting odd details. What the man kept on his desktop, for instance: a fountain pen; two objects that looked like metal bracelets; and a leaflet setting out that week's schedule of services at the Brompton Oratory. He had a bulbous face, baggy under the eyes with a tendency to floridity. Minto was vaguely put in mind of some sort of dog, a bloodhound perhaps. A lugubrious and unathletic bloodhound. Thornton-Bass shook his head balefully, and demanded: 'What makes a human being do something like that?'

Minto sat and contemplated the curator of German pictures. There was a tortured quality to the way the man asked the question that Minto was inclined to find affected and irritating. There was a certain glorying in the tragedy: the human spirit had been affronted by the incident, but it was an affront only to be understood in terms of the personal suffering Thornton-Bass had sustained, and sustained not without heroism.

'What indeed?' Minto echoed, involuntarily parodying the preciousness. How old was Thornton-Bass? Probably not more than a year or two older than Minto himself, but he had already taken up grateful residence in his natural habitat of middle age. He wore a blue serge suit, conservatively cut, ridiculously heavy for the time of year. Had it been a few degrees cooler there would undoubtedly have been a waistcoat, too, across which would have hung the inevitable gold watch chain. Minto could imagine how little he had changed over the years, how even as an undergraduate he would have affected the same style of dress and deportment, the same mannered harking back to an illusory golden age of good chaps, good clubs and good Catholic families. It was an act, of course, a self-comforting device, a means of remedying a self-perceived lack of social ballast. People were constantly constructing their own myths. Some even went on to believe them.

Thornton-Bass shook his head again. 'I suppose the man was deranged. I saw him briefly yesterday just after the incident.'

'How did he seem?'

'It was difficult to tell. In a strange way, he seemed not quite all there. I don't mean half-witted, but he looked odd . . . almost comatose.'

'Comatose?'

'Yes. As though he was in shock. The whole thing was quite horrible.'

'He didn't say anything then?'

'Not so far as I'm aware.'

'No declaration of political intent? Not done as a gesture of gay pride, or to save the whales, or anything like that?'

Thornton-Bass shook his head.

'And you're left to pick up the pieces.'

'That's it. The whole business is tragic. Quite tragic.' As he spoke, Thornton-Bass distractedly fingered the pair of circular metal objects which he picked up from his desk, teasing them, bending them first this way then the other in his anguish. What were they? He didn't seem the type to go in for executive toys. Were they by some follower of Brancusi? Or perhaps they were abstruse Catholic reliquaries, obscure aids to worship.

Suddenly aware of Minto's gaze, Thornton-Bass gave a sheepish little laugh and dropped them back on to his blotting paper, adding elliptically: 'Ah, yes. As you have probably detected, I'm no great admirer of the internal combustion engine.'

'I'm sorry?'

'Bicycle clips.' He paused, then added: 'So much faster through all this hideous London traffic. If I had my way the motor car would be banned from the face of the earth.'

It fitted in, of course. And you could be quite sure Thornton-Bass didn't ride a mountain bike. It would be studiedly antique, with a capacious wickerwork basket attached to the front handlebars. He probably set out on it at the crack of dawn each morning in order to take in *en route* an early celebration of Mass, which he undoubtedly pronounced 'Marse'. Minto had done some checking before he came. Strange that this absurdly mannered and self-conscious throw-back to *Brideshead Revisited* was in fact a considerable scholar in his own right, a fluent German speaker, and an international authority on German Romanticism.

'Tell me a little more about the Böcklin,' said Minto.

'The Böcklin. Yes.' Thornton-Bass gave a sharp whistling intake of breath to convey the pain the subject continued to evoke in him. 'What makes the whole thing so unspeakably awful is that it had only been on view for eight weeks. We bought it in February, you may remember, and it had been in the hands of the restorer for three months after that. Nothing drastic: just a light clean and the removal of some old overpaint. It was in pretty good condition.'

'I hadn't realised it was such a recent acquisition.'

'It was a tremendous *coup*. We bought it at auction. It came from the Marriott collection, you know.'

Marriott. It wasn't the first time he had heard the name. But it was unexpected to hear it in this context. 'Leslie Marriott?'

'Exactly.'

'I didn't know he was a great collector as well?'

'Not a great one. But he had a lot of pictures. This was one of his best. It's no secret that the German nineteenth century is one of our weaker areas at the Royal Gallery. This painting plugged a major gap.' He looked up, momentarily amused by his own colloquialism. 'And it's unique, you know: the only surviving example of Böcklin's second version of his most famous subject, *The Island of the Dead.*'

Minto made the sudden eye contact he'd been seeking. 'What did you pay for it?' he demanded. That one's for you, Elaine. Art and money and violence indeed.

Thornton-Bass looked perplexed. 'I ... er ... well, I don't know whether I can give you that information just like that.'

'Oh, come on. It's a matter of public record, surely?'

He said grudgingly: 'Yes, I suppose you're right.' He sighed, as if what he was about to reveal was in some way distasteful, as if he didn't himself like to soil his hands with financial considerations. 'I believe it was one point five million pounds.'

'One point five million.' Minto made an elaborate note in his book, rather enjoying the role of the tactless relation at the sickbed who asks about the size of the patient's estate.

Böcklin. He paused, recalling the few odd examples of the artist's work that he had once encountered. They had been in Basel, in the museum, where he'd filled in a spare half-hour before an interview he'd gone to do with Yehudi Menuhin last year. He remembered mysterious rocky landscapes in which misshapen goatmen fought prancing centaurs, and Germanic naiads leered across vertiginous chasms. 'Böcklin's quite a Teutonic taste, isn't he?' he ventured. 'Personally I find him rather heavy-going, a little hard to take.'

'Really?' Thornton-Bass peered at him with a mixture of surprise and mistrust. As if he'd just queried a religious truth, perhaps impugned the doctrine of transubstantiation. 'But this picture was one of the great examples of imaginative symbolism. It's very, very special. Almost Wagnerian in a way, and highly atmospheric.' He pushed a transparency towards Minto, adding, 'That's how it looked, before ...' and tailing off with a hopeless gesture. The man was craving some sort of sympathy, wanted some sign from Minto of appreciation of his tragedy, of the terrible blow he had sustained. Maybe it was true. Maybe he had fought long and hard to secure this Böcklin for the collection. Maybe its acquisition had been a moment of intense personal and professional pride. Maybe losing it now was like seeing someone very dear to you mown down in a road accident. But still Minto was disinclined to give him what he wanted. His instinct rebelled against the demand made upon him. Grieve on your own, but don't involve me, he thought bitterly. Go and light a candle in one of your incense-laden churches. Without saying anything he took the transparency and held it up to the light.

Involuntarily, he shivered. He didn't like it. This was more than symbolism. It was decadence. There was something macabre about the mysterious green light which bathed the landscape, and the twisted figures in the foreground. He suddenly realised what was disquieting about it: a suspicion that the artist had set out deliberately to create something suggestive of evil. It was the intention behind it that was distasteful, a sense that the man who had painted this picture was at home among the rocks and the skeletons of his imagination.

Minto dredged into his memory for something he'd once read. 'Wasn't Böcklin one of Hitler's favourite artists?' he asked.

Thornton-Bass mused on the point for a moment. 'I believe so,' he murmured. Then as much as a reassurance to himself as a reprimand to Minto he went on: 'Still, it's very bad art history to hold an artist responsible for his later admirers.'

Hitler, thought Minto. Hitler and Marriott.

Minto asked: 'So this is the second version of *The Island of the Dead*, is it? I think I once saw the first version in the Basel Museum, could that be right?'

'That's correct.' Thornton-Bass blinked back at him, impressed by this chance piece of knowledge, and determined to redress the balance by imparting more of his own. 'In fact the first version was painted by the artist five times in the 1880s. The one in Basel that you've seen; one in Leipzig; one in the Metropolitan Museum, New York; and two formerly in Berlin, probably destroyed. One of those was actually in Hitler's private collection. All five have in common the horizontal composition and different colorations from the very striking green light of this second version. And what makes this second version so pre-eminently desirable is that it's unique, as I say: there are no other examples of it. We were very lucky to have it here.'

'So would I be right in saying that your picture represents a very distinctive variation on the original theme?'

'Absolutely. Apart from the rather startling vertical format, there's also what one might describe as a narrative development.'

'How do you mean exactly?'

'Well, there's an extra dimension to the story. You've got the same dramatis personae as in the first five versions, the silent boatman labouring over his oar, and the mysterious shrouded figure who is his passenger. But here for the first time the white-shrouded figure turns back, and you see that his face is a skull. He turns back and engages the spectator directly with that mocking death's-head stare. It's a horrific and unforgettable moment.'

It was, reflected Minto. Once seen, that figure stayed with you. This was the stuff of nightmares, playing on the fears that haunt the margin of reality and fantasy. Here was the revelation of the great inevitability. The revelation of the triumph of death.

'Not an easy picture to live with,' he suggested.

'Perhaps not,' agreed Thornton-Bass. 'But enormously powerful.'

Minto paused. 'I suppose one could imagine it having a pretty powerful effect on a suggestible mind. On a mind perhaps already a little unhinged?'

'What are you saying?' Thornton-Bass put his spectacles back on and gave him a troubled glance.

'I don't know, I'm thinking out loud. But supposing someone mentally unstable came into a room and caught a glimpse of that image for the first time. It just might tip him over the edge, don't you think?'

'I find that a little fanciful.' The suggestion seemed to annoy him, as if Minto were implying some sort of contributory negligence on the gallery's part. 'Anyway, the man responsible wasn't seeing it for the first time.'

'Oh?'

'He came in the day before yesterday as well.'

'How do you know that?'

'One of the security guards recognised him. She gave a statement.'

'What did she say?'

'That he first came in on Monday and sat in front of the picture staring at it very intently for about ten or fifteen minutes. Then he left rather suddenly.'

'Really? Could I speak to her?'

'Well, I suppose it might be possible.' Thornton-Bass eyed him suspiciously, as if speaking to the staff did not in his judgement fall within the range of activities suitable for a gentleman. 'If you imagine that would help.'

'It would.'

'I'll have a word with the head of security and see what can be arranged.'

'I'd be grateful.'

Minto frowned. There was a story here. Something more than met the eye, something hidden. But how to get to it? Comatose, this man had been, after the violence. He'd come in the day before and sat and stared at the picture for fifteen minutes, as if transfixed. Why?

Minto was beginning to feel impatient with the blubbery figure opposite him, with his tortured posturings and fraught expressions of dismay. 'I wonder,' he asked, 'could I see the picture itself now?'

'Well, I ... I suppose you could. It's in the conservation department.'

Minto rose. 'Will you lead on?'

Thornton-Bass got up uncertainly, then, in another irksome affectation of middle age, waddled off down the passage.

There was a girl in a white coat in sole occupation of the conservation department when they got there. Rather a pretty girl, though her legs were too thin.

'Ah, Emily,' said Thornton-Bass, 'I've brought with me Mr Maitland. He'd like to look at the . . . at the Böcklin.' He added a little archly: 'Mr Maitland is a gentleman of the press.'

Minto nodded at her and she looked away nervously.

'It's over here,' she muttered.

The three of them gathered round the white-topped table on which the poor battered remnants of the painting lay. The image was still recognisable, but it was criss-crossed with the rips of a knife, some of them clean-cut and one or two of them jagged gouges. The canvas had been removed from its stretcher like a casualty from his clothes. Its tattered pennants were held back in place with light strips of rice-paper, a little like first-aid bandages. Intensive care? Or the mortuary? There was something appalling about this destruction. It was the wantonness. The sense that it had been wrought by human agency, not by some random accident of fate.

'What's the prognosis?' said Minto to the girl.

'It's still too early to say.' She spoke rather softly, in a precise and carefully modulated voice. 'There's considerable paint loss in the more jagged gashes, of course. The cleaner cuts are much easier to repair. It depends what we can do with these.' She gestured towards a series of plastic envelopes, each one carefully annotated.

'What's in those?'

'Paint flakes, meticulously gathered up from the floor of the gallery after the incident. There are hundreds of them, some hardly bigger than a pinhead. It may be possible to reconstitute a certain amount by working through these envelopes.'

'My God, how would you do that?'

'Computer technology, maybe.' She turned serious eyes on him. 'There've been some extraordinary developments in that field, particularly in America. But it's still agonising, painstaking work. It won't be quick, you can be sure of that.'

Minto looked back at the canvas. Was there any pattern to the explosion of stabs across the image? Could anything be deduced from the way the violator had set to work?

'He was angry about something, wasn't he?' said Minto, to nobody in particular.

'Or frightened,' murmured Emily unexpectedly.

And then Minto saw it. Caught the direction of Emily's gaze. Followed it into the centre of the picture, to the point where the white-shrouded figure turned his face to the spectator's view. Turned to the murky green light his sightless skull and made his hideous revelation, of the eternal power of death. And at this lower central point, the rips stopped. The face was completely undamaged. Grotesquely, obscenely undamaged.

Thornton-Bass cleared his throat. 'Where is the stretcher now?' he enquired.

'It's on the table behind you,' Emily told him. They all turned to look at the wooden structure which had been the support over which the canvas was stretched. Emily went on: 'It's reasonably intact, you see. A few nicks from the blade of the knife, but the basic construction's sound.'

She lifted the flat, rectangular object with its central crossbeam and tapped it to indicate its solidity. Minto glanced at it, then stared back, intrigued.

'What's that label on the back?' he asked.

'That modern one?' Thornton-Bass paused and frowned. 'Oh, that's a Courtney label.'

Courtney again. The man had got everywhere, done everything. The more you delved the more you found his hand at work in all the deals of any significance that had taken place in the art market over the past two or three decades. His influence was pervasive. 'When did Courtney sell it?'

Thornton-Bass frowned. 'I think Marriott must have bought it from him direct. But some time ago. Fifteen, twenty years, perhaps?'

So Marriott bought from Courtney. Interesting. Minto filed the fact away for future reference. 'And where did Courtney get it from, I wonder?'

'It's not entirely clear as yet. We are still piecing together the full provenance.'

Minto nodded. Courtney had the reputation of having played his cards close to his chest when it suited him to do so. You didn't get information out of him if he didn't want you to have it. That much he had gathered. It was what was making this piece on Courtney so bloody difficult to put together. Difficult, but tantalising. And now Minto had added one more fact to his store. One more fact worth investigating. Leslie Marriott had been a client of Courtney's.

'What's that?' demanded Thornton-Bass suddenly. He snatched the stretcher back urgently from Emily's surprised grasp. He was animated now in an unfamiliar way. A scholarly animation which transcended his other preoccupations.

'What have you found?'

'Look, there: underneath the brown tape on the back. It must have been dislodged by one of the slashes of the knife on the canvas.' Gently Thornton-Bass prised the brown paper adhesive away and beneath was revealed the edge of an old label, demonstrably more ancient than the Courtney one which was by contrast attached on top of the brown tape. 'Another dealer's label,' he muttered. 'This is fascinating. We would never have known about this if it hadn't been for . . .' A dim realisation of the inappropriateness of exultation in this context caused his voice to tail off. But by gentle probing he managed to reveal the full extent of what was inscribed. Minto peered over his shoulder and read:

'Galerie Voermann, München. A. Böcklin, Die Toteninsel.' A stock number was followed by the date 'October 1924'.

'Extraordinary,' said Thornton-Bass. 'Let's get that photographed, Emily.'

Surreptitiously, Minto had already made a note of it.

'So,' Thornton-Bass was saying, 'if there's nothing else you need to see here, I think I must be wending my way back upstairs. I've got quite a lot on my plate today.'

'Of course you have. I'm very grateful for all the time you've given me. It's been very helpful. Perhaps you'd like to hand me over now to your head of security so I can ask that guard a few questions.'

Thornton-Bass seemed momentarily disposed to argue, but finally gestured him to follow.

On his way out Minto turned and smiled at Emily, and added: 'Good luck with all this. I'm lost in admiration for the amazing work you're doing.' She blushed and looked away. If all else failed, he was thinking, he would be reduced to writing nine hundred words on how computer technology might be able to save the ravaged Böcklin. And if

Elaine McBride didn't like it, she knew what she could do with it.

The man who showed him into the keepers' rest-room was small and balding and sweated a lot.

'Maureen's in here, mate,' he declared. 'You can have a chat with her and you won't be disturbed for half an hour, not till the next shift comes off.' He opened the door with considerable officiousness and announced: 'Maureen, this is Mr Maitland, come from the ... er ... what paper did you say?'

Minto told him.

'I'm a *News of the World* man myself,' he said defiantly.

'More like the bloody *Sunday Sport*,' muttered Maureen with a wink at Minto. She was plump and wore a lot too much make-up; her breasts sagged unappealingly beneath the sad green blouse of her uniform. 'So long, Brian,' she added encouragingly. The man paused at the door. You could see he wanted to stay, to witness the interview, but on the spur of the moment he couldn't think of any good reason for doing so. In the end he sloped off with an ill grace, like a spoilt child.

'So what do you want to know, love?' asked Maureen.

'I'm doing a piece on the mutilation of the Böcklin and I think you can help me. I want you to tell me what happened yesterday. And the day before. I want you to tell me everything you can remember about the man who did it.'

Maureen paused, casually unfastening one of the buttons of her blouse, then she told him.

Told him how she'd first set eyes on the bloke the day before yesterday, how he'd come in smartly dressed like and sat in front of the picture for a good quarter of an hour staring at the bloody thing as if he'd seen a ghost. How he'd reappeared the following day, yesterday, about 3.15, looking much more dishevelled, and then the next she knew he was at it like a mad thing, stabbing and slashing at the canvas with a ruddy great kitchen knife. How he'd dropped the knife and crumpled into tears – imagine, a grown man weeping like a child – then been led by Robbie to the bench. How she'd rung the alarm bell and finally the police had come. How they'd marched him away within three feet of her, and as he'd passed her, they'd been pulling him along, because he was hardly able to put one foot in front of the other he'd been that shattered.

But what she didn't tell Minto was the word she'd heard the bloke mutter, over and over again, almost under his breath, as they dragged him past her towards the police van. She didn't tell him because it hadn't seemed to mean anything. Not then, not now. What possible significance could there be to such an unintelligible combination of sounds? A sound like 'Adolf', or maybe 'Rudolf', repeated over and over again on the lips of a sad and loony old man. What interest could those sounds be, when the sad and loony old man has just been arrested for slashing a picture worth one and a half million pounds?

5

For a moment Minto wondered if he had come to the right place. The first thing that struck him about the room he had been directed to was how small it was, how cramped; how parochial. He'd paced down sweaty, institutional corridors to reach it, found himself in an environment difficult to define. Provisionally he'd identified it as part school and part hospital. And part something else. He sensed an obscure reek of incarceration, and realised it was part prison as well.

'Is this court three?' he asked the harassed-looking functionary at the doorway. She was a haggard woman with short grey hair and unforgiving eyes; grudgingly she agreed it was. She spoke with the hostility of that branch of officialdom which views the surrender of any information as a direct threat to its own personal survival.

'Is there . . . is there a public gallery?' The truth was he'd never been to court before. It was unfamiliar territory, and it made him uneasy, sapped his confidence. All he could draw on was the experience gleaned from films on television, Ealing comedies, Perry Mason, that sort of thing. There had definitely been public galleries in the films he'd seen: people shouted from them, cheered, screamed abuse, or fainted in them when the verdict was brought in. Invariably they would be called to peevish and ineffectual order by the judge. Sometimes existence can only be sustained by recourse to the simplest clichés. There is a need for nature to imitate art.

'Just take a seat on those benches,' she told him, and turned away, her patience exhausted.

What benches? Those benches? They looked very basic: there were three of them, on the floor of the court, facing the raised dais at the far end of the room at which the magistrates presumably presided. The benches were already full of people, and he managed with considerable awkwardness to squeeze himself in at the end of the last one. There was an unwilling ripple of shuffling human flesh down the line, and he caught a sudden sharp smell of perspiration. It was even hotter today than yesterday. And there was a tension here, too. He sensed it the moment he sat down. An anticipation, laced with insecurity. An apprehension.

Sunlight shafted through the windows, set high in the walls above eye level. He watched the dust-motes dancing like tiny snowflakes. He thought: what are these people doing here? Gathered together to pass judgement on another human being, to impose society's punishment on a man who has threatened the fabric of that society. What had he done, this malefactor? He was accused of an act of violence against one of society's icons. He'd attacked a painting in a museum. A supreme icon, but for the purposes of calculating the severity of his crime an icon sanctified less by artistic merit than by financial value. Money. That was what it came down to, didn't it? That was what it had to be reduced to, in order for the people gathered here to be competent to deal with it.

The police. What did they know of the arcane imagination of Arnold Böcklin? The police were here, of course. Indeed two constables and a policewoman were actually his neighbours on this bench. They sat there shirt-sleeved and impatient, turning notebooks over and over with strong and febrile hands. The officer next to him had an elastic band that he toyed with abstractedly, winding it round his book, then his fingers, then his wrists, the action expressive of pent-up energy, of frustration at the constraint of legal procedure. He had coarse, close-cropped hair, and as he leant forward to concentrate on his elastic band, he revealed a red, pock-marked neck. He had a two-way radio, a notebook and keys to a souped-up patrol car. His field of activity was physical rather than cerebral. He wasn't equipped for art. How could he cope with *The Island of the Dead*? He could impose a speed limit on it perhaps, but he couldn't compute its evil.

Minto looked about him. Ahead, beneath the magistrates' dais, stood a table stacked with legal reference books. These were the tools of the trade. The means whereby the system could be mobilised, precedents established, and justice could be satisfactorily quantified. Crime must be evaluated in terms of concrete facts, not ethereal concepts; in terms of the cost of the picture ruined, not the quality of its creation. At the table sat a man, his fingers drumming in a moment of idleness. On the benches in front of him huddled a strange mixture of people, unified by no discernible common thread.

There was a neat, smartly dressed woman in early middle age, who betrayed her anxiety only through the occasional distracted playing of her fingers round her ear-rings. What was she, wondered Minto? A headmistress, perhaps; or a doctor; or a senior civil servant. Why was she here? An aura of competence emanated from her. An aura of competence undermined by an uncertainty as unfamiliar as it was niggling to her self-esteem. Next to her crouched a workman in overalls, staring straight ahead, a rolled copy of the *Sun* sprouting from his back pocket like a growth. And beyond them lounged an eye-catchingly beautiful black girl in her late teens, nodding her head to the rhythm of a Walkman. As he watched, an official approached her and demanded that she switch it off. She complied with an ill grace, her jaw continuing to work on gum, her foot still moving in time with the remembered music.

Minto looked at his watch. Proceedings were due to begin in three minutes.

He glanced at the court schedule, a typed sheet which he had acquired at the entrance to the building. Thomas Donat. That was the name of the first defendant of the afternoon, the man who stood accused of criminal damage to a picture in the Royal Gallery. Who was Thomas Donat? What would he look like? Would he be dragged in like some crazed, wild thing, strait-jacketed, spilling abuse and incoherence across the courtroom? Some ghastly piece of human wreckage, the mental equivalent of the broken, mangled body dragged from a car crash or bomb explosion? Suddenly Minto dreaded the prospect of seeing Thomas Donat, wished himself away from it all, anywhere, back in his flat, at the paper, in a cinema. What had all this to do with him? For a moment he felt dangerously exposed, unprotected by the cloak of civilisation with which his job as an arts feature writer normally endowed him. He thought of Elaine McBride. For a moment this random juxtaposition of art and violence was more shocking than he'd been prepared to believe.

Then it started: the usher announced in a loud voice: 'The court will stand.' And three people, two women and a man were filing in from a door at the back of the room and taking their places on the dais. The magistrates. They were undistinguished, surprisingly ordinary. Where was the majesty of the law, Minto wondered? The older woman, the chairman presumably, sat down in the middle. She had ruddy cheeks and wispy grey hair, and looked like the sort of person who might run a village post office. She peered cautiously out into the courtroom as if bracing herself for some instant challenge to her authority. Flanking her on either side sat the younger woman, tight-lipped and frosty, and the man, bespectacled, in his thirties, his eternal undermanagerhood evinced by the battery of pens arrayed in the outer breast pocket of his jacket.

Raggedly people began to sit down again. Minto was aware of a movement to his right and looked across to see a door opening and another man being led in. A man in his sixties with silver-grey hair. A man dressed in a crumpled grey suit and a tieless white shirt buttoned at the collar who walked with a slow, shuffling movement. A man with two days' growth of beard, who none the less still retained the vestige of good looks: there were strong lines to his face and dark deep-set eyes, eyes which momentarily ranged round the room and registered an emotion that Minto could only analyse as profound mystification. Mystification edged with fear. His first sight of Thomas Donat. Thomas Donat, enemy of society. Thomas Donat, violator of works of art. The defendant swayed slightly, an arm went out to support him, and he was allowed to ease down gently into a chair.

An unfamiliar reaction suddenly welled up within Minto. He was unprepared for it, so it hit him hard. He looked across at Donat and was for a moment overwhelmed by the tragedy of the man. A great wave of human sympathy broke over him, knocking the mental breath out of him, leaving him gasping for air. That poor bastard, sitting there all alone, unprotected against the world. It was the pathos of the cornered animal. It was the pathos of the uncomprehending victim of an accident. And in some obscure way he sensed it was the pathos of betrayal. Shocked, as much by the fact of his reaction as by its force, he tried to rearrange himself, take himself in hand. He looked across at the magistrates, looked up at the sunlight shafting in through the windows, looked anywhere to take his eyes away from the man in the dock. This just wouldn't do. He was Minto Maitland, arts feature writer of a leading Sunday newspaper. He was thirty-two, unmarried, self-sufficient, and able to do without all this. He didn't need it, it needn't touch him.

But it did.

The clerk of the court, the man who had been sitting at the table stacked with reference books, was now addressing the magistrates' bench. He spoke crisply, confidently. 'This case is number one on your worships' list this afternoon. Thomas Donat. This man was arrested yesterday at 3.35 p.m. in the Royal Gallery, London, West Central One. He stands accused of criminal damage to a picture in the collection of the gallery, the property of the nation.'

The chairman of the magistrates cleared her throat awkwardly and said something barely audible to the clerk. The clerk nodded wisely, then murmured in reply: 'We are in no position to take this further at this stage. Because of the value of the picture concerned, this is not a matter for this court . . .'

There was a second interruption from the village postmistress, as she shuffled through the sheaf of papers in front of her with a mixture of anxiety and irritation. 'What is the value of the picture? We . . . er . . . we don't seem to have a note of it here . . .'

A moment of uncertainty afflicted even the clerk of the court, who hitherto had given the impression of being the man in real charge of proceedings, gracefully humouring the bench of magistrates into the illusion that they had some control over what was going on. The matter was resolved by the counsel for the Crown Prosecution Service who rose to his feet and asked permission to contribute the relevant information.

'Yes, yes,' said the chairman impatiently.

'The value of the picture is one point five million pounds.' He paused, for the figure to sink in, then added, with a flourish: 'Sterling,' and sat down, well pleased with his contribution.

'Thank you,' said the chairman, making an elaborate note.

So. It was established. One point five million pounds. And every one of those one million five hundred thousand pounds was an extra weight of damnation against the man. Every one of them magnified the severity of the crime in the eyes of the law. And every one of them increased the vehemence of the punishment to be meted out to him. The arbitrariness of this line of reasoning upset Minto. If only Thomas Donat had reserved his violent attack for some other, less valuable object in that room in the gallery. If only he'd slashed with his knife at the fire-extinguisher, or a catalogue, or an exit sign. Then, although the violence of the act would have been the same, he would probably have been let off with a caution. It was the money that counted.

But then another thought struck Minto. Perhaps this speculation might be missing the point for a different reason. Perhaps Thomas Donat had always intended his violence for that one picture. Perhaps it was a premeditated act, directed against that specific target. But if so, why? Why *The Island of the Dead*? And why *The Island of the Dead*, second version? These were not the questions that the court would answer, nor even, he suspected, get to grips with at all. But he himself, having laid eyes upon the man responsible for this outrage, having sensed and shared his grief in the most unexpected way, knew intuitively that there was more to this than some mere random vandalism. That acts like these have explanations as well as punishments.

The chairman of the magistrates drew herself up to her most commanding height and addressed the prisoner: 'We are refusing jurisdiction, and we are not going to hear your case in this court. We will be committing it to the Crown Court. In the meantime we will decide the question of bail.'

The other two magistrates nodded cautiously, as if they

sensed a trap but were not yet competent to identify where it might lie.

The Crown Prosecution Service lawyer bobbed up again. 'I have to submit the strongest possible objection to the granting of bail in this case.' He was a small, balding man with heavy spectacles. He gave the impression now of going through the motions, of mouthing a set text. He continued: 'The defendant stands accused of an act of grotesque and gratuitous violence against a highly valuable work of art, a painting by . . .' he paused, and checked his notes '. . . by Arnold Böcklin, valued at one point five million pounds. If he is not restrained in custody, there is every possibility that he may commit more acts of violence against persons or property.'

Now a new player in the drama was on his feet. The counsel for the defence was a tall, gangling young man. Minto had made an earlier enquiry of the paper's legal correspondent as to what sort of representation the defendant could count on at this stage. Apparently this man would be the Legal Aid duty solicitor. He was likely to have conducted a brief interview with his client perhaps quarter of an hour before the case. What could he possibly have gleaned in that time?

'Your worships, I respectfully submit to your attention the report of the police doctor who attended my client when in police custody earlier today, together with the report of the duty psychiatrist in attendance today at this court. You will see that neither authority in his assessment finds any evidence that my client is normally of a violent disposition but that when examined he was diagnosed as suffering from a relatively high degree of shock. Furthermore, although my client's memory of the incident is confused, he has expressed his profound regret for what took place in the Royal Gallery yesterday, and wishes to help the authorities in any way he can. I would therefore like to apply for bail on behalf of the defendant on the grounds that he represents no further threat to persons or property, and is more than willing to comply with any requirements for medical or other examination that may be made by this court.'

The gangling figure sat down, and there was a momentary silence. The magistrates began muttering together, then the chairman leant down to the clerk for more consultation. Minto caught the words 'further psychiatric reports', which were followed by much sage and relieved nodding from the bench. But all was clearly still not well. The chairman looked across at the defendant with a perplexed expression on her face. She asked him: 'Am I correct in thinking that you are not a British passport holder and that you are not normally resident in this country?' She managed to phrase the question with enough surprise and disdain to suggest that this was an error almost as serious as the charge he was already facing.

Unwillingly, Minto's gaze was drawn once more to the forlorn figure in the dock. He sat there, apparently for a moment unaware that he was being addressed. Then he looked up with sad, tired eyes, and gave his head a little shake. It was not so much a reply as a desperate attempt to clear his mind, to comprehend what was being demanded of him; the fog in the man's brain was almost visible, wafting about the familiar landmarks of his mental existence, occasionally clearing sufficiently for momentary recognition of a fact about himself, then thickening again to consign him to perplexed obscurity. Minto experienced an almost physical pain in watching him.

The lanky defence lawyer rose again. 'My client is a Canadian citizen,' he confirmed.

'Is he staying in this country on business?'

'No, I understand he is here on a family visit.' All attempt to elicit response from the defendant had been abandoned now. It was as if they were discussing someone who wasn't in the room; or perhaps a backward child not capable of answering for himself. Thomas Donat sat on, crouching a little forward in his chair, bemused by what was passing over his head. A Canadian, thought Minto. Visiting his family. A curious background for a man who had just committed a violent attack on other people's property. Let alone a violent attack on a very valuable picture. And a totally uncharacteristic action at that. It didn't make much sense whichever way you looked at it.

'Is there anyone prepared to stand bail for the defendant?' enquired the chairman.

'Yes, madam.' The defence counsel was leafing through

papers, and found the information he sought. 'My client's niece, Mrs Leila Parsons. At whose house the defendant has been residing since his arrival in this country.' He gave an address in Putney.

Minto made a discreet note of it.

'Is Mrs Parsons in court?'

A quiet voice from in front of Minto said, 'Yes, madam. I'm here.' And the neat, well-dressed woman with the ear-rings half rose from her place. Intrigued, Minto watched the reaction of Thomas Donat. For a moment the man stared at her with amazement; then a half-smile of recognition crossed his face, before his features relapsed into a preoccupied glaze.

There was more confabulation between the chairman and the clerk of the court.

'Are you prepared to give financial surety?'

'As far as is within my means, yes.' She spoke gently, but with a certain authority. She gave the impression of substance, of not being someone easily trampled upon. Analysing what he heard, Minto realised that although her English was perfect, something in her intonation suggested that Mrs Parsons was not speaking her native tongue. Was she perhaps Canadian, like her uncle? Or was she of some obscurer extraction which he couldn't immediately define?

'Are you prepared to undertake that the defendant will live and sleep at your home during the period of his bail?'

'Certainly I am. He has been staying with us since his arrival in this country. We'd expect to continue to look after him. I can assure you he will be safe with us.'

There was something impressive about the way she said it. Minto had been half expecting that Mrs Parsons's assurance would be to the effect that Donat would not run away while in her care. But no: she'd simply said that he'd be safe with her. Safe.

The court remained suspended in a state of indecision. The lawyer for the Crown Prosecution Service spoke again about the inadvisability of allowing such a potentially dangerous criminal to roam the streets. The clerk of the court offered further discreet advice to the three magistrates above him. Finally the justices announced that they were to withdraw for a few minutes to consider the case. They filed out awkwardly, as if anxious to suppress any implication of defeat in their retreat.

When they re-emerged, the chairman announced that they were prepared to grant bail to Thomas Donat on condition that he lived and slept at the Putney address of Mrs Leila Parsons, pending his appearance at a Crown Court. He was also to surrender his passport and make himself available for such further psychiatric consultation as the authorities might direct.

Minto walked slowly from the courtroom in an unaccountable state of elation at their decision.

When he emerged into the sunlight he stood still for a moment, relieved to be back amongst normality, away from the fetid atmosphere of arbitrariness and constraint of the building he had just left. But at the same time he felt perplexed. Where did all this leave him? No further forward in the pursuit of Thomas Donat; no nearer to unravelling the mystery of why he had attacked the picture. He was going to have to write this wretched article in the near future, but what the hell was he going to say? The proceedings he had just witnessed had been remarkably unproductive of good copy. OK, Elaine, it's no go, a non-starter: the man's just a nutter, a hundred-per-cent fruit-cake. He walked into the gallery on a two-day pass from the loony bin, laid into this picture at random, and now the men in white coats have caught up with him. Let's kill the idea now. It could have been a good one, but let's be big enough to admit defeat when there's no way forward. All right?

But no, it wasn't all right. One thing that his recent experience in court three had convinced him of was that Thomas Donat ran deeper than that. There was something subtler in his motivation, something that he was either hiding or for the time being incapable of expressing. Yes, but Minto could still wash his hands of the business, couldn't he? Draw a line under it now, walk away from it on the pretext that he'd reached a dead end. But the bugger of it was he didn't want to. He wanted to know more. He wanted to be there when Thomas Donat finally unburdened himself. God damn it, something in him wanted to help the guy.

He needed a drink. He walked for two or three minutes, turned up a side-street, and came upon a pub that was still open. He ordered brandy, then sat down as far away as possible from the group of garrulous builders congregated round a fruit machine, settling himself at a table by the window looking out into the road.

Thomas Donat. Canadian, late sixties, in London on a family visit to his niece in Putney. A family man, anxious to keep in touch with relations over the Atlantic, setting aside time to fly over to spend a week or two with them. Thomas Donat, a man described by both the police doctor and the court duty psychiatrist as being apparently of a non-violent disposition; and yet a man who had walked into one of London's leading public galleries yesterday afternoon with an eight-inch kitchen knife and stabbed a painting by Arnold Böcklin into near destruction. Thomas Donat, who had sat there today with an awful resignation, an animal ensnared in a trap, no longer resisting, just staring about him with sad, bemused eyes.

He was depressed and disturbed. Thomas Donat had engaged his sympathy and he hadn't been prepared for it. He wasn't used to having his emotions hijacked in this way. He felt threatened, intruded upon. He couldn't function properly unless he was in control. He was only secure so long as he felt certain of his continuing ability to uncouple from whatever or whomever he had become, by his own judicious decision, connected to. His relationships had to be regulated by a periodic testing of that uncoupling mechanism. And apart from anything else, it was so bloody unprofessional for a journalist to feel like this about someone he was meant to be investigating objectively. It was something that he would prefer Elaine, for instance, not to know too much about.

He'd just finished his drink when he looked up and saw her through the window. At first he thought she was just another woman out shopping, because all he registered was a figure clutching a John Lewis carrier bag in her hand. But then he recognised the neat dark blue jacket and skirt, and the competent, well-groomed cut of her greying hair. Christ, it was Mrs Leila Parsons.

She'd stopped still now, and was staring at something. She glanced round momentarily, and he saw the look of horrified despair on her face. Then he realised what she was staring at. A car, presumably her car, parked at a meter. Parked at a meter with a big yellow clamp round its wheel.

Without thinking, he ran out and went straight up to her.

'I'm so sorry – is this your car?' he said.

She nodded, wordlessly.

'Is there any way I can help?'

'I don't understand it,' she murmured miserably. She was grappling with herself, trying not to give in to it all. 'I put the right amount of money in, I swear I did. But it doesn't seem to have registered properly. And now they've clamped me. It couldn't have happened at a worse time . . .' Her voice tailed away and he was suddenly afraid that she was going to cry.

'They're bastards, those people. Real bastards.'

'You see, I just don't know what to do now.' He sensed the sudden wave of despair breaking over her, threatening to engulf her. The tension of the day, the effort of coping with the unfamiliar ritual of the court, of coming to terms with her uncle's appalling aberration, of alleviating his agony, all of it had become too much. She'd met all the challenges so far and dealt with them. But this was one too many, this extra unfairness. This was the point when her normally extensive reserves of resilience and resolve gave way. This was the moment of crumbling. Her voice was tiny now, barely above a whisper: 'I have a sick relation with me. Someone I've got to get home urgently.'

'Look,' said Minto, 'I'd very much like to help you. I realise you don't know me, but you can trust me, I promise you. Here's my card, take it . . . you see, I'm an art critic' – the modification came instinctively to him, sounding less aggressive than journalist – 'I work for this newspaper, I'm perfectly respectable.' He gave a little laugh to put her at her ease, but she was past such comfort. She took the card, clutching it anxiously in her hand and running over it with unseeing eyes.

Minto went on: 'Give me your car keys, and go straight back with your sick relation in a taxi. The main thing is to get him home. I'll wait here and get the car released for you.' She stood there dubiously. Was one part of her subconscious mind wondering how he knew that her sick relation was a man? It had slipped out by mistake. But if it signified, she disregarded it. There were too many other problems occupying her attention. She shook her head in an effort to pull herself together and take a decision.

When she spoke she was unable to suppress the gratitude. 'Oh, God. Would you really do that for me?'

'Of course I will.'

'But you may have to wait ages.'

'Don't worry about that, I've got nothing particular to do this afternoon. You go and catch your taxi. Just leave me the keys and your address. And perhaps your driving licence too.'

She paused, then handed them all over, scribbling the information on a scrap of paper from her bag. It was superfluous, of course. Minto already had the address in his notebook, but he had to play the game or he'd lose her. Despite everything, he noticed, her handwriting was neat and clear. She said: 'I'd call my husband to cope with this, but he's away on business. In Brazil.' She gave an odd little laugh, at the outlandishness of the destination. Then, abruptly, as if she could bear the complications of the situation no longer, she was gone, hurrying back along the pavement in the direction of the court.

Minto stood there for a moment, imagining the crumpled and fearful figure waiting for her at the door, waiting to be taken away to the temporary refuge of her house, waiting to be driven away to the one welcoming landmark of his London experience. Then Minto turned back into the pub. The first thing he did was ring the police to arrange for the clamp release. The second was to order another drink.

He sat down again. He would be in this pub for a couple of hours at least. Time to gather his thoughts. It had been a disturbing day, what with the interview with Elaine, the visit to Thornton-Bass, the courtroom, and now this. There were many unanswered questions, many things niggling him. For a moment he was back in the conservation studio at the gallery, staring down at the stretcher of the Böcklin, the physical scaffolding from which the picture had been detached. And there it had been. The Courtney label. Discreet, but unavoidable. See, it was announcing. I'm behind everything, if you only look.

Marriott.

There was something he could do here, to fill in the time. He pulled out his mobile phone again and called Charles Benson. He demanded the bones of the Marriott cutting file. Yes, here. On the telephone, why not? Balancing the slim machine on his shoulder, he wrote notes in his pad.

'Leslie Marriott,' read Benson. 'Born Bermondsey 23 July 1920. Died last year in the South of France. Created KBE 1983 for services to British industry and for charitable works. Mostly donations to the Conservative Party, I suspect. Knighthood stripped from him in 1989 when sentenced to two years' imprisonment for fraud and false accounting—'

'What does that mean?' demanded Minto.

'He got caught.'

'Doing what?'

'Cooking the books. Illegal share dealing. He was stupid. He got greedy. He didn't just milk the cow, he bloody raped it.'

'You city boys have a graphic way with words. Anything else?'

'Well, there was some talk at the time of an arms deal or two, even drug money. But nothing was ever proved.'

Minto folded away the telephone, put his pen down and drained the rest of his glass.

He had things to celebrate. As a journalist, anyway, he had plenty to give thanks for. He was establishing murky connections in the past of Sir Alexander Courtney; connections with Marriott, a known criminal; connections linking both men to *The Island of the Dead*. Connections which were at the very least suggestive, and certainly worth further investigation. On top of that, hadn't he just succeeded in infiltrating himself into the very heart of the family of the man responsible for the crime of violence which he was simultaneously investigating? It was a *coup*. A scoop. An act of supreme professionalism.

But he wasn't happy.

Suddenly he wished that he hadn't got involved, that he'd gone to interview Saul Bellow instead. He wished he'd never set eyes on Thomas Donat. That he hadn't undertaken to return the car, hadn't got his emotions engaged. It was dangerous, all this. Very dangerous indeed.

6

'I really am most exceptionally grateful to you, Mr Maitland.'
Leila Parsons stood in the doorway of her neat Victorian villa
in Putney. She wore a cool white blouse, a blue cotton skirt
and low shoes. She was composed now, emanating neat
practicality. Minto guessed she was used to being on top
of the situation, that her momentary lapse into the wholly
uncharacteristic sort of panic which had persuaded her to
entrust the care of her car to a complete stranger was an
incident she would prefer to put behind her. That was the
way she functioned. She didn't like fuss. Even disasters
like yesterday's must be coped with sensibly. Other people
snapped. She made a point of always coping. Until the
clamping, that was. 'Won't you come in for a moment? So
that we can settle up on what I owe you.'

Minto judged that any attempt to refuse payment would
be a mistake. Acts of altruistic philanthropy arouse suspicion
when they involve unsolicited donations of money as well as
time. To reveal that he could easily reclaim the expense from
his newspaper would be to blow his cover. He smiled and
followed her in. But he felt uneasy. He was deceiving her,
of course. This neat, practical woman with the flecks of grey
in her hair had just been through a harrowing twenty-four
hours. Her husband was abroad on business. Single-handedly
she had just brought home an uncle who was on police bail for
a sickeningly violent offence. And here was Minto, pretending
to be someone he wasn't in order to get a story out of her.

She led the way through the house. A pleasantly leafy small
garden beckoned out of the french windows. 'Won't you come
out? It's such a lovely evening, isn't it? I was sitting out here.
Can I offer you a drink? I've got some beer in the fridge.'

'That would be nice.'

She disappeared inside again, and Minto looked about him. It was seven in the evening, but the sun was still warm. It had been another glorious day.

She came back out with a tin and a glass. 'This is the sort of weather that is wasted on a city, don't you think?' she said.

He smiled at her. 'I don't know. Out here you can almost imagine yourself in the country.' It was true. It was hard to connect these peaceful surroundings with magistrates' courts. With police cells. With the frenzied mutilation of a canvas in a stifling picture gallery.

'Won't you sit down, Mr Maitland?'

He lowered himself into a deckchair. How to play it, without revealing himself as a calculating shit? To be a calculating shit is one thing; to be revealed as one is quite another.

'I hope your sick relation is feeling a little better,' he ventured.

'Oh. Yes, thank you. He's resting upstairs. He's . . . he's very tired, actually.'

Minto poured out his beer and took a long draught of it. It was pleasantly cold and refreshing. He felt something brushing against his legs and reached down to find a ginger cat rubbing against him.

'I am so sorry. Does he bother you?'

'Not in the least. I like cats.'

'He's a lazy old so and so,' said Mrs Parsons fondly as the animal padded away and stretched out in the sun.

'Actually, I've always preferred cats to dogs. I admire their independence.'

There was a pause. She gave him an uneasy look, then murmured, 'It's funny you should say that.' She picked up her own glass abstractedly and wiped the bottom of it to avoid its staining the top of the table. 'That's exactly what uncle Thomas said when he arrived last week.' For a moment she closed her eyes reminiscently. 'Strange, how well he seemed then. So delighted to be here. You wouldn't have thought he had a care in the world.'

She was speaking as much to herself as to him, but Minto felt uncomfortable. He paused awkwardly, then said; 'Mrs Parsons, I haven't had a chance properly to explain myself. It was difficult in the brief time that we met earlier today.'

He saw a shadow of doubt cross her eyes. Careful now. Don't ruin it. Don't lose her trust. 'You see I was in court number three at Marlborough Street this afternoon . . . in connection with another case. I happened to see you and . . . and your uncle. So I realised the dilemma you were in when I came across you later with your car clamped. I'm so sorry. It must have been a wretched time for you.'

She sighed. There was an element of relief in that sigh. 'So you know about all this. Well, you've been very kind. Yes, it's been a terrible time. What happened in the Royal Gallery was all so . . . so utterly . . .'

'Unexpected?'

'Yes. That's exactly it. Unexpected.' She seized gratefully on the word. 'My uncle is a sweet man. I've never known anything like this to happen to him before. It's just not in his nature to be violent.' She seemed pleased to talk. Minto sensed that it was a release for her. That with her husband abroad on business there hadn't been a chance until now for her to stand back from the events of the past twenty-four hours, to objectivise them by speaking about them. To get them under control.

'Are you close to him? Do you know him well?'

'I'm close to him, in the sense that he's my late father's first cousin. But no, I haven't seen much of him since I left Canada.'

'When was that?'

'Oh, longer ago than I care to remember. I came over as a student in 1967. I met my husband and married him in 1970. I've been here ever since. We've been back four or five times on visits when we picked up contact with uncle Thomas, but not so much since my father died. Still, he's always been such a kindly, gentle man. Very welcoming whenever we did see him.'

'Does he come over here much?'

'Not at all until now. This was his first visit. He wrote to me in spring saying he was thinking of coming to England to see the sights, so of course I told him he must stay with us. He arrived last Friday.' She shook her head, baffled by the sequence of events she was describing.

'And you say he was OK when he arrived?' Minto leant forward, cradling his beer. He didn't know whether he hated himself more for the possibility that his concern was simulated or for the possibility that it was real.

'He was fine. A bit tired, perhaps, at first, but by Sunday he seemed in great shape. We drove out to Windsor and had a look round the castle. He took a lot of photographs, he was really enjoying himself. As far as I could tell.' She paused, seeming to doubt for a moment whether any of her perceptions about other people could be relied upon again. Then she went on: 'Well, we dropped my husband at Heathrow to catch his flight to Brazil on our way home, and came back here. The next day Uncle Thomas went off by himself, saying he was going to do a few sights. Buckingham Palace, he said, the galleries, that sort of thing.'

'That was Monday, the day before yesterday. How was he after that?'

'Well, that's the point. He came back that evening in pretty bad shape. He seemed very withdrawn. Even a little bit . . . well, I know this is strange, but even a little bit frightened.'

'Frightened of what?'

'I couldn't tell you. He wouldn't say. I asked him if everything was all right, and he said yes, but it clearly wasn't. Then yesterday, late morning, he set off again without saying very much. Frankly he looked a bit rough. Dishevelled, if you like.'

'Did he say where he was going?'

'No, he didn't.' She gave a bitter little laugh. 'I suppose I should have probed a bit more. I would have done, if I'd realised at that point what he was taking with him.'

'What do you mean exactly?'

'Half an hour later I decided to make myself a sandwich and when I went to cut the bread I couldn't find the bread knife.'

The ginger cat stretched, yawned, then pulled himself up to amble purposefully into the undergrowth.

For a moment Minto paused, remembering the stricken canvas that he had seen that morning in the Royal Gallery.

Laid out in bandaged tatters on the table. Laid out like a corpse. He waited for her to go on.

'I don't suppose I'll ever get that knife back,' she said at last. 'It's crown evidence now.'

'I'm so sorry. It must have been the most appalling shock for you. Did the police ring you?'

'Yes. About half-past six last night, from Vine Street police station.' She smoothed her skirt and looked up briskly, as if to indicate that brooding on it wouldn't get anyone anywhere. 'Of course I went down at once. To give what assistance I could.'

'And how was he when you got to him?'

'He seemed sort of mystified more than anything else. I suppose it must have been shock. He didn't say very much. I think he found it very difficult to get any words out at all.' She paused and frowned. Minto suddenly realised she was moved by what she was saying and was haunted by the spectre of a further loss of control. She swallowed and went on: 'You see, it was rather sweet in a way: although he hardly spoke he kept touching my hand with his in a gesture of ... of reassurance, I suppose. He seemed to be trying to communicate that something very awful had happened, but he didn't want me to worry because he would be all right. In the end he would be all right.'

'You've no inkling what this has all been about?'

She shook her head and said, 'None at all.' But she said it rather too quickly. Minto sensed the shutters going up. Maybe he had asked too many questions for a casual passer-by, even for a casual passer-by who had turned into a Good Samaritan. Or maybe he had just asked the wrong sort of questions.

'I'm sorry,' he said. 'You must think me dreadfully inquisitive and intrusive. Please forgive me. It's just that ... well, seeing your uncle in court I felt so sorry for him.' He waited. Had he judged it right? He decided to go on: 'You see, I was looking at him in court: there was this sweet, innocent elderly man. And there they were describing this horribly violent attack on the picture. And the two things just didn't seem to add up. They didn't go together.'

She smiled back at him. 'Tell me something, Mr Maitland,' she said, 'what was it that you said you do?'

'Oh me? I'm a writer . . . an art critic. A reviewer, that sort of thing.'

A cloud of doubt crossed her eyes. 'What was an art critic doing in a magistrates' court?'

Before he could answer he saw her looking past him, suddenly distracted. She got up. Quickly. Urgently.

Minto turned and saw why. There, in the french windows, his hand outstretched against the doorpost to support himself, stood Thomas Donat. He wore a thin dressing-gown over trousers and slippers. He had shaved, cutting himself once or twice, and made some attempt to brush his hair. He narrowed anxious eyes against the setting sun and swayed slightly.

'I . . . I heard voices,' he said softly. Now he listened for it, Minto could hear the accent. There was Canadian there. And an underlay of something else as well.

'You should be getting your rest, Uncle Thomas. You shouldn't be down here, you must be exhausted.'

He shook his head slowly. 'Couldn't sleep,' he murmured and shuffled forward.

Minto was out of his chair now, guiding the old man by the elbow to a chair in the shade. He sat down with painful slowness. There was something infinitely sad in that movement. A hopelessness. A devastation. He looked up uncertainly at Minto.

'Uncle Thomas, this is Mr Maitland. He's been very kind to me. He rescued my car for me this afternoon.'

Thomas Donat nodded, apparently comprehending at least that Minto was a friend. That was enough to be going on with.

Minto said, rather more heartily than he had intended: 'Are you feeling a bit better, Mr Donat?'

Donat narrowed his eyes again in that expression of mystified concern which was momentarily familiar from the courtroom. Minto thought he wasn't actually going to speak, but finally he said: 'Yes, a little better,' and Minto felt strangely gratified.

'Would you like a drink, Uncle Thomas?' asked Mrs Parsons.

He shook his head, but smiled back at her with a bleary gratitude.

'Well, what a lovely evening,' said Minto.

They sat in silence for a moment. The sun was still warm and the foliage was lush. A bee buzzed about the hollyhocks, and Minto drank another deep draught from his glass.

There was a rustling in the bushes in the far corner of the garden. It was not a loud noise, but it was disruptive, disturbing. It carried across the grass to them with an unmistakable urgency. With a repressed hostility. It was a fevered, anticipatory rustling. The sound of one animal stalking another. Of haunches flexing. Of an imminent attack.

They all sensed it. The menace transmuted itself through the leaves. Minto sat up straighter and put his glass down on the table. And then came the small explosion of energy as the cat leapt for its prey. A crashing through undergrowth. And the anguished, heart-rending cry, of the little bird caught in the cat's claws. Helpless. In its death throes.

Everyone sat transfixed. In the gentle silence of the evening it had been impossible to disregard the sounds of abrupt and wanton carnage. A moment later the cat emerged from the undergrowth with its trophy held triumphantly between its teeth. The tiny bird hung limp and bloodied, its plumage bedraggled.

'Oh, God,' said Thomas Donat, trying to rise up from his chair.

'No, don't get up, Uncle. That wretched cat. There's nothing to be done now, I'm afraid.'

Minto himself felt an overpowering desire to help. Somehow. Without knowing what he was going to do, he went forward to investigate. The cat, its eyes flaring, its ears back, dropped its trophy and retreated defiantly before him. Minto crouched over the mangled bird. It was still twitching feebly.

'But the bird,' breathed Donat. 'It is alive still?'

There was a spade leaning against the wall nearby. Minto took hold of it and used it to lift the mortally injured bundle of bloodied feathers to a less visible corner of the garden.

'No, it's dead,' lied Minto over his shoulder. 'I'll just give it a decent burial.'

When he came back to sit down, he laughed, trying to set things right again. He said, 'One always forgets that nature is so . . . so violent.'

Violent. The word hung in the air. Threatening. Dangerously evocative. For a moment he visualised the kitchen knife. And the ribboned canvas.

He glanced across at Thomas Donat peering miserably after the cat as it slunk behind the bushes sniffing for the prey that had been taken from it. He wished the old man wouldn't look like that.

Then Donat spoke. He spoke with such an unexpected clarity and conviction that both Minto and Leila Parsons stared back at him in surprise. He said: 'It was a long time ago.'

'What was, Uncle Thomas?'

Donat brought his hand slowly up to his cheek, and held it there for a moment. Tenderly. As if the cheek itself were sore.

'You see, she hit me.'

'Who hit you?'

He brought his hand down to the edge of the chair, as if to steady himself. Minto could see it clench round the aluminium armrest. 'It was her. It was Greta.'

'Greta? I don't think I know Greta.' Leila Parsons paused, perplexed, shrugging at Minto. Minto's heart leapt. The action included him in a conspiracy. He was on her side. He had won her trust. 'Who is Greta? Is she a friend of yours in Canada?'

He shook his head. 'No, not in Canada.' He paused. 'Before that. She must be dead now, I never saw her again. You see, it was all a very long time ago.' The anxiety was still there, ingrained in every line of his face, but his voice was stronger. There was a gathering momentum. As if talking was regenerating him.

It was Minto who said, 'Do you want to tell us about it, Mr Donat?'

'Yes. Yes, I do. I have been thinking much about it and now I want to speak of these things. It is better that you should know. I want to tell you about Greta and my life with her in Budapest.'

'In Budapest? In Hungary?'

'Yes, in Hungary. It happened many, many years ago.'

And he narrowed his eyes again. As if peering very intently down a mine shaft. A single mine shaft.

By November it was cold in Budapest. A city of extremes, reflected Thomas as he lay on the bed next to her. The oven heat of August had given way to the icy winds of late autumn, and by four o'clock in the afternoon the grey skies had already massed heavy with the threat of snow. How could you keep an equilibrium in the face of such contrasts of weather? No doubt someone at party HQ was working on the problem; Central Committee had it in hand. Soon there would be an announcement that Socialism had triumphed over the climate. A detachment from the Writers' Union would be seconded exclusively to produce pieces backing the party line on the matter: poems on the one season as opposed to the four of them would ensue, polemics against capitalist inadequacies in the regulation of mean temperatures. Such bourgeois and unegalitarian concepts as summer or winter, as hotter or colder weather would have been eliminated from the people's consciousness.

Until such reconstruction became possible, it remained bitterly cold. Thomas drew on his cigarette and cast his eye about the apartment. To call it an apartment was an exaggeration. It was just a room, really. A room with a pair of fine high windows which looked out on Béla Bartók Street and spoke of grander, more opulent times. A room with a bed and a desk and three chairs. And a gramophone. The precious gramophone that creaked out the jazz from his record collection, most of which he had borrowed from Tibor. Downstairs there was a bathroom shared with the eight other tenants of the house. There was a paraffin heater in the corner, vainly labouring to counter the effect of the wind which insinuated itself irresistibly through the pair of fine high and ill-fitting windows.

They had just made love. She had pulled a blanket over her now, and she still had a thick jersey on. Even passion had not warmed them sufficiently to jettison all their clothes, but her skirt and underclothes lay abandoned in a heap on the floor.

She shivered slightly and murmured, 'I'm freezing, do you know that, Tamás?'

He didn't reply at once but continued to stare up at the ceiling, fighting the surge of disconsolate resentment which was rising up within him. Nothing was any good, was it? Not as things stood. He still taught, went through the motions with his students at the literature department of the university. Two weeks ago he'd had another article published in the *Szabad Nép*. An article on modern Hungarian music. A weak and feeble article which had miserably pulled its punches, failed to address the central questions. Why, for instance, was the work of Bartók, Hungary's most famous composer, the man who'd given his name to this street, no longer played in his home country? But on the other hand, if he had addressed these questions then the article would undoubtedly have been rejected. Maybe he should rewrite the piece along the lines on which it should have been written, and submit it to the magazine edited by Tibor's friend the poet Tamás Aczél. If the authorities hadn't closed it down by the time of the next publication date.

But the truth of the matter was he couldn't give his mind fully to any of these concerns. Not so long as Greta was making him so unhappy.

'Why don't you speak to me, Tamás?' she pressed him again.

'Because it's hopeless,' he said at last, his eyes still on the ceiling.

'What is hopeless?'

'Everything. Everything about us is hopeless.'

'What are you trying to say?' She propped herself up on her elbow and contemplated him.

'That either we should see more of each other. Or less. Like this I'm not happy.'

She frowned while she assimilated what he was telling her. 'We've been through all this before, for God's sake. I don't like it any more than you do. If I could make more opportunity to be with you, I would seize it with both hands. But it is difficult for me, you know that. I am not like you: I am not a free agent. I have to be careful.' She paused, and drew back behind her ear a blonde lock of hair that had fallen across her cheek. Then she added, pleadingly: 'But surely a little time together is better than no time at all?'

He sighed. He was up against that wall again. He decided to try it one more time: 'Christ, Greta, my darling, if only you'd let me prove it to you: I could make you so happy. Why don't you leave him, for God's sake? Then we could see each other the whole time instead of once every three weeks like we do now.'

'It's not so easy as you make it sound.'

'I think it could be. If you want something enough you can make it happen.'

'You must understand something: it's not so easy to leave a man like Peter.'

'No. I don't understand that.' He felt angry now at the absurdity of her husband. At the absurdity of her being married to him. 'What's so special about Peter? You don't still love him, do you? Don't tell me after all this time that you're worried about hurting his feelings?'

'No. He has no feelings.' She laughed bitterly. 'Not real feelings. It's not because I want to save his sensitivities, far from it. It's more that I don't think you've quite grasped what you're dealing with in Peter. You see, in his own way he's a powerful man. I don't know what he might be able to do to me. Or to you.'

'Greta, darling, I'm not going to let him hurt you. And I can stand up for myself. Look, I'm not a weakling.'

'I'm not talking about that sort of power. I'm not talking about him coming round and beating you up. If he wanted to do that, he could get others to do it for him.'

There was silence for a moment. Thomas was aware of the wind whistling through the window and the flickering of the paraffin stove. For a brief moment he glimpsed something in his heart which he hated her for having insidiously planted there. He sensed fear.

He reacted with anger again, as one does when confronted with intimations of one's own cowardice. He shook his head impatiently. 'These are just excuses. Why don't you admit it, why can't you be honest with yourself? Ultimately you're not prepared to leave him, are you? Well, I can't say I blame you. This apartment isn't exactly the lap of luxury. You're more comfortable where you are. Look, I don't know what power it is that this famous Peter wields, if he's chief commissar for party paper-clips or what, and frankly I'm not very much interested, but it seems to me you've taken a good look at your Peter's house up in Buda, whose address you never see fit to give me, you've taken a good look at the villa on Lake Balaton that probably goes with his job and decided that you'd prefer not to give it up if all you've got as an alternative is this place.'

She was crying now, turned away from him. 'I do not give you our address in Buda because what good would it do?' she sobbed. 'It would be dangerous if you tried to contact me there. It would bring us both into trouble.'

'So you keep telling me.'

'You're not kind, Tamás,' she whispered.

He knew he was not being kind to her. He hated the feeling. But she had caused it, hadn't she? She had caused it by all this mystification about her husband. She had caused it by her seeming reluctance to hand herself over to him full time. She had caused it by being so desirable and yet so irregularly available. She had caused it by making him angry. Because she'd caused it, he couldn't find it in his heart to comfort her. Not yet.

She was sitting on the edge of the bed now, slowly pulling her stockings back on. She ran her hair back into place with her fingers, dabbing her eyes with a handkerchief. Surreptitiously he watched her. What did he really know about her? Did he know anything more now than he'd discovered on that first day of intimacy on the Danube? Why had she been so parsimonious with her company in the long autumn weeks since? Once they had gone to the cinema together and sat all the way through an appalling Soviet film, the sort of propagandist garbage that most of the audience sniggered at under the cover of the darkness. He had ached for her, tortured by her proximity. And then immediately afterwards she had said she had to go, couldn't stay with him any longer, even though he knew from the taste of her lips in the blackness of the auditorium that she wanted him almost as much as he wanted her. After that there had been four or five occasions when she had found the opportunity to meet up with him in the apartment here, frantic couplings curtailed by her self-imposed deadlines. What was she up to? What was the truth about her husband? What did she really want from her relationship with Thomas?

As he watched the graceful movement with which she stood and began to slip back into her skirt, he felt the beginning of the melting of his resentment. All right, he thought, maybe this has gone on long enough. He was beginning to relish the prospect of his contrition and her forgiveness, savouring it before he set it in motion. Then something even more urgent began to assert itself, and he reached out for her, pulling her back down on to the bed.

'No, Tamás. No, not now.'

She struggled momentarily, but she fell alongside him. She hadn't properly fastened her skirt, and she put up only an imitation of resistance as he eased it up over her thighs again. He began to caress her earlobe with his tongue, and watched as her lips parted in an involuntary gasp of pleasure. Parted to reveal that distinctive gap in her front teeth. He ran his hand up her stockinged leg, reaching the flesh of her inner thigh.

'Greta,' he breathed.

'No, no,' she murmured, but the protest was mechanical rather than compelling, more like an adjunct to her excitement than a denial of it, and as she said it her legs parted wider. He began to squeeze her gently, rhythmically, in the way that he had learned pleased her.

Then came the rapping on the door. Instinctively they fell apart.

Again he sensed it in himself. Fear. Fear of the unexpected caller. Fear of the AVO car drawn up in the street outside.

'Who's there?' he called.

'It's me. Tibor. Quickly, open up.'

He was relieved, then annoyed. 'It's a little inconvenient . . .'

'Let me in. This is important.' Tibor's will could be rock hard. It wasn't so much that he was persuasive as single-minded. Utterly single-minded. Even Greta must have sensed it, because she was sitting up again on the edge of the bed, adjusting underclothes, smoothing down the crumpled skirt. The carnival was over before it had started. Their *rapprochement* was incomplete.

'For God's sake, wait,' called Thomas. He shrugged helplessly at her. She waved him on with a gesture that acknowledged the supervention of an irresistible fate and the passing of a moment of ill-judged lust.

In fact, as Thomas struggled with his trousers it was Greta herself who got to the door first to let Tibor in. Maybe she was curious. After all, this was the first time she had met him.

'Oh, hello.' He stood for a moment in the doorway, running quick, appraising eyes over her. His cheeks were flushed. He was always excitable. Excitable and, once set on a course of action, impervious to embarrassment. He'd said as much to Thomas on their first meeting the summer before last, soon after his release from the prison camp. Look, he'd declared, when you've been holed up in a place like that for three years, you don't bother too much with social niceties any more. Life's too short.

He walked past her and greeted Thomas.

'This is important, Tamás, you've got to come now.' Tibor was painfully thin. It was a legacy from those years in the camp, an imprisonment from which he had been released and rehabilitated as part of the Nagy regime's New Course. The New Course involved the party's unprecedented admission that mistakes had been made in the past. Tibor's release was a tacit admission that his confinement had been a mistake too. Good of them, wasn't it? Tibor had said with the heavy irony that Thomas had found so endearing in the man. But Tibor was not healthy: his hair was thinning and his eyes were watery. God knew what he had been through in that camp. Thomas had never probed the question, justifying his reluctance to himself as fine feeling. But in fact it was cowardice, wasn't it? He knew Tibor was braver and more durable than he was. He didn't want to learn any more details of Tibor's sufferings. The details would force him to confront his own inadequacy.

And there was another thing, another anxiety that preyed on his mind about his friend, though Tibor himself never referred to it: if Tibor's imprisonment had been a mistake according to the New Course, how was it officially viewed now, now that the New Course had been largely swept away with Nagy's deposition and the reinstatement of Rákosi? You couldn't help feeling that Tibor was a marked man. You couldn't help looking at him and thinking, how much longer before they pull him in?

Thomas was on his feet now, doing up his trousers and pulling on his shirt. Tibor was not the man to be fazed by the interruption of a friend's love-making. Not when he clearly had something of consuming absorption on his own mind.

'Tibor, not so fast. First I want to present you to Greta Kassák. Greta, this is my friend and colleague Tibor Monos.'

She nodded at him distantly, and said, 'I'm pleased to meet you. I've heard about you.'

He raised a hand in acknowledgement, but barely looked at her again. 'Delighted,' he murmured. 'Now, Tamás, you must listen to me.' His thin limbs were galvanised by a tenseness, a perceptible anticipation. 'I've come round straight away because there is a wonderful opportunity for you at short notice. The Writers' Union is making a deputation this evening. It is a group of twenty, but Gregor has pneumonia, and so we want you to join us. It's imperative that we should have a full complement to voice our protest to the Central Committee.'

'Wait a minute. What is this deputation, explain it to me?'

Tibor lowered himself into the chair at the desk and tapped out the last cigarette from his packet. He lit it with a shaking hand. He had almost no fingernails to speak of.

'Got a drink?' he demanded.

Thomas handed him a glass, filling it with a precious measure of palinka. Then he turned, bottle in hand, to offer some to Greta.

She had her coat on and she was standing near the door. Her eyes were dry now, and she had recovered some of her self-possession.

'I won't keep you,' she said. 'You have business to discuss, I can see that. I have to go anyway.'

There was a hardness to her tone which he had not

heard before. A hardness precluding receptivity to his own contrition.

'Greta,' he said pleadingly.

'No, I have to go.' She leant forward and kissed him briefly on the cheek, at the same time disengaging the grip of his hand on her arm. She slipped away through the door and he heard her footsteps clattering down the stone stairway. Running away from him. He would have gone after her, chased her into the street. But there was Tibor. Tibor, sitting there, taut with urgency. Tibor, challenging him to do his duty.

He stood for a moment, bottle still in hand, agonising. Tibor said, 'Come on, pour yourself some of that and sit down. We've got to talk.'

Thomas obeyed, pensively, and Tibor added, 'Look, for God's sake, I wouldn't come bursting in here if it wasn't important. I'm sorry if I interrupted anything, but for shit's sake there'll always be another time, won't there? And be honest with me: doesn't there come a point when the freedom of your country should be more important to you than a quick screw.'

'It's not like that,' he said.

'That's your trouble, isn't it, Tamás? The quick screw always has to be the grand passion. Forget it, huh? It'll only lead to trouble.' Tibor paused to drain his glass. 'Now listen, let me explain about this evening. You're going to join us, there are twenty of us from the Writers' Union, and we're going on a deputation to meet members of the Central Committee. It's a great chance to discuss our memorandum, to get our point of view across to the bastards. And listen: we understand Rákosi himself may be there.'

'Rákosi?' This was something. The party chairman himself, meeting a deputation of writers. You might have expected the commissar for literature at a pinch. Or more likely some self-important official from the Ministry of Culture. But Rákosi. That was extraordinary. So extraordinary that it made him uneasy. Thomas could not quite suppress in himself the suspicion that Rákosi's attendance was also a little bit ominous, too.

'There, I thought you'd be impressed.' Tibor seemed

unmoved by the implicit danger. Tibor saw it simply as an accolade, a reward for persistence, a gratifying acknowledgement that the sniping he had been orchestrating was beginning to draw the fire of the big guns. 'They're taking us seriously at last. Now do you see what an opportunity I'm giving you? This'll be something to tell your grandchildren about. The day I met Rákosi.'

'The day I met the bald git,' said Thomas. He'd been wondering if the fact of his meeting with Rákosi wouldn't in itself be the guarantee of a grandchildless future. But the joke made him feel a little better, lent him a momentary confidence. Tibor laughed too.

'Come on,' he said, 'we'd better get going. This is going to be better than spending the afternoon in bed with a scrubber.'

'She's not a scrubber.' Thomas paused, dissatisfied with the simple denial. 'Actually, she's the wife of a high-up party official.'

Christ, why had he said that? In some pathetic attempt to match Tibor's achievement in producing the party first secretary to be grilled by the Writers' Union? Was cuckolding a party official perhaps as splendid an anti-establishment gesture as pleading for intellectual freedom in front of Rákosi?

Tibor turned back, already out on the landing. His interest was briefly engaged. 'God almighty, what's a woman like that doing with you, I wonder? What did you say her name was?'

'Kassák. Greta Kassák.' Talking about her to Tibor hadn't been a good idea, he sensed that already. He felt disloyal to her now, as though he'd cheapened their intimacy by publicising it. He should have kept his mouth shut. But he'd wanted to prove to Tibor that he was capable of acts of daring, too.

Tibor shrugged, to indicate the name meant nothing. Then he was on his way again, clattering downstairs with surprising speed and agility. Once they were in the street, he said: 'I don't know who she is, but I know her type.'

'Who?'

'Your precious girlfriend. The Kassák woman.'

'What do you mean, you know her type?'

'She's bored. She's looking for kicks.'

'You're wrong, you know. There's more to her than that, you should talk to her. She feels very strongly about things.'

'What sort of things?'

'She feels very strongly about Hungary, for a start. She wants the Russians out.' It was true, he told himself. She'd found that Soviet war memorial on the Danube Bend as obscene as he had. Surely she had. But what were the other things she felt strongly about? Not rocking the boat? Keeping the house on Balaton? Having her cake and eating it? 'She can be very outspoken, you know,' he added.

'Why's she stay married to this party tosser, then?'

'Christ, I don't know. Give her a chance.'

Tibor slowed his pace for a moment and looked into Thomas's face as he spoke. 'Just be careful, Tamás, all right? I can see this one bringing you nothing but trouble.'

But then Tibor knew nothing about women. Nothing at all.

On the tram he sat wedged between Tibor and an enormous peasant woman, whose bulk and baggage spread over two seats. Baskets and bundles were strapped to her in all directions. She sat there immovable, breathing stertorously like some lumpen beast of burden. Intellectual freedom. Artistic integrity. Oh yes, she'd be very grateful to the Writers' Union for its deputation, wouldn't she? It would make all the difference to her existence to know that they were fighting for the independence of cultural life in Hungary. Who were they trying to fool? This was an act of supreme self-indulgence, wasn't it? And probably an act of supreme foolhardiness, too. Put your head above the parapet and you'd only get it blown off. Who'd thank them for it? Not this woman. The only social change she'd be interested in would be an increase in her turnip crop.

Shit. He suddenly felt very depressed. He thought of Greta, wiping the tears from her eyes. He thought of his own cynicism and frustration. Then he thought of Tibor and his three years in the camp. Now he felt ashamed of himself. Christ, there came a time when you had to get out and do something. Otherwise how could you ever change anything?

For reassurance he turned in the direction of his companion. Tibor was staring very intently out of the window, frowning slightly, absorbed in his own thoughts. He envied him his unblinking conviction, his confidence in himself.

'Where are we going?' asked Thomas.

'Republic Square.'

'What, party headquarters?'

'That's it.'

There was silence between them for a few moments. The tram drew to a halt and a mass of passengers pushed their way in. Women jostled each other, clutching their string shopping bags. Thomas caught the tantalising whiff of fresh-baked bread. Another man, standing very close to them, was reading *Népsport*, and arguing with a friend.

'Don't make me laugh. Of course Puskás is the best inside right in the country. He's the best bleeding inside right in the world.'

'I'm telling you he's lazy.'

'Lazy? I wish there were a few more lazy like him in the Honvéd team.'

'Look, I'm not saying he's a bad player. I'm just saying he only tries when he feels like it. That's not so good for the rest of the lads in the side. He's got to pull his weight every game if we're going to win the Olympics.'

'Pulled his finger out yesterday, then, didn't he? Six-one, look.' The score in the paper was emphasised with a jab of the finger. 'He got two and Hidegkúti got four.'

Tibor nodded his head in the direction of the dispute. 'Nice to see people buying the only newspaper in Budapest where you can believe what you read,' he said in a low voice. 'Pity it's only the football results.'

Thomas laughed, but Tibor was pulling at his sleeve, talking with sudden urgency.

'You know what I thought, when I was in there, when they had me, in that camp? When they were trying to make me believe things that I knew were not true?'

'What did you think?' The old tenseness had returned to the pit of Thomas's stomach.

'I thought that these lies they were giving us were like dead things. Immobile, inflexible. It's only truth that adjusts, it's only truth that is alive. With truth you have to make daily revisions, it changes with reality. Lies on the other hand are never renewed. Have you realised that, Tamás, do you understand what I'm telling you?'

Thomas took a deep breath and said, 'It's because I understand what you're telling me that I'm coming with you now.'

It was a curiously unreal sensation, the arrival at party headquarters. The deputation had assembled round the corner, in a bar, and moved off together mounting the steps to the front door of the building in a phalanx. Thomas recognised quite a few faces, although he didn't know them well. There were one or two former colleagues from the *Szabad Nép*; and then there were the leaders of the group, men like the poet Tamás Aczél and George Hámos, the editor of *Irodalmi Ujság*, the newspaper that had been suppressed earlier in the year. With much coughing and shuffling of feet the group was led into the hallway of the headquarters. It was stark and highly lit. Across one wall hung a large Hungarian flag with the hammer and sickle superimposed upon it. What had Tibor once said? Like a suppurating blemish on the face of your lover. Below it hung the inevitable portrait of Rákosi.

They were greeted politely enough by functionaries, men whose lapels bristled with party badges. A phoney *bonhomie* prevailed. It was almost as if the writers' deputation were a visiting football team being welcomed by the home side. Here were the common courtesies as a prelude to well-regulated competition, competition that would end with everyone shaking hands when the final whistle blew. Someone put a pen in Thomas's hand and asked him respectfully to write his name and address down in an official-looking book, just as a record of the occasion. He complied almost without thinking.

Then the writers' party were led through into the chamber.

And at a stroke the mood was changed. Suddenly the men they were confronting were dangerous.

They were hand-picked, of course. Specially selected. Only the most rigid party activists had been allowed in to make up the gathering which met the deputation. And they had been primed, worked up into a pitch of anger and resentment, so that the moment the group of writers were ushered into the chamber it was like walking into a wall of hostility. It was a physical thing. It even got to Tibor. Thomas watched him as he sat down ahead on the benches set aside for the visitors, facing the fifty or so who comprised the reception committee. Tibor had been one of the first in, but now he was momentarily confused, knocked off balance by the menace. You could see from his taut, white expression that even he had not bargained for this, that the reality of confrontation had come as a shock. Thomas watched his friend take himself in hand almost at once, gripping the back of the bench very tightly with spindly knuckles and concentrating his watery eyes on the opposition. Refusing to be intimidated. Refusing to be diminished.

What had they been told, these party activists? Thomas took his own seat in the row behind the deputation's spokesmen and gazed at them, wondering for a moment how they had been persuaded into such hatred. They were simple people, of course, none of them of great intellect. Dead from the neck up. What you had to do with these blockheads was isolate them from each other in your imagination. See them as individual, deeply inadequate units, not as a coherent team. Then they became comic, absurd. One by one they were laughable; ignorant, blustering time-servers, men who could only see salvation in the unthinking toeing of an increasingly illogical line. But it was hard to sustain the intellectual gymnastics necessary to separate them up and break their power. Once you let it slip and saw them *en masse* then they were threatening again.

A minute or two after the deputation was installed, there was a sudden scraping of chairs and everyone abruptly stood up. A door at the opposite end of the chamber opened, and there was Rákosi himself coming in with three henchmen. He moved oddly. There was something physically repellent about him. He was as bald as his photographs suggested. But in the flesh he had an obese, slug-like quality.

He smiled as he sat down. A self-absorbed smile. The smile of a man who lived in the luxury of a Buda villa guarded from the outside world by armed men for twenty-four hours a day.

He said nothing. It was one of the henchmen on his right who set proceedings in motion.

Thomas did not know the name of the man who stood up in the row in front of him to put the deputation's case. He read slowly and carefully, as if a single slip would undermine its cogency: 'We respectfully ask the Central Committee to ensure compliance with the resolutions of the Central Committee and of the Party Congress so as to suppress the anti-democratic methods by which organs and functionaries conduct affairs, methods that disfigure the party's cultural policy, paralyse our intellectual life, and undermine the party's prestige and influence . . .'

There was an orchestrated murmuring of dissent from the body of the chamber. Like angry waters on the lake.

The writers' spokesman cleared his throat and continued reading from his prepared text: 'We also urge the committee to reconsider the abusive administrative measures and guarantee the writers, journalists, and other intellectual workers a climate of Communist frankness and honesty, or, in other words, the opportunity to produce without disturbance creative works capable of serving the cause of the people and of Socialism.'

At once a party activist was on his feet. He was visibly shaking with anger.

'I would like to ask the comrade to be more specific about these alleged abuses which prevent him and his colleagues from working in a spirit of Communist frankness and honesty.'

The banning of Imre Madách's *The Tragedy of Man* was brought forward as an example of unwarrantable cultural interference. This play was a national classic, and it was being suppressed. And what about Bartók? *Bluebeard's Castle* had been played to acclaim at concert houses across the world. So why were Hungarians being denied the opportunity to enjoy it too?

These were errors too fundamental to be dealt with by a mere foot-soldier. At a signal the original questioner, still racked with fury, obediently yielded place to the man sitting on the right of Rákosi himself.

'I don't think the comrade has quite thought out the full

implications of what he is saying.' The man who spoke had thin wire spectacles which glinted in reflected light. It was impossible to see his eyes. His voice was calmer than that of the previous speaker, but it was a smooth and dangerous calm. 'Presumably he would agree that the purity of the party is of paramount importance, that it must be preserved at all costs; that we must deal firmly with those elements not conducive to a mood of Socialist optimism?'

All eyes were turned on the writers' spokesman, who bowed his head to signify reluctant agreement. Words, thought Thomas. Words. We are all drowning in a sea of meaningless verbiage. Strip away the words, and what are you left with? A bullying state; a cowed people.

'In these difficult times we must be at our most vigilant to counter those reactionary forces which lurk ready to impair the party's progress,' continued Rákosi's right-hand man. 'It is surely self-evident that the inherent pessimism and *petit-bourgeois* tendencies of the works in question are unhelpful in creating the climate of resourcefulness and endeavour which will ensure that the people, by forging a glorious partnership between workers and intellectuals, will go on to reap the full benefits of Socialism.'

Vigorous applause broke out instantaneously from behind the speaker. Like the crack of gunfire.

Tibor was on his feet now, his slim frame swaying against the might of the enemy drawn up before him. Thomas felt a sudden urge to pull him back down below the parapet, to save him from this dangerous exposure.

'Comrades,' he began, investing the word with a mordant irony, 'I have one further instance of cultural intervention which I wish to bring before you. In recent years a word has been robbed from our language. An ugly word, some may say, but a word of which it grieves me to say we are in need if we writers are to treat of reality in the constructively critical way we have been encouraged to follow in recent Party Congresses and Central Committee resolutions.' He paused momentarily, savouring the interest that he had aroused on both sides of the room. 'The word I have in mind is "rape".'

Rape. For a moment even the susurrations of disapproval

were silenced in shock. A forbidden word. A dangerous word. Not a meaningless, dead word, not a word to drown in. But a suppressed and therefore even more lethal one.

A new voice was raised in reply. It was Rákosi himself who was speaking now. 'Socialist writers must have better things to concern themselves with than such subjects,' he said firmly. 'In a Communist society such as ours this phenomenon has no relevance any more. Therefore the word has no use.'

'But with respect, that has not always been the case.' Thomas could see the small beads of perspiration on his friend's forehead as he framed his words. 'If it is the duty of the Socialist writer to draw attention to abuses in society, to deal with the reality of life, then this is a subject which must be touched on.'

'What is there to write about?' demanded Rákosi.

Tibor swayed again, then visibly steeled himself. 'We must face the fact that the soldiers of our Soviet allies have not always dealt well with Hungarian women. Particularly not in the villages.'

The unspeakable had been spoken. The inconvenient historical fact had been swept out from under the carpet, exhibited shamelessly to the public gaze.

Unexpectedly Rákosi laughed. It was not a kindly laugh. It was the laugh of a man dealing with a tiresome small child whose ignorance provokes ridicule.

'You writers really have no idea,' he said, shaking his head, 'absolutely no idea. Look, let me explain something to you. In Hungary there are, let's say, three thousand villages. Supposing the Russians violated, say, three women in every village. Nine thousand in all. Is that so much? You writers have no idea of the law of large numbers.'

He smiled round to his supporters behind him. Once again they thundered their applause. In amusement. In relief.

How could you deal with men like this? thought Thomas. They were not human. There was something missing inside their heads. You couldn't talk to them. You couldn't reason with them.

He rubbed his eyes with his hands, and as his fingers passed slowly by his nostrils, he was jolted with a memory of unexpected poignancy. Mixed with his own fearful sweat he smelt her again. Her scent, her body, there on his fingertips. From that afternoon. From the bed.

Those few hours seemed an age away.

'What? You signed the book?' Tibor berated him on the street corner later that evening, his breath turning to steam in the lamplight. 'You can't have been such a fool as to sign that book.'

'I didn't think.' Thomas was perplexed. His spirit was sinking. 'What harm could it do?'

'What harm could it do?' Tibor paused, shaking his head. 'It emphasises your existence to them. Underlines your identity. There it is in black and white, in your own handwriting, the fact that you were a member of the writers' deputation that came up with such unorthodoxies tonight. That came up with such perfect proof of its own unsoundness. That caused them all such grief, from the bald git downwards.'

Thomas tried to laugh it off, but he sensed Tibor's concern. That worried him. 'I'm a small fish, I think,' he said. 'They won't bother with me.'

Tibor shrugged. His pinched nose was red in the cold. 'I wouldn't bet on it. It's not difficult for them to trace you now.'

It wasn't difficult, thought Thomas. Particularly as he'd also put down his address in that wretched book when he'd signed his name.

Suddenly he knew they would be coming for him. He knew it in his bones. They'd be there, hammering at his door in the middle of the night. It was only a matter of time. The AVOs would pull him in. For questioning. And worse. He'd be an easy target. And he'd told them exactly where to find him. It was all his own fault. He could have wept.

Tibor took pity on him. 'Look, take this key. It's a room in Vendel Street. It's safe, no one knows about it and the people there won't give you away. Hole up there for a while, till this dies down. Don't go into work, get someone to call into the university and say you're sick. And look, Tamás: don't go back to your own apartment for

the time being. There's no point in looking for trouble,
is there?'

On balance Thomas felt there wasn't. He thanked Tibor,
and made to go on his way. In the direction of Vendel Street.
In the direction of his new home. He was grateful. But more
than anything, he was scared.

Tibor called him back for a moment. His eyes were smarting
against the foggy night as he told him: 'Look, keep it quiet, OK?
Don't draw attention to yourself for a week or two. I'll be in
touch with you, discreetly, but don't make unnecessary contact
with people. And, Tamás, do me a favour: leave that scrubber
of yours alone. She must be risky, given her background. I
mean it, Tamás. Don't complain. It won't do your dick any
harm to give it a bit of rest.'

A bit of rest. Suddenly that was something his whole body
ached for more than anything in the world.

Dusk was beginning to fall in Leila Parsons's garden. The cat
had long since melted away into the evening undergrowth, and
a cool breeze was whispering through the acanthus bushes.
Thomas Donat's voice fell silent. Minto looked across at him,
at the features of his face sagging in exhaustion. He'd never
seen a man so pale and tired, as he sat there wrapped in
his dressing-gown. The strange thing was that although Leila
Parsons had been with them throughout, present as every
sentence of the narrative formed on her uncle's anguished
lips and floated softly across the shadows, Minto had the
impression that the words had been directed towards him,
that she was merely an eavesdropper on their conversation.

'I think you'd better get some rest now, Uncle,' said Mrs
Parsons gently. 'Really I do. Come up with me now.'

He allowed himself to be led away upstairs without even
a glance back at Minto, even when Minto called after him,
'Goodnight, Mr Donat.'

Had it helped? wondered Minto in the taxi back to his flat.
This stream of reminiscence – starting with Greta Kassák on
the Danube pleasure steamer and leading on to Tibor Monos
and the extraordinary deputation to the Central Committee
– had it eased Thomas Donat's spirit at all? And why

had this undamming of memory suddenly taken place this evening, without warning, in a quiet Putney garden? The story Donat had been describing encompassed events of forty years ago, events from another world, before the tyranny of Communism had been swept away, before Donat himself had been transported on to another existence in Canada, half-way round the globe; was there some connection between these events in Hungary at that time and the one specific violent incident in the Royal Gallery yesterday?

Minto recognised one thing: if there was some connection, it must be uncovered as soon as possible. No other way would peace be restored to the mind of Thomas Donat.

7

The next day it was mercifully cooler. Grey clouds were massing, presaging rain. From Elaine's fourteenth-floor office the sky seemed very close.

She was standing by the window, highly groomed as usual. She always looked as though she'd just stepped out of the hairdresser. It was disconcerting, that sort of glossy American-style perfection. Disconcerting, because it meant nothing beyond an expression of its own efficiency. It perfectly reproduced the constituent features of female beauty without achieving that beauty. No doubt her limbs were perfectly in trim, regularly massaged and worked out. No doubt her skin and teeth were in great shape for her age. But what did it all amount to? Blandness, not inspiration.

'So how's the piece on the crazy man in the gallery going?' she demanded.

'It's not. I'm sorry.'

'Not going? How d'you mean, not going?'

Her attitude annoyed him. 'I've looked into it in detail but there's very little to work with.'

'Surely you can put something together.'

'There's really no story. The man's an out-and-out loony. Look, I've seen him, I went to the magistrates' court yesterday. He's barking. He was hardly able to string two words together, let alone a coherent sentence. They'll either lock him up or deport him, it doesn't make much odds either way.'

'So what about the picture?'

'What about it?'

'Is it a write-off?'

'They're not sure yet. I get the impression they can probably salvage it.'

'And there was no significance in his choice of that particular picture?'

'None at all.' Minto had his pen out now, was turning it idly between thumb and forefinger. He'd noticed the habit in himself before: it was something he often did when he was being economical with the truth. 'It just happened to be the nearest one.'

'Do I get the message that your heart's not in this piece, Minto?'

'Look, it could have been, OK? It was a great idea. But there's no meat to the story, as it turns out. There's no mileage in an out-and-out nutter. For God's sake, Elaine, readers are bumping into out-and-out nutters every day of the week as they walk down the street, they're sick of them. There's no novelty value to madness.'

She considered the point of view for a moment, then reached for the bottle of mineral water and poured herself a glass. She didn't offer him one. Finally she said: 'So I still need a piece from you this week. What's it going to be?'

He smiled back at her, suddenly disproportionately relieved. 'Don't worry. There's another angle to all this that could be more intriguing. There's the conservation angle. They're going to try to reconstitute the picture from literally thousands of little flecks of damaged paint. It's the most extraordinary undertaking, it may involve computers. I think this is the line to pursue.'

'I don't know. It sounds a bit technical.'

'I think I can give it a little topspin. There's quite a pretty girl who's part of the conservation team.'

'Photogenic?'

'Could be.'

'OK, we'll try and get Rory down there this morning for a few shots. I guess it'll have to do.' She didn't sound convinced. Minto felt inclined to try to placate her further.

'Look, one or two other leads have turned up in the meantime. On Courtney, I mean. There's more to that man than meets the eye, you know. I'm working on one or two skeletons in the cupboard. If it all comes together I reckon the Courtney piece could be a winner.'

'This is the modern Duveen guy, huh?'

'You could call him that, I suppose.' He could hear Elaine's brain working. She'd already composed the title for the piece. In her mind's eye she was designing how it was going to look. He resented her intrusion. He could hear her now, if the Courtney piece turned out as good as he hoped it might. 'Yeah, sure, Minto's feature was great. I knew it was going to work the moment I suggested it to him. Courtney seemed the kind of guy who might have a few secrets to hide, know what I mean?'

'OK, sounds good to me,' she said now. She paused, still not entirely satisfied. 'But first, get me something on this Royal Gallery business, won't you? Even if it's just the restoration angle?'

As he was turning to go, she added: 'I suppose you've asked her out, have you?'

'Who?'

'This girl from the conservation department.'

He was about to say no, her legs were too thin, not my type, but he stopped himself. Instead he smiled back at her without replying and shut the door gently behind him.

Ridley was at his desk as Minto passed by. Ridley had his feet up and was smoking, staring into the middle distance.

'Morning,' said Minto.

'Morning, old cock,' said Ridley expansively. 'How's it all going? Got the Courtneys taped, have you?'

'I'm working on it. I've got lunch with Theo Denton today.'

Ridley brought his feet down from the desk and sat up straighter.

'Denton, have you?' He gave a little whistle. 'Backs to the wall time, then.'

'Denton's gay?'

Ridley giggled. 'I'll tell you what they say about Denton, old boy: when he came out of the closet, he took the hinge with him.'

Minto shrugged. 'And I thought I'd try and get a word with Max Courtney, too.'

'You've chosen a bad day for that, I'm afraid. It's the big old master sale at Sotheby's. You won't get anything out of Max Courtney today.'

Won't I? thought Minto. In his heart he despised Ridley. He'd given up, with his frayed shirts and his greasy hair and his bloodshot eyes. He'd thrown in the towel. You could see the way other people's energy made him uneasy, aroused his negativity. Once, going through the files, Minto had come across something Ridley had written fifteen or twenty years ago. It had been a review of a Degas exhibition. After reading it, he'd looked twice to check on the name of the author. Because it had been good, that piece. Bloody good. And now all the man did was regurgitate auction-house press releases. It was sad, really. But Minto was not staying around to be infected by Ridley's defeatism.

'Well, I'll go and see if I can pin him down at Sotheby's this morning,' he said, moving off. 'I've got one or two questions for him.'

'Just be careful, old boy,' muttered Ridley. 'Bloody careful. You're going swimming in the piranha tank.'

It was the first time he'd been to a major sale at Sotheby's. He found a place standing at the back of the room and marvelled at the size of the gathering, at the numbers of people massed together for the occasion. The clientele was not dissimilar to that of Courtney's memorial service. There was the same sleek opulence, the same odd intermarriage of Bohemia and Belgravia. Only now there was a greater variety of nationalities intermingled: French, Italians, Americans. Like worshippers before an altar, rows of seated bidders were drawn up to face the rostrum. But the atmosphere had a different sort of charge to it from the church; some people looked preoccupied, some looked furtive, some looked studiedly casual, but in everyone you sensed the tension, the anticipation just below the surface. Buying fantasy was a serious business.

As a prelude to the sale of each lot, two porters would place the picture to be offered on an elegant easel. The auctioneer would turn momentarily to look at it, then slickly set the bidding on its way. Now it was a tiny flower painting, the image barely discernible at this distance, set in a thick black frame. 'Two hundred thousand pounds for this Balthasar van der Ast. Two hundred and twenty thousand, thank you, sir. Two hundred and forty thousand. Two hundred and sixty thousand. Two hundred and eighty thousand.' The bids kept coming, now from the room, now from the telephones, a bank of which were set up along one wall and manned by a line of elegant auction-house personnel. Here sat exquisite young men and young doe-eyed blonde women, their ears clamped to receivers, connected like up-market croupiers to a far-flung range of rich and secretive punters who were communicating to them their clandestine desires. These were the punters too discreet to be seen in the open. These were the punters for whom anonymity increased their ardour, like love-makers impassioned by the cover of darkness.

At £500,000 the bidding became more taut, more staccato. It rose in tens of thousands in a tense final exchange between a telephone bidder and a buyer in the room. It juddered precariously to a halt at £580,000. For a moment the auctioneer's hammer was held in unbearable suspense at the top of its arc while the question was demanded of the blonde on the telephone whether her bidder was all done. 'Against you, Rosemary,' pleaded the man on the rostrum. 'Against you, Rosemary, at five hundred and eighty thousand pounds.' Except that he said 'pines' now, the excitement of the moment elongating his drawl. And then the hammer crashed down abruptly and with finality. What made this picture worth £580,000 and that one £80,000? wondered Minto. What, for that matter, determined that the Böcklin's value should be set at 1.5 million pounds? It was an arbitrary judgement, like setting a price on a man's courage, or a woman's virtue. In a world where the worth of all things could be expressed in financial terms, then maybe all things could be bought and sold. And maybe all men, too. In the end.

He felt Ridley at his side, before he saw him. Smelt his alcohol-laden breath, sensed the sweaty nearness of the man, as he pushed in next to him. 'Thought I'd come and join you,' leered Ridley. 'This sale might be worth a paragraph or two at the weekend.'

Minto nodded.

'See who bought that last lot?'

Minto shook his head.

'Your friend. Over there. On the aisle, in the fifth row.' Minto followed Ridley's gaze down the lines and caught a glimpse of the squat, dark figure, in profile as he turned to whisper to his companion. Max Courtney. And the man next to him, his head bent solicitously to catch Courtney's words, was Winter.

'How did you see that?' demanded Minto.

Ridley smirked. 'You get to know a trick or two when you've been to as many sales as I have.'

At the end of the auction Minto left Ridley and followed Winter and Max Courtney out. They walked fast so that without running he only caught up with them half-way down Bond Street.

'Mr Courtney,' he said.

Max turned upon hearing his name, but did not shorten his stride. The weather was still grey, but he was wearing dark glasses. 'Yup?' he barked.

'My name's Dominic Maitland. I'm writing an article about your father, and his role as a creator of today's art market. I'd really appreciate it if I could ask you a few questions. Could you spare me a few minutes?'

'Not now,' said Max. Something about the way he said it riled Minto. It wasn't just that it was offhand, but calculatedly offhand. Deliberately rude.

But Winter interposed. Deftly. Deferential but steely. 'Perhaps you should give Mr Maitland a moment, Max,' he suggested in a soft, dangerously gentle voice. He had a lined, tanned face and very thin lips. 'The sale's ended early, and there's a little time before lunch. Maybe we should hear something about the sort of piece Mr Maitland is thinking of writing.'

Courtney didn't say anything for a moment but kept walking. Fast.

'I'd be very grateful,' encouraged Minto. 'I'd like to get my facts right.'

Max gave a little, cynical laugh, as if he doubted the capacity of any journalist to succeed in that aim. But he'd caught the hint of the threat Minto had intended to imply. 'OK,' he said, staring straight ahead of him. 'Come in now. I can give you fifteen minutes.'

In an office beyond the main gallery of Courtney's, Max gestured to Minto to take a chair, and settled himself back in his own seat behind the desk. The desk seemed somehow too big for him, and Minto decided it had been his father's. Max had probably moved in here soon after Alexander Courtney's death. To assert himself at once. To show he wasn't afraid, not too young at thirty-four. Now he stared back just a shade too belligerently, just a shade too determined to prove that business was continuing as usual. He took off his dark glasses and smiled the sort of smile that humourless people sometimes imagine will do as a substitute for charm.

On the shelf behind him, in its ornate silver frame, stood the photograph of Alexander Courtney. Minto recognised it as the image he had encountered two days earlier in the viewing room after the memorial service. Its repositioning here was making a point. A point for his benefit. That face again: hard, unyielding; not without charm. But those eyes, they were the give-away. Penetrating, unrelenting, uncharitable eyes. Elements of the father's face were repeated in the son, without adding up to the same impressiveness. Max's eyes were aggressive rather than intelligent, arrogant rather than irresistible, and his father's lean good looks were already compromised by an incipient fleshiness. Alexander Courtney had been six foot two; Max was shorter by several inches. Max spoke with a drawl. Needless to say, no expense had been spared in securing Max the very best sort of education. No doubt Alexander had taken pleasure in creating in his son a perfect specimen of the English gentleman. And in the process had saddled him with all sorts of other baggage. Did Max sometimes wonder about his own Austrian origins? Or did he prefer to rest on the laurels of his mother's eminently respectable Barrymore lineage?

These were questions that could all come later.

'Do you mind this?' asked Minto, indicating his small tape recorder. Sometimes he used it, sometimes he didn't. Interviewees occasionally found it pressurising, which could be a disadvantage. Or an advantage. With Max Courtney he reckoned it wouldn't make any difference, and the evidence might be useful later.

At once Minto was aware of the shadowy figure of Winter. Moving smoothly across to Max's side and pulling open a drawer. Out came another cassette machine. Winter flicked a button and the tiny spools began to turn. 'A double-check,' he said, and retreated to a chair in the corner. Max wasn't smiling any more.

'Have you found it difficult,' enquired Minto, 'following such a successful father?'

Max Courtney frowned. 'Taking over here hasn't been easy, but you wouldn't expect it to be, would you?' He spoke brisk, clipped words, intended to convey dynamism but suggesting a certain tension, too. 'I can tell you one thing, though. If anyone's equipped to do it, I am.' He paused for effect. 'You know why?'

Minto shook his head.

'I'll tell you why. I worked with my father for twelve years. Closely. In those twelve years I've learned more than most dealers learn in a lifetime. It was an education to work with him. To learn his methods. To understand his angle on things.'

'So you don't dispute the estimation of your father that he was the leading dealer of his generation.'

'My father was a genius,' said Courtney simply. A look of unqualified admiration crossed his face. It was like the sun coming out between clouds.

Minto decided to humour him. 'What did he have that other dealers didn't, do you think?'

It was a question that Max Courtney must have been asked before, because he replied immediately, without reflection: 'Guts, that's what he had. Plenty of them. It takes guts to start from nothing and build up what he built up. It takes guts to back your hunch and risk your last fifty thousand pounds for a filthy dirty picture catalogued as "French School" that you think is going to turn into a Fragonard. It takes guts to bid a hundred thousand pounds you haven't got for a picture you think you can sell for a hundred and fifty by the time you have to pay for it. My father had the courage to follow his instincts. And his instincts were always right.'

'Always?'

'Whenever it mattered.'

'Could you give me some examples?'

Max gave an ironic little laugh, as if the answer were self-evident. 'My father was famous for being able to judge the pace of the market better than anyone else. He always saw the recessions coming. Unlike anyone else, he was always ready for them. In 1974, by the time of the Arab oil crisis, he was carrying practically no stock at all. Same thing in 1980. And then in 1990 when the music stopped playing he was about the only dealer in the world who'd left the dance floor in time. We'd made no major stock purchases for the previous twelve months. Offloaded most of the expensive ones by the time the crash came. It was uncanny the way he got that right.' He paused, then added with an affectation of casualness: 'And of course there was the Tokyo venture.'

'What, the gallery he opened up there in 1983?'

'That's it.' Something about the Japanese enterprise was giving Courtney pleasure. He leant forward meaningfully across the desk and demanded: 'You know why we haven't got that any more?'

'Why not?'

'Because my father only took a seven-year lease on it. Got out at exactly the right moment, the moment the Japanese stopped buying Impressionists. We had seven years of fantastic trading. And then we were out, clean. Just like that. And when the Japanese stopped buying Impressionists, boy did that market die. He knew, you see, when he started. What the cycle was likely to be. He had that instinctive foresight, the foresight that no one else had.'

Minto looked across at the photograph again. For a moment he wished he'd met the man he was investigating. He'd clearly been exceptional. But how exceptional? Minto was

not inclined to accept the version of Max Courtney in
every detail. But he didn't yet know enough about the
background to see where the gospel according to Max
might be challenged. Minto's view of human nature was
based on the assumption that every man has a weakness.
He could see no reason why Alexander Courtney should
prove any different. It was just a question of uncovering
where that weakness lay.

'I've heard it suggested,' went on Minto, 'that your father
frightened people. Could he be a bit of a bully?'

'Who told you that?' There was an anger in the tone. And
a wariness.

'I can't remember. But was it true?'

Max frowned again. He seemed about to reply when Winter
stepped in. Winter, with his calm, reassuring voice, from the
background: 'Really, Mr Maitland, you make it sound as
though Sir Alexander was some sort of godfather in the
Mafia. The idea of him going round frightening people is
patently absurd.'

'What do you think?' persisted Minto to Max Courtney.

There was silence for a moment, then Max shook his head,
almost as if to clear it. He spoke firmly, to reassure himself
as much as Minto: 'No one who played straight with him
had anything to fear.'

Minto decided to change direction now. 'Did you see what
happened to that picture in the Royal Gallery earlier this
week?' he asked. 'The Böcklin?'

At that moment the telephone rang intrusively on Max
Courtney's desk. He picked it up and muttered with a barely
suppressed violence, 'I said no bloody calls,' and slammed
the receiver down again. 'I am sorry. What did you say?' But
Minto had the definite impression he remembered perfectly
well. That he was playing for time.

'I said, did you hear about that Böcklin being attacked by
a man with a knife in the Royal Gallery?'

'The Böcklin?' He paused. 'The one that was attacked? I
think I saw something about it, yes.' What was it Minto
observed in the man's eyes then? Anger? Suspicion? Or,
stirred by the faintest whisper of memory, like the breeze

in the cypresses beside the open tomb, just a glimmer of fear?

'You sold that picture once, didn't you?'

'Before my time, if we did.'

'Courtney's definitely sold it. It has your label on the back.'

'Really?' Confidence was returning. 'I think you'll find that a large number of top museums in the world have pictures with our labels on their stretchers.'

'But am I right in thinking that this picture was sold to Leslie Marriott?'

Marriott. The name hung there for a moment. Like the flickering flame of a candle. Would it die? Or would it burn?

This time it was Winter who replied. 'It's possible. The records would have to be checked, but it would take time. You have to realise that our archive has become a significant repository of information for art historians. We get so many enquiries about our old stock numbers that we're having to introduce a fee for the service of looking them up.' Winter laughed urbanely at the tenacity of scholarship.

'But your firm sold quite a lot of pictures to Marriott, I believe?'

Again that momentary cloud of unease in Max Courtney's eyes. 'Leslie Marriott was a big collector. He came to us like anyone else, to buy the best.'

'He was also convicted of fraud. And maybe he was guilty of other things, too. Pretty bad things.'

'I think you'll find a lot of that was just rumour-mongering. Some guy carrying the can for a lot of other people's transgressions.'

Then Winter, ever the voice of reason, added: 'Come on, Mr Maitland, if we're going to be held responsible for every one of our clients' misdemeanours, none of us are going to get very far, are we? Presumably you don't run a check on your newspaper's readership to make sure none of them have got criminal records?'

Minto smiled politely. But he was thinking of something

else. He was remembering his conversation with Thornton-Bass about one of the examples of the first version of *The Island of the Dead*. That had been the property of Adolf Hitler. No doubt the dealer from whom the Führer acquired it would have justified himself with a similar argument.

The truth was, if you looked in the files, you found that Leslie Marriott had been a bad man. A fraudster, with a question mark over many of his dealings. And he'd had a connection with Alexander Courtney. Maybe closer than these people were prepared to admit. A hunch was formulating in Minto's mind. There was an underlying defensiveness to Max Courtney. Somewhere along the line he had something to hide. Minto could smell it. And Minto's instinct was that it might relate to Marriott. That was the connection to be investigated. That was the story to follow up.

And there was another thing, a personal element. The more he saw of Max Courtney the less he liked him. He didn't like his manner, and he didn't like his bluster and aggression. He didn't like sons who had assumed positions of power unwarranted by their own ability on the back of the privilege of their fathers' wealth. And at the same time he had a strong feeling that if he'd ever met Alexander Courtney he wouldn't have liked him much either. Digging up the dirt on the Courtneys would give him a certain degree of personal satisfaction, too.

'I'm interested by your father's early days,' Minto said now. 'Who could help me there?'

Max shrugged. 'He opened his first gallery in 1958. It grew from there.'

'And before that?'

'As a boy he came over with his mother from Austria before the war. She was a remarkable woman.'

'Did you know her?'

'No. She died in 1957. But apparently she brought my father up single-handed, because her husband, my grandfather, died in the early thirties in Vienna.'

'Did your father talk to you about his first years in Austria?'

'Not much, no. After all, he was only ten or eleven when he got here, so I don't think he remembered much about it. As I understand it, my grandparents' family was just about wiped out during the war. I believe my grandmother's sister died in Buchenwald. You don't dwell on that sort of thing, there's no point. That was my father's attitude, and he was absolutely right. There was nothing left to link him to Austria after his mother died.'

And he was too busy becoming an Englishman, thought Minto. Marrying into a good English family. Perfecting his accent. Drawing a line under his foreign past. Quietly consigning it to the shredder.

'And the early years in London? The late fifties and sixties, when the business was being built up? Who could tell me more about that time?'

'There are people here who could fill you in on a few details. Diana Maybury's been with the gallery in London for twenty-eight years. Bill Ryder may have been with us even a year or two longer.'

Loyal servants, thought Minto. They're not going to rock the boat, coming up to pension time. There won't be much to learn from them. 'I thought I might have a word with Theo Denton,' he suggested casually.

Max Courtney sat up straighter. 'You can talk to him by all means.' He was making a considerable effort to control himself, you could tell from the way he was fingering the paper knife, turning it over in his hands. 'But just bear in mind that my father sacked him. For incompetence.'

Winter stood up now. There was a new edge to his voice as he said: 'Look, Theo Denton's a bitter man. An unreliable witness, OK? Treat what he says with a pinch of salt. I wouldn't want you to get into trouble with our lawyers. No, I wouldn't wish that on anyone.'

'Pretty hot-shot, are they?' said Minto. Mocking. Annoyed at the threat.

'Bloody hot,' said Max Courtney, smiling his charmless little smile.

Minto had looked up the figures before he'd come. Courtney's employed forty-two people in London. Another thirty-three in New York. And eighteen in Paris. And Max Courtney was running the whole show now. Nominally, anyway. With Winter's help. By art-market standards, it was a big business. But it had to stay big. It must continue to deliver even though its founder and driving force was no longer there. It mustn't lose its successful image, its reputation for providing the best pictures. And selling them. Maybe the pressure was on Courtney junior. Maybe it would make or break him. The last thing he needed was bad publicity, anything that knocked the good name of the firm. He was nervous now. But was he nervous in general, or about something in particular?

Then Minto allowed himself to think of her. Let her flood back into his memory, with her angry, low-lidded eyes. Standing in the gallery here, with her back to the wall by the Corot.

'And your sister,' he asked, 'was she never given the chance of joining the business?'

'My sister lives abroad. She has other interests.'

'Are you close to her?'

'Of course.' For a moment it seemed as though he was going to go on; he paused, then thought better of it. Instead he laid down the paper knife and reached across to flick off his cassette recorder. 'I'm afraid time's up. I'm sorry, I have to go out to lunch now. It was a pleasure to meet you.'

As he got up to leave, Minto said, 'So you think your archives might reveal something about the history of the Böcklin *Island of the Dead*? The Royal Gallery picture?'

'Like what precisely?'

'Well, we know who bought it from you, don't we? We know Marriott did. But where did you get it from?'

Courtney shrugged. 'That may or may not be revealed in the records.' He moved to the door and held it open for Minto. 'You'll have to consult the archivist. No doubt your paper won't mind meeting our administrative charge.'

'Thanks. I'll bear that in mind.'

It was Winter who saw him out of the gallery. 'Good luck

with your article,' he said as he shook Minto's hand. 'We'll be interested to read it.'

Minto smiled back at him but said nothing. I bet you will, he thought to himself.

8

'I hope your paper's picking up the tab for this little extravaganza?' Theo Denton peered beadily at Minto over the top of an effete pair of reading glasses, glasses which he had been using to study the menu with the same absorption as if it were an old master drawing of doubtful attribution. His voice was precious to the point of self-caricature.

'Of course.'

'Then I shall have the *foie gras*.' He smiled with satisfaction. His eyes were shrewd rather than sympathetic. 'I'm not going to apologise for failing to wear a tie to lunch with you. I can see no reason why one should dress up for the press.'

'Quite right,' Minto assured him. 'I would have been horrified if you'd worn a tie.'

Denton cocked an eyebrow at him, but said nothing. How clever are you? you could see him calculating. Because if you're clever, you'd better watch out. Because I don't like people being clever with me.

'Did you used to wear a tie when you worked with Alexander Courtney?' persisted Minto.

'With Sir Alexander, you mean.' Denton enunciated the title with a disdainful irony. Then he pondered the question, massaging his neck in that meditative fashion which Minto already recognised as characteristic. You saw a lot of Denton's neck. He favoured a crew-neck woollen jersey worn next to the skin in a style calculated to combine bohemianism with a whiff of the waterfront of Marseille. He'd thrown an old tweed jacket over the top, but you could still count the lines on his throat, see the ravages of time on his wrinkled skin. 'I suppose I probably did,' he replied batting an eyelash of distaste. 'But then I was a lot prettier and more innocent in those days.'

'When did you first meet Courtney?'

Denton frowned. 'Before I answer that, I'd like to make a little pronouncement. Nothing too testing, dear heart. Just a very basic condition we should get straight at this stage.'

'Go ahead.'

'You should understand one thing, then. Whatever I say about Courtney now is entirely off the record. As far as I'm concerned, I never spoke to you. Certainly not about Courtney anyway. If you quote me on him, I shall deny it flatly. Understood, my sweet?'

Minto nodded. Was it the hot-shot lawyers Denton could see on the brow of the hill? Or was it something else?

'So what line are you going to take about Courtney, in this article of yours?' demanded Denton. 'Tell me that. Where are you coming from, as the Americans so picturesquely put it?'

'How do you mean, what line?'

Theo pursed his lips and contemplated his three-quarters-empty Bloody Mary. 'What's it going to be: greatest dealer of the century, that sort of stuff? Businessman of genius, entrepreneurial hero? Single-handed saviour of the nation's heritage?'

'I wasn't going to be that critical,' laughed Minto.

Theo didn't laugh back. He was the one who made the jokes. 'I always used to find it just a teeny bit strange,' he went on, 'that Courtney should have received that knighthood for services to the preservation of the nation's heritage. You would never have found heritage considerations holding him back if there was any question of an advantageous deal, would you? The item would have been out and off to America before you could whisper 'export licence', particularly in the early days. It's a bit like making some duke who's devoted his life to the wholesale massacre of pheasants President of the Royal Society for the Protection of Birds.'

Minto sipped his own Bloody Mary thoughtfully. 'So what sort of line do you think I should take on the man?'

Denton's eyes suddenly grew bright with venom. 'Shit of the year,' he muttered. 'If you like, shit of the decade.'

'It's interesting you should say that, because reading

through the files you find that no one's ever been very critical in dealing with Courtney. Courtney somehow always managed to engineer himself a pretty good press. He always came out smelling of roses. It's a public relations triumph.'

Theo sniffed. 'He was a very rich man, don't forget. And in my experience the press are infinitely venal.'

Minto laughed. He thought of Ridley. How many drinks would it take to buy off Ridley? 'OK,' he said. 'So what I want to do now is set the record straight. Dig a bit deeper. Uncover a few of the skeletons.'

Denton looked at him. Now there was malice in his tone. 'Don't underestimate what you're up against, sweety. It'll take more than your clear blue eyes and your classical profile to dig the dirt on Courtney, you know. A pretty face is no substitute for rigorous investigative journalism. I can't do it for you. I can only point you in the right direction.'

Minto suppressed his annoyance. He knew Theo's type. Vicious, for the sake of it. For a moment he glimpsed the despair of the ageing gay facing a future of loneliness; sensed the self-destructive bitterness of a man compelled by his nature always to launch the pre-emptive strike, to get his retaliation in first. To hurt before he was hurt.

'Well, point me in the right direction, then. You were about to tell me about the early days. How did you first meet him?'

Theo shook his head. There seemed to be something oppressive to him about the question. 'Were you going to order the Sancerre?' he demanded irritably.

'If you like.'

'I do.'

Theo must be humoured. Minto succeeded in attracting the attention of the wine waiter almost at once, and the man reacted with the brisk obsequiousness always elicited by the request for an expensive bottle. 'Go on, then. About Courtney.'

Denton sighed, then took a deep breath. 'Very well then, dear heart, you asked for it: here come the Denton memoirs. Should I call them "Enemies of Promise", or does something tell me that title's been used already?' He paused, for theatrical effect. Minto reflected that this man might have made a pretty good actor, had not all his dramatic energy gone into playing himself. 'So let me skip lightly over the first quarter century of my life and dive straight in at Chapter Three. What shall we call that chapter? Yes, I think that one would be "The Courtney Years". You see, I first came across Courtney in the early sixties. He was already a force to be reckoned with. He had his first gallery in Bruton Street. And maybe one in New York by then, too. I'm not sure. He always had such excellent connections on the other side of the Atlantic. He really worked on them, you know. He'd go back and forth like a yo-yo, and that was something unusual in those days, when London and America seemed much further apart. He had tremendous energy and drive.' Denton paused to drain his Bloody Mary. He yielded praise reluctantly. It was as if it hurt him, and the drink was some sort of a consolation for the pain. 'Courtney had made his name selling some very expensive Impressionists, but he was branching out into the old master field as well. That was where I came in.'

'What were you doing then?'

'Me, dear heart? Oh, I was beginning to flower.' Theo spoke with some satisfaction, and Minto had a momentary vision of Ridley's unhinged closet. 'Quite the child prodigy, if I say it myself. I came back from Italy in sixty-one and joined the old master department of one of our leading auction houses. Frankly, I was too clever for them; I had a much better eye than any of that crew of posturing chinless wonders. So when Courtney asked me to join him, to develop his old master business, I jumped at the chance. He talent-spotted me, if you like.'

'So he didn't have such a bad eye himself?' suggested Minto. It was meant as a joke, a bit of flattery, but Denton rounded on him with unexpected fierceness.

'He was a bastard and he was probably a crook. But he had the best bloody eye in the world. Don't let anyone tell you otherwise.'

Minto absorbed the advice, then asked, 'What do you know about his history before you met him, though? Where had he sprung from? Because he wasn't English by birth, was he?'

'No,' said Theo with some relish, as if the man's weak point had been unintentionally exposed. 'No, he wasn't. Although you would never have guessed it to look at him. Just sometimes when he spoke, when he was excited, his accent betrayed him. You heard a little hint of *Mittel* Europe then.'

'His mother had taken British nationality when she came over?'

'Oh, yes, no doubt. But he would never have talked about that to me. He grew more English than the English. I found it all rather pathetic, personally, that obsessive desire to develop himself as a pillar of the British upper classes. He bought a country house – Hartsmore, an old Barrymore property in Wiltshire – and lived the life of a country gent. He hired shoots, went to Ascot, all that sort of carry-on. Then, Christ almighty, you should have seen what a fever pitch of excitement and sycophancy he worked himself up into when he got the knighthood. I remember a photograph of him shaking hands with Mrs Thatcher, you should look it up on the file, it can't have been more than eight or ten years ago. Talk about a dog wagging its tail. It was quite revolting to look at.'

'So he was a bit of a snob?'

'Yes, in the way that foreigners get to be when they decide to become fully paid-up members of the British establishment. Look at Chips Channon.'

'What, the man who was accused of putting the interest of his adoptive class before the interest of his adoptive country?'

'Something like that,' said Theo, cool again. Minto realised he'd committed a *faux pas*. He'd come out with the line Theo had been preparing for himself. Theo must be allowed to make the jokes.

'So when did Courtney actually start as an art dealer?'

'Late fifties, I'd have said. Before my time, anyway. I was in Italy up till sixty-one enjoying an extended student life.' The wine waiter had come back and filled their glasses. Theo broke off to drink and nodded appreciatively, for a moment mellowing almost visibly. 'Yes, those were the days. When

I was up at I Tatti putting Berenson straight about one or two of his more flagrant misattributions. Poor old thing, he quite lost it later on, you know.'

'You see, when you look in Courtney's cuttings file there's remarkably little on his early days. Who'd know about that, I wonder?'

Theo eyed him laconically. 'I think he took a lot of those secrets with him. Maybe he confided things to his closest family. Maybe he said something to Winter. Then again, maybe he didn't.'

Minto thought of Max Courtney. Remembered the aggressive, obstructive eyes staring back across the desk that was too big for him. And Winter: discreet, calculating. And unyielding. Finally he thought of Isabella, and wondered once again why she seemed so bored and resentful. And why she needed to keep playing games.

And Theo Denton. Was he always this edgy? Or was it something specific to do with Courtney? It was almost as if Courtney himself was constricting him, as if the man's influence was repressing him at a distance, from beyond the grave. Embittering. And menacing.

Minto decided to continue his questions. Gently.

'So when you joined Courtney, he was already successful. How had he done it?'

Theo smiled, as though enjoying a private joke at Minto's expense. He said, 'Can you reach the bottle from where you're sitting? I seem to have run dry.'

Minto leant over and filled his glass, dripping cold water from the ice-bucket over the tablecloth. It was as if Denton needed this as a prelude to what was coming. He had decided to impart wisdom, to play the role of the grand old queen.

'Let me explain to you a few of the facts of life of the art market. As to a layman, my dear Mr Maitland of the sky-blue eyes and the perfect profile. You ask how Courtney first made his money.' He rubbed his neck for emphasis.

'Impressionists, my dear. How does anyone make money in this taste-forsaken world? Courtney was one of the first people to understand the nature of the appeal of Impressionist painting to new money, particularly American new money. Look, basically Americans like colour in pictures. Impressionism gives it to them in hefty dollops, with a veneer of art-historical sophistication. It's reassuring to these first-time collectors to read about the Impressionists having been rejected in their own time by an ignorant public. By paying huge sums for them two or three generations later people can be made to feel they're both righting the wrongs of history and stating their cultural superiority to their ancestors. Courtney grasped all that and made his first million through supplying Americans with Impressionist pictures from Europe, and thereby supplying them with a myth to believe in, a comforting myth of their own discrimination.

'Let me see now: when was the Goldschmidt sale? 1958, I think. That was a watershed, a turning point. The moment when Sotheby's invented Impressionism. They sold a collection of just seven great Impressionist pictures for more than three-quarters of a million pounds. It was an incredible sum for those days. But Courtney wasn't far behind. I don't know if he was going already by fifty-eight, but by fifty-nine he'd made a bit of a name for himself. Yes, that's right, I remember now. I was looking through a copy of *The Burlington Magazine* for 1959 the other day, and I happened to notice there was a full-page Courtney advertisement offering a Cezanne for sale then. As usual, Courtney's timing was impeccable.'

'In what way, particularly?'

'By the late fifties a lot of Americans were beginning to make money again. Large amounts of money. The United States government had introduced legislation allowing rich collectors to write off a portion of the current value of their art against their income tax if it was to be left to a public museum on the owner's death. So they all rushed in and bought Impressionists.

'You know what Courtney said to me once, soon after I joined him? Come with me, he said, this will interest you. I'm going to show you a picture which explains the whole Impressionist market. I went with him into one of the private viewing rooms, and he unveiled this Monet. It was one of the poplars series. You know, sinuous lines of trees receding round a riverbank. Rather beautiful, I thought, in a superficial sort of way. What do you see when you look at that picture, he demanded? Trees, water, sky, I said. No, no, what image do you see there? There's a secret image, a subliminal message. I peered at it but I couldn't understand what he was getting at. Look at those tree-tops, he said, the way they form a perfect "S" in the picture space as they go back into the distance. Then look at those two very firm trunks cutting vertically through them in the foreground, almost from top to bottom of the canvas. You know what that is? It's a dollar sign, isn't it? That's what Monet's all about: money.'

Minto watched while this time the wine waiter refilled Denton's glass. 'But Courtney cared about pictures, didn't he?' he asked. 'As well as money, I mean?'

'Yes,' said Theo. 'He cared about pictures. He felt strongly about them, you're right. He had this almost visceral reaction to them. He was quite funny about it, sometimes. I remember some inordinately pretentious American woman standing in front of a little Boudin he was offering her and her quoting old William Lurcy's lines at him: "Ah, Mr Courtney, don't you agree, the priceless temptation of art gives one everything – delectable stings, a hint of pepper and sun, the effortless crunch of teeth into a morsel of canteloupe ..." And you know what Courtney replied to the old hag?'

Minto shook his head.

'He said: "Personally I find it simpler than that. When I see a good picture, my arse tightens."'

Minto smiled, registering Theo's pleasure at the story. 'What was Courtney like? To meet, I mean?'

Theo narrowed his eyes thoughtfully, as if he were conjuring up an image of the man. 'Good-looking. Tall. Blond. And very determined. My dear, you sensed that determination the moment you came into the same room as him. It was an almost physical thing. I remember our first meeting quite well, actually. I had brought a picture round from the auction house to show him. He was already powerful enough to demand that: auction houses sent pictures from forthcoming sales round to him if he requested them. Gave him his own private views. He made me sit down and wait while he looked at the thing. Then the telephone went. There was a client on the line, someone to whom he was trying to sell another picture. Well, he turned away from me to speak, but I could hear him perfectly clearly. Maybe he let me overhear intentionally. Anyway, it was an absolutely outrageous performance of charm and salesmanship. My dear, could he turn it on. By the end of the conversation the deal was as good as sealed. It was what the Americans call awesome. And do you know, something I've never forgotten? As he put the receiver down, he licked it. Yes, licked it. Licked it in the most suggestive way.'

So this was Alexander Courtney. Shit of the decade. The best eye in the world. The man who licked telephones. The man who frightened people.

And here was Theo Denton on Courtney. Full of hate and resentment. Edgy, too, at the memory of the man. And yet, despite everything, unable to suppress a measure of admiration.

The *foie gras* was cleared away and Denton's Dover sole was brought to him. He poked at it, trying to fault it; forked a little into his mouth and thought better of it.

'So how did things go once you started working with him?' ventured Minto.

'How did they go? Pretty well at first, though I say so myself. I brought in one or two absolutely sensational things. A little Duccio, I remember, that we sold to Norton Simon. And a Rubens sketch: God, it was a ravishing picture, I would have killed to own it myself, but it went to the Los Angeles County Museum. For a time I suppose we complemented each other quite well. Generally speaking I found the pictures, and he sold them. But after a year or two the problems started.'

'Problems?'

'Yes, problems. You see, with Courtney, everything had to be done his way. He wanted to have control. Not just over the business, but over you as well. He wanted to own people, to dominate them. He was insufferable: trying to muscle in on everything I did. My pictures, my deals, my clients, the people with whom I'd built up a relationship of business trust over the years. Finally he started trying to find fault with me, trying to trip me up. In effect he accused me of incompetence. My dear, I may have been accused of many things in my time, but incompetence? Never! You should have heard what Bernard Berenson once said about me. Berenson thought I could develop into one of the great art historians of my generation. Well, nobody accuses me of incompetence with impunity.' The veins on Denton's neck stood out in an excess of self-righteousness. 'The very idea!'

Oh, shit, thought Minto. Is this all it amounts to? Hell hath no fury like an old queen scorned? Perhaps Denton had simply not proved up to the job. Perhaps Courtney had perfectly legitimately given him the push. Perhaps Denton had nursed an unreasoning grudge ever since, had made a career out of spouting off against him from the moment of his dismissal.

But then Denton said something which regalvanised Minto entirely. Put a completely different complexion on the interview.

'And I realised that I didn't trust him,' he murmured, pushing aside the half-eaten sole and reaching for the wineglass again. 'Not after the business with Marriott.'

'What, Leslie Marriott?'

'The very same.' Denton paused, fingering the glasses that hung round his neck. Savouring the impact he had made.

'What was the business with Marriott?'

'I don't know how much I can say. Not even today, I'm still not sure.'

'They're both dead now, both Courtney and Marriott,' urged Minto. But he kept a grip on himself. Said it casually. He was worried that if he showed too much excitement and enthusiasm Denton would choose to go quiet. The pleasure of the pain inflicted on Minto by withholding what he sensed he wanted desperately to hear might outweigh the pleasure of the scandalous revelations he was on the verge of making. He had that kind of viciousness, lurking just below the surface.

But Denton wanted to speak now. Perhaps the wine had got to him, loosened his tongue. Or perhaps there was something deeper, some unanswered question, that he genuinely wanted to get straight in his own mind. He leaned forward and lowered his voice. Minto could smell the mixture of alcohol and stale aftershave as he said: 'You see, it never quite added up. There were a number of disjointed incidents that I could never quite put together, make sense of, so to speak ...'

'What were these incidents?'

'Well, for a start there was Marriott himself. I never liked him. He was the worst sort of arrogant, jumped-up, self-made little man you could ever wish to meet. Sleazy, greasy, with slicked-back hair. Always talking about his "girlies" and what he planned to do to if they let him have his way with them. And, my dear, the ties he used to wear. No, no, no.' Denton waved an admonitory finger at the very memory of them. 'He first appeared on the scene about 1966, I suppose. He'd already made a packet in the property market, or so he said. But he was expanding into other interests. That's what he told me, soon after I first met him. Well, of course we now know what those probably were, don't we?'

Minto nodded. The rumours about the arms deals and the drugs money had never gone away. At the time of his trial for illegal share trading the papers had had a field day. One of his more recent 'girlies' had even sold her story to the *News of the World*. In passing, Minto had marvelled at the sexual appetite of the man. Or alleged sexual appetite. But those were the sort of exaggerations you didn't choose to sue about. They might even buy you a little kudos in your new surroundings when you were bound for a couple of years' detention at Her Majesty's pleasure.

'Marriott was a great admirer of Courtney,' went on Theo. 'Courtney had the knack of attracting the custom of that type of new money. He knew how to play up to it, win its trust. Edward Purchas was another example. Not that I'm impugning anything against that man's reputation. Pure as the driven snow, dear, that one. Financially speaking, anyway. I don't know about his private life, though I've heard a few rumours. But that's by the by, and not for repetition.

'Anyway, back to Marriott. He and Courtney became thicker and thicker. I was increasingly excluded from their dealings. Just once I had a little peep into their secret world. It must have been, what, end of seventy-four, because in 1975 I finally moved on from Courtney's and started my own gallery. Couldn't stand it any longer. Courtney was away on business in the States. I was minding the shop. Deacon, our financial controller, came through on the line saying there was an unattributed payment just arrived in the bank account of three hundred and eighty thousand dollars. He needed confirmation that this was the proceeds of the Degas sale. Courtney for once was unobtainable, but I had a hunch that this Degas had been sold to Marriott, so I decided to do some checking through the Marriott files off my own bat.

'Well, the Marriott papers weren't in the general filing where you would have expected them. I was curious. I hung around after everyone else had gone home on the pretext of waiting for a call from America. Then I went into Courtney's own private office. Most of his private correspondence was held under conditions of unbelievable security, and I was no good at picking locks. My fingers are too delicate, don't you see? Everyone's always said I've got artist's hands. But I was lucky: I found the Marriott file in one of his desk drawers, a drawer I did have a key for because I'd come across it in his secretary's office. When I opened it I found some very interesting material. There was a list of companies, about six or seven of them, all offshore, registered in Panama, Cayman Islands, Netherlands Antilles, that sort of thing. It was fairly clear that when Marriott bought pictures, he bought in those names. I even found the Degas invoice, made in the name of one of them. But the odd thing was, there was the Degas, meticulously described. But the price wasn't three hundred and eighty thousand dollars. The bill was made out for one hundred and eighty thousand.'

'So what did you do?'

'I was careful, dear heart. Courtney wouldn't have been exactly overjoyed if he'd got the idea that I was somehow checking up on him. So I just mentioned it to him in passing, when he was back. It was three hundred and eighty thousand you got for the Degas, wasn't it, I said. He said, of course, and that was that. So somebody was on the fiddle, weren't they, my sweet? At the very least, a little bit of money-laundering was going on, wasn't it? Two hundred thousand dollars was being meticulously dry-cleaned.'

'Did you take it any further with Courtney?' Minto tried to conceal his excitement. Here was evidence of Marriott having used dubious offshore companies to channel what may well have been dirty money into the art market. Here was evidence of the connivance of Courtney.

'I didn't, no. You see, by then relations between us weren't good, to put it mildly. I didn't feel at ease with him. I was beginning to feel I couldn't trust him. I knew I was probably going to be on my way quite shortly. Maybe I was even a little bit frightened of him.'

Frightened of him. That word again.

'Why were you frightened of him?' The question needed to be asked.

'Oh, my God, I don't know.' Theo paused, thoughtfully, then added: 'Well, maybe I do. There were a couple of other incidents, earlier on. But I don't think I can tell you about them without a glass of grappa. To give me courage.'

He smiled. But only half-jokingly.

When he had it in his hand, he said, 'You see, the thing about Courtney was that in the end he cared more about things than about people. There was a streak of inhumanity in him. Perhaps that was the clue to him.'

'What exactly happened to make you think that?'

Again Theo rubbed his neck and frowned uneasily. 'Well, for instance, there was one thing . . . very minor, but it always stayed with me. Just once he asked me to stay a night at Hartsmore. It was just after he'd bought it, in about 1970, and he was very proud of the house and garden. He wanted to show it off. It was June, and I got there in the early evening. I found him in the garden, beside an ornamental pool. He was scouring through the water with a net on a pole, pulling out the goldfish. He was throwing the healthy ones back in, but the more blackened, wizened ones he was separating off. "What are you going to do with those?" I asked. They were flapping around in a bucket. "They're coming over here into this ditch," he said. "Into their own little Buchenwald." And he laughed, very loud indeed, as if he'd said something riotously funny.'

Buchenwald. Where Courtney's own aunt had died.

'Then there was the other time,' went on Denton, 'one evening in London a year or two later. We'd just sold a Salomon van Ruysdael rather well, and he was full of good humour. I'd never seen him in a mood quite like that before: he was almost sentimental. I got the strange feeling he wanted to confide in me. "Come on," he said. "Let's celebrate. I'll buy you dinner at Wiltons. Just the two of us." Well, in the past I'd seen him drink quite heavily, but he never got drunk. But now there was a sort of light-headedness about him. Towards the end of the meal he said to me: "You know how I deal with shits like Marriott?" I was surprised, it was the first and only time I'd heard him refer to Marriott like that. "I always keep one jump ahead of them. They can never quite catch up with me. In the end, I always know more about them than they know about me.'

'Then, quite suddenly, he said something extraordinary. I don't know if there was some hidden connection of thought with Marriott which brought it on. I've never been able to work it out. But without warning he leant across to me, like I'm doing to you now, and he growled: "You know, I killed a man once."'

The words hung in the air on Theo's grappa-scented breath.

Killed a man. Courtney, smooth West End art dealer, was claiming to have killed a man.

'I can tell you one thing, my sweet,' Denton continued, 'I believed him. If you'd been there, you would have too. He spoke with absolute assurance and conviction. Not boasting, you see, not confessing. Simply imparting information. The awful thing was that just occasionally you got the feeling about Courtney that he was a little unbalanced. That feeling you sometimes get about supremely self-confident people, people who are used to getting their own way, that they've lost any sense of discrimination between right and wrong, that they see themselves as being above the conventions that govern normal people's lives. There's something rather terrifying about that when you meet it in a very powerful man.'

'Did he tell you who he'd killed?' insisted Minto.

'Well, I pressed him a bit, because I was quite drunk too.

But all he said was, it was a long time ago, and asked for
the bill.'

Minto was struggling to make sense of what Denton had
told him. A different picture of Alexander Courtney was
emerging. A more chilling dimension. The goldfish. And the
boast about the killing. This was a man who cared more for
things than for people.

'Did you yourself have any more contact with Marriott?'
he asked Theo tentatively.

Theo frowned. 'Only once. And that was later. Ten years
later, probably, it must have been in the early eighties. I
had my gallery in Bury Street then. I had very little to do
with Courtney by that time. Our ways had diverged. He was
expanding all over the world, and I was concentrating on
developing my own small but highly discriminating clientele.'
He looked up, defying Minto to challenge the assertion. Under
other circumstances Minto might have been inclined to ridicule
its preciousness. But now he knew that he must keep his
mouth shut. 'Anyway out of the blue I got this invitation
to the opening of a Courtney exhibition. Normally I just
chucked them away, but I was curious about this one. It
wasn't Courtney's normal style. It was a Tissot exhibition,
you know, all that Victorian high life. Just for the hell of it,
I decided to go along.

'It was the usual glitzy crowd. I nodded at Courtney, but
distantly. Played the ice queen, in fact. A role I can play extra
cuttingly, I don't mind telling you. The pictures were pretty,
but not real art. I tend to go along with Ruskin about Tissot,
dear heart. Ruskin said Tissot's pictures were just like painted
photographs. He talked a lot of sense, Ruskin, even if he never
actually recovered from the trauma of seizing a handful of
Effie's pubic hair on his wedding night. But I digress. No,
the point is, I was on my way out, when who should I bump
into but Marriott.

'He greeted me and asked me what I thought of the show.
Well, I'm not one of those bitchy old queens who go round
knocking other dealers' pictures. I said I thought it was
interesting, but not Courtney's normal style. He said that
was just where I was wrong. He said he thought Tissot

meant more to Courtney than any other artist. He said it with a sort of triumph, as if he was scoring a point off Courtney, showing off his knowledge of something about him that Courtney didn't know he knew. "I'll tell you something else," he added to me, "if you want to understand a bit more about Courtney, look at Tissot. You can learn a lot about him by studying Tissot.'"

'What did he mean, do you think?' asked Minto.

The air was thick with the scent of cigar smoke. Unbidden, the waiter returned and refilled Denton's grappa glass. Denton fingered his reading glasses fastidiously as he watched the liquid rise up to the rim.

'I've never really worked it out, what he was trying to say or why he was saying it to me,' admitted Theo quietly. 'Maybe he was a bit drunk. But there was clearly quite a lot to the relationship between those two. Maybe Marriott knew more about Courtney than most people.'

Minto nodded. 'But what do you think he meant about Courtney and Tissot?'

Theo massaged his neck again. 'That's a tricky one. I've thought about it a lot. I just don't know what he was on about.'

'And in the end Courtney stayed one jump ahead,' mused Minto. 'Because Marriott got caught. And Courtney didn't.' He was already building theories. Constructing hypotheses. Hidden links, discreet conspiracies. Maybe even already imagining an unwitting role for Thomas Donat in the web of deceit.

He called for the bill, and almost as an afterthought he asked Theo: 'Do you remember Courtney selling Marriott the Böcklin, *The Island of the Dead*?'

'I don't think I do, dear heart. What Böcklin was that?'

'In the Royal Gallery now. Didn't you read about it? Some madman mutilated it earlier this week, took a knife to it.'

'Oh, that picture.'

'I saw it yesterday. The stretcher's got a Courtney label on it. The Royal Gallery bought it at the Marriott sale.'

'Well, I don't remember it at Courtney's. But then again, I wasn't party to everything that passed between those two, not by a long chalk. And the fact that I can't recall it from the Courtney stock doesn't prove anything either. Courtney had a number of pictures which he occasionally sold from his own private collection. That could have been one of them.'

Minto nodded. He was going to need to know more about the history of that picture. Both in order to nail Courtney, and in order to set Donat free. He pocketed the receipt from the plate in front of him and made to move off. 'That was extremely helpful, thank you for talking to me,' he said.

But Denton didn't seem disposed to follow him. He stayed sitting where he was. Immobile. Like a cross between an ageing matelot and a buddha. 'Well, Mr Maitland, you may be a very promising young journalist, but I can't help feeling you've rather slipped up this afternoon.' Denton eyed him with malignant glee.

'Oh, in what way?' Gently, thought Minto. Don't overreact. Let him enjoy his little game.

'There's one question you appear completely to have forgotten to ask me. A fairly obvious one, I would have thought.'

'What's that?'

'You haven't asked me if I still have the photocopies.'

'What photocopies?'

'The photocopies I took of the Marriott file when I found it in Courtney's drawer twenty years ago. The photocopies I took because I thought there might be a time in the future when they would come in useful. The photocopies I kept but never brought into play because frankly I judged it too risky given the dangerous nature of the two gentlemen involved.'

'Oh, my God,' murmured Minto. 'You took photocopies.'

'Yes, I took photocopies.' Denton paused. Once again he was savouring the impact of his words. 'You see it just occurs to me, in the afterglow of this excellent little lunch, that since, as you so rightly pointed out earlier, both the gentlemen concerned have now passed on, conditions might be a smidgen more favourable to their publication. You'd like to cast an eye over them, I take it?'

Dry-mouthed, Minto admitted he would, very much.

'Can I tempt you to an afternoon of mutual pleasure frolicking in my small but commodious apartment in Pimlico? I don't want to boast, but I have a king-size bed.' He pronounced it 'baird'.

Minto smiled weakly. 'I really don't think you can.'

'I feared not.' He allowed a moment's silent regret to elapse, and drained the last of the grappa. 'Then maybe we shall have to soil our hands with some of your newspaper's filthy lucre.'

'We'll have to see if we can come to some sort of an arrangement about that.'

'I'm sure we can,' declared Denton. He got up and staggered off towards the lavatory. 'Let's be in touch,' he called over his shoulder.

As Minto walked elated away from the restaurant, he couldn't decide whether he'd glimpsed a seam of steel beneath Denton's preciousness. Or if all he'd witnessed was the last ragged cannon volley of a sinking vessel.

9

'This is the art market,' wrote Minto, 'that rarefied meeting point of commerce, snobbery and connoisseurship; where taste meets vulgarity, where wide boy meets Old Boy. Where aesthetic Etonians service taste-challenged new millionaires, urging on the socially insecure expensive pictures whose acquisition will simultaneously confer the twin badges of financial substance and artistic sensibility. In this maelstrom of charlatanry and sophistication there are some pretty smart operators. And none was smarter than Sir Alexander Courtney.'

He paused, glancing up from his word-processor to the familiar view of the backs of terraced houses which he saw from his study window, watching the grey skies gather round the television aerials. It had been a pretty full forty-eight hours, what with Thornton-Bass, the courtroom, and Thomas Donat's revelations yesterday, then Max Courtney and Theo Denton today. He'd come home this evening to try to put things in perspective. To sort out what was and was not relevant. About Donat. About Courtney. About Marriott. Courtney had sold pictures to Marriott. Marriott was a crook. Donat had attacked a picture Courtney had once sold to Marriott. Maybe it was just a coincidence. But connections must be investigated, if only to eliminate them.

Almost as therapy he'd begun to hammer something out on the screen about Courtney. It was very provisional, that opening. But it got him going, at least.

'Sir Alexander Courtney, by the time he died earlier this year, was the doyen of the London art trade. Honoured by Mrs Thatcher for his work for this country's heritage, widely acknowledged as the leading "eye" of his generation, he sold more pictures to the world's top museums and collectors than most of his competitors put together. To meet him was to shake hands with the perfect English gentleman. He married into the Barrymore family, he sent his son to Eton. And yet with Alexander Courtney all was not quite as it seemed.'

Suddenly he was aware of someone behind him. Sensed someone else in the room rather than saw them. He wheeled round. Christ, it was her. Frankie.

She leant forward and kissed the top of his head, but he shook himself free. 'You know I find that bloody annoying, people reading over my shoulder when I'm writing.'

It had been a mistake to let her have a key, but it had seemed like a good idea at the time. Back in the distant history of two or three months ago.

'So how was Birmingham?' she enquired.

'Birmingham?' He paused, collecting his thoughts. 'Oh, Birmingham. That was fine.'

'So how about the "great to see you again, Frankie, I really missed you" bit?'

'Look, I've got things on my mind, OK?'

Normally she laughed a lot. It was part of her technique for making you feel good. But now she wasn't laughing. She stood there, confronting him, in tight blue jeans and a white T-shirt. He recognised that this was a perilous moment in their relationship, the moment when he registered her attractiveness but found himself unmoved by it. He knew too well how those jeans would roll off her limbs, how she would step out of them, bending to ease them over her ankles. There was no mystery left to her body. How could that be, when three months ago its revelation had seemed like the most miraculous discovery? He remembered how much he'd wanted her then, how he'd marvelled at the line of her long brown legs as they were exposed to him for the first time, how her touch and her scent had once had such novelty. And therefore such excitement.

'Thanks, Minto. You really know how to make a girl feel welcome.'

Minto grunted. Why couldn't she leave him alone?

'You know what?' she persisted. 'I reckon there's something missing with you. There's a dimension lacking in you, a whole dimension of feeling. In the end, you just don't give very much, do you? Is it because you don't know how to give it? Or because you just haven't got it to give?'

He didn't say it, but he wanted to. Just because I don't feel it for you, it doesn't mean I can't feel it. But because he had to say something, because he was confused, he exclaimed: 'For God's sake, Frankie, you're talking like some third-rate American soap! What is it that I'm meant to be giving? Or not giving, as the case may be?'

'The very fact you have to ask that question proves my point.'

Minto shrugged.

'What is it, then?' she went on. 'What are these things that are on your mind?'

He could have told her: the Courtneys, for a start. Father and son. One dead and one alive, but together they were hiding something, he was sure of it. Then there was the poor old Hungarian with the sad eyes who had attacked a picture in the Royal Gallery and touched his heart. And finally there was something else. Something he certainly wasn't going to talk to her about.

There was Isabella Maurbach.

So all he said was: 'It's been a bugger of a day, and I've got work to do.'

She sighed and turned to leave the room herself. 'Want me to make you some supper later?'

He shrugged. He didn't feel like taking anything from her ever again.

Twenty minutes later the telephone rang. He reached over and picked it up.

'Hello, is that Dominic Maitland?'

'Speaking.'

There was a momentary pause while the familiar but not immediately identifiable woman's voice at the other end prepared itself. Gathered strength for what was coming. 'This is Leila Parsons here, hello. I'm fine, thank you. Look, I'm terribly sorry to bother you again so soon after your enormous kindness.'

'Not at all. How can I help?'

'I really wouldn't impose on you normally, but it's uncle Thomas. He's troubled, you know. He seems to want to talk, but he seems to have a block about communicating with me. Finally I got him to admit that he would very much like to have another word with you.'

'With me?'

'Yes.' There was a slight catch in her normally calm voice. An edge of desperation. 'I don't quite know what it is, but it seems to me – and I'm no psychiatrist of course – but it seems to me that he feels better about unburdening himself to someone who's not the family. Someone he trusts, but someone with a bit of distance.'

A bit of distance. Minto could provide that. He was expert in it, according to Frankie. 'Would you like me to drop in?' he said.

'Oh, could you?' There was genuine gratitude now.

'Actually I have to come in your direction this evening,' lied Minto. 'It's no trouble. I'll be with you in forty minutes.'

As he went into the other room putting his jacket on, Frankie said, 'What, are you going out now? I thought you said you had to work.'

'Something's come up. Something important. I've got to go.'

She ought to understand. She really ought to be pleased. In a way his going was proof of the dimension of feeling in him whose existence she had questioned.

He was going because there was a story here, he told himself. An imminent revelation. But more important, he was going because he minded about Thomas Donat.

It wasn't just that he minded, he reflected as he drove across Putney Bridge. It was that he minded minding. The emotion was unfamiliar to him, and he resented it. Minto was the ice-cool outsider. The observer who kept his distance, didn't get involved. But at the same time the observer who knew it all. He was the prober who could see through other people, tease the truth out of them in interviews. He was the revealer of hidden agendas, the man who discovered the secret burial grounds and disinterred the bodies. But now he was compromised. Ensnared. He didn't care enough about Frankie. And he cared too much about Thomas Donat.

It was during that short car journey that his defences finally caved in and he thought about his father. He very rarely thought about his father. Why now, for God's sake? But he knew the answer, knew it perfectly well if he was honest with himself. That answer had to be confronted. The truth was, Thomas Donat reminded him of his father. Thomas Donat, with his look of troubled mystification, of suppressed panic. Thomas Donat, in the dock, desperately trying to make sense of what was happening to him. Desperately struggling to keep a hold on reality. Minto had seen that look before. On his father's face, as he lay in that hospital bed, dying of cancer.

Of course, his father had been a bad father and a worse husband. Everyone agreed that his mother had endured an intolerable marriage and the best thing that had ever happened to her was her release from it when the divorce came through. Minto had scarcely seen his father after the age of ten or eleven. But when he had heard he was dying, he had gone to him. Minto had been twenty-three. He barely recognised the pathetic figure lying there in the bed with the emaciated cheeks. The bravado had gone, the recklessness that had made him such an impossible husband and such an exciting companion. All that you saw in the eyes was this drugged confusion. At first he thought his father hadn't recognised him. But for a moment the eyes had cleared and an agonised smile had played on his lips. It was almost unbearable to witness. Then his father had reached out a bony hand and touched his forearm. 'Will your mother come?' he'd whispered.

Would his mother come? He wasn't close to her any more. She had grown increasingly silly under the influence of her smug second husband Gavin. Gavin, who only cared about his garden. Minto found his mother more and more infuriating and didn't normally see her very often even then. He went to call on her specially, and while Gavin was out tending his tomatoes he'd made the suggestion to her. 'It's out of the question,' she'd declared. 'After what that man did to me. I've no wish to see him, dying or not. And anyway, you know what I feel about hospitals. They're infectious, full of disease and germs. The less time you spend inside them the better.' For a moment he saw her no longer as his mother, but as a sad, scared, middle-aged woman, inventing bogeymen to justify her fear and resentment.

Minto went to visit his father once more, just before he died. His father reached out the same claw-like hand and touched Minto's arm. 'Your mother?' he mumbled. That harrowing look of pleading. Forlorn. Desperate.

'She couldn't come. She's not well.' He hated saying it, and he could barely get the next words out: 'But she sent her love.'

Had the lie made any difference at all? Had it impinged even marginally through the fog of his dying father's consciousness? As he'd left the hospital, he'd hated them all for the intolerable emotional demands they'd made on him. He had vowed never to get into that situation again. Never to expose himself to people, never to render himself vulnerable. It wasn't just that he'd minded. But he'd minded minding.

It was still light when he got to the house in Putney, but the evening was colder and greyer than on his last visit. Leila Parsons came to the door wearing a jersey and a tweed skirt.

'Thank you for coming,' she said. She smiled at him with the sort of relief people show to doctors on house calls. A tall balding man hovered awkwardly in the background. 'This is my husband Howard. Howard, this is Dominic Maitland who was so kind to us yesterday.'

Howard Parsons offered a half-hearted handshake. Minto could see he was ill at ease: used to leaving things to his wife. Used to her coping. Half resentful of the attention her sick uncle was eliciting from her, but determined that the matter should not become his responsibility.

'Difficult business,' he muttered.

'Awful for you, I'm sorry,' said Minto.

'I'll leave you to ... er ...' He edged away into another room without finishing his sentence.

Weak, thought Minto. Not her calibre. He fancied himself as

something of a connoisseur of marriages between unequals. The subject intrigued him. Sometimes you meet a man the initial judgement of whose merits you feel compelled to revise upwards upon meeting his wife. Sometimes, on the other hand, you come across a woman whose sole failure of otherwise impeccable good sense has been her choice of husband.

'Uncle Thomas is in the drawing-room,' said Leila Parsons a little too briskly. 'He's waiting for you.'

He half rose when they came into the room. He looked smarter today: he wore a clean shirt and tie, his hair was brushed with a straggling parting, and he had shaved. But his eyes still looked sad and bemused. He sank down again into his chair and shook Minto's hand from his seat.

'Are you feeling a little better today, Mr Donat?'

'Better, I think. Certainly a little better.' Thomas Donat smiled back at him with the sudden brilliance of light through a momentarily clearing fog. Minto was painfully reminded of the hospital bed. The unmistakable institutional smells of the ward. The crabbed hand coming out to clutch his arm.

'That's good. You look better.'

'Can I get you a drink?' asked Mrs Parsons.

'I won't, thank you,' said Minto. Thomas also shook his head.

'Then I'll leave you to chat for a while,' she said, and closed the door softly behind her.

Minto looked at the forlorn figure in the armchair. He seemed superficially relaxed, until you noticed that one hand was clasped around the armrest so tightly that his knuckles were white.

'Did you want to tell me some more about . . . about what you were telling me yesterday?' suggested Minto gently.

Thomas nodded slowly. His mouth opened but no sound came. Minto sensed the man needed encouragement, but knew he must hit the right note if that encouragement was to be effective. Minto was groping in the dark; trying to operate some unfamiliar computer without a manual. Unless he tapped in the right code, he couldn't even log on to the system.

'Do you want to tell me about Greta again. About the

woman you took on the pleasure steamer up the Danube?
Who you saw that autumn in your apartment in Budapest?
What happened afterwards with Greta?'

Thomas closed his eyes. And, involuntarily, his hand
went up to his cheek once more. No, not that shaft. He
had looked down that shaft. He had told the kind young
gentleman everything he had seen down that shaft. He must
move on. Approach the darker areas. There the seams of
memory became dangerous, treacherous, leading you through
labyrinthine tunnels which might at any moment collapse and
leave you stranded without oxygen to breathe. But he must
take courage. He must try. He had finally convinced himself
that only by talking of these things might he find a measure
of relief.

'You should know how it was when I left my apartment,'
he said slowly. 'When I became a ... what can I say? ...
a refugee in the other apartment, the one which Tibor had
found for me.'

'Tell me,' said Minto. 'I should like to know about that.'

It was ridiculous. He'd overreacted. It had been the pressure
of the events of that one momentous evening which had
unbalanced his judgement. You don't expect to meet Rákosi
every day, do you? Nor to be faced by such a wall of
hatred and suspicion as he had encountered in the Central
Committee chamber. It had been an unnerving experience.
But, with hindsight, surely not one of such significance that
you had to flee your home and lie low for weeks afterwards.
Like a fugitive. Like a coward.

And there was something else. A thought that had crystallised in the time he'd idled away here, mulling over the events
of that curious interlude spent as a last-minute member of the
Writers' Union deputation. A thought that had crystallised
into a conviction as he went back over the exchanges, as
he remembered the bigoted fury of the party activist and
the smirking complacency of Rákosi, recalled the beads of
perspiration on the forehead of the unbowed Tibor Monos.
The truth was important. Important to Tibor, to him, even to
the peasant woman preoccupied by her turnip crop, although

she might not yet realise it. He was grateful that he'd been part of it that evening, pleased he'd had the chance to show solidarity with his colleagues' views. He'd learned something there. He'd learned that he wasn't prepared to sit back and let the waves of meaning-robbed verbiage break over him any more. He wasn't prepared to let the authorities get away with their emasculation of language. These men needed to be challenged. The New Course set in motion by Nagy and then derailed by Rákosi and his henchmen needed to be reinstated. Reinstated and accelerated.

It was the fourth morning of his exile. He looked out from the window of his unfamiliar quarters and watched a new day unfolding. A tram rattled past, packed as usual, with passengers even hanging on to the outside of the doors. Two horse-drawn carts laden with vegetables clattered by more slowly. A mist shrouded the distance, softening the outline of the buildings. The innocuousness of the scene was intolerable. This was a city unconcerned with his misdemeanours. Life went on. What was he doing, cowering here, in a cage of his own making? What was he doing, running away from shadows?

And what was she doing now, what was Greta doing?

In the long tracts of inactivity that he had suffered here in this room he had thought of her often. The memory of their last meeting assailed him like a recurring physical pain. His anger. Her tears. The lost tenderness of the *rapprochement* which he hadn't had the time to consummate. The hardness of her voice as she left him. He could still hear her footsteps receding down the stairs.

He still knew so little about her. He didn't even know exactly where she lived. It was in Buda, that much she had let slip. If her husband were as important as she maintained, then no doubt she lived well up there, in a comfortable house. Maybe even with a garden. But she hadn't felt it safe to let him contact her there. She'd never given him the address, nor the telephone number. Not when he had pleaded for it, breathless with heat and passion at the end of their day out on the Danube.

'No, Tamás,' she had told him, 'these things are too dangerous. It's not worth it to run the risk.'

'How can we get to meet again, then?' he had demanded.

'Give me a little time. I must work it out. It's all so new . . .
all so unexpected, what has happened today. I never thought
it was going to get this far. Not so quickly.'

'Nor did I.'

'We must be careful.'

'You do want to see me again, don't you?'

'How can you ask?' She had smiled up at him through her
perplexity.

'OK,' Thomas had said. 'Then here is my address if you
cannot give me yours. You must get messages to me there
about when and where we can meet. Remember, don't take
long. Otherwise I shall die.'

They had come by post, those messages. They were short,
as if scribbled in the few brief seconds when a watching head
was turned away. And painfully sporadic. 'Meet me at the
Corvin Cinema, 2.30 Wednesday afternoon. All love. G.' Two
or three weeks would pass before the next: 'Thursday, four
o'clock at your apartment. Can't wait to see you. G.'

I know the type, Tibor had said. She's just looking for
kicks. She's bored.

Was that the explanation? Was he just a diversion for
her? Was she ultimately unwilling to rock the boat of her
own marriage for his sake? Or was there some other less
obvious restriction to her life which she had not divulged?
She was twenty-five. She had no children, that she had told
him. That couldn't be a factor. Did the absurd Peter have
some other hold over her? Peter Kassák. He tried to envisage
the man. After his experience of the party activists the other
night, he could see him in the guise of the questioner who
shook with fury as he queried the deputation's thesis that
cultural life was being interfered with. A molten blockhead
with a ridiculous little toothbrush moustache. An unthinking
machine, programmed only to follow the party line with a
remorseless determination.

He has no feelings, Greta had told him.

Well, then? Why did she stay with him?

Was it the holiday villa on Lake Balaton? Was it the
security which his position gave her? The security to play

around. The security to indulge herself. To play the armchair patriot, railing at Soviet interference in her country but not lifting a finger to upset the status quo from which she derived such benefit. To play the armchair lover, too. Controlling the situation to her own convenience. Keeping her paramour on a string: close enough for pleasure; distant enough to cause no danger.

No, he didn't believe it. Not one word of it. She was passionate, not calculating. She gave herself to him as an act of love. Not as an act of scheming experimentation. She was a creature of impulse. His mind went back to one of their conversations in his freezing bedroom in Béla Bartók Street, as the paraffin heater flickered and the gramophone scratched out the rhythms of Dizzy Gillespie.

'Tamás,' she had said, gazing intently at him, 'tell me something: are you an intellectual?'

'Well, I teach at the university. I am a writer. I suppose, yes, I am an intellectual.'

'And what is an intellectual?'

He thought for a moment, then he told her: 'I guess an intellectual is someone who takes himself seriously.'

'So you take yourself seriously.'

'Probably too seriously.'

'It's true,' she nodded thoughtfully. 'You are a serious man.'

'It's a fault when you take yourself as seriously as I do,' Thomas had continued. 'You are too close to yourself, you see too much of yourself. You end up either grossly overrating or grossly underrating your own importance.'

'Which do you do?'

'Obviously I overvalue myself. Or I wouldn't have dared to make love to you.'

She had laughed delightedly. 'You're very silly, you know that, Tamás? But maybe that's why I love to be with you, because you take yourself seriously. Me, I am the opposite. I take things at face value. I do not take things seriously, I do not look for hidden meanings. Perhaps I am a simpler person than you.'

Perhaps she was. Perhaps that was it. But God, he needed to see her again. Very soon indeed.

It was crazy, really. Once he got outside, he found he was suddenly nervous. He found himself going to the most absurd lengths. He walked close to the wall, away from the pavement's edge, avoiding the eyes of passers-by. His own room on Béla Bartók Street was only twenty minutes' walk away. But the next thing he knew he was taking a tram. In the opposite direction, out beyond the Eastern railway station. After six or seven stops he got out and walked about a bit. Aimlessly. But making sudden, unexpected movements. Darting into shops, and re-emerging by another exit. Doubling back along the road he'd just taken. After an hour or so of this, he had convinced himself he was not being followed. He laughed at himself for being such a fool. That was a good definition of egotism, wasn't it? Of taking yourself too seriously? To be so convinced of your own importance that you were under the illusion of constant surveillance. It would be a good story to tell against himself at some future date. She'd find it funny. It would make her laugh.

Once he had crossed the bridge back into Buda he began to walk faster. He couldn't wait any longer, he needed to know. The anticipation was intolerable. His whole being was concentrated on the uncertainty. This was why he'd left his sanctuary, why he'd jeopardised his safety. He couldn't have borne another hour in that place without knowing. The hope was more agonising than the disappointment. He pushed through the door of the block in Béla Bartók Street and ran up the four flights of stairs to his old door, arriving panting, fumbling the key in the lock.

He stumbled into his old room and there it was. Lying on the floor just inside the doorway. Exactly as he'd hoped against hope it would be. Exactly as it might have lain for days if he had not come. A letter from her.

'I must see you,' it read. 'Gellért Hill. Sunday, three o'clock. Sorry, sorry. All love G.'

On the way back down old Mrs Varadi the house gossip who lived on the ground floor accosted him. He was still euphoric and the words didn't really sink in at once. She was tugging at his sleeve and saying: 'Mr Donat, Mr Donat, did they find you?'

'Did who find me?'

'Those men. Two of them, there were, they came late last night and knocked on your door. They made such a filthy racket I called up to them to be quiet as you obviously weren't in. They came back down and asked me if I knew where you were. Well, I didn't of course, but I said could I give you a message from them. They said not to worry, they'd catch up with you later.'

She stood there, all eager and pleased with herself like some indolent dog wagging its tail.

'Thank you,' said Thomas quietly.

'Going out again now, are you?'

'Yes. Yes I am.' He swallowed hard. 'And if anyone else calls, tell them not to bother. Tell them I may be away for quite some time.'

He walked out into the street slowly. Thoughtfully. Keeping close in to the buildings. Away from the pavement's edge.

He was glad she had chosen Gellért Hill. It was the highest point of the city, a limestone rock rising more than a hundred metres straight up from the bank of the Danube. On a clear day like that Sunday it gave you a spectacular view, both north and south, of the way the river snaked out in each direction. You could see the processions of barges barely moving on the silvery surface. And you could see beyond the roof-tops and the chimneys to the woods, massing on the river's banks and islands and drifting on to the horizon. Up here he was free, he could breathe. He was above it all. Above the turmoil of the city. Above the clanking trams and black smoking exhausts of the lorries. Above the blockheads and the language-manglers, the time-servers and the party-toadies. Above the secret policemen and the poets. Above the watchers and the watched.

He was leaning on the balustrade looking out to the north, absorbed in the view, when he felt a hand on his arm. He turned and she smiled up at him. She was wearing a grey raincoat, tightly belted to emphasise her waist, and her head was wrapped in a dark blue scarf. The cold lent her features an extra definition. Her eyes were sharp and clear.

'Look,' he said, pointing out beyond the city, 'isn't that a magnificent view?'

'Can you see as far as the Danube Bend?' she laughed.

He squeezed her arm. 'I think I can even see a little village with a landing stage and an inn. Wait a minute, beyond that there's a field – a field with a barn.'

'You have very good eyesight.'

'I have a very good memory.'

She took his arm and they walked for a moment, peering up at the gigantic statue at whose pedestal they now stood. This was the coronation of Gellért Hill, the image you could see dominating the city whenever you looked up at it from the swarming streets of Pest. Now, close to, the monumental black form of a woman holding a palm to the skies looked faintly absurd, a monstrosity. 'That's a big lady,' murmured Greta.

'She's better from a distance,' observed Thomas.

'Who is she?'

'Liberty.'

'And is that better from a distance, too?'

'That's hard for us to tell.'

'Why?'

'Because we've never been close enough to the real thing to be able to make a comparison.'

'We're shackled, you mean.'

He looked at her quickly. Was she remembering the time he'd used the word before, and regretted it? On the boat, last summer? 'Shackled,' he repeated. 'That's about it.'

'Well, then, Tamás,' she continued, 'in that case I have some good news for you. At least I hope you will find it so.'

'Good news? Tell me the good news.'

She giggled at his enthusiasm. 'There are two things. The first I will tell you now. The second later.'

'What is it, Greta?'

For a split second he stared into the chasm. An unaccountable glimpse of horror, a brief presentiment of the depths opening up to receive him. Don't say it, Greta. Whatever it is, don't say it. It will lead to disaster. It can't do us any good.

'I can be free tonight,' she said softly. 'I could stay with you. If you wanted, that is.' She paused, uncertain of him. Perhaps she saw something fleeting in his eyes.

At once the moment passed. He embraced her hard, running his hand up and down her back. 'I can't think of anything I want more. I have been wanting it ever since I met you.'

'So have I.'

'Does this mean your husband's gone away again?'

She shook her head dismissively. 'Let's not talk of him. He's not important.'

He felt her arm tightening round his waist.

'Look,' she breathed, 'this is the statue I prefer. This one here.'

Flanking Liberty was another cast, of a muscular naked athlete struggling with a mythical beast. It was smaller by comparison, but still more than life-size. Greta gazed up at it, suddenly absorbed, running her eyes meaningfully over the thighs and tensed haunches of the naked warrior.

'What do you like about it?' he asked her.

She smiled slowly, showing him the gap in her two front teeth. 'His body reminds me of you.'

She turned against him and opened her mouth to his. As he kissed her, he felt her hand running up and down the inside of his leg. It wasn't a gentle or calculated movement. It was a tense, involuntary spasm of carnality.

'Christ almighty,' he murmured, and guided her to the steps which zigzagged in unexpected patterns through overgrown public gardens all the way to the foot of the hill. After a single flight he drew her off the path into the shadow of a clump of bushes. 'No,' she breathed, pulling away. 'Let us go to your room. It will be better to wait. More exciting.'

So he hurried her over the bridge and, in a miasma of suppressed lust, on through the thoroughfares of Pest to the simple refuge in Vendel Street. As soon as he had kicked the door shut they fell upon each other, pulling the clothes from their bodies, leaving a trail of debris around the room. 'I want you to be like that statue for me,' she whispered, as they sank down on to the bed and she drew him to her. 'As big and as hard as the statue.'

Trains. He could hear them, distantly, setting off on meaningless journeys. There was something comforting about the clanking of those engines in the dark, and the slow rhythmic pattering of the trucks and coaches they drew behind them to unknown destinations. He listened to them as he clung to her beneath the covers of the single bed. It was later that night and their bodies were entwined in each other, flesh against flesh. He felt the softness of her breasts squeezed against the matted hairs on his chest. He felt her calf wound round his thigh. Her angles were a source of unsuspected delight. He ran his hand round the voluptuous curve of her buttock, marvelling at the geometry of love-making.

'So,' she whispered into his hair, 'you're on the run.'

'I'm dangerous. You must beware of me.' He was on the edge of sleep. Half-conscious. Wholly happy.

'Have you been so very, very bad?'

'Some people seem to think so.'

'Your great friend Tibor has been corrupting you, has he? Leading you astray?' For a moment he sensed something unfamiliar beneath her playfulness. A harder edge. A suspicion. Or perhaps a jealousy.

'No. If anything he's been protecting me. He gave me the keys to this place.'

'This is Tibor's flat?'

'No, it's not actually his flat. But he comes here now and then. He's brought me things.'

She paused, assimilating what he said. He sensed that there was something about Tibor which simultaneously annoyed her and roused her interest. Then she sighed, and spoke again: 'So, does this make up for it?'

'For what?'

'For my being so difficult. For making you angry when we last met. For not seeing you enough?'

'I'm sorry,' he breathed. 'I was unkind. I should be the one making it up to you.'

'It wasn't my choice, you know. It was the only way. You

must take my word for it now, but maybe one day you'll understand.' They lay on in each other's arms in silence for a while, then she murmured, 'So do you still think I'm hanging on to Peter for his villa on Lake Balaton?'

'Of course not. I was being stupid. You must forgive me.'

'Tamás. Listen to me.' She pulled a little away from him. He opened his eyes to see her lit by the moonlight. She was staring hard at him. As if trying to memorise the geography of his face. 'I promised you the second piece of good news. Do you want to hear it?'

Suddenly the abyss was there again, brutally exposed. The vertigo. Don't. Don't say it. If you say it we shall fall. And if we fall we die.

But he couldn't help himself. He nodded slowly.

'I'll leave him for you. For good. Just tell me that you want me and I'll come to you.'

'Greta.'

It was a noise like gunshot. Like a machine-gun.

Someone was beating on the door. Very hard, in quick, explosive bursts. Heart-stopping bursts. Not like the other time with Tibor, when he'd had the chance to think whether or not to open the door. This knocking allowed no deliberation. He leapt up instinctively, without knowing what he was doing, so that when they broke in he was standing there naked. Just standing there. Helpless. Unprotected and unprotecting. He heard her scream. Just one short, sharp scream, before the room was full of men.

One of them switched on the light. Two more took him by the arms. Roughly, pushing him against the wall.

'Tamás Donat?'

AVO men. He caught a glimpse of their notorious blue uniforms. So this was how it happened. This was what it was like. He felt that momentary dissociation from the self that sometimes occurs in supreme crisis. He'd heard about it often enough, how they came at night, when their quarry was least prepared, when defences were more easily breached. But this was what happened to other people. It wasn't meant to happen to him. Not now. Not here. He was meant to be safe here, wasn't he? Something had gone badly wrong. For them to come now, tonight of all nights. For them to come when she was here. Invading their intimacy. It was the ultimate intrusion. For a moment his fear gave way to fury.

'What do you want, you bastards?'

Another of them hit him very hard on the cheekbone. 'Get your clothes on, scum. You're coming with us.'

He fell to the ground. They threw his trousers and shirt towards him.

He never actually exchanged words with her again. There were so many of them, in the way, crowding out the small room. He remembered odd details, like the fact that one of them was smoking a cigarette, holding it tip downwards between nicotine-stained thumb and forefinger. Like the way another of them spat contemptuously on the floor. Like the way a third kicked over his small pile of books and ground his heel over the papers he had been working on that morning. He called her name as they bundled him downstairs. But he never heard a reply. He hadn't even had time to put his socks on.

It was to Andrassy Street that they drove him, to AVO head-quarters. To the building with the long grey forbidding façade which you normally hurried past as if it wasn't there.

How long did he spend at Andrassy Street? It was one of the great unanswered questions of his memory, like asking a car-crash victim to remember the time he had spent in a coma. It could have been days. It could have been weeks. In another sense, it was years of his life. Looking back, all he could be certain about was that by the time he finally re-emerged he was not the same man they had taken in.

Shivering, sockless, dragged from her embrace, he was sped through the city. They drove fast. Wedged between two uniformed AVO men, he was aware of the twinkling lamplights which rushed past as the car accelerated through deserted streets, juddering over tramlines. He was aware of a receding glimpse of freedom. And he was aware, miraculously, of a sudden surge of steel within him. The steel was sharpened by anger, honed by an adrenalin of fury, a determination that the people who were doing this to him should not get what they wanted out of him. And the steel was solidified by a setting of conviction. Now, at the moment of ultimate test, he knew he must stay strong. What was happening to him now meant something. His oppression by these men stood for something much more significant than his own individual plight: it stood for the oppression of the truth by the system. So he must stand firm. He must stand firm for Tibor. To prove that what Tibor had suffered had not been in vain. He must stand firm for her, for Greta. To prove that their affair meant incomparably more than her marriage to that party automaton. And he must stand firm for himself.

As they arrived he asked, 'Why are you bringing me here?' But no one answered.

They manhandled him out of the car and in through a back door. Then he was pushed down two flights of stone stairs. Down. Down into the black subterranean world that was to crush his horizons and consume him. Briefly he was impelled into a tiny interview room, where, after a moment's solitude, he was joined by another uniformed AVO officer. He was a small, dark, oddly meticulous figure, with the shrivelled skin of a desiccated plum. Very carefully he sat down opposite Thomas at the table. In silence he went through a ritual of removing from his breast pocket a spectacle case, taking out spectacles, placing them on his nose, then clicking the case shut.

'You are Tamás Donat? Writer? Lecturer in literature at the Budapest University?' His voice had a high-pitched, whining quality. Crabbed, like some bitter schoolmaster, disillusioned by years of his own inadequacy. With no pleasure left to him but the assertion of power over the weak and helpless.

Very slowly Thomas reached inside his jacket for his identity card and pushed it across the table. Saving his strength. Pacing himself.

The interviewer paused, peering at the file in front of him. He blinked, from the file to the identity card and quickly up to Thomas's face, before lowering his gaze again. Finally he said, 'You need time. An opportunity for extended self-criticism. You know that, don't you, Donat? And I'll tell you something:

you're a lucky man. You're going to be given what you need. Time for reflection.'

Then he snapped the file in front of him shut, removed his spectacles, and went through the same elaborate ritual of replacing them in their case. For a brief moment he looked up and rested his eyes on Thomas. They were dead eyes. Not just empty of humour, but devoid of life. Dead as the lies he peddled. Don't give in, Thomas told himself. Don't let them win.

They led him down more stairs, down into the bowels of the building. A door was opened and he was shoved inside a cell. A small bare cell, lit by a single unremitting bulb. A cell that was to be his world for an incalculable length of time.

The bulb burned on remorselessly. It was never switched off. At first it exercised a sort of fascination. It was the focus of his existence, the one energised, animated element in his world. A substitute sun. But gradually its light became a distraction and then an unending source of menace. Did it never wear out? Did it never flicker and die? Would it never grant him relief? When he lay down to sleep he had to close his eyes tight, clenched in a vice. He would turn his face resolutely to the wall in the doomed battle to exclude the all-pervasive glare.

How long was it before he lost all sense of time? Another unanswerable question. Cut off from all contact with the outside world, all source of natural light, the demarcation between night and day rapidly broke down. He had nothing on which to pin his understanding of the passage of the hours. They brought him food and drink of the most basic kind; but they did so at irregular intervals so that no framework for a disciplined existence could be established by the arrival of his meals. His slops were emptied for him too, but again without pattern. This space, his space, this three-metre by two-metre cage of white-walled windowless infinity, this was his world. His world of the single unremitting bulb.

And yet he survived. He gathered himself into himself, set himself tasks, established his own routines. He exercised regularly in the cramped confines of his room, imposing upon himself highly disciplined sequences of stretches and jerks. The physical effort was gruelling and unfamiliar, but he persisted. His instinct told him that he could not afford to relax his regime. He knew he must give his mind to things, too, attempt feats of memory, make work for his brain. He tried systematically to enumerate the books in his bookshelf at Béla Bartók Street. He laboured to recall the names of all twenty-four boys in his class as an eleven-year-old. He went through all the poetry that he had by heart. Latin, Hungarian, German; even a little bit of English. He thought of the fury of the party activist blockhead; of Rákosi orchestrating the laughter of the party faithful; of the dead eyes of his AVO interrogator. And he knew he must not let them win.

When he'd exhausted other people's poetry, he composed some of his own. Sheer doggerel, a lot of it, but the discipline of memorising it as he put it together gave him another vehicle by which to journey through these seemingly limitless tracts of time. Sometimes he thought of his parents: his father who had gone off to the war in 1941 and never come back; his mother, and how peaceful she had looked that summer morning laid out dead on her bed.

Often he thought of Greta, too. Recalled her clothes, identified her entire known wardrobe. The thin cotton dress she had worn on the voyage upstream to the Danube Bend; the skirt and jersey she wore in autumn; the belted raincoat and scarf in which she had met him on Gellért Hill. He went over and over conversations they had had, the two of them. Analysed every detail of their affair. Greta. Somehow he convinced himself of an enduring and unbreakable correlation between the agony of his solitude here and the ultimate reward of extended possession of her. For every hour he spent here now, there would be a hundred to live with her in compensation. So the longer he bore it now the greater the deposit of future happiness he was building up for himself.

He savoured his own strength. It fed off itself. The experience was bringing to the surface some deeply buried hermitic instinct within him. Perhaps in some other life he'd been a Trappist monk.

Sometimes he heard screaming. It was the noise of a man screaming in pain and it came from an indeterminate distance away. Not next door, but not far. Agonised, piercing screams. Screams dredged from the pit of despair. But there were ways of coping even with that. Very calmly, very clinically, you dissociated all emotional content from the noise. It was aural disturbance. It had no human significance. No more significance than any other natural phenomenon, like the wind howling in the rafters. Sometimes it was there. Sometimes it wasn't.

At some incalculable juncture in this immeasurable confinement, they came for him again. Without warning. He heard the footsteps in the corridor outside. The door opened. He sat up, expecting food. But no. Two of them entered his cell, pulling him to his feet. Where am I going? he heard his own voice asking. It was strange to use his voice again, to be directing questions to real live people as opposed to talking only to himself. But even now no one bothered to reply.

He was led up twisting stairs. Down passages. And then suddenly a door opened and he was in daylight. It was cold and it was raining. But this was unquestionably daylight. And it was unutterably beautiful. He'd never seen anything quite so beautiful in his life.

They held him. Tight, by the arms. Not that he struggled. He knew there was no point. They were taking him somewhere. The car drew up in the courtyard, in the grey drizzle, and his two guards prepared to bundle him in with them, into the back seat.

With an enormous effort of will he stopped himself. No further down this shaft. Here he must turn back, for this way lay madness. That car journey led to the unspeakable things, the horrors he was not going to talk about even to this kind young gentleman. No. No further. He blinked, and smiled apologetically across at Minto.

'Forgive me,' said Thomas Donat, 'I have taken much of your time with my . . . with my stories.'

'Not at all. I find them very interesting. You tell them very vividly.'

'You are kind to listen to them.' He swallowed. 'They are

just reminiscences. An old man's reminiscences. But it helps to speak of these things . . .'

It was dark outside, and through the window opened to the garden a breeze flapped the undrawn curtain.

'I understand,' murmured Minto. And the picture, he ached to ask; what about the picture? What about *The Island of the Dead*? Stop these agonised memories of the distant past and tell me why you lashed out at that picture. Tell me all the things I need to know, give me the connections. Tell me about Marriott. Does Marriott mean anything to you? Where does he fit in?

But he knew it wasn't the time for questions. He could see the old man's eyelids were heavy, his shoulders hunched with exhaustion. And Minto was sensitive to these things, wasn't he? 'But she sends her love,' he'd whispered at the hospital bedside. Once, a long time ago.

'I'd like to hear other things about your life,' said Minto quietly. 'Can I come again tomorrow to hear some more? Would that be all right?'

He sighed, and nodded. 'Yes, you should come again tomorrow. But now I am tired. I must go to bed. Goodnight, Mr Maitland.'

Thomas Donat pulled himself slowly to his feet.

And Leila Parsons came in. Came in a little too promptly. God knew how long she had been listening outside.

It was past midnight when Minto got home. There were no lights on in the flat, and he shut the front door softly behind him. He stood there for a moment in the hall, still unsettled by what he had heard. He had stopped for a drink on the way home from Putney, downed a couple of whiskies in an effort to dispel the intensity of Thomas's narrative, to make sense of the procession of images from the story he had just heard. Thomas's exile in the strange apartment; the exhilaration of the rendezvous with Greta Kassák; Greta lying in his arms when the AVO men burst in. The AVO men, who had come to take him away. And Greta, naked in Thomas's bed, watching it all. Witnessing his arrest. Greta. What was the connection between this woman in Budapest forty years ago and the slashing of the picture called *The Island of the Dead*?

Minto walked slowly along the passage to his own bedroom door. When he went in, he found Frankie lying there. He was simultaneously annoyed and relieved. She was already asleep, one long leg thrust out exposed beyond the covers. There was a wantonness about the position, an abandon, which suddenly moved him. She lay on her stomach, and at the top of her thigh the sheet bunched up over the mound of her buttock. She was naked.

Minto undressed quickly and slid in beside her warm body. She didn't wake, but as she sensed him close to her, she turned slightly and spread herself round him with an instinctive animal sensuality. Her somnolent eagerness was in itself exciting, more so than the identical movements in her waking state. Frankie; Greta Kassák. Like this they're all the same. The same curves. The same flesh. The same hot breath.

Afterwards there may have been a few whispered words of tenderness. Or maybe merely of apology.

And Minto went to sleep thinking of Isabella Maurbach.

10

Minto called her next morning.

He arrived early at work, sat for a moment at his desk, and took the card from his pocket. He stared at the name. He stared at the address in Munich. He could not wait any longer. He was surprised by his nervousness as he dialled. And when she wasn't there, and he had to leave a message asking her to call him back, he was surprised by his own disappointment.

After all, Isabella Maurbach was the original spoilt bitch. He'd classified her, defined her. That should have made her easier to handle. But it didn't. And he couldn't quite explain to himself why.

He had a nine-thirty appointment in Elaine's fourteenth-floor office. There she sat, looking fresh and well-groomed. As usual. There were two other men with her.

'OK, Minto, I asked these guys in because I figured they might have useful input, reference the matter you raised yesterday afternoon. You know David Bridges from our legal department? And Ray Vinea, of finance?' Elaine beamed across at him. He didn't trust that smile.

'Hello,' said Minto without enthusiasm, and shook them both by the hand. Bridges was a certain type of Englishman, he could tell even before the guy opened his mouth. He could tell from the heavy brogue shoes and the lines of diffident anxiety on his forehead. This was a man who'd never taken a risk in his life and wasn't likely to start now. Vinea, on the other hand, wore heavy spectacles and a deep tan. He was one of the American money experts who'd been drafted in after the take-over to exert a bit of discipline. To pull things together. The three of them took seats in a little semi-circle facing

Elaine at her desk. There could be no mistaking who was in control. The worker bees paying homage to the queen.

'I've filled David and Ray in on the background to this one, Minto,' continued Elaine, pouring herself half a glass of mineral water. 'Basically your contact Denton claims to be in possession of material which could be relevant to the piece you're researching on Sir Alexander Courtney. He's demanding payment for the release of this material. Perhaps you would give us your evaluation of the information he's offering?'

David and Ray turned towards him. Pens at the ready, hovering over files. Bridges looked studiously concerned; Vinea assumed an expression of profound scepticism.

Minto took a deep breath. 'Look, potentially this stuff's dynamite. It can establish a link between Courtney and Leslie Marriott, prove that Marriott was using the purchase of works of art as some sort of money-laundering operation, as early as 1975. Nothing of this came out at the trial. It would be a whole new dimension to the story. At the same time it would be pretty sensational if we could provide conclusive evidence of Courtney's involvement, too.'

Bridges shook his head nervously. 'We'd have to be jolly sure of our ground before we went to press on that one.'

'Courtney's dead now, don't forget,' Minto reminded him.

'But he's left behind some pretty powerful interests. Some powerfully protected ones, too.'

So you're frightened of the hot-shot lawyers as well, are you? thought Minto. 'Of course we must tread carefully,' he agreed. 'But that's why we need Denton's material. It will give us the data to check out. On that basis we'll know if his story's got the legs.'

'But what exactly does this material consist of?' demanded Vinea. 'As I understand it, there are just a few names of offshore companies which may or may not have been used by Marriott. They could be perfectly legitimate.'

'We won't know unless we check.'

'Are we being offered anything else?'

'Yes. There's this phoney invoice issued by Courtney for

one hundred and eighty thousand dollars for a picture which cost three hundred and eighty thousand dollars.'

Bridges frowned. Vinea said, 'That's quite a discrepancy. I agree that on the face of it that might constitute money-laundering. But where do you get the corroboration that three hundred and eighty thousand dollars was actually received? You'd need detailed access to the Courtney books of the time. Have you got that?'

Bloody interfering American with his designer spectacles and his healthy skin. 'Of course I haven't got that. Not yet. But I need the stuff from Denton in order to make a start, don't I?' said Minto. 'Look, I don't know why you're making such a big deal out of this. It's a fairly straightforward transaction. In return for a financial consideration, Denton's prepared to make over to us Courtney's Marriott file. With the proviso of complete anonymity for him.'

Bridges muttered something about dangerous precedents and legal minefields. About journalists being sent to prison for failing to divulge their sources. And not just journalists: editors, too.

Elaine assumed one of her stock executive expressions. This time it was of Intelligent Concern. She demanded, 'So how much is Denton asking for here? You never mentioned a figure.'

'He's hard up, I know that,' replied Minto. 'And he's got a drink problem. I don't think it would take much. Perhaps three or four grand?'

It was a shot in the dark, but he could tell he'd hit the right target area. Not too much to rule the matter out of court. Not too little to cast doubt on the quality of the information on offer. Bridges sucked on his pen. Vinea looked unconvinced, but could offer no more than a slow shake of his head.

'The way I see it,' continued Minto, gathering steam, 'this could materialise into just the sort of serious investigative story that has made this newspaper's reputation in the past. You know, exposing corruption in the British establishment. I mean Courtney's aspires to be tremendously establishment. Don't forget that Alexander was knighted by Mrs Thatcher.'

And maybe once he killed a man, he added under his breath.

'This could be four thousand pounds down the drain,' insisted Vinea. 'We have to face that possibility. That's the bottom line. I mean it may not seem much to you people chasing after your exclusives and your exposés. You win some, you lose some, that's your attitude. If this one doesn't work out, you just move on to the next. But my department has to account for this money. How reliable is this guy Denton? You say he has a drink problem.'

Minto drew the line at vouching personally for the miserable old queen. He remembered the bleary, malicious eyes leering back at him across the restaurant table. There are some masts to which you avoid nailing your own colours too conspicuously. 'All I can tell you is he worked with Courtney for the best part of ten years. He should know, if there's anything to know.'

'If there's anything to know,' repeated Vinea.

Elaine clipped the top of her mineral water back into the bottle with the palm of her hand. Clipped it in decisively.

'Well, I'm inclined to run with this one, guys,' she announced. 'I give it tentative approval.'

'It needs the formal OK of the finance department this afternoon,' warned Ray, obstructive to the end.

'Understood,' agreed Elaine. 'Minto, you should have your go-head later on today. Don't move on Denton till then. Meanwhile, David, you put some sort of legal form of words together for Denton's signature. To protect our asses.'

Bridges nodded. That was what he was good at, thought Minto. Protecting his ass.

Bridges and Vinea filed out of the door, an Anglo-American alliance of singular charmlessness, thought Minto. He made to follow, but Elaine called him back. That smile again.

'I hope you appreciate what I'm doing for you here,' she told him.

'Thanks,' he said shortly.

'You'll make this a good one for me, won't you?'

Correction, thought Minto. I'll make it a good one for me. 'I'll try,' he said.

'And while you're waiting for the Denton OK, just finish that Royal Gallery restoration piece, would you? On the picture that loony tried to take apart? Rory went up yesterday and got some shots of your girlfriend in the conservation department. All I need now is your nine hundred words.'

'You'll have it by lunchtime,' said Minto.

That afternoon Thomas Donat sat in the Putney drawing-room watching Minto warily. The two previous nights had brought him blessedly deep sleep, but last night had not been so good. The horror of the past had seeped slowly but irresistibly back into his consciousness; gradually his dreams had overwhelmed him. After a certain time he had found it too dangerous to close his eyes for fear of the memories that passed before them. So he had stayed awake from dawn, reassuring himself with the sounds of the gathering birdsong and the distant reverberations of the jets on their final descent towards Heathrow. In that other place long ago there had been no birdsong, no aeroplanes; only the desolation of that light bulb. He realised it had been a mistake to go so far back last night, to penetrate so deep down that most perilous shaft. To get so close to the ultimate horror. He rubbed his eyes with the inside of his palms and smiled weakly at the familiar face of his visitor.

'It is good of you to come again, Mr Maitland.' He was pleased to see the kind young man once more. It was true that talking to him had been an obscurely therapeutic experience up till now. But he was worried. He had encouraged him to come this afternoon, to make the familiar journey out to Putney. Now how to explain that the story could go no further? That although he had approached it boldly, his courage had failed him, and he now recognised its revelation would be intolerable?

In fact it was Minto who resolved the problem. Minto, who feared that the Budapest narrative might be a cul-de-sac; Minto, who in his impatience to advance the stream of reminiscence to a time when the connection with Marriott might be established, gave him his let-out. 'How did you come to leave Hungary?' he asked gently. 'How did you end up in Canada? Do you think you could tell me about that?'

'How I came to leave Hungary.' Thomas nodded, considering the proposition. Nodded eagerly; and Minto misread his enthusiasm for urgency rather than relief.

Oh yes, thought Thomas. This was fine. This he could manage, to take up the thread again in November 1956. On Thursday 1 November to be precise. As long as he drew a curtain across the month of October that year, and all the events that had preceded it.

Thursday 1 November. All Saints' Day. He woke at seven, when it was still barely light, and tried to calm the turmoil within himself. There was still the sporadic chatter of machine-gun fire in the distance, but it was a residue, like the water dripping from trees after a storm rather than the rainfall itself.

Oh yes, he had made the decision: that was irrevocable. He had gone to bed in its resolve, and now this morning he knew nothing had changed, that he had to do it. And do it now. But it gave him pain. A deep, piercing pain that cut right down to his roots, penetrated as far back as the furthermost limit of his memory. You do not leave your own country without tears. You do not easily cut yourself off from everything that is familiar, from the place where you have been born, brought up and schooled, the place where you have worked and lived and loved and hoped, even though you know there is nothing left for you there.

All Saints' Day. He reached for the tiny radio. The one that had been Tibor's. The one that he'd taken possession of because he knew Tibor would have wanted him to have it. Radio Budapest was broadcasting Mozart's *Requiem*. As a tribute to the dead. For a moment he peered out of the window, transported by the beauty of the music, thinking of the people he'd seen die in the past few days. Some of them had surely been saints, if sanctity is to be measured by courage. Dear God, had he not seen with his own eyes thirteen- and fourteen-year-olds confronting Russian tanks in Béla Bartók Street? He had watched in disbelief as they flung their petrol-filled milk bottles at these armoured leviathans, those monsters that crawled the streets on caterpillar treads like evilly magnified insects. He had felt his heart leap in triumph when he'd seen one of the cockpits explode in flames from a particularly well-aimed missile. And he had stared immobile in horror as another tank had caught three of these children in its sights and mown them down like dolls.

He knew death well now, in closer proximity, in greater quantity than he had ever imagined he would have to face it. He'd seen it in many different forms, serene and agonised, peaceful and bloody. For a moment, up here in the room with the paraffin heater and the once-elegant windows through which the wind continued to blow, he covered his eyes with his hands and stood still. Maybe if he never moved again it would all stop, all go away, and he would be able to forget the misery and the suffering. And, worst of all, the sickening sense of ultimate futility. The absolute conviction that, however much they struggled, they were doomed. All of them.

He shook his head. What to take? One small suitcase, that was his prescribed limit. He stuffed into it his warmest clothes. A few books. The cross his mother had always worn about her neck. And, as an afterthought, that photograph of Greta he had taken that day last year on the pleasure steamer. It was absurd to bother with it, but he took it none the less, crammed it into the breast pocket of his jacket. Then he shut the door on his apartment for the last time and clattered down the stairs. He knocked on Mrs Varadi's door and gave her Tibor's radio, presented it to her in farewell. She looked at him with tired eyes and murmured hollow thanks. You could see she would have preferred the gift to have been a loaf of bread. There comes a point when you need bread more than technology. Mrs Varadi had reached that point. Still he shoved the radio into her hands. She would have more use for it now than he would, where he was going.

It was clear that morning, mercilessly bright. There was no autumn fog to provide a decent shroud to this mortally wounded city. As he walked slowly towards his rendezvous in Móricz Zsigmond Square, he gazed at the evidence of recent

conflict. The sharp November sunlight revealed in higher
definition the ferocity and scale of the fighting they had all just
lived through. Corners of whole buildings had crumbled under
the onslaught of artillery; bricks and masonry lay in dusty
piles like rock-falls down a cliffside. Elsewhere the façades
of houses were pockmarked with bullet holes. Windows
were shattered and hastily patched up with newspaper and
cardboard. All that newspaper. All those printed lies. At last
they had come in useful for something.

He passed the wreck of another Soviet tank, skirted round it,
and almost trod on the body of a spread-eagled Russian soldier
in its shadow. No one felt like burying the Russians. They
lay where they had fallen. Someone had emptied a bucket
of lime over this one. For health reasons. Even in death the
Russians were still a threat. Despite himself, Thomas peered
for a moment at the face of this man, contorted in a grimace
of death. His features were Mongolian. Dear God, Mongolia:
to have come all that way, from that far outpost of the Soviet
empire, for it all to end like this. In the gutter of an unknown
European city.

But then again, perhaps this was the man who had fired the
vicious volley which had cut down the children. Thomas tried
to persuade himself that it was. Tried to persuade himself that
somewhere in all the mayhem justice was being done.

Thomas moved on, and at the corner of the street he
paused, his attention caught by a cardboard box on the
pavement. There were coins, even a few notes, lying in this
box. Perhaps as much as five hundred forints in all, made up of
many different donations. Just lying there, open to the public,
for anyone to dip a hand into and pillage. And yet no one
had touched it. There was a note pinned to it in explanation:
'For the families of the Freedom Fighters,' it read. Freedom
fighters. The full weight of the tragedy of Hungary weighed
down on him for a moment as he pondered the words, and
he could barely move. He could smell it, his country's misery:
it was compounded of the dust of the fallen masonry, of the
lime that doused the corpses, of the gunpowder that had
dealt death indiscriminately. Then Thomas put his hand in
the pocket of his raincoat and came out with ten forints. He

dropped it into the box. It was his farewell. His libation to his country. His alms to fate.

Imre was waiting, pummelling himself against the cold. He stood next to the motor bike and the side-car in which he had offered Thomas a lift to Sopron. Imre had been his pupil at the Eötvös Lóránt College. He was on the student revolutionary council. He grinned proudly, gesturing to the machine.

'Sure, I can give you a lift,' he had said last night. 'For you, Mr Donat, it would be a pleasure. You were always on our side, from the early days. We knew you were one of us.'

'And you're going to Sopron?'

'Yes, to Sopron. I'm going across to meet the Students' Council there. They're in complete control of the town, it seems. I go to co-ordinate our next moves. It's crucial to present a united front, for everyone to act together. We've achieved so much already. And I'm going to collect a short-wave transmitter they're prepared to let us have. They're like gold dust, those things. A lot of our problems here have sprung from poor communications, you know. If we'd had more transmitters we'd have tidied up the Russians and those AVO bastards a great deal quicker than we did.'

Thomas had nodded wordlessly. The boy's optimism made him miserable. More miserable than he could say.

They'd agreed to meet at eight this morning.

Now as Thomas climbed awkwardly into the open side-car, clutching his suitcase, Imre asked him: 'Why do you need to get to Sopron? You didn't say.'

Of course Thomas could not tell him the real reason. That Sopron was nearly in Austria, only a few kilometres from the final escape. That Sopron would carry him to within a few steps of getting out of all this. Leaving behind the unspeakable things. The things that were too horrible to remember. And the things that were now too poignant to tolerate any more. Like this boy's boundless optimism. Like his innocent bravery. Thomas had to get away from those things, too, before he infected them with his own crushing sense of futility. So he muttered something about an old aunt who lived in Sopron. An old aunt, his dead mother's favourite sister, who needed visiting to check if she was still all right. He owed it to his mother's memory to make the journey, he implied.

They rattled off over the cobblestoned, battle-pitted roads of the city, negotiating the larger obstacles like overturned lorries, rattling over the tramlines, dodging a three-legged dog ambling across the street with its nose to the ground. Imre drove with a suppressed energy, opening up the throttle to its fullest pitch whenever a clear piece of road presented itself. On the outskirts they stopped briefly at a checkpoint manned by students. Imre was waved through almost at once. 'See,' he said happily, 'we are getting better organised. Every day things are taking more shape. Now every road is guarded. None of those AVO bastards will sneak out through here.'

Thomas nodded. It was impossible to say more against the noise of the motor. But a few kilometres further on they had to slow down again. A line of Soviet tanks was drawn up in file along the road. They were stationary.

As they drove slowly past them, Imre waved his fist and shouted, 'Get back to Moscow, you shit-arses!' He laughed exultantly, then bawled down to Thomas: 'The silly sods have probably broken down. So much for Russian engineering!'

Again Thomas didn't reply beyond a smile and a wave of his hand in vague acknowledgement of the joke. The truth was he didn't think the tanks had broken down. Nor did he think they were on the way to Moscow. He didn't like the way they were facing away from the direction of the Russian border. Facing back into Budapest. *Reculer pour mieux sauter*, he recalled, but he tried instantly to stifle the phrase. Suddenly he had an image of Russian tanks like this drawn up on every road out of Budapest, halted on their apparent exodus. Halted, and surreptitiously turned about. To form a noose of steel about the city, a noose that would soon be tightened.

But what could he say to Imre? He suddenly wanted more than anything to protect him, to prolong his hope. He couldn't bear to see him disillusioned. He never wanted to see anyone disillusioned again: it only reinforced his own sense of isolation and despair. So they drove on in silence, and Thomas clutched his suitcase even closer to him and turned up the collar of his raincoat as it began to rain.

At Sopron, he thanked Imre and shook him by the hand. The rain had stopped, but it was cold, bitterly cold. A freezing east wind blew, swaying telegraph wires and whipping up leaves. Thomas shivered. It was a wind from Russia. 'Good luck,' he said. 'I hope you get your transmitter.'

'We'll meet again in Budapest,' declared Imre with confidence, running a hand through his long black hair. His cheeks were smeared with engine oil and he looked as though his face was blackened for combat duty. He grinned in exhilaration. Thomas suddenly realised that Imre was stimulated by this life on the edge. Here was a man completely fulfilled by what he was doing. Whatever happened later Imre would look back on this period as one of tremendous happiness. It was his taste of freedom. For that much he was grateful on Imre's behalf.

'I hope so,' said Thomas.

That night he went through the border into Austria. He left Sopron under the cover of darkness in the back of a peasant's horse-drawn cart. He walked the last six kilometres along a narrow track, lugging his suitcase, his absurdly urban luggage, trying not to think of the people and the memories he had left behind in Budapest. He caught his breath when he saw the guard tower. He stood still, peering up at its shadowy silhouette. It should have been manned by the green AVOs, the border police, but it looked empty. He stood still, debilitated by sudden and unaccountable fear. What if some solitary sniper lurked up there? What if he was going to die at this last moment of all?

Then he heard voices talking in German beyond a clump of trees a little way ahead of him. Safety was only a few steps on. He stumbled forward at a run, then paused again. This was the last time he would feel Hungarian soil beneath his feet. For a moment he was tempted to reach down and clutch a handful of earth as a final memento of his country, a constant reminder to take with him wherever he went from now on. But then he thought, no. Let that be an end of it. There must be no looking back. If I look back I'll see the things I'm escaping. If I look back, I'll destroy myself.

Besides, it was a bitingly cold night, and the ground was probably frozen.

He marched forward with his eyes set on the future. He decided then that he was going to get right away from all this, not just out of Hungary but out of Europe too. He was going to Canada. Canada, where his cousin János had made a life for himself. Canada was where he wished to go, to be near János. Henceforth he would be Thomas, not Tamás.

He had to be patient, of course. When he was met by the Austrian border guards he was taken to a refugee centre in woods not far from Vienna. There he lived in a camp for three weeks. When his papers finally came through he was sent on to England by train, where there was another wait in a camp at a place called Detling, near Maidstone.

'So you see, Mr Maitland,' he observed thoughtfully, 'it is not quite true that I have never been to England before. I passed through in December 1956.'

'How long did you stay?'

'Not more than a week or so. Then there was another train which took us up to Liverpool.' At Liverpool they had embarked on the voyage to Nova Scotia.

'I will not easily forget that journey,' he murmured to Minto, closing his eyes as he sat hunched on the Parsonses' sofa.

'It must have been exciting.'

'No, not exciting. It was hell.' He gave a little laugh. 'Hell on earth. Do not forget that we Hungarians are not by nature sailors. We have no seaboard. No navy. Admirals, yes, in the past, but no sea. So we were sick, most of us. Sick as dogs.'

He shook his head ruefully. He remembered one other thing about that voyage. It must have been the fourth day or so, when things were calmer. He ventured out on to the deck and stood for some time watching the ship's passage through the grey waters, catching distant wafts of salt spray and straining his eyes for any sign of land on the apparently infinite horizon. And suddenly he was reminded of that other boat trip, on the gentler summer Danube, when the dragonfly had danced on the surface of the water and she had sat opposite him in her thin cotton dress and gazed out at the fishermen on the bank. Very slowly he took from the breast pocket of his jacket the photograph, her photograph, the one he'd taken with him on a last-minute whim. He held it in the wind for a moment, ready to let it go. Ready to watch it flutter into the enormity of the Atlantic Ocean. His final link with the past would be severed. But he didn't. He shook his head and put it back into his pocket. Everything else could go, but not this.

By the time he reached British Columbia, Thomas felt that he had indeed travelled half-way round the world. Once there, he said, he felt little temptation to look back.

'And how was Canada?' asked Minto. 'Was it easy to settle in, or was it all utterly alien and unfamiliar?'

'I was fantastically lucky, fantastically I tell you.' Thomas's eyes gleamed with sudden animation. 'First of all I had my family nearby, János and his wife. And then there was already a little Hungarian community in the area, people who helped me like I was their brother, welcomed me and made me feel at home. And I liked Canada. It was a young country, a flexible country. Not like Europe, not so set in its ways. Not like England would have been, if I had come here. I understand that now, now that I have spent time in London. It would not have been right for me to have come to England.'

It was true, thought Minto. Thomas Donat had lived for nearly forty blameless years in Canada but within a week of arriving in London he had taken a knife and carried out a frenzied attack on a valuable picture. But why? You couldn't put it down simply to the English climate, or even to the innate inflexibility of the people.

Donat continued: 'In Canada they found me a flat, and then they found me a job even, teaching in the faculty of Eastern European literature at the university.' He nodded reminiscently. 'Perhaps you do not know this, and I may make this little boast: by the time I took retirement two years ago I was the number two in the whole department. It is not so bad, that, for the little man from Hungary to get so far?'

'I'm sure it was what you deserved.'

'Who can say whether we get what we deserve.' He was silent for an interval, apparently pondering the question. 'But yes, I worked hard. And I have been happy in Canada.'

'You have never married?'

'No, I never ... never felt the need.' His hand went unconsciously up to his cheek, and stayed there for a few seconds, as if protecting an area of sudden tenderness. 'Oh yes, I have had my lady friends, some of them very charming. But in the end I found I didn't need them; not one only, anyway, and not permanently. You see I cultivated a very considerable self-sufficiency. It ... it seemed the safest way.'

The safest way. Minto looked out into the leafy garden, averting his eyes from the older man. He was suddenly embarrassed. Embarrassed because he knew exactly what Thomas meant.

'Yes, I worked hard.' Thomas nodded judiciously. 'And I cannot complain. I have been lucky. A fortunate man.'

He stared back at Minto, with a fair imitation of content, as if he had just spoken his own epitaph. And defied anyone, Minto included, to challenge it.

Minto looked up, realising that the narrative had drawn to a close. He had been caught unawares. Was that really all? The full story? And suddenly he felt cheated. There had been nothing about Marriott. Nothing about Courtney. And nothing about *The Island of the Dead*. He was let down, for a moment even resentful, obeying the immediate inclination to blame others that a man feels when he has followed his own instinct only to discover it faulty.

Up till now, Minto had been sparing with his questions, allowing Thomas to tell his tale in his own words. No interruptions; only occasional promptings. But now he had to do it. Now he had to become more specific, if he was to guide Thomas into more productive directions. So he cleared his throat and said: 'Do you ever remember meeting a man called Leslie Marriott?'

Thomas held his head on one side, screwing up his eyes in an effort to conjure some flicker of recognition from his memory. Despite his frustration, Minto was touched by the evident desire to help, the wish to provide him with an answer that he would welcome. But none came. In the end the expression on Thomas's face was pure bafflement.

'No, I regret. I have never had the pleasure of knowing this gentleman.'

'And what about Alexander Courtney? Does that name ring any sort of bell?'

'Alexander Courtney?' Again the perplexed frown, and the emphatic shake of the head. 'No, I am sorry.'

'It doesn't matter.'

But, oh God, it did matter. Because all that left him with was one last stark alternative. The final resort. The question he could not put off any longer, the one he was always going to have to ask sooner or later, if he couldn't coax the answer out of Thomas in the course of his anguished narrative.

He swallowed hard, then asked it. Slowly and clearly. So there could be no mistake.

'So when had you seen that picture before? *The Island of the Dead?*'

The silence was appalling. He watched the expression of unbridled horror cross Donat's face, draining his cheeks of colour. Slowly his head fell forward, and both his hands went up to his ears in a belated attempt to exclude what he had just heard. To deny that the words had even been spoken. To negate the betrayal.

'Mrs Parsons,' Minto called, opening the door to the hall. She wasn't listening outside this time. But she came gliding downstairs with a sort of suppressed urgency.

'I'm terribly sorry,' he offered in explanation, 'I seem to have overtired him. All this reminiscence, it's ... it's taken it out of him.'

'Don't worry.' She was kneeling beside Donat now, giving him a drink of water. 'Of course he's very tired, he's been overdoing it a bit. And you've been so terribly kind.'

He'd been so terribly kind, he thought as he drove back into central London. He'd been so terribly kind, he told himself as he turned the key in the lock of his flat. He'd been so terribly kind, he repeated, as he rewound his answerphone and listened to the messages.

There was one from Elaine, thanking him for his piece on the Royal Gallery outrage and telling him that the finance division had given him the formal go-ahead to negotiate with Denton. There was another from Frankie announcing, like a sort of challenge, that unless she heard from him by ten o'clock she wouldn't come to him that evening. And there was one from Isabella Maurbach, asking him to ring her back on a Munich number.

Isabella Maurbach. The daughter of the man who preferred things to people.

The woman who liked to play games.

11

'Who is it?'

The voice at the other end of the telephone was thick with ill-tempered sleep, but Minto had no qualms about having woken Theo Denton. Maybe it was not yet nine o'clock, but two days ago the man had made him a business proposition. A demand for money. He should be pleased to be getting such a swift response.

'It's Dominic Maitland.'

'Oh.' Denton cleared his throat noisily. Buying time. 'What do you want?'

'I wanted to develop the discussion we had at lunch. To make you a financial proposal for the material you offered me.'

'What material?'

'The material you mentioned. Photocopies of a file you have in your possession.'

'I don't remember mentioning any photocopies.' What Minto should have been feeling was irritation. Impatience at the inability of this hungover old queen to focus his mind first thing in the morning. But that wasn't what he felt. Because there was an ominous clarity to Denton's voice. A resolve underlying the preciousness.

'Oh, come on, let's not play games.'

'I assure you, I'm not playing games. I'm telling you. I just don't know what you're talking about.'

'For God's sake, Theo. I'm talking about lunch, on Wednesday. You told me a lot of things. A lot of interesting things. I want to follow up on them.'

'Did I?'

'You bloody well did.'

'If I told you things, it was probably just the drink talking.'

He gave a light little laugh which didn't quite ring true. 'The drink does that to me sometimes. Stimulates the old imagination, dear heart. That's the way I am, you'll just have to bear with me.'

'Christ almighty,' said Minto. 'Don't you understand? I'm ringing you up to offer you money. Bloody good money if you'll give me a sight of the Marriott file. Are you telling me you're turning down three thousand pounds for a few photocopies?'

'I think you must be confusing me with someone else.' There was a pause. Minto imagined him rubbing his neck. Then a shriller, more hysterical edge gathered in Denton's voice. 'Look, it's absolutely intolerable of you to pester me like this. You ring me up at some God-forsaken hour, ranting on about photocopies and files and financial arrangements, trying to put words in my mouth. I'm not interested in it, do you understand me? I don't want to hear from you again. Not from you, or any of that other wretched crew.'

That other wretched crew?

'Who are you talking about?'

'I don't want to discuss it. Just leave me alone.'

There was a click. Theo had rung off. Christ, thought Minto: the man's frightened. He's been got at. For a moment he stood there, pondering the outlandishness of the situation, struck by its enormity. Someone had threatened Theo Denton since their lunch on Wednesday. Someone had demanded his silence. Someone was trying to hide something, to suppress it. And although for a moment Minto's memory conjured the image of the ranting Max Courtney, the one that stayed with him longer was that of Winter. Winter with his insinuating smile.

Very gently, he put back the receiver and stared out of the window. Fear was just a little bit infectious. Even down the telephone.

He took the plane to Munich that afternoon.

There wasn't much to keep him in London now. Not Theo Denton, anyway. Not even Thomas Donat, not after last night's excessively penetrative questioning. And not Frankie. Certainly not Frankie.

Of course he cleared the trip with Elaine. It was an

understood thing that an article like the one on Courtney would require an expense budget. It must be properly researched, and research demanded travel, after all. And this trip to Germany was crucial, he assured her. He had a number of people to see. Who? No one she'd know, but important people. Such as? Well, Frau Dr Englehart for one, widow of the last proprietor of the Galerie Voermann and guardian of its archives. Maybe the stock number culled from the reverse of *The Island of the Dead* would reveal something about the picture's past and a connection with Courtney. He was due to see Dr Englehart at three o'clock tomorrow afternoon. Anyone else? Well, yes, there was the other appointment. The one he'd fixed for tomorrow morning at eleven o'clock at an address in the smart Munich suburb of Grünwald. The one he'd arranged when he called back Isabella Maurbach. The daughter? Yes, Elaine, the daughter. Hey, that's great, that you got to the daughter.

'Yes, Elaine,' he'd agreed. 'It's great that I got to the daughter.'

He peered out of the aircraft window at the afternoon sun lengthening the shadows across the car-parks of Heathrow airport, and thought about Isabella. She had sounded cold on the telephone. Cold and distant. Yes, he could come and see her if he wanted. If he happened to be in Munich. But there was no point in his making a special journey because she hadn't much to tell him. Wait a minute, he'd felt like saying: what about Denton? You were the one who put me on to him. You were the one who told me to go and see him. Now just as things were getting interesting he's been muzzled by your precious brother and his mates. You can't just walk away from that. There's something going on here, and you've got to tell me what you know about it. But he said nothing on the telephone, sensing it was better not to. Safer. It must all wait till he could tell her in person.

And there was another question that was bothering him, too. One he'd been asking himself repeatedly the whole week. One he was no closer to solving than the moment when Elaine McBride had called him in to discuss an article on the violation of a picture in the Royal Gallery and first put it to him.

Why?

Why had Thomas Donat, an apparently harmless and gentle sixty-nine-year-old Canadian national, a retired academic paying his first visit to London, set out one morning from his niece's home in suburban Putney where he was a guest, taken a bus to the Royal Gallery, and there savaged a picture called *The Island of the Dead* with an eight-inch kitchen knife? Why, when his previous known life was seemingly unblemished by any recorded act of violence, had this mild-mannered man run so disastrously amok? What chance coincidence of circumstances had precipitated this ugly and terrible explosion?

Minto reached for his briefcase and brought out the transparency. The image he had kept since Michael Thornton-Bass had pushed it into his hands in the Royal Gallery the morning after the incident. He held it momentarily to the sunlight through the cabin window and despite himself he shivered. There it was again. *The Island of the Dead.*

He searched for a clue in the picture, something which might have triggered the appalling reaction in Thomas Donat, some element which could have made a connection, direct or tangential, in his mind. A connection which, once established, had set in motion the horrific sequence of events whose aftermath Minto had witnessed. He remembered the picture lying on the slab. In ribbons. The paint flaking where the knife had gouged rips into the canvas. Then he saw again the half-comatose, half-mystified figure bent forward in the airless heat of the courtroom. And he wondered.

Then again, maybe the whole thing was random. Maybe there was no significance to the choice of picture. Maybe it had just happened to be there at the moment of his brainstorm. Maybe the picture itself was the innocent victim.

Innocent? Was this picture innocent?

He ran his eye over the glowering sky, the charged pattern of darkening clouds, then let it fall down the vertiginous angle of the rocky cliff-face. Evil was ingrained in the very stones of the landscape. An insidious, decadent evil. It whispered in the cypresses. It lurked in the cavernous blackness of the entrance to the mausoleum. It played about the softly gliding boat, pulled at its shadowy boatman and finally burst out in the leer of its eyeless corpse.

He laid the transparency aside, and drummed his fingers on its glossy surface. The picture. He knew he had to penetrate its mystery. To trace its past. To sound the distant bell whose resonance Thomas Donat had caught again this week in the Royal Gallery.

He was going to Munich to search for some answers.

And for the first time Minto half acknowledged to himself that maybe he was going to Munich for another reason. Because he was frightened to stay in London.

Munich was rich. The city exuded a sleekness and a moneyed opulence which simultaneously repelled and attracted Minto. He left his hotel and strolled down Maximilianstrasse in the sun, watching well-heeled women drawing up in large Mercedes and shimmering into expensive clothes shops. The streets themselves seemed built on an extravagant scale, grand and wide and elegant, as if people had always done well for themselves here and had the time and confidence to cultivate a sense of space. Even the churches looked chic. Minto stood for a moment gazing at the façade of the Theatinerkirche, marvelling at its deep yellow colouring. As the taxi drove him from his hotel to the address she had given him he thought, she's a rich girl in a rich city, Isabella Maurbach. A very rich girl indeed, probably, now that her father has died. When the door was opened to him by a Filipino maid who showed him into a large white drawing-room and asked him to wait, he saw no reason to revise his opinion.

Minto looked about him. There was a curious anonymity to the atmosphere. Certainly the room was expensively decorated, with thick cream curtains and a luxurious pale blue carpet which, with that distinctively continental intimation of plenitude, finished vertically a few centimetres up the walls at the edges of the room. The immaculate sofas, so white and pure that it was hard to believe they had ever been sullied by human contact, were separated by a low glass table on top of which stood a small modern sculpture of a half-eaten apple.

Beneath the table, in two neat piles, lay magazines: *Weltkunst*, *Interiors*; half hidden, a copy of *Hello!*. Along one wall stood a heavy German seventeenth-century chest; and above it, in that once daring juxtaposition of old and modern which had now become a cliché, hung an Expressionist print in violent colours. But even the violence was muted by fashionability. The creamy blandness of the Utrillo above the fireplace set the tone more truly.

It was the surrounding blandness which drew him to the one unexpected element in the room, a small picture hanging to the right of the window. This one didn't quite fit in. It was different. You didn't notice it at once. It was almost as if it was hiding in the shadow of the curtains. But once found, it sent out a different signal from its setting. It was small, not more than forty-five centimetres by thirty. It was upright in format and showed an elegant woman in a smart English drawing-room of the 1870s, all velvet curtains and potted plants. The woman was self-possessed and yet at the same time a little mysterious; she was coping, distantly, with the advances of a stiff and immaculate white-tied suitor who was bending forward over her shoulder as she reposed on a chair. The suitor's eyes were absorbed by her; but her own eyes stared out of the picture space with a dreamy distraction. A little half-smile played about her lips. It was by James Tissot.

Minto turned away, perplexed, and walked to the grand piano which occupied one end of the drawing-room. So here was Herr Maurbach's monument; his trade mark. For a moment Minto felt curious about the man and peered amongst the cluster of photographs standing on the top to find his image. It was not difficult to identify him. In his portrait he wore rimless spectacles and had the high forehead and aquiline nose of a musician. The photograph was posed with the soft, contrived lighting of a studio publicity shot. This was the sort of picture that appeared in countless opera-house programmes. It told you very little about the man and a lot about his profession. What was he like in private? Did he rant and rave? Was he passionate and temperamental? Was he a tortured spirit, did he suffer for his art, did he throw things about the house? Looking around the room with its immaculate finish, its clinically clean fireplace unblemished by anything so soiling as a log of wood, Minto found that at least was hard to believe.

He ran his eye over the other photographs. There were nameless women in headscarves, and smirking men in loden coats. He was about to move on when he caught sight of one of Alexander Courtney. Courtney at ease. On holiday. It was taken, he guessed, in the mid-1970s on board a boat of some sort. He was sitting with his arm round a teenage boy clearly identifiable as the young Max. Courtney himself smiled confidently back at the camera, affluent, tanned, with the thickened torso of middle age. Max, too, smiled. A smile of pleasure in his father's company. An unquestioning, uncomplicated smile. The third person in the photograph was a girl of perhaps thirteen with long dark hair that fell about her shoulders. It took him some moments before he realised this was Isabella. She sat on the deck, her knees drawn up towards her chin, her back resting against her father's bare legs. She was looking away from the camera, perhaps into the distant horizon of the sea. Her brow was puckered into a frown. How could one interpret that frown? Was it petulance? Was it indifference? Or was it a susceptibility to distraction, a tendency to daydream? Was she ultimately a soul sister of the woman in the Tissot? Was that the reason why the Tissot struck the one genuine note in this otherwise bland desert of a room?

She came in then, just as he was turning away from the piano. Yes, this was her: the girl in the photograph, now grown up into a beautiful woman with short-cropped hair. When he registered she was frowning at him, he recognised the resemblance even more clearly. Frowning. Still disconsolate, twenty years on.

She stood still for a moment just inside the doorway, as if the effort of actually addressing him, of any sort of social oiling of the wheels of human contact, was suddenly too much for her. He had forgotten how tall she was. Her father's height had passed to her rather than to Max, he saw that now. She waited, long-legged in elegant jeans. She had a thoroughbred face, with those flared nostrils and eyes covered by long-lashed lids; still the same eyes, hard to catch because they would not meet his. He realised then that she was driven by a condition whose outward manifestations replicated those of shyness. But this wasn't shyness. At certain points in his first encounter with her he had provisionally identified it as boredom. Now he knew it wasn't that either. It was something different again. Something to which he couldn't yet quite give a name.

He walked forward with his hand outstretched. 'Hello. It's good of you to see me again.'

For a moment he thought she wasn't even going to do him the courtesy of bothering to take his hand. Finally she did, with a gesture of supreme uninterest. 'I hope you had a good trip,' she said. Again the crystal English accent, unexpected in this Munich drawing-room. And a wintery coolness; a determination not to let him impinge at all on her.

'I hope my visit isn't a terrible inconvenience to you,' offered Minto, smiling brilliantly at her.

She shrugged but didn't answer. 'Would you like some coffee? Or a drink?'

'Coffee would be nice, thank you.'

She went back to the door and called through crisply to the maid. Then she said to Minto, 'Won't you sit down?'

Her formality annoyed him. He wondered if this was perhaps another of her games.

'Have you lived in Munich long?' he tried again.

'Nearly two years.'

'What brought you here?'

'My husband.'

'Your husband?'

'He said it was a good base for him. He travels a lot. As I told you.' The reference to their previous meeting, intended as a reprimand, was none the less a flicker of light in a dark tunnel.

The maid brought in the coffee and put it down on the table between them. He helped himself to sugar and milk and stirred his cup. Then he leant back in his seat and said, 'Well, shall we talk about your father?'

She reached forward and took a cigarette from the case on the glass table. Minto was about to make a move to light it for her, but she did it herself with a brisk flick of her lighter. 'Why?' she said, inhaling and leaning back in her chair. 'Why should we do that?'

He took a deep breath. 'I'm writing an article about your father. I wanted to ask you a few questions.'

'Oh yes,' she said. 'Of course, you're a journalist.' She spoke the word with a blend of amusement and disdain, as if it were the punchline of some feeble joke.

'I'm sorry. I know you make it a rule not to talk to them. But I thought you were prepared to make an exception in my case.'

'Did you?'

He laughed again. To give her the chance to laugh with him. 'Don't worry, I work for an impeccably serious journal. Not a tabloid.'

'I've always felt that journalists are probably much the same whoever they work for.'

For a moment he wondered if they'd got to her too. If they'd pressurised her to stay silent just as they'd pressurised Denton. But he knew that wasn't true. There was something different going on here. She was being obstructive for her own private reasons. She wasn't driven by fear. Perhaps by anger; perhaps by something else. 'That's not quite true, you know,' he said.

'You journalists, you really enjoy your hatchet jobs, don't you?' she went on, momentarily animated by bitterness. 'You just want to cut my father down because he rose up so much higher than you ever will. And he got there on his own merit.'

'I'm not doing a hatchet job. Your father intrigues me, that's all. He's worth writing about. I want to know more about him.' He paused, then added: 'In a strange way I think you do, too.'

She looked up at him quickly; something in her eyes registered that he had hit home. Then she stubbed her cigarette out and shook her head. 'Journalists make me sick,' she declared.

'Why?'

'What gives you the right to intrude into other people's privacy? What makes you so wonderful that you can set up as judge and jury on your fellow human beings?'

Minto did not answer her question. Isabella's aggression was an advance on her indifference. Her anger obscurely encouraged him. He smiled back at her and shrugged. She made to go on, then caught his eye and looked away.

At last she said wearily: 'So what sort of shape is this article on my father taking?'

'An appraisal of his career in the art world. What drove him. What made him so successful.'

'And have you spoken to my brother?'

'I've spoken to your brother.' Minto paused, debating how to go on. Remembering Max sitting there, aggressive, humourless. Remembering Winter, loitering silkily in the background. Pulling the strings. 'Frankly, he wasn't that helpful. He just gave me the official version, as if he was spouting a press release.'

'A press release.' She repeated the words with the same scornful amusement as before. 'That would figure. And what was in this "press release"?'

'Oh, the landmarks of his career. The names, the dates. The annual profits. But I wanted to get a clearer picture of what he was like as a man.'

She looked up. 'As a man,' she repeated. Unhelpfully. Deliberately unhelpfully, with a sort of insolence. An insolence that he found suddenly exciting.

He said, 'I must tell you that I took up your suggestion. I spoke to Theo Denton.'

Was there a quickening of interest? Was there a barely perceptible glint of curiosity in her eye? 'What did he tell you?'

'He told me a lot of things.' Minto paused, observing her.

'Let me guess, all right? He said he was a bully and a snob. He said he bent the rules a bit. Anything else?'

'Well, yes there was actually.' Minto ran through the options. Denton had told him that Courtney frightened people.

That he made jokes about Buchenwald. That he'd once killed a man. But those weren't the revelations to hit her with now. 'Denton said that he preferred things to people.'

'He said that, did he?' She was staring very hard at the cigarette case. Opening it, cradling it in her hands. Chewing her lip.

'Was it true, do you think?' he asked softly.

'I don't want to talk about it,' she said abruptly, snapping the box shut.

He smiled with a show of imperturbability. It was one of her games: the less he reacted, the more she would tell him. He got up from the sofa.

'I like your Tissot,' he said, walking over to the side of the window to look more closely at the little picture.

Unexpectedly she rose too and followed him over to where he was standing.

'Yes, it's beautiful.' The way she said it was almost shocking. It was the first unforced, spontaneous remark she had made that morning. It was like hearing with momentarily perfect clarity a voice on the radio that up till that time has been distorted by interference. Her enjoyment of the picture was genuine and uncomplicated. Unlike the rest of her performance today.

He looked at the woman in the painting. He registered again the elegant fashionability of her dress as she sat there, cool and distant. Now Minto stared more closely into the scene he saw that her suitor was offering her something. An ice perhaps. But she was paying him no attention. Her gaze was drawn elsewhere, into an area denied to both the viewer and her admirer.

'She seems a difficult conquest, this lady,' observed Minto. 'She's not giving the poor guy a very easy time.'

Isabella Maurbach turned away abruptly. 'It's hardly surprising,' she said. 'It's only too clear that the man's an unspeakable bore. Why should women have to put up with boring men?' She walked back to the sofa and sat down again.

'Have you had the Tissot a long time?'

'About ten years. My father gave it to me.'

'Of course. He had a Tissot show, didn't he? In the early eighties?'

'I really can't remember the year.'

'It was unexpected, that show, I thought.'

She looked at him curiously. 'Why?'

'Well, your father made his name selling Impressionists, didn't he? He also developed a very successful old master arm to his operation. But I wouldn't have thought that the nineteenth century was particularly his milieu. At least not this sort of nineteenth-century painting. This very English, very Victorian subject matter.'

She breathed deeply. She didn't try to hide her annoyance. She shook her head like an impatient teacher dealing with an especially backward child. 'My father had passions for individual painters. Tissot was one which happened to catch his fancy.'

'I wonder why particularly.'

'I'd have thought it was clear enough in his case.'

Minto sensed something in her tone. A bitterness. And yet simultaneously something unfamiliar: a tenderness, too. 'Tell me,' he said encouragingly.

'Look, you say Tissot is very English in his subject matter. But don't forget he was also a foreigner himself. A Frenchman. An alien.'

'So?'

For a moment he thought she wasn't going to go on. That she'd lost interest in the subject. That she wished to close it. But at last she said: 'I think that maybe my father rather identified with him. My father was fascinated by England. He loved the place. A lot of the time he took great trouble to appear more English than the English. But although he would never have admitted it, he was always a little aware of his own foreign roots.'

She glared back at him, as if furious that he had prised the revelation from her, intruded so unscrupulously on her privacy. And yet at the same time she was triumphant. Look, she was saying: I'm intelligent, when I choose to be. I understand the way people work. Even my own father. Especially my own father.

'Did he tell you that?'

'Of course he didn't.'

Minto tried once more: 'But he talked to you about Tissot, did he?'

'A bit.' She picked distractedly at the cushion cover next to her. 'I've told you. He was interested in him. Interested in his life.'

'Really?'

She did not reply immediately but got up again and walked to a bookshelf in the corner of the room. She moved with an affectation of lazy indifference. An affectation which Minto suddenly realised couldn't quite disguise an enormous natural grace. She pulled out a book and brought it back to him.

'There you are,' she said, taking her place on the sofa once more. 'As you can see, his interest went some way back.'

The book she had handed to him was James Laver's *Vulgar Society*, a life of J. J. Tissot. Minto opened it curiously. On the flyleaf was the inscription in a neat handwriting 'To Alexander Courtney, from his mother, Christmas 1955. 11 Strandwick Mansions NW3.'

Minto stared at it for a moment, entranced. Here was the earliest physical relic of the man that Minto had yet chanced upon. Christmas 1955: before his mother died. Before his art-dealing career took wing.

Isabella Maurbach reached across to retrieve the book from Minto, as if she begrudged him more than a few moments' possession of it. 'I removed it from my father's library after the funeral. It was funny. I just went in and took it. I had this sudden desire for some memento of him to bring back here with me. A book like this seemed perfect.'

She laughed, a slightly bitter, suddenly disenchanted laugh. 'My father once even wrote an article about Tissot, you know. He didn't write much, my father, he was never very interested in expressing himself on paper. But that article was an exception. It's not too bad, either.' She seemed to be relishing her patronising stance, enjoying the granting of lukewarm praise. It was almost as if she was settling some private score, exacting some sort of revenge. There was this ambivalence in her attitude to her father, this simultaneous desire to attack and protect him.

'He wrote an article about Tissot? I'd be very keen to see it. Do you know where it was published?'

'I can't remember.' The wall was coming down again. 'You've got researchers, presumably. They'll find it if they're any good.' Then she added, as a concession: 'Maybe in the exhibition catalogue, if you're interested.'

Minto searched for another opening. He was beginning to lose patience with her changes of mood. The turning on and off of the tap. 'And you,' he asked, 'when did you leave England?'

'About five years ago.'

'You came out here then?'

'No. I went to live in Paris.'

'Tissot in reverse?' He spoke jocularly.

She considered the point. 'Not really, no.' Her lack of warmth was devastating. Maybe it wasn't so much like a tap being turned off; more like the sun going in.

'And what did you do in France?'

'I studied for a while. Later on I met my husband there.'

'You liked France?'

'Of course I liked France. It was very refreshing after England. The French are much less repressed than the English, they express themselves much more freely. I like their sense of grandeur.' She paused, then went on with a renewed aggression, 'You know the difference between French and English artistic feeling, don't you?'

'No.'

'Just look at the difference between Versailles and the Tower of London.'

'But the Tower of London is a prison.'

'Exactly.'

'That's not very patriotic of you.'

'I don't feel very English. I always reacted against it: all those cucumber sandwiches and absurd repressions. I had to get away.' She had to get away. From what, exactly, Minto wondered? What was she trying to prove to him? Or what was she trying to prove to herself?

'And what about Germany? How do you feel about Germany?'

She shrugged. Apparently that was going to suffice for an answer. For a moment Minto was angry. He saw a spoilt rich woman sitting in front of him. A spoilt rich woman playing games. Playing games like the one she'd played with him in the gallery after her father's memorial service. He felt like shaking her, knocking some sense into her. Or some manners at least. He decided to press her: 'After all, you're coming back pretty close to your roots by living here in Munich, aren't you?'

'How do you mean?' There was a flicker of interest in her eyes.

'Your father was Austrian by birth, wasn't he?'

'By birth,' she admitted grudgingly. 'But it didn't signify very much. He never talked about it.'

'So you don't know any of the Austrian side of your family?'

'Look, my father's father died when he was four years old. Then my father came over to England in the thirties with his mother, and his mother was killed in a car crash before I was born. Kaput. All gone, just like that. I never knew them. If we have relations left in Austria now, I'm not aware of them.' There was a hard edge to her voice. The sort of bitterness that is a shield against pain.

'But you're half Austrian. Don't you feel some sort of sympathy with people here?'

'Not really.' She laid her cup on the table with finality, to indicate that her interest in the subject was closed.

Now, thought Minto. Now was the time to force the issue. He thought of the disconsolate girl sitting on the deck. With her back to Alexander Courtney. Peering out to sea. He said, 'Did you not feel that close to your father?'

'Whatever makes you say that?'

'I suppose because you left England. Whereas your brother stayed on and went into the business.'

'You don't understand very much about people, do you?'

Minto fought to keep his self-control. He succeeded well enough to detect in the moment of panic which had prompted her to lash out that he had touched something in her.

'OK, then. Tell me what I don't understand.'

She swallowed. Composing herself. 'Contrary to what you think about my relationship with my father, Mr Maitland, I left England because if anything I was too close to him. I needed to put some distance between us. He and I were very alike. I knew him too well. I could see through him.'

'Your brother says—'

'My brother's judgement is clouded by idolatry. He worshipped my father. But he didn't understand him.'

'And you did.'

'And I did.' For a moment she had been animated, but now she was retreating into herself. Perhaps she felt she'd been unnecessarily revelatory. But at the same time there was an unexpected look of triumph in her eyes. And of pride, too. My father was clever, she was saying. And I'm clever too. Like him.

At the door she gave him her hand, formally.

He shook it, thinking how infuriating it was that she should play the grand lady with him now, after all her bad manners and her hostility. But he held on to her hand a fraction longer than he'd intended. And through the touch of her flesh, he realised suddenly how tense she was. This was more than shyness, more than boredom. More than rudeness, too. He sensed something else: a hint of desperation. A panic, even. This was a woman on the edge. A beautiful woman on the edge, only just controlling herself by sustaining a front towards him of alternate indifference and aggression.

She let go, and her hands dropped back to her sides, into the pockets of her jeans. She sighed and said, 'Look, I'm sorry. I haven't been in a very good mood this morning, have I?'

Minto decided the time was past for politeness. 'You haven't actually, no.'

She smiled back at him, for the first time looking him full in the eyes. 'Well, you seem to have survived the ordeal, anyway.'

He laughed. Her complicity was exciting, intoxicating, enough to knock him off balance. The sun had come out again. 'When do you think you might be in a better mood?' asked Minto. 'I'd like to talk to you more, you know.'

She nodded. 'I think we must, don't you?' It was an odd way of putting it. As if the situation was driven by its own dynamic. As if there was no avoiding a sequence of events that lay inexorably before them.

'Will you have dinner with me tonight?' He half surprised himself when he said it.

'What, I have dinner with you?' And for a moment he thought, what am I doing? What have I said? This is another man's wife. This is trouble.

But she went on decisively: 'OK. You can pick me up here at eight o'clock.'

12

Frau Dr Englehart was an elderly, white-haired woman who lived half an hour outside Munich, in a house prettily sited overlooking Starnbergersee. She had an almost indecently healthy complexion, the sort that you sometimes find amongst Alpine people, redolent of open air and a lifetime of washing in cold water. Once inside, her rooms were all bare wood and plain functional furniture, an asceticism which Minto guessed was a mirror of her cast of mind. Her conversation was brisk, at times almost hectoring. She had a tendency to lecture, and a capacity to see issues in black and white; Minto suspected that she was one of those people for whom old age had clarified rather than blurred distinctions. Here on the edge of the lake with its crystal waters, bright summer light and icy winter winds, it was as if her vision had grown preternaturally sharp. Her vision, but not necessarily her compassion.

'You are art historian yourself, Herr Maitland?'

'Not by training, no. I'm a journalist. I'm researching an article for my newspaper.'

She nodded regretfully, as if to imply that time spent with anyone not qualified as an art historian was time wasted. 'This article, please: what does it concern?'

'It concerns a picture by Arnold Böcklin. The second version of *The Island of the Dead*. It's recently been acquired by the Royal Gallery in London.'

'*The Island of the Dead*? It is on view in London now?'

'It isn't, actually. Not any more. You see, the tragic thing is it's just been mutilated . . . in a sort of accident.'

'Mutilated?' Dr Englehart seized on the word, removing her spectacles and narrowing her eyes in disapproval. 'Mutilated? How did this outrage occur?'

'There was an attack, with a knife.'

She drew in her breath with a sharp little sound of dismay. 'By a madman, of course.' It wasn't a question but a statement.

Minto decided not to argue. 'I suppose so,' he said.

'And what do you wish to know about this picture?'

'Earlier this week I was able to inspect its stretcher, and I found it had an old Galerie Voermann label and stock number on it. I wonder if it would be possible for you to look it up in your records?'

'So. This is one of our babies, this Böcklin.' She paused, with a certain amount of satisfaction. 'Very well, show me the details.'

She put her spectacles back on and peered at the paper Minto handed her.

'*Ja.* This is one from the early nineteen twenties.'

'Do your records go back that far?'

She turned on him with some severity. 'The Galerie Voermann archive is complete right back to the founding in 1892. Hans Voermann, the great-uncle of my late husband, established the business in that year. He was always a most meticulous keeper of records. My husband Manfred was in control of the gallery from 1953 till his death in 1981. He too had a very tidy mind. Oh, yes, very tidy. It was a sadness to us both that our son Rolf had no interest to keep the business running. So when Manfred died I took over the archive and have kept it – how do you say? – serviceable here in this house out of respect to his memory.'

'It must be a lot of work.'

'I have always been used to hard work.'

'I'm sure you have.'

'Perhaps you would care to see for yourself the operation of the archive. Follow me, please.'

She led the way out into the hall, and then purposefully up a flight of stairs.

'Do you chase, Herr Maitland?' She demanded over her shoulder.

'I beg your pardon?'

'I said, do you chase?'

'I'm not sure that I . . .'

'But of course you must chase. The British are a nation of chasers.' She paused a little breathless on the ascent to indicate a large nineteenth-century wooded landscape which hung over the stairwell. 'In these woods in Austria my family used to chase.'

'To chase what?'

'To chase the – how do you say it? – the untamed pigs,' she replied firmly.

Minto felt obscurely inadequate. He was neither an art historian nor a chaser of untamed pigs. He peered into the undulating tree-covered hills in the landscape hanging before him and wondered at its peculiarly Germanic quality. It wasn't just the style of painting that was unfamiliar. It was the very landscape which struck him as the product of an alien imagination. Nature creates landscapes, but minds make them too. And for a moment he remembered the landscape conjured by the mind of Arnold Böcklin.

As he followed Frau Dr Englehart from room to room, Minto realised that the whole of the upper floor of her house was devoted to the archive. Even the single used bedroom was walled by neatly shelved files. She slept in the midst of this monument to her family's endeavour.

'Come,' she said, 'first we must consult the stock number index.' She bent forward frowning over the cards, then drew one triumphantly from its drawer. 'There we are: A. Böcklin, *The Island of the Dead*. Your number is correct.' Minto felt relieved, as if he had come up with the right answer in a school arithmetic test. 'And here it gives us the invoice number which relates to this picture.'

He followed her out to another room and a separate index, which in turn led her to an invoice file perched so high that Minto himself had to mount a pair of library steps to reach it down.

She smoothed out the copy of the bill for his inspection. 'You see, Herr Maitland, I was not in error. The date of this sale was May 1925.'

'And this was the buyer?' Minto ran his finger along a name and address written in such perfect German script that it was at first sight illegible. The handwriting was alien, a little like the landscape had been on the stairs.

'That is the buyer. Count Barodi, of Budapest.'

'A Hungarian?'

'*Ja*, a Hungarian.'

Minto paused, aware of distant echoes. 'Is that unusual?' he asked.

'Not so strange, no. There were still many good collections in Hungary in the early part of this century.'

'I hadn't realised.'

'But certainly. There was for instance the Hatvany collection which included important Impressionist works. The Baron Hatvany was an early owner of the famous picture by Manet, *A Bar at the Folies Bergère*. It hung in his collection in Hungary until the early 1920s when he had to sell it. I believe to pay a gambling debt.' She gave a little scornful laugh at such fecklessness.

'And do you know more about Count Barodi?'

'I must confess, I do not remember his name before from our records. Wait, I will check.'

She re-emerged from another file shaking her head. 'No, you see this was his only purchase from the Galerie Voermann.'

His only purchase. How had it come about? Had this lone Hungarian aristocrat, fleetingly passing through Munich one early summer's day in 1925, caught a glimpse of this picture on a chance visit to the gallery? Had it gripped his imagination so powerfully that he had felt compelled to own it? Or perhaps some other visitor to the gallery had seen it and said, the man who'll buy that picture is Barodi. Barodi in Budapest. He likes that sort of thing. What kind of a man was Count Barodi?

'So Barodi bought the picture in 1925,' mused Minto. 'I wonder how long it remained in his collection?'

Dr Englehart shrugged. 'I do not know. Of course the big Hungarian collections were gradually dispersed.'

'When?'

'Either in the years before the last war, or during it. Most of those which remained after that were confiscated or plundered by the Communists.'

Minto nodded. There was still a chasm to be accounted for

in the history of the picture. Count Barodi bought it in 1925; Alexander Courtney was in possession of it by the 1960s, when he sold it to Marriott. But the chances were that the picture had spent a fair amount of the intervening period in Hungary.

In Hungary. Where Thomas Donat had lived until 1956.

There. That was the connection. It hit him suddenly, with force. He stood at the upstairs window, trying to assimilate its implications, peering out at the shimmering lake where two distant windsurfers were scudding across the glistening face of the water. He had been wrong. The time and anguish he'd expended two days ago probing Thomas Donat's escape and ensuing life in Canada had been wasted. The evidence now pointed to a link with the picture having been established before that. In Hungary. In circumstances which Thomas Donat, with his sad eyes and gentle hands, had not yet been able to describe to him. He must get back to Donat. Start his questions again. Now he knew more precisely where they should be targeted.

'So,' continued Frau Dr Englehart, 'when did this Böcklin come to England? Do you know that, Herr Maitland?'

'I'm not sure, but I think it must have been at least thirty years ago, if not more.' He turned away from the window and added: 'It was sold by Courtney's in London. Did you perhaps know Alexander Courtney?'

He saw her stiffen. Saw something in her expression flinch. '*Ja*,' she murmured. 'Alexander Courtney.'

'You met him?'

'Just once. I did not trust him.' She said it flatly, without emphasis. But with conviction.

'He was very successful and charming by all accounts. Why didn't you trust him?'

'I do not know for sure.' She paused, then said in the same flat tone, 'But I think perhaps he was an evil man.'

'Evil? How do you mean?'

'Manfred had bad contacts with him. Bad experiences.'

'Why? What did he do to Manfred?'

She paused. Minto was aware of the regular spraying of a sprinkler watering somebody's lawn. In the distance a dog barked. 'I will tell you the story,' she said at last. 'Then you can make your own conclusions.'

He nodded, and waited for her to pull back a stray strand of white hair behind her ear. To compose herself.

'It happened not long before Manfred died. Perhaps it was the spring of 1980. Anyway, Alexander Courtney came to the gallery in Munich to see us. He introduced himself and told Manfred that he understood we knew of a good Monet, a landscape, which might be for sale. He had a client for it. He quoted the number in the catalogue raisonné, the complete list of the painter's works compiled by Wildenstein. Here it simply said that it was in an unnamed private collection. It was true that Manfred knew the owner. She was the wife of an old client of the Galerie Voermann who had recently died; she was a sweet lady, this widow. She lived in Lucerne, but Manfred told Courtney nothing of this. Manfred rang her up, confidentially, and she told him that on no account was this picture to be sold, she had no intention to dispose of it. So later that day Manfred informed Courtney that it was not for sale, there was no business to be done. As far as he was concerned, that was – how do you say it? – the finish of the affair.

'But three weeks later Manfred had a bad telephone call from the lady in Lucerne. She was in much anguish, Herr Maitland. A man had been bothering her, intimidating her; suggesting that things would go badly for her if she did not sell this picture. Her son, too, apparently had been threatened. She was frightened. Manfred was very upset. He advised her to go to the police. He called Courtney in London. When he remonstrated with Courtney, Courtney became abusive. He told Manfred he would put the matter in the hands of his lawyers if Manfred mentioned the subject again. Once more Manfred was very upset. He became ill. Yes, I think that this was the beginning point of his final illness.'

'Was there any proof that it was Courtney who had been intimidating the lady in Lucerne?'

'Nothing to prove it, I suppose. But Manfred was very unhappy about this. He was very much suspecting.'

'What happened to the picture?'

Frau Dr Englehart shrugged wearily. For a moment she seemed very old. 'This I do not know. A few months later Manfred was dead, you see. It was not possible to follow the matter up.' Then she brightened. The spirit returned to her. 'But I hope very much that this lady kept her picture and enjoyed it into a rich old age.'

'I hope so,' smiled Minto.

But he was curious. 'Could I see it?' he asked.

'What, this picture by Monet?'

'Yes. Do you have the photograph from the catalogue raisonné?'

She reached up for the volume from a nearby shelf. 'I have not forgotten it,' she declared. You could see her determination to prove how retentive her memory still remained. She leafed purposefully through pages and then pointed triumphantly at the harvest landscape of 1891. 'There. That was the one.'

'Private collection,' it said. Minto made a discreet note of the catalogue number.

Not long after he took his leave of Frau Dr Englehart. He walked through the sweet-smelling garden lapped by the lake itself. He turned to take a last look at the view across the water, with the windsurfers and the mountains beyond. There were worse ways of spending your old age than as the guardian of the archive of a family business in a setting like this.

'So, Herr Maitland, I hope my information has been of some help to you.'

'Definitely. Thank you so much. I'll send you a copy of the article when it comes out if you'd be interested.'

'I would like to see it. And you'll mention, perhaps, the name of the Galerie Voermann?'

'Of course.'

She smiled at him. Grateful. Momentarily like a child who has been promised a treat.

As he approached the gate beyond which his hired Opel awaited him, he was suddenly visited with such a clear vision of Isabella Maurbach that for a moment he had to pause and compose himself. His desire for her was almost like a physical pain.

* * *

Thomas Donat blinked in the sunlight shining through the curtains and pulled himself up painfully from his bed. He sat for a moment on the edge, disorientated, feeling the stiffness in his limbs and the heaviness in his heart. For a moment he pretended to himself that he was back in Vancouver, that he had never come to London. That none of this had happened. But there was no comfort in that delusion. Then he reached for his shoes, easing his socked feet into them. He looked at his watch. It was 6.15 in the evening. He recognised the unfamiliar noise that had woken him from his fitful dozing. Those were bells. Church bells ringing. Tolling across the neat back gardens and the prim red-brick villas of Putney. After all, it was Sunday. He had never been religious. He found it an infinitely melancholy sound.

'Did you ever do that, Tamás? All that church stuff?'

She had asked him that once. As they'd docked at Szentendre on their way home on that blistering summer day on the Danube Bend. As they'd looked up at the church towers of the town, almost absurdly picturesque in the mellow sunlight.

'What do you mean?'

'Did you go and make your prayers to God? Did you have to listen to the priests?' She giggled at the idea and squeezed his hand.

'Yes. But it was a long time ago. When I was a child. I don't think I ever took it seriously. Did you?'

'I was taken to the church once or twice. With my grandparents.'

'Did it mean something to you?'

She shook her head. 'Those things were not real, were they? They were fairy stories. I want real things. I want it all to depend on myself, not something mysterious above me, controlling me.'

'I think you're right. In the end we've only got ourselves. We are masters of our own fate. We've got to take control, make our own opportunities in life. And profit from them.'

She giggled again. 'We profited from them today, didn't we?'

The trippers were piling back on to the steamer. Laughing. Pushing. Filling up the space on deck and constricting their movement. She withdrew her hand from his, as if they were now in public again.

It was true, what he'd told her. In the end we've only got ourselves to rely on. He'd always believed it. Only once had his resolve failed him. Only once had he been defeated, all those years ago in Hungary. It was too much to ask of him that he fight that battle again. Now, as an old man. He could not face it. But then again he wasn't sure that he could suppress the revived memory of that defeat for ever.

The room was oppressive. He went to the window and pulled the curtains to one side, staring out into the lush greenery of the suburban garden. He ran his eyes over the acanthus bushes and the lilac tree, but he didn't see them. He didn't see them because he was concentrating too hard. Concentrating too hard on keeping the lids on the final shafts of memory. The ones he had determined never to reopen. Not for the police doctor. Not for the magistrates' court. Not for his loving niece Leila. Not even for his friend Mr Dominic Maitland.

But now he had to think hard. To be strong. Because an insidious voice was urging him in another direction, telling him that there was an alternative strategy. Another way of coming to terms. Maybe if he could not suppress the memory, he must purge it. Perhaps the lids needed to come off one more time. Perhaps he needed to stare down those shafts just once more. Unflinchingly. In order to confront the horrors face to face. But he hadn't the courage. Not to go through all that again. Not to feel the lacerating panic he'd succumbed to in the Royal Gallery. Not to have to cope with the sick despair which had enveloped him when Mr Maitland had asked him the question when they'd last been together. The question about when he'd seen the picture before.

And if he hadn't the courage, then what was left? What would his life be if he no longer had control over it?

Outside the evening sun was lengthening the shadows. The same evening sun that had lengthened the shadows at Szentendre, nearly forty years ago. He pulled on his jacket, straightened his collar and walked slowly down the stairs.

At the sound of his footstep, Leila came out of the

drawing-room door. As she always did, as if she was waiting for him. Like a nurse. Like a gaoler.

'Do you want something to eat, Uncle Thomas? Or a drink, perhaps?'

He shook his head. 'I thought I would go out. To get some air.'

'Come and sit in the garden. It's lovely out there at this time of day.'

'No.' He was quite definite. 'I must go out. To walk. To think a little.'

She looked at him dubiously. 'What, into the street? But I really don't think you're strong enough. I don't think it's wise.'

'Not far. I will not go far. But I need to go, to clear my head. I will be all right.' He was almost pleading now.

'I don't know about this . . . I could come with you, perhaps? We could walk together. Up to the Common and back?'

He shook his head wordlessly. He didn't want to hurt her. But he had to go alone.

Then Howard's voice interrupted them from the drawing-room. Impatient. Irritated. 'Oh for God's sake let him go, if he wants to go. It might do him good.'

'Very well,' she said. Standing aside, to allow him access to the front door. To the outside world. 'But don't be too long, please. And be careful. I am worried about you.'

Making an enormous effort, he smiled back at her. To reassure her. Then he pushed out of the door, head bent, exhausted by the exertion of the smile.

Why had she come?

Minto contemplated her surreptitiously as she studied the menu in the dimly lit whiteness of the fashionable Munich restaurant. He'd taken trouble to find somewhere good, done some research. But when he'd told her where they were going she'd shrugged and said he didn't have to: she'd have been perfectly happy in the local *Bierkeller*. It wasn't as if she had taken great pains to dress up. She wore jeans and a dark polo-neck jersey. She looked as though their rendezvous at eight o'clock had taken her by surprise, as though she had just broken off from whatever she'd been doing and flung on a jacket to meet him when he called for her in the taxi. As though she was saying to him, look, this is no big deal. Don't get ideas.

But once she had eased herself into the back seat of the cream Mercedes, once she had settled herself there next to him and the taxi-driver had accelerated away from the house, from that moment he was conscious of an unspoken ambiguity about her presence with him, an ambiguity that was the more disturbing for her resolute determination not to acknowledge it. Why had she come? Perhaps she was bored with the opulent loneliness of her life in this smart suburb of this rich city, perhaps she was exasperated by her husband's frequent absences on tour. Perhaps she had imagined that alternative male company for an evening might temporarily relieve the tedium of existence. But if that was so, then why had she chosen as her companion her father's persecutor, the journalist she saw as a hatchet man? Why, for that matter, if she was so sensitive about her father's reputation, had she originally pointed Minto in the direction of Theo Denton and his damaging revelations?

And why was Minto here himself? He could no longer preserve the illusion that he was merely the sharp-eyed observer of humankind's weaknesses and foibles, sitting down to dinner with one more specimen for his dissection. That here he was, the dispassionate professional conducting an interview, merely trawling for information. His excitement gave him away. No, this was Minto spending an evening with an attractive, wilful woman. A woman who was in the process of breaking loose from her moorings: not just from her husband, but from other, deeper, more complicated entanglements, too.

She ordered gravadlax and when they brought it to her she chased morsels of it round her plate with a fork then abandoned it largely uneaten. Finally she looked across at him and said: 'Tell me something. Something that's always interested me about journalists.'

'What's that?'

'Why are you all so obsessed with each other?'

'I'm not aware that we are.'

'That's how it comes across, you know, when you read a British newspaper. It seems to me that there's a sort of professional deformation afflicting journalists. You're all so smugly self-regarding.' Her eyes were gleaming now. Once again he felt oddly exhilarated by the rising wave of her anger. 'Admit it,' she went on, 'you write much more for each other than for the public, don't you? You're only really interested in what other journalists will think of your articles. Very often you're writing about other journalists anyway. Talk about incestuous. And of course because you are the media, you have a unique opportunity to air and disseminate your own self-satisfaction.'

'Come on,' he said. 'All professions are internally competitive and self-regarding in that way. I bet your husband's constantly measuring himself against other musicians. Speculating about what they think of his performance.'

'What do you know about my husband?' There was a sudden edge to her anger.

'Only what you've told me.'

'I've told you nothing.'

'You've told me that he likes Bach. And he's away a lot.'

'And you think that makes you an expert on him?'

'Not at all. I was only . . .'

'I'll tell you one thing about Gerhard: he's a hell of a lot better pianist than you'll ever be a writer.' She spat the words out. Venomously. Not so much with any regard for the truth. Not so much to protect her husband, but to hurt Minto.

'You're probably right.' Minto kept his head. 'But you can't be absolutely sure about that until you've actually read something I've written.'

Without warning she smiled at him. 'Like this profile on my father?' The wave of her anger had broken.

'I've got to write it first.'

'I'm not being much help to you, am I?'

'I've known easier interviewees,' he laughed.

'Is that what you want me to be? Easy?'

He shook his head. He didn't want her to be easy. She was much more exciting as she was. Angry. Wild. Unpredictable.

A little later he asked her about her mother. For a moment he wondered if she would close up again at the question, push him away, but instead she became articulate, as if expressing herself was a release. A way of controlling the situation. A therapy for her tension.

'She was very English. Very cool. Very self-sufficient. She'd been brought up in a traditional way, I think. All her family were the same. They found it difficult to let themselves go.'

'And were you close to her?'

'Less so than to my father.'

'Was it a good marriage?'

'It wasn't unhappy. Well, not like the marriages of the parents of other girls at school. I think seventy per cent of my year came from broken homes. But looking back I don't think my parents communicated very much. On the other hand, perhaps that's what kept them together. The fact that she didn't make many demands on my father.'

'And that suited him?'

'I think so.' She paused, frowning. Trying to get it right. As if taking pleasure in speaking of her own parents analytically, dispassionately. Asserting herself over them. 'But don't misunderstand me: my father was proud of her. He spoke of her as his adornment.'

'But not his passion?'

She looked at him. Appraisingly. 'I know how your mind works. You're trying to put words into my mouth. You want me to say he looked on her as a trophy of some sort. A thing. Not a person.'

He laughed. 'You're too clever for me.'

She laughed as well. 'Am I, Minto? Am I too clever for you? I wonder.' He felt elated. It was the first time she had called him by his nickname.

'I suppose my mother was a classic sufferer from the English disease,' she went on later.

'What is that?'

'A surfeit of repressions. It's not confined to English women, of course. English men are just as bad.'

'What are these repressions you keep talking about?'

'Oh, I don't know: constant embarrassments. Why are the English so embarrassed by everything?'

'Like what?'

'Like sex. Like their emotions. Like art.'

'That's quite a list.'

'Let me tell you something. What my father said to me when he heard I was getting married to Gerhard. He told me he was delighted I was getting married to a German, that I'd made a wise choice. English men didn't make good husbands, he said. In his experience English men could be divided into two categories: the frigid and the coarse.'

'And which am I?'

She paused. She took a piece of bread and began to tear it into strips on the white tablecloth. Finally she said quietly, 'I hoped you might not be either.'

He reached out and touched her hand. She let him hold it for a moment, then withdrew it abruptly.

He said, 'And why do you say the English are embarrassed by art?'

'Because they're so unnatural about it. So frightened, in a way. It's much more respectable to be interested in golf or cricket or shooting. In England if you say you're interested in art then there's something a little bit suspect about you.'

He thought back for a moment to St James's Piccadilly. To the church packed to the aisles with the rich and well-connected. To the West End art world honouring one of its own. 'Your father knew plenty of English people who didn't think art was a little bit suspect,' he said.

She shrugged. He noticed the lobes of her ears. Little physical details of her were impinging almost subconsciously on his brain. 'Art was OK to my father's cronies so long as it remained a means to an end.'

'A means to what end?'

'Making money, of course.' She said it heavily, without amusement. As if Minto had compelled her to confront an error of taste, a sick joke.

'And you'd include Marriott in that category?'

'What, Leslie Marriott?' There was no flicker of emotion at the mention of the name. 'Probably. I never knew him myself.'

'He did a lot of business with your father.'

'Maybe. I never knew him.'

'Do you ever remember a picture which your father once sold to Marriott, a picture called *The Island of the Dead*?'

'No, I don't.' Again no glimmer. No distant calling of the birds above the rocks. No sightless eyes mocking across the years. 'It must have been before my time.'

'Theo Denton told me some interesting things about your father's business relationship with Marriott, you know.'

'Denton did?' She sat up straighter now. Stopped tearing her bread into little strips beside her plate. 'So tell me. What did Denton say?'

'Do you really want to hear this?'

'Look, I'm not a child.' For a moment she had never looked more like one. Eager. Animated. Like a child about to be told a secret which had fascinated it all its life. 'Tell me.'

'Denton was implying that your father's art-dealing business was a vehicle for Marriott's money-laundering.'

He waited, curious and apprehensive about how she would react. All she said was: 'And you think he's right?'

'I do now. After what your brother did.'

'What did my brother do?'

'He leant on Denton. One moment Denton was telling me about Marriott's picture buying, and claiming he had photocopies to prove Courtney's had been supplying Marriott with false invoices; and the next day he was refusing to speak to me. Denying we'd ever talked. No, he'd been got at. Threatened. And I think it was Max who got at him.'

'Max,' she said thoughtfully. Distantly, as if Minto were no longer there. 'Or more likely Winter. It's always Winter who knows how to handle these things.'

'So you think they were behind it?'

'Quite possibly. But if they were worried about my father's

business dealings with a man like Marriott, they're fools.' She
said it very clearly. In her voice like crystal. With absolute
conviction.

'Why do you say they're fools?'

'Because they've got it wrong.' Again her tone carried
certainty. 'No, that's not the story. They don't need to
bother with it. My father was too clever to get embroiled
in something like that. Not something so obvious. No. It's
something else.'

'What is?'

She paused. 'What I thought you were going to find out
for me.'

He watched her hands. They were still but tense, gripping
the table in front of her. She had long, sinuous fingers
and short unvarnished nails that maybe she still bit now
and then.

'Wait a minute. Let me get it straight, what you're telling
me. You sent me to Denton in the hope that he'd reveal to
me some secret about your father. Something you thought
Denton knew about him and you didn't?'

She laughed a little bitterly. 'Maybe.'

'But what makes you think that there is a secret about
your father you need to find out?'

'Christ almighty.' She was suddenly close to tears. Fighting unseen battles with demons Minto could only guess
at. 'Because he started to tell me. Once, six years ago.
Soon after my mother died. And I wouldn't let him. I
didn't want to know, then. I didn't want the responsibility. I didn't want the imposition. I didn't want the burden.'

'And that was when you left for France.'

She nodded. Ran away, he thought. Out of range.

'Well, I don't know,' he said. 'Considering your views on
journalists, you're pretty unscrupulous in the use you're
prepared to make of them.'

'What do you mean?' Her nostrils flared out when she
was angry.

'I'm saying it's ironic. That in fact you needed me as a
journalist.'

She shook her head and said softly, 'No. I needed you as a friend.'

Minto had come to terms with her anger. He found her tenderness more difficult. He felt adrift, lost. Somehow outflanked by her, in her power.

He saw it then, too. How her father's death had forced her to confront his memory. To confront the self-perceived inadequacies in her relationship with him. To remember the demands he had made on her, and the times she had failed him. He saw how he himself had come into her life as simultaneously a threat to her father and a means to helping her come to terms with his memory, a potential balm to her feelings about him. To her feelings about the father she had once been so close to. The same father she had in some mysterious way come to mistrust as well.

The father she had had to get away from.

Minto knew with a shock of recognition what she was going through. He knew it because he had been through the same experience himself only a few days ago. Been through it when Thomas Donat in his gentleness and his anguish had forced Minto to confront his memories of his own father. Suddenly there was a profound sympathy between him and the woman in front of him. He wanted to communicate it to her. He wanted to reassure her.

'Do you mind if I tell you something?' he said.

'What?' She spoke warily. She was looking at him differently now. As if he were dangerous.

He paused, on the brink. Uncertain whether he was going to say something conciliatory about her father. Or something else. The words that came out in the end were: 'I want to tell you that I find you very beautiful.'

She stared back at him with that look he'd seen before. The one that made him think she was going to hit him. 'You bastard,' she said.

'What's the matter?'

'You know.'

'I don't know. What is it, for God's sake?'

'You bloody well do know. You know perfectly well how all this is going to end, don't you?'

They went back to the tall modern neon-lit hotel where he was staying and there, in the characterless setting of his bedroom, a room indistinguishable from two hundred others under the same roof, all decorated in the same beige pastel colours and each hung with the obligatory single Impressionist reproduction, they sat for a moment, she in her roll-neck jersey and jeans and he in his shirt-sleeves.

'Drink?' he said, reaching across to unlock the minibar.

'No.' She said it firmly. With such decision that he thought she might be about to repent her decision to come up with him, to make her excuses and leave. But when she got up it was only to come to sit next to him on the bed.

He realised his heart was beating very fast. He kissed her. She pushed him away. Then he kissed her again, and her lips responded.

When they made love she alternately clung to him and ground against him angrily. Using his body, as if this act of love were the consummation and ultimate expression of all the resentment he had built up within her.

After it was over, as they lay back sweating on the sheets, he found himself suddenly achingly curious, on the point of framing the question 'Have you done this before?' But he stopped himself in time. Instead he said simply: 'How did that happen?'

She wasn't looking at him. She lay staring away from him, chewing her thumb. 'Maybe because I'm bored,' she murmured, addressing the wall.

'Yes?'

When she said nothing more, he reached out a hand to take hers, but she jerked it away from him. 'There's another reason, besides all that,' he persisted.

Then she did take his hand and kissed it, murmuring pleadingly: 'Don't say it. Don't say anything. Not yet.'

As he lay there next to her and they drifted off to sleep, he was happy. He told himself that ultimately she was different from her father. That in the end, although she might fight it, she preferred people to things.

13

She left in the early hours, just as the sun was rising. Sleepily he tried to persuade her to stay, but he had already learned that it was pointless to argue with Isabella when she had made up her mind. 'Ring me later,' she breathed, almost as some sort of concession wrung from her in exchange for a swift and silent exit. He got up and peered out of the double-glazed window that wouldn't open in an effort to catch a glimpse of her. He couldn't see her, but he dimly caught the sound of one of the taxis drawn up in a line in front of the hotel starting its engine, and he knew she was on her way. He gazed out across the somnolent city for a moment, watching the cold yellow light of morning bathing the roof-tops. In the distance he heard a church bell strike six o'clock, suddenly very clear. Munich, at sunrise. He felt a wave of pure elation sweep over him; and then a curious undertow of vulnerability. He recognised that what was happening to him was very dangerous. And suddenly beyond his control.

He went back to sleep and when he awoke again at 9.30 a.m. the tempo of the day was different. The first thing he did was call his number in London to check his answerphone. 'Mr Maitland? I'm sorry. I don't know where you are, but could you call me urgently as soon as you get this message. I . . . I have some bad news and I really need to speak to you. It's Leila Parsons.' She hadn't needed to add her name. He'd recognised her voice immediately. It was her tone that was unfamiliar. Panicky. Desperate.

He was awake now. With a sick feeling of apprehension he sat on the edge of the bed and dialled the Parsonses' number.

'Oh. Mr Maitland. It's so good of you to ring back. I seem to be imposing on you constantly, but something rather awful's happened. I . . . I thought you would want to know.'

'My God! Is it Thomas?'

'Yes . . . yes, it is.'

'What's happened?' Minto had a sudden, sharp presentiment of evil. Of events over which he might once have been able to exert some influence now spiralling away into chaos. Beyond his control.

Leila Parsons answered softly. 'I'm afraid he had an accident yesterday evening. He went out for a walk by himself and he was knocked down by a car. They took him to hospital, he's in intensive care. He's not conscious yet.'

'Will he . . . will he be all right?' Minto's mouth was dry. He'd drunk a lot of wine last night. Here, with Isabella. While back in London Thomas Donat had been mown down in a traffic accident.

'They say it's a bit early to tell. He's critical, whatever that means.' She gave a little mirthless laugh.

'I am so sorry,' murmured Minto.

Hospital. Intensive care. His own father, with the crabbed hands and the desperate eyes. Now Donat. Donat, gazing at him with the same bemused and anguished expression.

'I should never have let him go out alone. It was unforgivable of me.' Leila Parsons's words came out quickly, in a rush of mortified guilt. 'He said he was fine, that he wanted a little fresh air, that he preferred to be alone. So I let him go. Of course I never should have, he was weak and still a little woozy. He must have stepped off the pavement without looking properly.'

'Is there anything I can do, do you think?'

'Oh, dear.' There was a profound sadness in her voice. 'There's so little one feels it's possible to do for him. He'd reached a point almost beyond help, it seemed to me. But one thing I do know is that he set great store by your visits. I hate to impose on you again. You really must say if it's difficult or inconvenient. But I'm sure he'd like to see you if . . . I mean when he comes round again. Could you bear to go and see him in the hospital? I know it would mean a lot to him.'

'Of course I will. Do they have any idea when he'll be able to have visitors?'

'Another forty-eight hours or so, they said. All being well.'

'I'm due back in London today,' he told her. That had been his plan, anyway. Until last night. What had last night changed? He still wasn't sure. He couldn't get his mind round that problem as well. He ran his tongue round his lips and fancied he could still taste her mouth on them. 'I'll ring you this evening,' he added. 'For the latest bulletin.'

'Thank you,' she said. 'I feel better talking to you about it. You see—' She stopped, apparently unable to finish the sentence she had begun. The silence was painful, even over the telephone.

Minto offered what comfort he could. 'Listen, you mustn't blame yourself about Thomas. Accidents happen. It wasn't your fault.'

'Oh, God,' she was talking faster again. 'I didn't think things could get any worse, not after what we've already been through. But last night was awful. Somehow it wouldn't have been quite so bad if there had been any witnesses to what happened.'

'Surely the driver must have given some account.'

'That's just it: the car that hit him never stopped.'

'What? It was a hit-and-run?'

'It didn't stop. It just drove on. He was found lying in the road two streets away from us by a passing pedestrian. The pedestrian – a nice man who'd been walking his dog – said he'd heard the noise of a collision half a minute earlier and then he'd heard a car accelerating away, but he wasn't able to give any description. The police said this sort of thing's happening more and more. Often it's just teenagers joy-riding. It's enough to make you cry.'

'Listen,' said Minto, 'it was an accident. OK? Accidents like this are happening every day. You're not to blame.'

As he put the telephone down, he wondered whom he'd been trying to reassure. Whom he'd been trying to exculpate. Leila Parsons? Or himself?

Because when he thought it all through, he needed reassurance. Whichever way he looked at it.

As he showered, he tried to face up to the implications of what he had just heard. He tried to imagine what had been going through the mind of that poor old man as he set out on his solitary walk through leafy Putney last night. Leila Parsons might blame herself for having allowed him out alone. But might not Minto also be held to blame, because of the persistence of his questioning at their last meeting? He could still see Donat, vividly, with agonised hands clutched to his ears. When? Minto had demanded. When had you seen *The Island of the Dead* before? Perhaps it had all been too much. Perhaps this impatience had precipitated something unbearable in the old man. Perhaps he had set out alone last night because he could go on no longer, because as a result of what Minto had forced him to confront he had determined to end it all under the wheels of the first passing car that he encountered.

That was bad enough, thought Minto as he dried himself and pulled on a shirt. What was worse was the alternative scenario. The other interpretation of the evidence. The one he'd been trying to repress as paranoid. The one that seemed increasingly and horrifically plausible.

What if it hadn't been an accident at all?

Supposing it had been planned. Supposing a car had been waiting for just this opportunity. Supposing Thomas Donat's evidence in regard to some incident long buried in the past had become too dangerous to some third party for Donat to be allowed to live to divulge it. And what if that evidence concerned a picture by Arnold Böcklin called *The Island of the Dead*? Paranoid, paranoid, Minto kept telling himself. And yet why hadn't the car stopped? And, hell, yes: why had Denton been silenced too? OK, he hadn't been run over. But who knew with what sort of violence he might have been threatened in order to prevent him talking further to Dominic Maitland?

Because violence ran through the Courtney family. The threat of it lurked about their dealings. Real, but as yet unprovable. He'd just heard how maybe Alexander had intimidated the owner of a beautiful Monet. The same Alexander who boasted of once having killed a man.

And this was the family of the woman to whom he'd just made love.

Isabella Maurbach. Née Courtney.

He knew he must get back to London. He lifted the telephone to confirm his lunchtime flight back. But he suddenly realised how much he wanted to see her again. Or at least to hear her voice. So he dialled her number, before anything.

'Mrs Maurbach, she no here,' the Filipino maid told him. 'She just left by car. She not back till later in week.'

'Gone? Where to?'

'She no say, sir. You want I give her message when she return?'

'No,' said Minto slowly. 'No, no message. Just say I rang.'

As he took a taxi to the airport, he tried to recreate her image in his mind's eye. To recall how she lay in his arms, the warmth of her body, the abandon of her limbs entwined with his own. To reconcile her contradictions: her elegance, and her boredom; her intelligence, and her rudeness; her coolness, and her desperation; the apparent hostility of her manner and the reality of her nakedness next to him. Her nakedness, grinding against him on the sheets of the hotel bed. He still had no clear answer to the question he had asked her after their love-making. How had it happened? Why had it happened? What did she want from him? Don't say it, she had told him. Not yet.

He took stock of the Courtney investigation so far. All he knew was that there were secrets in the life of Alexander which his son and the enigmatic Winter were eager to suppress; perhaps so eager that they would not stop short of having a man run down in cold blood. There were secrets in the life of Alexander to which his daughter had refused to listen when her father had begun to confide them. And now he was dead she wanted to know those secrets. Maybe Minto could help her find them out. No, she had said, they're not to do with Marriott. My father would have been too intelligent to get embroiled in something as obvious as that. No, Marriott's a mere diversion. It's something else.

She had been emphatic. And there had been something

compelling about her conviction. Perhaps she was right. Perhaps the real story lay embedded further into the past. He thought of *The Island of the Dead*. He remembered Count Barodi and Hungary. He thought of Thomas Donat all those years ago in Budapest. Perhaps there was something further back in the life of Alexander Courtney that linked in with all these elements, that would provide the key to his secret. If Marriott was not that key, Minto must delve deeper, to an earlier phase in Courtney's career.

But he felt vulnerable, and a little afraid. These were dangerous people. Suddenly all he could remember was her ranting in the restaurant last night: 'You bastard,' she had raged at him. 'You know perfectly well how all this is going to end.'

'You been away, old boy?' Ridley sat at his desk and blinked blearily up at Minto through cigarette smoke. He'd taken off his jacket to reveal braces and a pair of frayed cuffs. There was a sort of soiled style to him, though. As if he was dimly aware that the shirt he was wearing had once been expensive, and the trousers had come from a Savile Row tailor. A Savile Row tailor whose bill had never been paid.

'I've had a couple of days in Munich. Researching Courtney.'

'Been with the Krauts, eh? What did they tell you about Courtney, or shouldn't I ask?'

'A little bit here and there. I really went to meet Courtney's daughter. She lives in Munich.'

'Why does she live there, then?'

'She's married to a German.'

Ridley sniffed. Tolerance of foreigners was not his strong suit. 'Poor wretched woman. Attractive, is she?'

Minto hardly blinked as he said, 'Not my type.'

Ridley nodded morosely and stubbed out his cigarette. 'So what can I do for you?'

'You don't by any chance remember the Tissot show Courtney put on about ten years back?'

'I bloody well do. I reviewed it for *Art Monthly*.'

'Was there a catalogue?'

'Dirty great thick job. Packed with a load of balls-achingly dull articles. You know the drill, academics and other prats reappraising the genius of a rediscovered master.'

'There wasn't one by Courtney himself, was there?'

'I believe there was a short piece, now you come to mention it.'

'Can you remember what it said?'

'Not a word.' Ridley beamed up happily.

'You haven't still got the catalogue?'

'Right behind my head. Pull it down, old boy, I haven't got the energy. Second or third shelf. Little vanity of mine, I always keep the ones of exhibitions I've reviewed.'

As Minto took it away, he looked back and saw Ridley reach into his drawer for a bottle which he quickly tipped into a plastic cup before replacing it. The guy was plastered. But not so plastered that he didn't still take precautions to hide the evidence.

Minto shook his head and began to read the page which interested him.

Tissot and the Commune

Tissot is a mysterious artist. Books have been devoted to him, but no one's yet got to the bottom of him. The more I read of his life and work, the more he fascinates me.

He's almost unique in that he was one of the very few artistic bridges between Paris and London in the second half of the nineteenth century. In Paris in the 1860s he moved in very interesting circles: he was a close friend of Degas and Manet, and at the same time highly regarded amongst the Salon painters. A glittering career lay ahead of him. But after the Franco-Prussian war and the Commune of 1870–71, everything changed. He came to London, as an exile. And in London he built up a second, even more successful career as a painter of contemporary fashionable life. He was much admired, cutting a dashing figure in the drawing-rooms of London, while at the same time being treated with that element of suspicion that the English reserve for the very successful foreigner who inserts himself too easily into their society. Later in the decade there was a scandal with a beautiful divorcée, Mrs Newton, and when she died of tuberculosis Tissot went back to France. It all reads a bit like a Victorian melodrama.

The part of his life that has always intrigued me most is his experience in the Commune. This is the episode most shrouded in mystery, and yet surely one of the most crucial periods in that it appears to have decided him to come to London and start a new life away from France. I have studied this period in detail and have reached the conclusion that Tissot's behaviour and motives have been very much misrepresented.

There is no doubt that Tissot acquitted himself bravely in the defence of Paris when it was besieged by the Prussians in 1870. Thomas Gibson Bowles, in Paris as correspondent of the *Morning Post*, recounts how Tissot was in the front line of the fighting at Malmaison-La-Jonchère in November when seventeen of his company of sixty were killed or wounded. Manet writes to Eva Gonzales: '*Tissot s'est couvert de la gloire a l'affaire de la Jonchère.*'

After the siege and the capitulation of the city on 28 January 1871, the German army staged a triumphal entry into Paris then withdrew after the French government agreed to the conditions of peace. But the French government was then overthrown by the Commune in Paris, and the city was thrown into a nightmare of lawless insurrection. Certain accounts suggest that Tissot himself was an insurrectionist, a member of the Commune. There is no evidence to substantiate this.

The most reliable account is surely that of Bastard, Tissot's early biographer. According to him Tissot returned to his house in the Avenue de l'Impératrice at the beginning of the Commune in order to check on his collection of paintings. Although his property was in danger because of the fighting, he selflessly continued to work as a stretcher-bearer. At one point, having made his way to the Comité Centrale des Fédérés to ask for medical help and supplies, he found himself spontaneously opposing the minting of some museum silver which he heard being debated by the Communards. Appalled by the fighting, and endangered by his unpremeditated opposition to the Communards, he fled Paris for London, taking with him just a few treasured possessions.

Other conflicting accounts, some deriving from the memoirs of the painter Jacques Emile Blanche who was only repeating the garbled reminiscences of his aged father, just simply do not have the ring of truth. Is it likely that Tissot, who had fought bravely the year before, would dress up in the uniform of an officer of the Commune just to save his own possessions? I for one could not imagine it. Tissot was not a coward. Nor did he flee to London 'because he was hopelessly compromised by his connection with

Communard Headquarters', as some would have it. He did not arrive in England as a political refugee, because he had never been one of the insurgents and had nothing in common with them. He uprooted himself because he had simply had enough of Paris and wanted to see what London had to offer. Once there, he enjoyed a decade of deserved success.

The likelihood is that Tissot was the victim of a case of mistaken identity, frequent enough when a city is enduring the chaos of armed insurrection. In 1874 Tissot is recorded as having been cleared of any misdemeanours in the Commune by reference to the préfet de police in Paris. His name had been confused with that of '*un nommé Tissot [Antoine]*'.

Minto laid the catalogue aside thoughtfully. What had she said? Maybe my father identified with Tissot. Maybe they were both personable foreigners who had suffered the effects of English insularity. Suffered them, and to a certain extent triumphed over them. But still, it was an odd piece for Alexander Courtney to have written. There was an unexpected fervency about it. A passion. Minto leafed through the other introductory essays. There were seven or eight of them, on different aspects of Tissot's art and life. His history paintings; his paintings of modern life; his relationship with Degas; his relationship with the glamorous divorcée, Kathleen Newton. Perhaps Courtney had simply wanted to see his own name in print in company with more august scholars on a subject dear to his heart. A bit like a Sunday golfer who gets the chance to play a round with a group of top professionals. Even the richest and most successful have their vanities, after all.

But he didn't think that that was quite the explanation. Not with Alexander Courtney. Marriott had said it too, according to Theo Denton: you can learn a lot about Alexander Courtney by studying Tissot. It was an article to which Minto was going to have to return. He went to the machine and made a copy of the two relevant pages from the catalogue.

Then, as an afterthought, when he took the catalogue back to Ridley, he asked: 'You know the Marriott picture collection? It was sold at auction, wasn't it?'

Ridley blinked bibulous eyes at him. 'That's right. By order of the court, or something. Last year.'

'Have you got the catalogue there?'

Once more Ridley indicated the shelves behind him. 'Top left, I believe,' he said, staring glassily ahead.

Minto leafed through the pages with mounting interest. Then he saw it: a full-page coloured illustration with the description facing it. Claude Monet (1840–1926). *Harvest Landscape*, signed and dated 1891. It was the picture that Frau Dr Englehart had shown him. The Wildenstein catalogue raisonné number confirmed it.

He looked down to where the provenance was listed, the history of the picture. 'Purchased from Courtney's, 1980,' it said. Innocent enough information.

Unless you knew the circumstances of its acquisition by the sellers.

14

In the bleak hinterland off the Finchley Road rise a variety
of apartment blocks, from red-brick Edwardian to thirties art
deco, interspersed with the occasional ill-judged foray into
the contemporary style, all glass and slabs of discoloured
concrete. With his street map open on the seat beside him,
Minto drove amongst them, wondering at the lives they
concealed, the self-enclosed suburban dramas for which they
acted as a backdrop. It was another hot, airless day, and as he
accelerated down tree-lined streets where the leaves seemed
already to be wilting in the sun, past patches of grass long
since yellowed by the heat, Minto glanced up periodically
into the rear-view mirror. Part of him despised himself for
doing it, told himself that these were spectres of his own
imagining. But he had to check. He had to know if he was
being followed.

He was reasonably confident that no one was on his tail
by the time he caught a glimpse of the name above the
doorway to the block that he was seeking. Strandwick
Mansions. The name he'd noted written in the book on
Tissot which Isabella had shown him in Munich. The block
was one of the red-brick Edwardians, and the letters were
inscribed in that elongated art-nouveau style which must have
struck its original constructors as daringly modish. Now the
building had a dingy, uncared-for quality, like a middle-aged
divorcée who has let herself go. Minto paused for a moment
on the doorstep, reading the meaningless list of names by the
bells. He paused at number eleven, occupied apparently by
a Mr Michael Blair. An innocent, anonymous sort of name.
Doubtless that flat had changed hands many times since the
1950s. Finally he rang 'Caretaker' and a moment later he was
buzzed in and stood blinking in the murky hallway.

'I wonder if you can help me,' said Minto politely to the stocky male figure who emerged from the shadows. 'I'm doing a little research.'

'From the council?'

'No, I'm a . . . I'm a journalist.'

'What, from the newspapers then, are you?' The man had a little bristling moustache, and was not lightly going to allow his territory to be invaded. He was wearing shirt-sleeves and braces, brandishing a magazine in his hand. The door marked 'Caretaker' out of which he had just emerged now stood ajar, and Minto glimpsed beyond the evidence of a bachelorhood of unexpected neatness: a table with a chair drawn up to it and a single half-drunk cup of tea, in a saucer. His thin grey hair was cut to a military brevity. He'd probably been in the army in his youth; not very successfully, fancied Minto, but he could imagine that it had been the one significantly formative experience of this man's life. He stood there, in the slightly seedy surroundings of the communal hallway where the dying potted plant and the peeling paint spoke of defeated bourgeois ambition, of faded pretension to grandeur. He stood there, challenging and aggressive. But intrigued too, Minto could tell. Newspapers. They exerted a fascination. That being so, Minto knew how to up the ante with a character like this. How to ensure his interest, and his ultimate co-operation.

'I'll be frank with you,' declared Minto, man-to-man, half confiding. 'I'm working for television, actually.'

'Television, eh?' He drew himself up to his full height and stuck his chin out, as if Minto had just told him he was himself about to be beamed live into the living-rooms of the nation.

'That's right. I'm researching a programme at the moment, due for scheduling next spring.'

'Researching, are you? What sort of programme would that be, then?'

'I'll tell you, because I think you could be the man to help me, Mr . . . er . . .'

'Mr Jenkins.'

'Right, then, Mr Jenkins.' Minto paused, improvising wildly. 'We're doing a programme on people who've lived in the same house for forty years or more. We want to interview them, see what changes they've been through during that time. It's in our series *Living History*.'

'What, one of them documentaries, is it?' There was a hint of disappointment in his tone, implying that he would have been happier if Minto had been seeking locations for soap opera.

'Exactly. A documentary.'

'So what do you want to know, then?'

'I'll tell you what I'm looking for: I'd like to know if there's anyone in any of these flats who's been a resident here for forty years or so. Anyone whose memory goes back that far. If there is, I'd appreciate having a preliminary word with them now.'

Jenkins sucked his teeth meditatively. 'Forty years, you say?'

'That sort of length of time.'

'Well, I've only been employed here since seventy-nine myself. But it strikes me your best bet would be Miss Fulbrick. She's been here longer than anyone else, though I don't know if she's clocked up the forty years yet. You could speak to her.' He paused, then added a trifle enviously: 'What, she'd be appearing on the telly, would she? On the box, like?'

'Oh, it's early days yet. We're only at the research stage. But it would be a great help to have a quick word with her. See if she might be suitable for what we have in mind.'

Jenkins eyed him dubiously. 'She's an old lady. Doesn't get out much now. She has her good days and her bad days.'

'What number flat is she?'

'Nine,' said Jenkins. 'Second floor.' He frowned as he stepped back into his own doorway, paused there uncertainly. There was clearly something still on his mind. It didn't seem so much a reservation about allowing Minto to pass, more a desire not to let him do so without communicating something further to him. Something Jenkins considered important, information he was eager to impart.

'I met that Bruce Forsyth once,' he announced. He paused for the full impact of the revelation to sink in, then added casually, 'Know him yourself, do you?'

Minto shook his head.

'Lovely bloke,' reminisced Jenkins triumphantly. 'Got his autograph somewhere.'

'You're a lucky man, Mr Jenkins,' said Minto, and hurried on up the stairs.

It was difficult to say whether it was one of Miss Fulbrick's good days or bad days. It wasn't that she was uncommunicative. If anything, she was too forthcoming. It was just very difficult to keep her to the point. She showed no reluctance about inviting him into her sitting-room. She told him to sit down, then, manoeuvring her bent frame back into her own chair, she launched into an account of her hip-replacement operation, which diversified into confused memories of a woman called Olive, and an involved story about the malfunctioning of various kitchen appliances, a story which gradually petered out as the last threads of her narrative finally eluded her. It was almost as if she had been waiting for him, thought Minto. But perhaps in a sense she had. When you were old and starved of company, you fell on any potential conversation with a ravening and indiscriminate hunger.

Miss Fulbrick's living-room was scented with old age, that sad amalgam of furniture polish, imperfectly scoured dishes, and the nameless little failures of personal hygiene to which the solitary are doomed. It was a dated, careworn interior, where the furniture gave the impression of being too big for its surroundings. Miss Fulbrick, a thin, bent, white-haired figure with a nose like a beak, lived dwarfed by her heavy brown bureaux, threatened by her wardrobes and standing lamps.

'How long have you been living in Strandwick Mansions, Miss Fulbrick?' he asked her. And for a brief moment he was back in the opulent whiteness of the Munich apartment, cradling in his hand the book Isabella had given him. The book with the inscription on its flyleaf.

Miss Fulbrick peered uncomprehendingly back at him, then said with a sudden access of briskness, 'So they've sent you to investigate, have they?'

'I'm sorry? Investigate what?'

'The voices. The voices in the radiators.'

'In the radiators?'

'Yes, in the radiators. There are voices in there, trying to speak to me, tell me something. Not everyone's ears are good enough to catch them, but I've got exceptionally sensitive hearing for my age. It comes of being musical, you see. I've spoken to Mr Jenkins downstairs and he said he'd get it looked into.'

'What are these voices saying?'

'That's just it. I can't make it out. But they're definitely in there somewhere. Trying to communicate.'

Minto shifted uncomfortably, embarrassed. And a little uneasy. There are moments when the frailties of old age cross the boundaries of comedy and enter the territory of the macabre.

'Do you recognise the voices?' he suggested.

'No, not recognise, not really. You see they're distorted. Just once I wondered if it wasn't Mother in there, trying to tell me something. But I really hope it wasn't. She so hated confined spaces.' She paused thoughtfully, then continued on a tangential track. You could almost see her mind negotiating the points. 'It was the blitz, you know. The blitz. That was a time, people in the underground. They slept there you know. Mother wouldn't hear of it, of course. She said you caught diseases down there. All those human beings in such a close space. A breeding ground for germs, she said. So she stayed put. Wouldn't leave her own bed, she said, not on account of a few bombs. And you won't find me down the underground, not then, not now. Always preferred the bus, I did. Used to take the number nineteen every day for twenty-three years.'

'So you lived here in Strandwick Mansions during the war?'

'I should say not, dear, not here. Not in those days. We were up in Highgate, Mother and I. Mother always said the air was better up there. We had a grand piano in those days. Beautiful tone.' She paused, her eyes clouded by an unhappy memory. 'Too big to get through the door here, though, wasn't it. So we had to make do with that upright. I've always loved music, and Mother played quite beautifully. I used to give a few lessons in the evenings. And concerts! I don't get out so much now, but I used to go regularly, once or twice a week. Wigmore Hall, that was one of my favourites.'

It was hard to piece together the precise chronology of Miss Fulbrick's life. Minto tried again: 'So you moved here with your mother when? After the war?'

'She was never the same after the move. It slowed her down, you know. Some days she couldn't get out of bed at all. She'd been such an active woman all her life . . .' Miss Fulbrick peered out of the sitting-room window at the view which must have become so familiar to her. There was a line of terraced houses across the street and beyond, glimpsed across the roof-tops, a church spire shimmering in the heat. In the distance you could hear the plaintive chime of an ice-cream van.

'When exactly was the move?' Minto decided to punt. 'Late 1950s, could it have been?'

'Oh, no.' Miss Fulbrick turned her gaze from the window, shocked by the error into a moment of sudden lucidity. 'Earlier than that. It was 1953. We all went upstairs to the Gomezes to watch the coronation the week after we moved in. Funny little box it was in those days, you could hardly see the picture, but we all crowded round and thought it was a miracle. And she looked a picture, didn't she, Her Majesty? And the Prince, such a handsome man. Even though you could hardly see the inside of the Abbey on the screen, we all cried when she was crowned. So young and frail, she looked, and yet so beautiful and brave. It was the history being made, really, there before your eyes. Such a moving occasion. Mother said she never thought the day would come when she'd actually witness a coronation.'

'Were the Courtneys there that day?' It was a huge gamble, a shot fired at random.

'When?'

'When you all went to the Gomezes to watch the coronation?'

'When was that, then?'

'You were just talking about it. When the Queen looked so beautiful. Were the Courtneys watching too?'

Again Miss Fulbrick paused. Had any connection been

registered at all? Or had the thread been lost entirely? And then miraculously she nodded and declared with conviction: 'That Mrs Courtney. She was a strange one. No, she wouldn't have been there, not to watch the coronation. Mother said it was being Austrian. Didn't talk much. Kept herself to herself.'

'And what about her son? Alexander, wasn't that his name?' Minto felt as though he was propelling the old lady along a tightrope. At any moment she could be blown off by her own prolixity or the changing gusts of her erratic memory.

'Alexander, that was it. He was an odd fellow, too. A quiet one. At least you never saw much of him. No one quite knew what line of business he was in. Some people said he worked in the City. Other people said he was a merchant, had an office or a warehouse somewhere. Bought and sold things. But he never said much.'

For a moment the hazy image of the young Alexander Courtney grew a little less blurred in Minto's mind. It was still an unclear picture, but some aspects of it were crystallising. The merchant, buying and selling things. Pictures, perhaps, in a quiet way. Discovering an aptitude for the market. Training his own prodigious eye. Content for the time being to operate from a domestic base, apparently tied to his mother. Biding his time. But what had made him jump, given him the impetus to leap from small-time handler of unconsidered trifles on the margin of the art trade, as he seemed to have been at this stage, to the big-time dealer at the centre of things that he'd become by the 1960s?

There was only one answer. It must have been his mother's death. In the car crash. A tragedy, but at the same time a catalyst to action. A liberation.

'But he was living with his mother when you first knew them?'

She nodded. 'Oh, yes. They were both of them up there in flat eleven. As I say, they were a bit stand-offish, didn't seem to have many friends either. And he was away a lot.'

'Did they ever invite you round?'

'Oh, no.' Miss Fulbrick frowned at the suggestion. 'Mother

said they were aliens. Not that we knew them during the war, but Mother said they were the sort of people who would have been kept under police surveillance at that time as likely fifth columnists. You can't be too careful.'

For a moment Minto felt a little sneaking sympathy for the Courtneys, holed up here surrounded by xenophobic English neighbours, who whispered amongst themselves, speculating about their origins and trustworthiness. But then he remembered Alexander's subsequent history and realised his sympathy was wasted on such a man. A man who dominated people, intimidated them. A man of dangerous charm. A man who boasted he had once taken life.

Then without warning Miss Fulbrick made her revelation. Almost casually, she added with a little laugh of reminiscence, 'Of course, at the end there was the other one.'

'The other one?'

'The second man. The one that moved in with them.' Was she wandering again now? Was this a figment of her contorted memory, another voice from the plumbing system?

Minto taxed her: 'Another man who moved in with the Courtneys?'

'That's right.'

'Who was that?'

'The cousin. He came over from Vienna.'

'What, a cousin from Vienna came to live with them? When was that?' He could see her misting over now, wobbling. He mustn't let her lose her balance on the tightrope.

'Alexander . . .' she murmured. 'I once had a pupil called Alexander. All one summer. Mother called him Alexander the Great, because he was rather on the fat side . . . I blamed his parents. They would keep feeding him chocolate all hours of the day.'

Minto spoke quite sharply: 'Who was the cousin, Miss Fulbrick? The cousin of the Courtneys?'

She blinked, surprised by his tone. 'The Courtneys, yes. Oh, goodness me, the cousin. Late one night he came. The Gomezes saw him arrive, because they were returning home after midnight from her birthday dinner. He arrived with three large suitcases, got out of a taxi. The Gomezes said they thought it was Alexander at first because he had the same build and the same colour hair, but then Alexander himself came down the stairs to give him a hand up with the bags. Alexander introduced him to them as his cousin. His cousin who'd just arrived from Vienna.'

'When was that?'

She sighed. But she answered with an unexpected precision, as if a beam of light had illuminated the incident with sudden clarity: 'It must have been late 1956 or early 1957. Winter, anyway. I remember that because I met the cousin on the stairs once soon after he'd arrived and we exchanged a few words about the snow. I said it was cold, and he said it was nothing compared to the winters where he'd come from. He seemed a pleasant sort of fellow, a bit more forthcoming than the Courtneys themselves.'

'What was the cousin's name?' Minto pressed.

'It's a funny thing, I don't seem rightly to remember what he was called. But he explained it all to me, who he was.' She held up her bent fingers and counted the names off against them, in order to get it right: 'Let me see . . . His mother was the sister of Alexander Courtney's father. So Alexander and he were first cousins. That was it. But they'd never met before, what with him being over there and them being over here.'

'Did you talk to him much?'

'No, dear. I never got to know him very well because by the summer they'd all moved out.' There was a wistfulness to her tone, a sense of regret. Minto fancied that for Miss Fulbrick, at least, the unknown cousin had exerted more attraction than the young Alexander Courtney. Strange, if you remembered the magnetism of the man when older.

'Why did they move?'

She shrugged. 'All I know is they went up in the Hampstead direction. Near the open spaces. Mother was very envious of them, going up to higher altitudes, healthier she said it was. But of course no sooner had they moved than there was the car accident.'

'Yes, the car accident. How did you hear about that?'

'I read it in the *Highgate Times*. I kept the cutting.'

'You kept the cutting? Could I see it, do you think?'

'A cup of tea,' she said abruptly. 'A cup of tea, that's what you'd be liking, wouldn't you?'

'That's kind of you, but I'd love to see the cutting if I could.'

She didn't reply, but hauled herself laboriously out of her chair, and hobbled off to the kitchen. Minto urged himself to be patient. He'd got much further than he could have dared hope. He tried to imagine Courtney and his mother in these surroundings. With the Gomezes upstairs, flaunting their state-of-the-art television. With the young Miss Fulbrick and her invalid mother down in this flat. Here in Strandwick Mansions dwelt the Courtneys, assimilating Englishness. Did they sometimes wonder what life would have been like back in Austria? No, they probably eliminated such speculation from their imaginative repertoire. They'd determined to make a go of it here. Even though she was never quite accepted by the neighbours with her odd foreign ways; and he was an object of mystery and intrigued conjecture. A merchant? Or something in the City?

And then the arrival of the cousin from Vienna. Pulling up at night in a taxi with his suitcases, observed by the Gomezes. Moving in with the Courtneys. And moving on with them too, it seemed: for by the summer of 1957 the three of them had vacated their apartment and found new accommodation in the lusher pastures of Hampstead. Or had the cousin gone with them? Maybe that had been the moment he had chosen to go back to Austria. Anyway, that would have been the last anyone in Strandwick Mansions would have heard of them if it hadn't been for the accident. Alert little Miss Fulbrick had read about it in the *Highgate Times*. Probably rather relished the horror of it, ghoulishly parading it to her mother, racing upstairs to knock on the Gomezes' door with the news. Had anyone sent flowers to the funeral? Probably not, reflected Minto. In the end Mrs Courtney had been an alien, hadn't she. Not one of us.

Miss Fulbrick appeared in the doorway again, looking perplexed. 'Did you want something?' she asked Minto, as if she had never seen him before in her life.

'Just the cutting, Miss Fulbrick.'

'The cutting?' She said the word as if its meaning were lost to her, as if it were some arcane piece of specialist jargon.

'Yes, the one from the newspaper. About the Courtneys' motor accident.'

She closed her eyes and swayed slightly. Dear God, thought Minto, please don't let her faint. Please keep her upright. And coherent. Just a little longer. She blinked, then smiled at him.

'Yes, the accident,' she said firmly, and hobbled over to a large Victorian bureau and opened a drawer.

A moment later Minto was holding the yellowing paper in his hands, running his eye over the headline: 'Local Family in Fatal Car Crash',

Police are appealing for witnesses to a fatal car crash which took place on the A1 near Hendon at approximately 8.35 p.m. on Saturday evening. The driver of an Austin Seven, Mrs Frederica Courtney, 62, of Edgware Dwellings, Hampstead, died of head injuries after being involved in an accident with a haulage lorry. A passenger in the car, an Austrian national in his early thirties on an extended visit to this country, was also killed. The sole survivor in the car was Mrs Courtney's son, Alexander, 32, who escaped with severe bruising and mild concussion. He and the driver of the haulage lorry, Harold Gommersall, 37, of Doncaster, were released from hospital after overnight observation.

Police believe that Mrs Courtney's car may have sustained a puncture and veered into the path of the oncoming lorry with which it collided. The road was closed for four hours after the crash in order for police to clear the debris.

Mrs Courtney and her son had only moved into Edgware Dwellings within the past three weeks. A local resident told the *Highgate Times* that although he did not know the new arrivals well, they had seemed quiet, respectable people and the accident was a keenly felt tragedy.

Quiet, respectable people. A keenly felt tragedy. Minto paused, momentarily transported back into the past with the sudden vividness that an old newspaper can sometimes convey. So Alexander Courtney had been in the car himself. In the car in which his mother had died.

Severe bruising and mild concussion, the report said. In pain, but probably not unconscious. So the chances were he had been aware of the ambulance men pulling his mother's body from the wreckage, aware of it like some grim nightmare from which you hope to awake. That sort of experience never leaves you. It must have scarred him. Sitting bemused on the roadside as they carried away his dead cousin from Vienna. Sitting in the gutter next to Harold Gommersall, thirty-seven, driver of the haulage lorry, the other survivor.

Alexander Courtney, watching numb with horror as they removed his mother's bloodied corpse. And yet it must in some strange way have charged him up, galvanised him. Wrought in him the conviction that this was the beginning of the rest of his life. Because from then on it changed. From that point he never looked back; he was set on a career of spectacular success.

So that was the fate of the mysterious cousin. The one who'd smiled at Miss Fulbrick on the stairs and discussed the weather with her. He'd never got back to Austria. He'd been killed in the same accident as Mrs Courtney. A nameless Austrian national, lying dead on English tarmac. The man who had arrived in the night with his three suitcases, and stayed for nearly a year. The man who had been Alexander Courtney's cousin.

And if Alexander's cousin, therefore Isabella's cousin, too. A cousin she had never met; probably never even been aware of. He knew something about her she didn't know. He savoured the sensation for a moment: it gave him a brief and primitive sense of power over her.

'Did you ever see Alexander Courtney again?' he asked Miss Fulbrick.

'Who's that, dear?'

'Alexander Courtney. Your former neighbour. The man in the old newspaper you've just shown me.'

She looked at him blankly. Minto could tell she had finally fallen off the tightrope. There was to be no hoisting her back up today.

'Thank you so much for your help. Do you mind if I

borrow this cutting? I promise I'll return it to you in a day
or two.'

She lifted a tired hand at him. 'Take what you want,' she
said thoughtfully. 'Just bring it back when you come to do
the radiators.'

'Oh yes, the radiators. They'll be ... they'll be looked
into.'

'Wait,' she called as he made to let himself out. There was
an urgent tone to her voice he hadn't heard before, a hint of
desperation which gave a sudden flare of wildness to her eye.
'Have you thought about a priest?'

'A priest?'

'Yes, perhaps a priest should come.'

'What for?' Suddenly the musty shadows of the room
were oppressive, and he wanted to be out in the fresh
air.

'You see,' she said, with enormous concentration, as though
struggling to express an idea that might at any moment slip
from her grasp, 'it could be that what is really needed here
is not a plumber but an exorcist.'

An exorcist.

Maybe that was what they all needed, thought Minto
as he unlocked his car and climbed in. Not just Miss
Fulbrick, with the strangled voices in her central-heating
system, but Minto too with his paranoias and his hidden susceptibilities. And all the rest of them, as well:
the Courtneys, father and children, with their nameless
secrets buried in the past: Thomas Donat, with his bot-
tomless horror of a single painting; and the painting itself.
The Island of the Dead. That landscape needed exorcising
too.

As he drove back to his flat he began to put the pieces
together. To make some sort of pattern of them. The
picture had been in Hungary in Count Barodi's collection,
last recorded there after its purchase from Galerie Voermann.
It wasn't possible to specify when it had passed back into
art-market circulation, but one could guess. 1956 was as
likely a time as any other. Hadn't Thomas Donat described

the flood of refugees pouring over the border from Hungary into Austria in the weeks after the revolution? Refugees who'd fled with their most precious possessions into the sanctuary of the West. And what would such refugees have needed most upon first drawing breath in Vienna? Money, surely. Anything that could have been sold and turned into money would have been welcome. Like jewellery. Like a picture. Like *The Island of the Dead*. No doubt there had been dealers and opportunists lurking in Vienna only too happy to buy what was on offer at advantageous prices. Opportunists, perhaps, like Alexander's cousin, who, having acquired a number of potentially profitable items, bundled them into suitcases and set off to do business with his Anglicised relations in London. With his Anglicised cousin who was a merchant of some sort with incipient interests in the art market. His Anglicised cousin Alexander Courtney.

That's how it could have happened, couldn't it? It was plausible enough. And yet there were still big unanswered questions. It didn't explain why Thomas Donat had laid into the picture with an eight-inch kitchen knife. It didn't explain why Denton had been threatened into silence. It didn't explain what it was that the Courtneys had still got to hide.

It didn't explain why Minto was still looking into his driving mirror to see if he was being followed.

He parked the car outside his flat and in the communal hall paused out of habit to check through his post. Circulars and a bill. He ran up the two flights of carpeted stairs to his front door. He was immediately suspicious. The thin piece of thread he'd left drawn across his keyhole had been fractured. He'd been inclined to laugh at himself for the precaution that morning. It had struck him as absurdly melodramatic. Now he wasn't so sure. Someone had been through this door in his absence. My God, perhaps they were still there. He felt a little sick feeling of apprehension in his stomach. He tensed himself and softly turned the key in the lock. Once inside he edged along the passage. The drawing-room door was ajar. Had he left it like that? He couldn't be sure.

Finally he just pushed it open and burst into the room. And immediately the figure on the sofa jumped up.

'Oh, shit! It's you,' said Minto.

'Christ, you gave me a shock,' said Frankie. 'Where have you been?'

She'd been waiting for him. Just like that. As if she owned him. He felt foolish and angry.

'I wish you'd bloody well let me know before you turn up here. Give me some warning.'

'I did,' she said sulkily. 'I left a message on your answerphone. You can listen to it if you don't believe me: go on, play it back.'

Furious, Minto demanded: 'Have you been listening to my private messages?'

'Why shouldn't I?'

'Because they're bloody private, that's why.'

'Why can't you just be honest with me, Minto?' She was on the verge of tears, had been ever since he'd come in. 'There's someone else, isn't there?'

For a moment he saw her clearly. Isabella. Lying there in the Munich hotel room.

'There's no one else. I just need a bit of space, OK?'

'Don't lie to me: I want to know. You're seeing someone else, aren't you?'

He shrugged. He wasn't going to tell her anything. Isabella was none of her business. He didn't want to talk about Isabella to anyone. How could he? He hadn't even come to terms with Isabella himself. But part of his heart leapt in oblique anticipation. What had Frankie heard on his answerphone tape? Had Isabella called?

'Look, I'm not stupid,' went on Frankie. 'I've noticed what's been going on with you over the past two weeks. You've changed, something's been happening to you. You're not the same person.'

'I've got things on my mind.'

'She's in Putney, isn't she? There's someone in Putney? You're always sneaking off there. There's another bloody message from her now, she wants you to call her. Leila, or something.'

'I haven't got a girl in Putney. That's a work contact. To do with a story I'm writing.' But as he spoke he was aware only of an acute disappointment. So that was all. Leila Parsons. No message from Isabella.

'Christ almighty, you're a sod, Minto. You're not worth it, do you know that?'

He watched mutely as she flung the keys to the flat back at him and then moved round the rooms pushing her various belongings into a bag, even retrieving from the bottom of the cupboard a T-shirt whose scent had once evoked her so powerfully when Minto had picked it from the floor. Once. Several weeks ago. She worked methodically with that abstracted discipline that is the refuge of certain passionate people in moments of distress. When she had finished she stood still for a moment in the doorway, half expecting to be summoned back. But Minto stayed silent.

She was a strong girl, Frankie. She'd get over it.

'Good news,' said Leila Parsons on the telephone later that evening, 'he regained consciousness today. The doctors are much more optimistic.'

'Did you speak to him?'

'For a few minutes, yes.' Her voice sounded tired and tense, as though even the relief was numbed. 'He . . . he asked after you. He'd very much like to see you.'

'When?'

'Tomorrow, if you could manage it. A short visit, so as not to take up too much of your time . . . and so you don't tire him too much. But he said he was very anxious to tell you something. The rest of the story, he said.'

The rest of the story.

Suddenly Minto felt very frightened indeed. It wasn't just the realisation that what he would hear tomorrow might finally reveal the hidden evil of *The Island of the Dead*. It was also the nagging suspicion that the very communication of the secret would expose him to further evil. Its knowledge was dangerous. It would make him vulnerable. Vulnerable, perhaps, even to the sort of accident that Donat himself had sustained.

15

'Donat?' said the harassed woman at the hospital reception desk. 'Donat? I'll have to check.'

Minto looked about him. He was already beginning to feel uneasy in this place. Uneasy at the unfamiliar smell. Uneasy at the dilapidated decoration, the flaking paintwork. Uneasy at the concentration of suffering and grief that all hospitals constituted in his mind. It weighed on him. He imagined the man hours of pain sustained within this building, fancied that aggregation of distress ingrained into the very brickwork and plaster, so that you could not but sense it once you stood enclosed by these walls. It wafted out of them and penetrated into the marrow of your bones. He watched the people who milled about in this reception area. Visitors, many of them, some laden with gifts, others with brave smiles. But everyone moved with an edge of anxiety, an apprehension that they could not quite suppress. There were patients too, patients in dressing-gowns, who wandered with the disorientated air of prisoners on parole. You sensed a constant intimation of mortality.

There were people here who were going to die. And others here who were going to have to grieve for them.

'Donat did you say? Ah, yes, here he is. He's in Mandela.'

'Mandela?'

'Yes, Mandela Ward. Third floor, lift shaft B.'

Minto walked on down passages, past doorways. He marvelled at the people who actually worked here. There was a briskness, a matter-of-factness about them. They moved in a self-constructed vacuum of the feelings, immune to the emotional implications of what they were dealing with. He passed white-coated assistants who wheeled patients fresh from operations on drip-bedecked trolleys with all the insouciance of Smithfield meat porters. He asked the way of a nurse, who replied in the numbing tone of mindless efficiency that permitted her to handle the dying with the same involvement as a municipal gardener might tend sickly plants in a public park.

With a sudden vividness he recalled the feeling of personal dread with which he had approached his last visit to a place like this. His final visit to his father's bedside.

And then he was there, at the swinging doors which were the entrance to Mandela Ward. Peering through he recognised the forlorn figure of the man he had come to see in the last bed on the right, in the corner. He paused for a moment, drawing comfort from the thought that Donat's position at least gave him a measure of seclusion denied to the other occupants of this desperately public room. But when he walked closer he was shocked by the paleness and frailty of the face that lay on the pillow. The eyes were open, but stared up to the ceiling. Only the hand, clenching and unclenching as it lay above the sheet, betrayed a sign of life.

'Hello, Thomas,' said Minto. He said it absurdly heartily, but the old man's answering smile of greeting was unfeigned.

'It is good that you came,' he murmured. 'Sit down. Sit close to me.' His voice was weak but determined.

Minto drew up the chair and bent his head closer so that Thomas would not have to speak too loud. 'How are you feeling today?' he asked him.

Thomas shook his head and made a little movement of dismissal with his hand, jerking his bony fingers to indicate that those politenesses could wait, were not important. 'You see I have to talk now. It is time. It will help me to tell it to you. To tell it all to you.'

'I am listening,' said Minto, leaning forward once again.

The grey winter rain teemed down, overflowing from gutters. splashing from window-ledges. Thomas Donat stood still for a moment, incredulous at the open air, blinking in the miraculous daylight. Every drop of water that fell on his face as he turned it to the sky had an invigorating purity that made him yearn for the next. After the narrow circumscription of his existence in the cell, the dimensions of this wet courtyard presented a vista of unspeakable loveliness. But he was not to enjoy it for long. There was a car drawn up, and the two AVO men flanking him propelled him towards it. A door was pulled open and they threw him into the back seat. Then they drove, edging out furtively into Andrassy Street, turning right into St Istvan's Boulevard. It was morning, he guessed. He could see pedestrians on the pavements, women shopping in a desultory way with their collars turned up against the rain. An old man shuffled by with a string bag of vegetables. In a doorway he caught a glimpse of two girls giggling together as they lit cigarettes. Their mirth was an unfamiliar thing, at once exhilarating and disconcerting.

The car ground over Margit Bridge and into Buda. They began to climb, up through the leafy streets of Roszadomb. Up to the luxury villas. Up to the lotus-eating land where the party functionaries sunned themselves. To Rákosi country. To where she lived. To the territory of Greta Kassák, housewife. Suddenly he thought, they're taking me to her. I'm going to see her again. After all, I've just been allowed to see daylight. Why not her as well?

It was like a dream. They drew up in front of one of the well-appointed residences, and he was hauled out into the rain again. An iron gate opened, and he was led through a garden with a line of silver birch trees and a carefully tended lawn. There was an elegance to the house, a symmetry to its façade. The upstairs windows were flanked by well-proportioned green shutters, and opened on to a balcony of elaborate ironwork. Beneath the balcony, across the entire width of the house, ran the colonnade through which you passed to reach the front door. Thomas paused for a moment in the shadowy hall, before being guided into a large drawing-room. The touch of his guardians was still firm, but perceptibly gentler than it had been in the car, as if out of deference to the surroundings. As he came in, a figure rose from a sofa and turned towards him.

It wasn't Greta. It was a man, not much older than Thomas. A tall, fair-haired man in a smart dark suit, the sort of well-cut suit that was unfamiliar on the streets of Budapest. He smiled

at Thomas. He smiled with such charm that for a moment
Thomas was knocked off balance. He smiled with such charm
that Thomas knew he was dangerous.

Everything was unfamiliar. The charm. The suit. And the
decoration of the room. At first Thomas could not understand
the process of oblique association which put him in mind of
his grandmother. But that was it, of course: the room. It was
like his maternal grandmother's house, a long-gone dream
of beauty and opulence dimly remembered from his early
childhood before the war. The sort of opulence that was
now forbidden. An outmoded relic of discredited bourgeois
values. The sort of opulence which had been in danger
of contaminating him across the generations, rendering his
family suspect, class aliens at odds with the dictatorship of the
proletariat. Only the fact of his mother's marrying beneath her
had saved him from the aristocratic name which would have
ensured his earlier persecution by the Communist regime. But
perhaps it was some atavistic discrimination which enabled
Thomas now to recognise the quality of what he saw arrayed
before him in this room. Across the floor spread a rich Turkish
carpet. Against one wall stood a Biedermeier sofa of exceptional elegance. Two early nineteenth-century French fauteuils
were drawn up before the fire. Everywhere he looked glinted
gilt: in ornate mirrors; on the frames of pictures which hung
in profusion on the walls. Landscapes. Portraits. Still lives.
It was a vision of gold; perplexing after the greyness of the
Budapest interiors to which he had become accustomed over
the years. Almost incomprehensible after his incarceration.

'Ah, Tamás,' said the man. 'It is Tamás, isn't it?' His
manner was relaxed, almost lazy, as if Thomas were a
guest at a garden party. Only the man's eyes betrayed
him. His eyes were alert, hawklike. And unforgiving. His
eyes warned Thomas not to relax for a second, not to yield
control of himself. Thomas nodded warily.

'I am Rudolf,' the man continued. 'I hope we shall be
friends. Will you have a drink? Here, take this glass, let me
fill it. There. You must have been through a lot recently. And
I want you to try one of these cakes. Come, they are delicious,
I recommend them. That's right, take another.'

The cakes were indeed delicious. To be confronted by such food was like a flimsy dam yielding to a torrent. Thomas abandoned restraint and dignity as he swallowed two in quick succession, then a third. He was scrabbling for them, stuffing them into his mouth. Then he looked up and saw Rudolf watching him. Smiling. As if the witnessing of his own descent into the animal constituted some sort of personal victory.

'So, Tamás. Sit down. What do you need? A cigarette? Of course.'

Thomas's fingers were shaking as he held the tip to the light. The inhalation was ecstatic. He was light-headed, on a dangerous edge of pleasure.

'You like my house?' Rudolf stood in front of the fire, his hands in the pockets of his jacket, and spoke softly to him. His words were the honey emanating from a terrible strength. 'It is beautiful, isn't it? I am proud of my collection. So few people in Hungary today seem to appreciate the quality of the old things, don't you agree? I, on the other hand, have always loved them. I have been lucky, you know. I have been conveniently placed to pick up the things that people have had to leave behind, the things for which they had no use any more. I see you looking at my pictures: you have good taste, I congratulate you. They are my special favourites. They are the things I would save first if I found my house was on fire.' He laughed, amused at his own joke. 'Look, there is a little gem by Karl Spitzweg. And here is a landscape which I am almost sure is by Corot. You know Corot? The French master. He has such a pleasing sense of atmosphere. And there, there above the fireplace: there is something quite unique. Look carefully at it and you—'

'Who are you? Why am I here?' The words fell like smashed glass on the floor, cutting through this dangerous enchantment. Thomas had to know what all this was about. The uncertainty could be contained no longer. He couldn't bear this mellifluous flow of words. It had to be broken. And was it some obscure instinct of self-preservation that compelled him to break it just before they reached that picture? The one above the fireplace. The disturbing one, the one which, half glimpsed, he instinctively recoiled from, didn't want to rest his eye on. What did it all mean, this opulence? What was Rudolf trying to do to him?

'Don't be anxious, my friend.' The voice was still gentle, but there was extra persuasion to it. 'You want to know why you're here? You're here so that we can have a little talk. And I? I am your friend. I think that you will find that we have much in common.' He paused, and added suddenly, in English: 'You have read the plays of Shakespeare?'

Thomas was so surprised that he also answered in English: 'I have read some of them.'

'Do you know that line of Shakespeare: "The lunatic, the lover, and the poet, are of imagination all compact"?'

Thomas looked up at him, confused.

'Which are you, I wonder?' mused Rudolf softly.

Thomas mumbled something incoherent.

Rudolf nodded thoughtfully. 'You have been the poet, Tamás, that I know. And you have been the lover, too, in your time. But the lunatic? Let's just say that I am here to dissuade you from your madness.' He paused, then added, smiling: 'Shakespeare. So. Here is something we share at once then. An interest in other cultures and languages. You and I have an understanding.'

An understanding. Thomas said nothing. He felt obscurely that he had been trapped.

'But the main point is,' continued Rudolf, 'that your time of reflection and self-criticism has elapsed. I am sure that there are now matters which we can profitably discuss.'

He braced himself. He must look somewhere else, away from Rudolf. He must have something on which to concentrate his eyes in order not to lose control over his brain. He chose the mirror on the wall to the left of the fireplace. He dwelt among its lozenges and scrolls, followed the golden passages of its ornamentation with a minute exactitude, like a traveller in a mountainous landscape plotting a course between peaks and crevasses. So that he could inhabit some other world from the present one, establish some distance. So that he was not consumed by Rudolf's will.

Part of his brain heard Rudolf's voice addressing him.

Softly persistent, ultimately demanding. But resistible. Oh yes, resistible. So long as he retained the distance.

'I think you know what I am going to ask you. And I think you know what you are going to answer me, too. You've come to understand that what I am telling you is correct. My way is the intelligent way forward. Admit it now: all this time you've just been given for reflection, all this opportunity for self-criticism, hasn't it convinced you that you were wrong? Look, Tamás, you've been misled by other people. You were hanging out with a bunch of decadent subversives, and they infected you. It wasn't really your way, but you were corrupted. You see that now, don't you, Tamás?'

Thomas swallowed and stared very hard at a certain point on the mirror's frame, where there was a little concave shallow like the inside of a shell. You could shelter there, he thought. Find refuge. Find protection from outside attack.

'Come now,' continued Rudolf. 'Think about it. Is this way not better? Not better than your cell? Don't you like the cakes? The cigarettes? This is what you get when you can think straight. This is what you get when you have thrown off the infection of wrong ideas. It's not so difficult, is it, to come back to being one of us, to thinking straight again?

'Perhaps you're wondering how you can do this, how you can express your new, more sensible point of view. I tell you it will not take very much. Here, I have prepared just a little article for you to sign. I've done all your work for you, really, haven't I? This will be your journalistic rehabilitation, this piece. I can promise you publication in all the party journals, high billing in the *Szabad Nép* with this piece. Maybe you might even make a little broadcast on the radio, too.'

He felt the paper pushed urgently into his hand. Reluctantly he extracted himself from the gilded crevasses of the frame, disengaged his eyes from its undulations. He stared at the typewritten sheet that Rudolf wanted him to put his name to.

It was a miserable document. Even through everything he recognised its grossness. It was a recantation of every demand that the deputation of the Writers' Union had formulated,

a rejection of the memorandum presented to the Central
Committee. It conceded the absolute right of the party over
cultural activity, to suppress and encourage as it judged best.
It confessed to abject error, to the corrupting influence of the
bourgeois and revisionist thinking of men like Aczél, Hámos
and Tibor Monos. It was a broadcast of his own collapse.

'No,' he said slowly but with resolution. 'No, this is
not right.'

'Come on, you must be sensible.' Rudolf was still smiling,
still giving him the full force of his charm. 'Perhaps there is
something you should know which will help persuade you.'

'What should I know?' His own voice was momentarily
unfamiliar. After all, conversation was still a strange new
luxury.

'You should know that your friend Tibor Monos has not
had your stupid reservations. He has been convinced again of
the merits of the party's line. We picked him up soon after
we took you in. He has been persuaded. He has signed a
piece admitting all his errors. It was no problem for him.'

For a moment Thomas looked up and caught a glimpse
of the picture. That picture. The one above the fireplace.
His head reeled dangerously. Then he guided his eyes
resolutely away. Back to the mirror and its frame. Back
to its familiar sweeps and flourishes. Back to the security
of its distance.

'I do not believe you,' he said.

'I tell you that it's true.'

'I don't believe you,' he repeated.

There was silence. Thomas was obliquely aware of the
ticking of a French clock on a distant bureau.

Finally Rudolf said, 'So don't believe me.' His tone was
harder now. Angrier. 'It doesn't matter whether you believe
me or not. You will save yourself a lot of trouble if you sign
this piece. Go on, sign it now.'

Absurdly, Thomas almost felt like laughing. He sensed he
had won. Won a battle at least, if not a war. What sort of
victory it would prove to be he could not judge. But he knew
he'd done something momentous today.

In the end Rudolf told him: 'Very well. You need more time

to think. I wish you joy of it, going back to the place where you have been. And, Tamás, I'll tell you something. You'll be with me again soon, sooner than you think, pleading for a chance to sign this piece of paper.'

Rudolf turned away, as if Thomas were no longer in the room. The end of his interest was so abrupt it was as if an electric current had been switched off. Abrupt. And insulting.

He was back in that cell.

Timelessness began again. It was different, this second incarceration. There were longer tracts of near-unconsciousness, when he inhabited a shadowy world between sleep and waking. Periodically he had a grip on himself. He could still do it: he could still set the tasks and carry them through to a conclusion. But then he would relapse, for longer and longer stretches, into that nether consciousness lit by the continuity of the bulb. Sometimes he cried, for no very specific reason, huge sobs racking his body for hours on end. Sometimes he thought of Tibor. Sometimes he wondered if it could all be true, if Tibor had yielded to their pressure. Most times he still knew it wasn't. Anger, that was the answer. As long as he could feel angry about things his system was invigorated and his strength renewed.

He thought of Greta more than any of them. He could conjure her image on that day in the village on the Danube, at their first meeting in the bar of the Astoria, or at their rendezvous on Gellért Hill with her raincoat belt drawn tight about her waist. It was strange the way her memory could also galvanise him into resistance. Sometimes an insidious voice would tell him that he had only to do what they wanted, to admit error, to put his name to the confession, for him to be free to go again, free to seek her out and lay permanent claim to her. But each time this fantasy projected itself, it would short circuit. It didn't work on that basis. She wouldn't want him, if he'd asserted his right to her through weakness rather than strength. He wouldn't want her to want him on that basis. He must have her on his terms, not theirs. The temptation could not remain a temptation so long as he

convinced himself that in yielding to it he would destroy the
pleasure that he sought.

And then he was there again. It was like a familiar dream:
the ascent from the depths of his incarceration, the glorious
shock of daylight in the courtyard, the car journey across
Margit Bridge into Buda and up into Rózsadomb. This time
there were buds on the trees, definite signs of spring as the
driver swung them along the avenues of privilege, between
the villas of the party high-ups. And then the house again, with
its line of silver birch trees, its colonnade, its wrought-iron
balcony. He found himself breathing in the heavy opulence of
the room, Rudolf's drawing-room. And there was Rudolf once
more, happy to see him, greeting him like an old friend. There
was wine. There was food, delicious food. And cigarettes.
And charm again. Smoothly persuasive words, constantly
beguiling him. Through the cigarette smoke he narrowed
his eyes and concentrated on the ornate gilt of the mirror
above the sofa.

'Tamás,' the voice was saying, 'I have something here that
I want you to read.'

He made no reply. It was harder and harder to keep his gaze
locked on to that frame. He sought out the shell which had
given him refuge before, lost it, and then despite everything
found himself looking down at the paper Rudolf had put into
his hands.

'It is the confession of Tibor Monos. You told me you did not
believe that it existed. Now I think you should study it.'

For a moment he wavered, dizzy with uncertainty. There
was Tibor's signature at the end. But of course it was easy
to fake a signature. Immediately his anger flared: how dare
they think him so stupid, so easily deceived?

'No,' he said. 'This is not genuine.' But suddenly, from
nowhere, there was doubt. Eating at him. Weakening him.

Rudolf left him in silence for some time with the document
in his hand. Then he began again, in a harder voice with a
new element in it too. An element of wry amusement. As if
a humorous side to the situation had just occurred to him.

'There's something else, Tamás. Something I should have
told you earlier. But maybe I wanted to spare your feelings.'

Danger. Eyes back to the mirror. Establish the distance. Don't let him in too close.

'Can you hear me, Tamás? This is important.'

He nodded slowly. Some awful compulsion was pulling his gaze away from the mirror's frame. He didn't know how much longer he could resist. He knew he shouldn't listen to any more of Rudolf's words. But there was no getting away from them.

'You know how we found you, Tamás, don't you? You realise how we knew where to come looking for you in Vendel Street that night? You thought you'd lost us, didn't you, when we came round to Béla Bartók Street and you weren't there? But we were never going to lose you.' He paused, savouring the impact of what he was saying. Rejoicing in its horror. Teasing him with its inevitability.

'No!' breathed Thomas. He was moving his hands from his eyes to his ears in desperate little jerking movements, as if he couldn't decide whether to protect his hearing or his sight.

'How could we have lost you,' continued Rudolf softly, 'when we had someone working for us who was never going to lose you? Someone who was closer to you than any other human being, someone who was always going to lead us to you.'

'No,' he murmured again. But he could smell his own defeat. He knew what was coming.

'Yes, Tamás, it was her. It was Greta Kassák. She was working for us all along. It was all planned, the way she sought you out and played you along. Poor bloody fool, did you really think she loved you simply for your own blue eyes?' He spoke more harshly as he answered his own question: 'No such luck, you cretin. She was acting on orders. She'd taken you captive on our behalf.'

'But what about Kassák?' Thomas was stung into protest. 'Her husband, Peter Kassák. He was someone important, someone high-up in the party ... she was his wife.'

'Is that what she told you?'

'Yes, she told me that.' Thomas could feel his voice rising in intensity. He was a little out of control, and suddenly almost shouting. 'Peter Kassák was her husband. And she was leaving him for me. That's what she said.'

Rudolf shook his head. He advanced upon Thomas, put a hand on his shoulder. 'You poor bastard,' he said. 'Greta was not married to anyone, certainly not to a party high-up.' He gave a derisive laugh. 'Greta was an agent, an exceptionally skilled agent, working for the state. She was no one's wife. If she gave you that story, it was simply as cover. To appeal to your vanity.'

'Greta?' His gaze swam under the dreadful plausibility, and he whimpered: 'Not Greta?'

'Of course Greta.' Rudolf gave a little laugh of scorn, of irritation at such self-delusion. 'Don't be so stupid. You don't think she would have chosen of her own free will to go with you, do you? She did it out of duty to the state.'

Then it snapped. His eyes rolled away from the mirror. Irresistibly drawn to the right. To the picture above the fireplace. To the place he knew he shouldn't look.

They were steep, those cliffs. They pitched vertically from the inky-black waters, up to the heights where strange and predatory birds wheeled and circled about their impenetrable eeries. These were menacing rocks: monoliths with no restful plateaus; monoliths in their sheerness far more fearful than higher mountains with gentler inclines. They were unyielding absolutes. This was a landscape to break the spirit.

On those rocks he lost himself. In their contemplation he at last sensed his hold on himself loosening, gently but ineluctably, until all that hard-won control drifted away. Prised from him by the weeks of solitude. All but severed by the appalling revelation of Greta's apparent duplicity. And now lost for good in these evil rocks. He tried to seek a refuge in the cypresses which grew up tall beside the cliffs. But his eye was led inevitably down them, down to the entrance to the mausoleum, down further to where the inky-black water lapped against the shore. And there was the final horror. There was the boat, rowed by the shadowy oarsman, approaching the end of its journey to the island. Its white-shrouded passenger turned and confronted Thomas. All that was visible was the face, staring out at him with eyes at once sightless and mocking. In confirmation of the vanity of all he had striven for, all he had put his trust in. The death's-head. The skull.

They kicked him out the next day. Out of his cell. Out of 60 Andrassy Street. He stood miserably on the pavement for a moment, blinking in the irrelevant sunshine, like a shipwrecked sailor swept up on a shore that could offer no salvation. Sockless, in no more than the trousers, shirt and shoes which he'd been wearing when they took him in, he felt about him for some indication of his bearings. In his hand he clutched the identity card they had returned to him as they pushed him out, the identity card which restored to him his individual existence. He peered at it uncomprehendingly, as if seeking confirmation of his own significance. Some objective confirmation of it. Because when he looked within himself, he found nothing but an overwhelming sense of his own worthlessness.

He felt no joy in his release. His freedom was a mockery of the word, a negation of hope. The day before, there in Rudolf's hideous opulence, there, underneath those spirit-destroying rocks, in the sightless leer of the death's-head, there he had signed Rudolf's confession. There had seemed no point in holding out longer. Not now. Not after the words Rudolf had whispered to him. Not after the dreadful plausibility had sunk in.

For a couple of hours he roamed the streets, haggard, purposeless beyond an instinctive desire to keep moving, to reassimilate a sense of space. He was vaguely aware of people noticing him, then looking away in distaste. Perhaps they thought he was drunk. They wanted nothing to do with him. Any more than he wanted anything to do with himself.

In the end he drifted on to Tibor's address. Or his last known residence, anyhow, a room on the second floor in a street off St Istvan's Boulevard. He arrived there by some sort of homing instinct, not by any conscious decision of his own. It was simply that he couldn't face his own apartment in Béla Bartók Street, still less his temporary refuge in Vendel Street.

Where he'd thought himself safe. Where he'd passed half a night writhing in her arms. Where he'd heard the pounding of fists like machine-guns on the door. But what did it matter now? Now it had all been taken from him. Now they'd forced him to give them what they wanted. Now that Rudolf had broken him.

He knocked limply on Tibor's door. And a moment later he saw his friend's face. What did he read in Tibor's eyes in that split second when they stood, suspended by mutual shock, staring at each other in the doorway? Disbelief. Sorrow. And pity. Yes, pity. The sort of pity that the strong will always feel for a weaker spirit, that cannot exclude from itself some small particle of scorn. He knew the moment that he saw Tibor's eyes that Rudolf had been lying to him about that confession. That Tibor's signature had been a fake. And the strange thing was, he registered it almost without surprise. It was just one more symptom of his own submission to the will of Rudolf.

'You're being too hard on yourself,' Tibor told him later. 'Anyone would have cracked. Anyone would have given in. It doesn't make their cause any less wrong, or ours any less right, just because you put your name to a piece of paper.'

Thomas shook his head mutely, and Tibor, misreading the signal, went on: 'Look, the fact that they spent so much time achieving a meaningless victory over you is an indication of the inadequacy of their position. What after all are they going to do with what they have wrung out of you? Even if they do publish it, and frankly I don't think they'll bother now, it won't get them very far. OK, yes, they took me in too, soon after they got you. But they didn't get anything out of me. I'm used to their tricks now, inured to them. And I got the feeling they weren't trying as hard as they might have been. The wind's up them, you know. Changes are going to happen soon. Whether they like it or not.'

Thomas wasn't able to bear it any longer. He lifted sad, uncomprehending eyes to his friend and said quietly: 'No, Tibor. You do not understand.'

'I think I do, you know.' There had been an arrogance to Tibor, always. He couldn't help it. It was the arrogance of the man who knows his suffering has been greater than yours and cannot quite let you forget it.

Thomas shook his head. 'It's not the confession.' He paused long enough for Tibor to turn to him perplexed by the silence. 'It's her.'

'Her? Who do you mean?'

'Greta,' he breathed.

'Who?'

'Greta. Greta Kassák.'

'Oh, God. The Kassák woman, yes: your bored housewife. I'd forgotten about her.'

Thomas nodded miserably. 'He told me it was her. He said she led them to me. He said she was working for them all along.'

Tibor paused, considering the proposition, as an academic point. 'Frankly, now you mention it, it doesn't surprise me. You have to face the fact, Tamás: what was she doing with you in the first place?'

What was she doing with him in the first place?

Greta. Her memory was like a deep, infected wound. A wound that festered throughout that long, broiling summer, inflamed by the heat. A wound that refused to heal. A wound infected by the sweet poison of Rudolf's words, whose pain throbbed through his body, debilitating his mind so that his ambition was suffocated, and all the values that had sustained him were robbed of meaning. What was worth fighting for any more? She had deceived him. Nothing she had said had been true. Nothing she had said could be relied upon. The death's-head had won. The only constant in a world of vanity was the white-shrouded figure, turning back over its shoulder to mock him.

After a couple of days with Tibor he went back to Béla Bartók Street. To his room there. It was curious: Mrs Varadi poked her head out of her door on the ground floor and greeted him as if he was merely returning after a few days' holiday. But people were used to it now: the late-night knock on the door followed by the disappearance of a neighbour for an indefinite period of detention. You learned not to ask

too many questions; just to keep your head down and thank
God it wasn't you. He remembered the last time he'd thrown
open the door to his room here, and the elation he'd felt as he'd
seen her note waiting for him. Now there was nothing. No hint
of communication from her. Well, there wouldn't have been,
would there? She'd done her job. She'd led them to him. She'd
probably moved on to the next target, hadn't she? There'd be
no point in further contact with him.

And yet there was still a small part of him which couldn't
quite accept the betrayal. He felt a yearning to know what
had happened to her. He needed explanations. Later in the
week he made his way back to Vendel Street; he climbed
the crumbling stairway to the tiny room of his exile, to the
scene of his last passionate encounter with her. The room
was occupied by someone else. From the frightened eyes
of the stranger who opened the door to his knock, it had
been let to another fugitive from the attentions of the AVO.
There was relief in the expression of the new occupant when
Thomas explained his friendly intentions, but no illumination
on the Greta question. No, there had been no letters. No notes.
Thomas stumbled away, confused and miserable.

One early summer day, maddened by dreams of precipitous
rock-slabs, of inky-black seas, of faces that were alternately
sightless skulls and Greta's twisted features, he set off on foot
past Gellért Hill, along Attila Street, and up into Rózsadomb.
It was another of those days of intense heat, and he felt the
sweat beneath his shirt as he walked. He wasn't even clear
exactly why he was going, or precisely where. In the back of
his mind lay some barely formed desire to find her. To accost
her, in her house. Or in the house of her precious Peter. To
have it out with her once and for all. To begin the process
of healing. It was a sort of madness, of course for hadn't
Rudolf convinced him that her husband didn't exist? But still
he asked himself which of all these smart, fresh-painted villas
set back from the tree-lined streets might enclose her? How
could he possibly judge? How could he knock on every door,
demanding of each outraged party dignitary disturbed if this
was the house of Greta Kassák? Of Greta Kassák, housewife?
Of Greta Kassák, erstwhile lover of the subversive Donat?

Of Greta Kassák, AVO agent? Of Greta Kassák, AVO agent, who had submitted to the distasteful embraces of the criminal Donat only in the course of duty?

He turned left, then right, at random, down elegant avenues, past exclusive railings, losing himself in the labyrinth of privilege. And then he froze. Suddenly. He'd seen something horrific. Something whose memory he had suppressed, and now, glimpsed again, threatened to destroy him. There was the familiar garden with the line of silver birch trees. There were the windows with the green-painted shutters, the colonnaded façade, the delicate ironwork. There was the familiar path to the heavy front door. It was terrifying in its apparent innocuousness. This was the nightmare made flesh. Rudolf. This was Rudolf's house. By chance he'd come upon it. Beyond that door lay the sickening opulence. Beyond that door hung an image of a cliff-face. Beyond that door he could almost hear the call of the sinister birds that circled about their mountain eerie. And the death's-head. The dreadful, mocking death's-head.

He forgot Greta. He turned and ran. As if they were after him. As if Rudolf were coming for him again. Which, in a sense, he was. And always would be.

By the beginning of August he felt he had to get out. Out of the heat and the misery of Budapest. Even the news of Rákosi's fall from power failed to persuade him to stay. 'Look, things are happening now,' Tibor told him. 'The bald git's gone. Have you seen what's getting published in the *Literary Gazette* these days, it's fantastic. Christ almighty, those poems of Méry's. They're wonderful to read. Even my own small contribution has been noticed. Complete strangers come up to me in the street and want to shake me by the hand. People are really encouraged by what we're writing. It strikes a chord.'

Thomas smiled back at him, but shook his head.

'Go on,' encouraged Tibor, 'read this.' Tibor was still thin, but his eyes watered less these days. To please him, Thomas reached across and took the copy of *Irodalmi Ujság*.

The article was by Gyula Háy, and it was entitled 'Why do

I dislike Comrade Kucsera?'. It was a merciless indictment of
the mentality of the party functionary. 'Lies are not lies for
Kucsera,' read Thomas, 'murder is not murder, justice is not
justice, and man is not man. Kucsera preaches Socialism and
means a system which keeps him going. He preaches unity
and means unity for himself and a few others who are up
to the same game. He preaches democracy and means his
own hegemony. That is why I dislike Comrade Kucsera.'
For Kucsera read Kassák, thought Thomas. For Kucsera,
read Rudolf. For a moment something flickered within him.

But he knew he wasn't ready for this. Not yet. 'No,' he
said firmly. 'I've got to get away for a while. Got to sort
myself out.'

Tibor shrugged. Thomas could tell he despised him for his
fine feelings. 'Don't stay away too long,' he said, 'or you'll
miss your chance.'

'What chance?'

'The chance to make history.'

Before he could make history he had to make peace within
himself. So this time he didn't head for the Danube Bend,
where the memories were too painful. Instead he travelled
east, to visit his uncle Ferenc, his mother's brother, and his
aunt Maria, who lived a life of quiet penury in a tiny village
on the edge of the Great Plain of Hungary.

'Of course you must stay as long as you want,' Maria
said to him. 'And if you need something to do, you can help
György with the maize harvest. He's not a bad sort, György,
once you get to know him.'

Ferenc and Maria had left Budapest in the great deportation
of 1951. At twenty-four hours' notice thousands of people had
been evicted from their homes in the city. It had been an
enormous clear-out: the authorities had taken the opportunity
to get rid of all those they wanted out of the way, either
because of their aristocratic origins, or because of their wealth,
or simply because they happened to inhabit a dwelling on
which one of the party high-ups had his eye. Thomas knew
of a family who had been ejected solely because they were
the possessors of a telephone line. Such was the antiquated
state of the system that it was easier to move a favoured

functionary into a flat which already possessed a line than to install a new one elsewhere. Ferenc and Maria had been told to move out because of their class-alien status. Both came of landed families branded as hostile to the proletariat. They had found themselves herded on to a train at the Eastern railway station, allowed to take with them only what they could carry, and shipped to their new dwelling. This turned out to be the house of a peasant, György Matyas, who had two rooms to spare. As a punishment for some shortfall in his maize crop, these two rooms were commandeered and Ferenc and Maria billeted on him.

A potentially hostile domestic situation had turned into a surprisingly successful ménage over the ensuing five years, a ménage which would have been the despair of the authorities had they been aware of it. György Matyas took to his new lodgers, responding to them in an unfashionably feudal manner. By the time Thomas arrived that August, he found György's relationship to his uncle and aunt more reminiscent of the faithful family retainer than the landlord. He ran errands for them, did their shopping, cut their wood, and generally took pleasure in seeing to their welfare.

'Not a bad sort,' repeated Maria graciously. 'He has made over to us another room where you shall sleep. It is the room we keep for János when he shall return to visit us one day.'

János. There was something pathetic about their idolisation of this son, Thomas's cousin, who had made a run for it out of Hungary in 1939 and finally reached Canada, via England. In Canada he had settled. Who could tell what Canada was really like? There were photographs, proudly displayed on the fireplace, but those only deepened the mystery. Canada. It seemed an unimaginable adventure, as remote from the daily life of the Hungarian Plain as a fairy story. These two parents still entertained fantasies that one day their son would come back and stay with them. But each time he had tried to make the trip, there had inevitably been trouble with the visas. Still, they both lived on in hope.

'He asked us to come and visit him in Canada,' announced his aunt. 'Canada, Tamás, imagine that. But we're too old now for that sort of junketing. We leave it to the young ones. But he asked us. He made the invitation. He's a good son to us, always has been. See, your uncle Ferenc has the letter somewhere.'

Thomas forbore to point out that the likelihood of their ever being granted exit permits for such a trip was minimal, even if they had been able to afford it. He was the last person to undermine anyone else's self-constructed defences against reality. He knew how important these fortifications could be. It was peaceful to be here, and he was grateful for their hospitality.

'Look at this,' continued his aunt with pride. 'You won't have seen this. He sent it to us last Christmas, all the way from British Columbia. It's a photograph of Leila, our grandchild. She's six now. Isn't that something?'

She'd set it in an old wooden frame which was now pushed eagerly into his hands. The child looked pretty, but pensive. As if she were actually contemplating the strange, outlandish grandparents who gazed so often at her image in such rapt adoration.

'She's a beauty already. She takes after her grandmother,' said Thomas gallantly.

Maria flushed with pleasure and took the photograph back from him, kissing it tenderly before replacing it above the fireplace. Another relic in the shrine.

'How is life in the grand metropolis of Budapest?' demanded Maria later. Ferenc would sit silently and smoke his pipe on the small verandah on these hot summer evenings, but his wife was always fussing, cleaning things, pottering. And asking questions.

'Busy,' said Thomas non-committally.

'How's your teaching going? And do you still write your poems?'

'It's going along fine.' Thomas had told them nothing of his stay in Andrassy Street. There seemed no point in upsetting them.

'Your mother would have been so proud of you. Do you know that, Tamás?'

'That's nice to know.'

Finally Maria could restrain herself no longer. She sank down on to a chair and swept a strand of grey hair out of her tired old eyes and said: 'So what's on your mind? Is it a girl?'

Thomas did not reply immediately, so she went on: 'You're at that stage in life when a young man should start thinking about getting married. Is that what it's all about?'

Was it a girl? How could he begin to explain? He didn't want to speak about anything to do with Greta. Not here. Not now. Not with anyone. So he just said: 'No, there's no one special at the moment. There's been no time for that sort of thing. Perhaps I've been overworking these past few months. That's why the rest here will do me so much good.'

And simultaneously Ferenc growled: 'Leave him alone, for God's sake. He's tired.'

Some afternoons Thomas left behind the clump of acacia trees whose leaves cast dappled shadows on the low-slung cottage's whitewashed walls, and set out to walk into the baking landscape. He needed to lose himself, and it seemed that the ocean of maize and sunflowers into which he was plunging would never end, stretching out in quilt-like strips as far as the eye could see. As he walked he listened to the broad leaves of the maize rustling in the breeze and watched the fields of sunflowers swaying their golden faces to the sky. He marvelled at the long ranks of poplars that drew graceful lines across the plain. Marvelled at their serenity, and their pointlessness. Swallows sat in somnolent rows along the telegraph wires, resting from the heat, waiting for the energy to fly on. Sometimes he passed goats and geese, grazing haphazardly on rough patches of grass yellowed by the sun. And very occasionally an ox-cart would come creaking along the dusty road on a slow progress from nowhere to nowhere. There was something comforting in the absence of purpose. Something consoling about the eternal aimlessness of it all.

Finally on these afternoon walks he would rest, his back propped against a poplar tree, and he would think. Gazing up into the branches high above him, he would go over the events of the previous twelve months again and again. Trying to fit them into a pattern that made sense. Then, even more desperately, trying to fit them into a pattern that didn't make sense.

How had it happened, that first meeting with Greta? He had come into the café of the Astoria Hotel. It had been packed and stiflingly hot. Sod it, he had thought: no room. And then miraculously he'd noticed the table for three with only two places taken. A convenient, solitary chair vacant just at the moment when he happened to need one. Next to two attractive-looking women, one of which was Greta Kassák. Convenient. Or too convenient. A happy chance? Or a well-worked AVO trap?

If it had been a trap, then he had fallen right into it. The ensnarement had been easy. Within a couple of weeks she'd caught him. On to the steamer up the Danube. Into that field in the afternoon heat. She'd played her part well, he had to give her that. Given the chance of another career, she'd have made a consummate actress. Dear God, that slap in the face: how he'd been taken in by it. How he'd wanted to believe in it. And yet, and yet: perhaps that one gesture had been genuine. Perhaps it had been the one moment in their relationship when the woman had asserted itself over the AVO agent. When he'd touched unwittingly some residual feminine pride within her. Oh, Thomas, Thomas. Don't deceive yourself. What had Tibor told him? Your trouble is you always want to see the quick screw as the grand passion. Too much of a romantic at heart.

And after that, the irregular meetings of the autumn. That had been the agent keeping him on a string. Doing the minimum. Leaving the longest possible gaps between their encounters because ultimately they were only a job of work. It was not so difficult to fabricate tenderness provided you didn't have to do it more than once a month. Her husband's alleged position in the party hierarchy had been a convenient excuse. But what about Gellért Hill? What about her apparent change of heart? I'll leave him for you, she had said. If you want me, I'll come to you. Well, she'd had to say that, hadn't she. Her masters had demanded that she relocate the prey and stick close to him until the AVO men had the chance to make a discreet arrest. This had been the best means of achieving that. You can promise what you like to a man when you know he's going to be put away for long enough not to be able to hold you to the promise.

Good work, Kassák, they had no doubt told her afterwards. The dangerous subversive Donat is locked up. Out of harm's way. Thanks to you he has the opportunity to reflect. To discover the error of his ways. The state is very proud of you. Who knows? Rudolf had probably decorated her for her efforts. Given her a medal. And then, remorselessly, she had moved on to her next pre-allocated target. Where would it be? The bar of the Astoria Hotel again? Of course you may share this table. My friend and I were just leaving. What? Stay for one more drink with you? Well, since you ask so nicely, I don't mind if I do. And later would she slap his face, too, in a nicely judged show of outrage? Would some other man's cheek bear the imprint of her palm? The stigmata?

It was Ferenc who made the suggestion, one evening, when Thomas had stayed up late with him, drinking palinka and smoking. There had been long periods of silence, broken now by his uncle laying down his glass and demanding in his low growl of a voice: 'Why don't you go and join him?'

'Who, Uncle?'

'János, of course.'

'What, in Canada?'

'Why not? He'd put you up till you found your feet. He's a good boy, János.'

'Listen, I hardly know him. I'd be imposing on him. And his wife: I've never met her.'

'He's your cousin,' said Ferenc, as if that answered all argument.

Thomas smiled back at him. He realised why his uncle wanted him to go to János. The journey would be a bridge to the son he had lost, hadn't seen for nearly twenty years. He would be travelling vicariously, through Thomas. It would establish a more poignant contact than the irregular letters, if Thomas who was with him now, whom he could physically touch, could be envisaged in the foreseeable future physically touching János.

But Thomas had to be firm.

'No. It's an interesting idea, of course, but I couldn't possibly. Not at the moment. There's too much keeping me here in Hungary.' He paused, and realised that his uncle was still staring at him unconvinced, so he added: 'Unfinished business.'

'Unfinished business,' repeated Ferenc. He shrugged and tapped out his pipe. It was the action of a man who has learned by bitter experience not to entertain too much expectation of life.

16

On the last day of August Thomas received a letter telling him
his name had been reinstated as a lecturer in the arts faculty.
He had undergone an unfathomable process of rehabilitation,
it seemed. He did not pretend to understand it; but he was
miraculously a person again. He hurried back to Budapest
and re-established himself in his room in Béla Bartók Street.
He paused for a moment at the door before letting himself in.
But of course there was no note waiting for him. No note in
Greta's distinctively spidery handwriting.

The mood in the city was different now. At first he had
been inclined to put it down to something within himself: to
the shock of the return from provincial life, his unfamiliarity
with the pace of urban existence. But after a few days he
knew that something unusual was happening. Change was
in the air. Once the new term started, it was impossible not
to notice the fermenting unrest amongst his pupils. There
was constant talk of Poland, and what had been achieved by
student demonstrations in Poznan in June. The graffiti in the
faculty lavatory – always a reliable gauge of the groundswell
of popular opinion – had grown more and more outspoken:
Russians out. Death to Stalinism. Reform now. And various
colourful suggestions as to what the harder-line Stalinists
amongst the teaching staff could do to themselves. Was
there some correlation between the relief of the bladder
and effusion of political feeling, wondered Thomas, trying
to keep his emotional distance from it all. But he knew that
something was building up. Something very big indeed.

Walking back home one Sunday evening in late September,
he turned a corner and found himself immediately enveloped
in a crowd milling about a broken shop window.

'What's going on?' he demanded.

'It's the *Hétföi* Hírlap, the new paper,' a breathless young man in spectacles told him. 'It's just come out and I've got a copy.' He waved it triumphantly in front of Thomas.

'What happened to the window?'

'There was such a crush the newspaper vendor was pushed back through it. He couldn't sell his copies fast enough.'

Thomas took the paper from the young man who hovered anxiously at his arm lest he should become separated from this prized trophy. He glanced at the front page. The leading article demanded a clean sweep of the party leadership, and the public trial of Rákosi and the AVO chief Mihály Farkas. It was extraordinary that people were openly calling for such things, and even more incredible that the authorities were letting them get away with it. You could sense the spontaneous build-up of a huge wave of resentment and revolt, here on the streets of the city. When would the wave break? But as he handed the journal back and walked on home, Thomas felt curiously dispassionate, dissociated from it all. Numbed. As if what he had gone through earlier disqualified him from active participation in the events that he was now witnessing.

On the morning of Thursday 23 October, he arrived at the faculty and recognised immediately that there would be no teaching done today. Lecture rooms had been commandeered for meetings by students. Hastily printed leaflets were being handed out. There was word of a march, a demonstration, starting at Petőfi Square at two o'clock. On an impulse, Thomas walked on across Pest to find Tibor in his room at St Istvan Boulevard.

Tibor greeted him excitedly. 'Come with me,' he said. 'I'm going to Petőfi Square. Great things are happening today.'

'History being made, I suppose.' Thomas often found himself seeking refuge in cynicism these days. It was the only way he could cope with Tibor.

But the irony was lost on Tibor. 'I am sure of it,' he declared. 'There will be a bigger crowd out there today even than for the Rajk reburial two weeks ago. Were you with us then, I don't remember?'

Thomas shook his head. 'No. I heard about it, of course.'

The ceremonial reburial of Rajk, the politician falsely accused and executed by the regime in 1949, and now cleared of wrongdoing, had been a tremendous focus of political opposition. Tens of thousands had taken to the streets. Thomas had stayed indoors, reading essays.

Tibor turned to him. 'So you must come now. Everyone must come with us now.' For a moment they were back in Béla Bartók Street and Tibor was urging him to drop everything for the Writers' Union deputation. Except that then there had been a third person in the room. Greta. Flushed with interrupted love-making. Greta, straightening her skirt and preparing to leave.

'No,' said Thomas, 'no. I don't think I'm in the mood for it just yet. Maybe later.'

Tibor paused, his hand on the door. 'I do not understand you, Tamás. It's as if you are grieving for something. But there is nothing to grieve for now. The time for grieving is past. There is everything to win. Why can't you grasp that?'

Thomas shrugged. 'I have work to do. I have essays to read.' He gestured to the file which he held in his bag.

Tibor said, 'If you're not coming now, then do one thing for me, at least. Wait here for a couple of hours, and when someone called László knocks on the door, receive the parcel he is bringing me. Will you do this one thing for me? It's important.'

Thomas nodded wearily. He suddenly felt the most tremendous lassitude. But he owed his friend something. He would stay and work here in Tibor's room.

It was early afternoon when László came, breathless from running up the stairs. He was a short, dark, angry man dressed in the overalls of a factory worker. He pushed the parcel into Thomas's hands. 'You'll make sure Tibor gets this?' he demanded.

'Of course.' Thomas had been on the point of asking what it was, but stopped himself. It was a long thin object wrapped in brown paper. A walking stick, he'd surmised in his innocence, before he'd taken it in his hands. Then he'd felt the outline of a barrel and a trigger beneath the wrapping. László hurried off again. 'Have you seen the people on the street?' he shouted over his shoulder as he left. 'It's fantastic.'

Thomas laid the parcel across the table and went to the window. It was then that he saw them.

He had never seen such a crowd in such a confined space. Or only once before, at the Népstadion, for a football match, when a sea of humanity had surged out from the exits at the end of the game. Then it had been a sea of exultant humanity, shouting excitedly, going back over the goals they had just witnessed, savouring the victory of their national side. Ferenc Puskás had done it again, weaved his magical spell, and the Swedish defence had fallen apart. Three goals to Hungary in the second half. For a moment it made you glad to be alive. And proud to be Hungarian. But now the atmosphere was different. He looked down from the second-floor window on the swaying force of people moving up St Istvan's Boulevard. His brain registered that he had never seen so many hats on top of so many heads. But his heart registered something different; caught a little spark of the mood of these marchers. They were not exultant, but they were expectant. There was an air of apprehension, perhaps, but a sense of opportunity, too. An opportunity not to be missed.

Part of him was caught up by the thrill of that mass of people. Part of him felt it again: that pride in being Hungarian. It was not just a river of men and women; it was a river animated by a tide of feeling, of hope, of expectation, of determination. It touched his heart, and he felt an unfamiliar tugging, a sudden impulse to get out there too. To merge himself with his countrymen. To be part of this spontaneous upsurge of feeling, this expression of communal resentment and refusal to be pushed around any more.

Still, he might never have gone if he hadn't seen her.

She was across the other side of the street, hatless. In her belted fawn-coloured raincoat, drawn tight so that it emphasised her figure, just like the time on Gellért Hill. He only caught sight of her for a split second, but he was immediately convinced. Or as convinced as a man can be looking down from a second-floor window on to an energised mosaic of humanity and identifying briefly one particle of that mosaic.

He pulled on his coat, slammed the door, and thundered downstairs. What was she doing there? God knew. And what was he going to say to her when he reached her? Again he had no clear idea. But he was driven by an anger: he needed to confront her, to demand explanations from her. He wanted to see if he could dredge from her some tiny molecule of shame, some smallest hint of contrition. He had to address the appalling chasm between the appearance of her attachment to him and the reality of her revealed indifference. Between avowed love and enacted betrayal.

At ground level there was a cacophony. The thud of hundreds of pairs of feet advancing. A mixture of voices in excited conversation, occasionally raised in laughter. Even sporadic singing. Two men just ahead of him walked holding rifles. Here and there the Hungarian flag was carried aloft. Thomas pushed into the mass of people, infiltrating himself between the currents in order to reach the stream on the other side of the road where he had seen her. The marchers were not moving fast. There she was, about twenty metres ahead of him. He bumped into someone's shoulder, apologised, and pushed on. Steadily overtaking, rank by rank.

And then at last he was only two paces behind the slim raincoated figure. He stretched out his hand to accost her. She turned, surprised.

It was not Greta.

She had Greta's figure, there was no doubt about that. But when she turned her face towards him he saw only a pale, rather plain girl. A pale, plain girl with gapless teeth.

'I'm sorry,' he said and edged away.

But there was no going back now against this current. He was borne along like some miserable piece of flotsam on the tide. Up towards the Margit Bridge. Then suddenly he felt a hand on his own arm.

'It's Mr Donat, isn't it? Good to see you here, sir.'

He turned and recognised one of his pupils from the university arts faculty. He greeted him uncertainly, trying to hide his own despair. He found himself asking: 'Where are we heading for, Imre?'

Only then did he realise that, despite eveything, part of

him was curious to know the answer. There was something seductive about the surge of people to which he had involuntarily joined himself. Through close communion with all these fellow-citizens he sensed something seeping back into his heart which he thought he had lost. It was getting through to him, this mixture of hope and determination, an intermingling of individual aspirations which created an aggregate of optimism stronger than the sum of the parts.

'We're going to the Joszef Bem statue,' the boy told him. 'We're going to honour the Polish freedom fighters. Did you hear what they've achieved? Gromylka's in, and the Soviets have had to like it or lump it. If the Poles can get the people they want to run their country, then so can we.'

Thomas laughed. He'd intended it as a cynical chuckle of disillusion. What came out had an unexpected note of elation. Suddenly there were unimagined possibilities.

'Have you ever seen anything like it?' went on the boy, gesturing to the ever-swelling mass of marchers.

Thomas had to admit he hadn't.

'Look: the workers are just out from Csepel Island and they're joining us in numbers. This thing started off with just the students from the university. Now half the population of Budapest seems to be on the streets. Have you seen the list of our demands?' He pushed a poorly duplicated typesheet into Thomas's hand, and Thomas studied it as they walked.

They were unequivocal, those demands. Soviet troops were to be evacuated immediately. Elections were called for, by secret ballot, of all party officials from top to bottom, and of a new National Assembly with all political parties participating. Nagy, the pioneer of the more liberal New Course suppressed by Rákosi, was to be reinstated at the head of the government. Economic reform was to be accompanied by recognition of the workers' right to strike. That symbol of Stalinist tyranny, the statue of the man himself, was to be removed and replaced by a monument to the Hungarian national freedom fighters of 1848–9. The hated hammer and sickle was to go from the Hungarian flag, to be replaced by the old emblem of the arms of Kossuth.

'What do you think?' asked the boy.

Thomas shook his head. 'Wonderful stuff.' He paused, dizzy for a moment. Then suddenly there was the white-robed figure. There was the death's-head. Mocking him. Reminding him of the pointlessness of it all, of the vanity of human effort. Of the hopelessness of trust in anything. Or anyone. Of duplicity and betrayal. When he spoke again, it was in a lower voice. 'But this is unrealistic. This is a dream world. This we will never achieve.'

'I think,' said the boy, 'that if enough true Hungarians come out with us on to the streets now, we can achieve anything.'

Thomas looked at him. He seemed very fresh and young. God, how Thomas wanted to believe him.

Maybe it was possible. Maybe, when you looked at the sheer numbers of people on the street now. Maybe people in this sort of number, if they all wanted something enough, then they could achieve it. Surely it was worth the try, anyway. It would make those party high-ups think again. It would wipe the complacent smiles from their faces. And maybe, just maybe, it would even get to Rudolf. Beyond anything he wanted it to get to Rudolf.

'After this we're going on to Parliament Square,' the boy was saying. 'The government have got to listen to our demands. Will you be coming with us there?'

'I'll be there.' Now he said the words, there was no doubt any more. These people needed him. So long as there was any chance of doing something, he'd be with them. This wasn't about lone voices crying in the wilderness any more. This wasn't about single light bulbs in solitary cells. Here he was with thousands of other people. Thousands of them.

They were going to smash the party shit-heads. They were going to smash Rudolf. They were going to smash the death's-head.

And maybe in the process he'd find Greta. Learn the truth about her. Get her out of his system. Once and for all.

It was the beginning of the most extraordinary week of his life, a time when he lived more intensely than he had ever thought possible. He witnessed the extremes of the human

spirit during those few days: from selfless and exhilarating
heroism to the pitiful depths of cowardice; from extraordinary
restraint in the face of provocation to a bestial gorging in the
most primeval of urges; from moments of supreme elation to
passages of profoundest despair. He discovered an existence
far removed from the cerebral posturings of the academic,
a world where action was everything, where quickness of
body counted for more than quickness of mind. And in the
few brief moments he snatched now and then for thought,
he even began to convince himself that it meant something,
that it wasn't all in vain. That was the most precious
illusion of all.

From the Joszef Bem statue the marchers wound their way
back to Parliament Square. Darkness was falling. People came
out of their doors to join them. Thomas noticed one man
carrying a huge portrait of Stalin, which he very deliberately
held up high, in a parody of reverence. Then he drew it down
and put a match to it. A huge cheer accompanied the flames as
they consumed the image. After that a portrait of Rákosi was
given the same treatment. Thomas felt a huge reassurance, a
sense of submergence in the will of the crowd.

In uncountable numbers they assembled in Parliament
Square. Everywhere you looked there were people, milling
and swirling like the fields of sunflowers on the Great Plain
animated by the wind. The cry went up for the man who,
by general consent, had been deemed their best bet to lead
them to freedom: 'We want Nagy!' Imre was shouting the
simple imprecation at full volume, and suddenly Thomas
found that he was joining in too. He put the full force of
his lungs into it: the unfettered use of his voice was in itself
an emancipation. Finally, at about ten o'clock, Nagy made an
appearance on a distant balcony. Although his moustachioed
face was barely identifiable from where Thomas stood, the
man was greeted with ecstatic cheering. But when he spoke,
it was an anticlimax: he asked the crowd to disperse and
go home. That was it. It was a strangely faltering and
unimpressive performance. For a moment Thomas could
have wept at his lack of bravado, his lack of theatre. But
Imre said, 'The poor bastard's probably got some Communist

gorilla behind him telling him what to say and poking a gun in his back to make sure he says it. What can you expect?'

'So what do we do now?'

'First rule of any effective insurrection,' announced Imre confidently, as if he was a veteran of many: 'Get control of the radio station.'

The radio station. They were in the leading group which made its way to Sándor Street and the Radio Building. Already the mood was different. There was still intense excitement, but the crowd's temperature had risen. Word came through that Stalin's statue on György Dósza Boulevard had been pulled down. The authorities had been powerless to intervene as the crowd heaved on ropes till it crashed to the ground, then hacked the hated symbol of Soviet domination to pieces. This was action at last, not mere words. An envious thrill passed through Thomas. Why hadn't he been there, pulling on the ropes? He sensed others, also, galvanised by the news. Now there must be action here too. There had to be. They must get into the building and broadcast their demands. If necessary by force.

In the jostling mass, Thomas suddenly felt a firm hand on his shoulder, and his name being called. He jerked his head round and there was Tibor, grinning at him. He always remembered that grin. It suffused not just Tibor's face but his whole being. It was an unadulterated expression of delight at the sight of Thomas. At the sight of Thomas here. With the people. On the streets. 'So you came,' said Tibor, squeezing his arm with bony fingers.

'I came,' laughed Thomas. He felt as if he had just drunk four glasses of palinka very quickly. 'I came to make history.'

'It's incredible, isn't it?' Tibor's eyes were bright. Thomas reflected that he had never seen him looking so well. 'All these thousands of people. Talk about a spontaneous uprising. It's not just the students now, you know; and certainly not just the intellectuals. It's the workers, it's the bloody workers. They've all come out from the factories and just piled in here with us. It's a bloody miracle. Christ almighty! Look, we're going in!'

The heavy oak gates of the Radio Building swung open. Suddenly it was all too easy: the crowd surged forward. 'Let's go!' cried Tibor. He had pushed ahead into the vanguard of the protestors now, and Thomas hurried on in his wake, towards the gaping mouth of the entrance. It was almost as if Tibor wanted to be the first in through the doors to prove something. About intellectuals not shirking the front line, perhaps.

Thomas was vaguely aware of a crackle of noise. Simultaneously he saw Tibor trip, then slump, doubled up on the pavement. For a brief second he thought his friend had merely missed his footing. Then he noticed five or six others had done the same, were lying at odd angles on the cobblestones, and he realised the noise he'd heard was machine-gun fire.

It was Imre who helped Thomas pull Tibor into a shop doorway. 'The bastards!' said Imre through clenched teeth. 'Those were AVO men in there, I saw them. They just opened fire on an unarmed crowd.'

Thomas was shaking with shock. They loosened Tibor's collar. His face was very, very white, almost like chalk, and his head had slumped sideways. Thomas reached an exploratory hand inside Tibor's coat and when he withdrew it he found it covered with blood. 'Oh, shit!' he said, very quietly.

'Let me take a look at him,' said a voice above them.

They made way because he spoke with a certain authority. He was an earnest, bespectacled figure with hair already receding although no more than twenty-one or twenty-two. 'I'm a medical student,' he explained as he crouched down with them in the doorway. Thomas noticed two drops of perspiration running down his forehead as he pulled open Tibor's jacket to gauge the extent of the wound, then peered into Tibor's eyes. When he looked up again he shook his head. 'I'm sorry,' he said. 'There's not much we can do for him.'

'But, Christ, we must get him to hospital . . .'

'There's no point now,' said the medical student. His tone was regretful but firm. 'You see, there are a couple of others out there we can save if we get them in quickly. They must have priority.'

He put his head down and scampered across to a doorway

on the opposite side of the street where another casualty lay. When Thomas looked up he saw the oak gates of the Radio Building were closed again. He could hear the shouts of outrage from the crowd, milling up against the doors once more. But the noise was momentarily irrelevant.

'If we could only lay hands on guns ourselves,' muttered Imre. He stood up and looked about him, then edged off into the mass of people. It was as if he had already forgotten about Tibor.

Thomas hadn't. He stayed there, cradling the dying man's head in his arms, listening to the crowd ranting against the AVO men and throwing bricks at the windows. After about twenty minutes a driver wearing a Red Cross armband finally arrived to take Tibor to hospital. Between them they carried Tibor into the back of a baker's van parked two streets away. His body felt very limp. Thomas climbed in with him, the van smelling incongruously of fresh-baked bread. He sat there, still cradling Tibor's head. As the van driver started the engine he said to Thomas: 'They'll never be forgiven for this.'

'Who?' murmured Thomas. But he knew the answer that was coming.

'The AVOs. Firing on defenceless people. Firing on Hungarians, for Christ's sake, their own countrymen. They're worse than animals. They should be shot like dogs. And they will be, too. They'll be shown no mercy if our people get hold of them.'

Thomas didn't reply. Because it was at that moment that Tibor died in his arms. He didn't know how he knew it, but he knew it with absolute certainty.

They left the body at St John's Hospital. A nurse offered him a drink of water and asked him if he was all right. He looked down and saw a lot of blood on his own shirt. Tibor's blood.

He nodded his thanks to her. He was all right. He was all right because he still had the grin to remember. The one smile of sheer unadulterated delight Tibor had ever given him.

The Russians came the next day. The Soviets, in their tanks, to restore order. Normally they lurked in the hinterland outside the city, an unseen menace, the ultimate sanction, only to be deployed as the last resort. Who called them in? Some said Nagy, but Nagy acting under impossible duress; others said, no, it was the last crime of the monstrous hardliner Gero, shortly to be displaced as prime minister. But in their tanks they came, clattering through the streets, inhuman metal slugs with swivelling gun-turrets.

'We're ready for them,' said Imre.

Thomas had made his way into the arts faculty at ten o'clock as usual. It was partly habit, and partly because he didn't want to be alone. Not today. Not after what he'd been through. He left his blood-stained shirt soaking in a bucket in his room in Béla Bartók Street, and slammed the door behind him. He'd slept a few agonised hours, his dreams peppered with the sound of gunfire and the smell of fresh-baked bread. He had to get out. It was a still grey morning as he crossed the bridge into Pest. Mist rose up from the water, clinging to the buildings. No trams were running. There was a curious air of unreality, almost a peacefulness, if you closed your ears to the sporadic shooting from the direction of Parliament Square. The few pedestrians he saw moved quickly, subconsciously hurrying from cover to cover.

He met Imre racing along a corridor in the faculty. He was on the way to a Student Revolutionary Council meeting. As far as Imre was concerned, the situation was in hand.

'Look, the Hungarian army's coming over to us in droves,' he assured Thomas. 'We can take the Soviets, if we stand together. We can force them out.'

'And the Radio Station?'

'We captured it. About three a.m. We got our guns in the end, and disposed of a few AVO men on the way. The problem is, the bastards had sabotaged the transmitter. Our broadcasts aren't getting very far.'

Thomas nodded. Imre had changed overnight. He looked older. He wore a rifle over his shoulder and a belt on which were clipped three hand grenades.

'Where did you get those?' asked Thomas.

'City Police Headquarters in Ferenc Vigyázó Street. They joined our cause last night and distributed their weapons amongst us. Once they heard what the AVOs had been up to, that was. There's no great love for the AVOs amongst those regular police boys.'

'Is there . . . is there anything I can do?' Suddenly Thomas wanted to be part of all this. He wanted to immerse himself in action. He wanted to occupy himself so thoroughly that he did not have time to think about anything. Not about Tibor. Not about Rudolf. Not about the raincoated figure he thought he'd glimpsed momentarily across St Istvan's Boulevard yesterday afternoon.

'You should wear one of these for a start,' Imre told him, reaching into his pocket and producing a ribbon in the Hungarian tricolour. 'Here, take this. For identification.'

'Thank you.' A little awkwardly Thomas pinned it on to the lapel of his jacket. 'But what can I do?'

'Go in there,' suggested Imre, indicating a door. 'They'll find you something.'

For the next few days, Thomas barely slept. In the first chaotic hours of the confrontation with the Soviet army, communication was the problem. So he was given messages to run from control post to control post, in the frantic struggle to co-ordinate the insurgents' efforts. That afternoon on one such mission he saw a Soviet tank for the first time. The noise of its caterpillar treads clattering over the cobblestones was magnified by the enclosing walls of the houses. It was a terrifying, deafening sound, and he stood frozen in a doorway while the column of three wound its way on towards Margit Bridge. How could the revolution stand up to this sort of might?

Later he discovered the answer, watched joyously as freedom fighters took cover from tank fire raking through buildings, then dashed into the dead area in the very shadow of the caterpillar treads, beneath the range of the guns, and tossed their home-made petrol bombs up on to the bodywork. Once fire burned on the armour plating the heat inside the tanks became intolerable. The first Soviet soldier to lift his head out of the cockpit would be picked off by sniper fire. Sometimes his body would wedge itself in the narrow exit, so that his colleagues within could not get out before being overwhelmed by the heat; otherwise if they did manage to push a way through, they too would be finished off by snipers as they emerged.

Not all the Soviet tanks were hostile. The next day Thomas saw one Russian halt his machine in Széna Square and emerge from his cockpit waving a white flag. To the cheers of the crowd he tore the red star from his cap and flung away his gun. 'I didn't come to shoot Hungarians,' he announced, and lit up a cigarette. He allowed the rebels to commandeer his tank, to drape it in the Hungarian flag. The Hungarian flag that had itself been retailored: the hammer and sickle had been torn out, to be replaced by the arms of Kossuth.

Later Thomas came across another Soviet soldier sitting on the pavement, dazed and baffled. 'What is this place?' the soldier demanded. 'Why do they not speak German?'

'This is Budapest,' Thomas told him in halting Russian. 'Here we speak Hungarian.'

'Budapest? Not Berlin?'

'Yes, Budapest.'

'But they told us this was Berlin.' He shook his head in mystification. 'They told us we had come to fight Americans and Germans. To hold back the fascists in Berlin.'

Exhausted, Thomas wandered through the mangled streets of Pest. It was a comfort in a way, this exhaustion. It stopped him thinking too much. He was on his way back to the arts faculty building. Maybe there would be more messages to carry. But maybe tonight he might snatch a few hours' sleep back in Béla Bartók Street. He looked about him. Telegraph wires hung like ribbons in the breeze, everywhere there was broken glass, and at one point tramlines ripped from the roadway had been bent into futuristic sculpture.

He turned a corner, and immediately came upon a dishevelled little man in a beret and a torn coat. He was gesticulating, waving his arms about. Almost pleading. There was a wildness, perhaps a desperation in his eyes. He was standing next to something rather strange. It was a figure hanging upside down from a lamppost, a figure strung up by his feet in the cold autumn wind. But the corpse felt nothing. He'd been beaten round the head by the mob. Then he'd had a couple of rounds emptied into him. He hung there, like a carcass in a butcher's shop.

'Look at the bastard,' the little man was urging Thomas. 'He was AVO, of course. Got what he deserved. And, for shit's sake, what about this? It came out of his pocket. It's his payslip. Do you know what this AVO bastard was being paid? Nine hundred forints a month. Five times a decent worker's wage. And for what? To spy on decent citizens. To throw them into prison. To torture them. Scum, that's what they are. Shooting's too good for them.' He spat viciously at the corpse, then wheeled away in disgust.

Thomas walked on, feeling a little sick. It wasn't the death. He was inured to that. It was the mutilation. The blatant evidence of the breakdown of all civilised restraint. The outpouring of mindless, bestial anger. And worse, it was the chord it momentarily touched within him.

Ahead in Republic Square another crowd had gathered, and he wandered on to investigate. There were men with pickaxes, scrabbling away at the road, hacking at the cobblestones. One by one they were dislodging them and lobbing them aside until the space for a trench had been uncovered. More men appeared with spades, men in raincoats, digging remorselessly, perspiring in the cold October afternoon. What was this? A mass grave, perhaps?

Then Thomas looked up and recognised where he was. He saw the façade of party headquarters. It was like a pock-marked face: holes had been blown in the walls. Many windows had been smashed.

'What are you doing?' he demanded of one of the men labouring with his spade.

'We're digging them out, mate.'

'Who?'

'AVOs of course. We got a lot of the ones inside. But there's more hiding in there somewhere. We've been told there's a web of secret underground cells under here. We're going to flush them out, every last one of them.'

The crowd was urging the diggers on. Thick as some sort of pollutant fog, there was blood-lust in the air.

Thomas wandered on, trying to assimilate what was going

on. AVOs. For a moment he saw the single light bulb again, heard the screaming. Remembered his original interrogator at Andrassy Street, the man with the skin of a desiccated plum. The man with the emotionless eyes. Perhaps that had been him, hanging from the lamppost. And then again, perhaps it hadn't.

Closer to the headquarters building itself five more bodies lay in a line. More AVO men, flung from upstairs windows, then deluged in a mass of their secret dossiers thrown after them. They had died on impact, most of them. But one of them hadn't quite succumbed, it seemed. Maybe he'd twitched, even tried to wriggle away to safety. So someone had come along and finished him off. He'd had his eyes shot away as a final imprint of revenge. He lay there, sightless, staring up to the grey late afternoon sky.

Sightless, like a death's-head.

Thomas was resting back in the arts faculty that evening when Nagy came on to the radio to announce the withdrawal of the Soviets. God almighty! The unthinkable: the Russians were pulling out.

Imre was sitting cross-legged in the corridor, poring over a map of the city, annotating it with a red pencil. He looked up triumphantly. He was still wearing hand grenades on his belt. 'So what did I tell you? We did it – the Russians are on the run. They're finally on the run.'

Thomas smiled back at him, willing himself to believe it.

'We're going to be free. Do you know that? We're going to be free. And you know what the glorious irony of it all is?'

Thomas shook his head. He suddenly felt very tired.

'They brought it on themselves. Unwittingly, the party faithful dug their own graves.'

'How do you mean?'

'They brought it on themselves,' Imre repeated. 'You know what they'd instituted in the steel factory in Csepel? Those ridiculous party ideologues laid down that half an hour each day should be set aside for workers' debate on a subject from that day's *Szabad Nép*. They thought they were stimulating a spirit of Communist self-criticism. What they actually did was awaken people to the possibility of alternative points of view. Sowed the seeds of revolution. And then did you see those boys of twelve making Molotov cocktails as if they'd been born to it? They were taught that skill by those cretinous Russian military instructors in case we were ever invaded by the forces of the West. The beauty of it is the people who bore the brunt of it were the Russians themselves.'

Thomas nodded again. Remembering the twelve-year-olds that hadn't been so lucky. The ones mown down like dolls by the tank-fire.

'Now we can begin to build the Hungary we want,' declared Imre confidently.

'Tomorrow,' said Thomas. 'First I'm going to catch up with some sleep.'

He realised he hadn't been home to bed for four nights.

When he awoke the next morning, he found the shirt still soaking in the bucket of water. Tibor's blood clung to the material. It was past salvaging, and he threw it out. After that he lit a cigarette and stared out of the window for a while. Then he made his decision. It seemed very obvious once he'd made it. He realised the idea had been lurking in the back of his mind ever since the day Tibor had died. It was only now that he had the chance to formulate it as a concrete plan. He'd do it that afternoon.

The janitor let him into Tibor's room. Tibor's things were lying about just as he had left them, but he didn't waste time on the books and bottles, the abandoned pair of boots and the unmade bed. It wasn't part of the plan to get bogged down in the sad relics of the man. He paused to slip into his pocket Tibor's tiny radio. His eyes rested on the essays he'd abandoned uncorrected. He left them as they were. They seemed to belong to another life.

All he wanted was the brown paper parcel that Tibor had never had the chance to come back and collect himself. The brown paper parcel delivered by the man called László a lifetime ago.

He unwrapped it with a sort of pent-up fury. It was a simple shotgun, with a few rounds of ammunition which he forced into his raincoat pocket. Then he set off. He held the gun in his hands, his right forefinger poised over the trigger. In one sense it felt as though it fitted, as though his hands had been made for it. And in another way its unfamiliarity was laughable. He was a grown man playing with a toy. The dividing line between fantasy and reality wavered dangerously. It was only a short step from this point to aiming the barrel and tightening the finger. Squeezing the trigger. And meaning it. Then it wouldn't be a game any more.

He was on his own now. Before he'd realised exactly what it meant, he found himself, gun in hand, striding over Margit Bridge again. And then he was in Buda, climbing the hill towards Rózsadomb. Purposefully. As if he knew exactly where he was going. Occasional passers-by greeted him. Perhaps they were impressed by his gun. 'I hope you killed a few of the bastards,' called one middle-aged lady with a string shopping basket. Russians? AVOs? He raised a hand in silent acknowledgement and paced on. No, my dear madam, look at me. I am an academic, not an assassin. I have not killed anyone. Not yet.

How had it gone? A left turn after this street. Then, surely, a sharp right turn at the bottom. Or was it left again? Had he got it wrong? In a sudden fury, he decided that it wasn't possible to have got it wrong. Or if he had got it wrong, he was going to tramp the streets until he got it right. Until he found it again. A chill breeze blew. Snow was in the air. But there was no turning back, not now.

Yes, there it was. The relief flooded through him. A sense of triumph caused him to pick up pace as he approached his goal. There in the twilight was the line of silver birch trees. There was the elegant colonnade; there were the fresh-painted shutters. A light burned in a downstairs window. Rudolf's house. And Rudolf was in there.

And then it came to him with full force: of course, that was it. That was what he was doing here. He was going to kill Rudolf.

He was filled with a terrible elation as he pushed in through the gate and made his way along the garden path to the colonnade. The last time he had taken this journey there had been two AVO heavies at his back, pushing him on, directing his stumbling steps. Now he could measure his pace. Now he was going to dictate what happened. Destiny was in his own hands. The rifle butt and barrel which comforted his palms would impose his own will. He was going to make things right.

Everything was possible now. He'd seen the lines of AVO corpses. He'd seen the Soviet tanks retreating from the city. He'd seen enough of his countrymen wanting something badly enough for the miracle to happen. Hungary was going to be free. Free of Russian domination. Free of the insidious power of the secret police. And all because enough people had taken to the streets and asserted their will. Now he was going to assert his own personal will. He was going to set himself free. He was going to end the life of his tormentor. He was going to set himself free from Rudolf. And maybe thereby set himself free from Greta. His act of self-liberation was going to stand as a metaphor for his country's own release. Just this one final step and they would all be free.

He was at the front door now, the heavy wooden door that had been opened by another AVO thug on his last visit here. Now he leant against it and it opened with only a slight push from his shoulder. He stood for a moment in the light of the hallway. Feeling the gun in his hand. Reassuring himself.

He heard a voice calling out from the drawing-room. Rudolf's voice. Rudolf's voice, raised in enquiry as to the identity of his visitor. Rudolf's voice, unlike he'd ever heard it before. Because it had an edge of uncertainty.

When Thomas came into the room, Rudolf was standing by a table with a sheaf of papers in his hand. He was wearing a heavy overcoat, as if he was on his way out. He turned abruptly, and his sleeve caught a glass which crashed noisily to the floor.

'I have come for you, Rudolf,' said Thomas quietly. He had to speak quietly to conceal the breathless excitement which was consuming him. To hide the terrible elation.

Rudolf swore. It was the first time Thomas had seen him unfeignedly angry. On the run. 'What are you doing here?' he demanded. His eyes were on the gun.

'I have come for you,' Thomas repeated.

'You fool. What are you: some one-man execution squad?'

'No. I'm not an execution squad for myself. I am here on behalf of my country. If I shoot you, it is Hungary shooting you. Not me. For crimes you have committed against this country.'

Rudolf's gaze was still on the gun. He took a couple of tentative steps backwards towards the fireplace. The fireplace. For a moment Thomas wavered. Don't look up. For God's sake, don't look up now. Avoid the rocks. Forget those cruel cypress trees. Whatever you do, don't let your eyes rest on the figure in the boat.

Rudolf was speaking again. 'You're a fool, Tamás Donat. Do you really think that you and your fellow-traitors can make an iota of difference to what happens here? Do you think that your few pathetic gestures of resistance will carry any weight in the end? You're pissing into the wind. Don't you see it? You'll be crushed.'

Thomas kept his eyes locked firmly on Rudolf. He wasn't going to look to left or right. Or up. 'You're wrong,' he said. 'You're on the way out. The Soviets are retreating. They're not staying here now.'

'Dream your dreams, little man.' Rudolf's self-assurance seemed to be returning. 'Your little insurrection will be knocked flat in weeks. Days probably. The Russians will be back, in force. Don't make any mistake about that.'

'So why are they leaving, then?'

'Do you know your French, Tamás? Of course you do, you who are such an accomplished linguist. Do you know the phrase "*Reculer pour mieux sauter*"?'

'You have to say that.' He raised his rifle in Rudolf's direction. 'But you're wrong.'

Rudolf backed off even further. He was standing on the hearth of the fireplace, almost against it now. It was as if he were drawing Thomas's gaze ever closer to the one object in the room which he didn't want to look at. As if he were doing it deliberately, to break the spell of his power. As if it were a battle of wills.

Then Rudolf smiled. Horribly. When he spoke it was with

that insinuating persuasiveness that Thomas remembered from before. 'You know, you're deluding yourself.'

Concentrating very hard on returning the stare Thomas said, 'No, I am right.'

'Tamás, Tamás. You were wrong before. You're wrong again now.'

He felt his hand on the barrel, and his forefinger on the trigger. He swallowed hard. 'How was I wrong before?'

'Don't deceive yourself. You were wrong about her, weren't you? You were wrong about Greta . . . about Greta Kassák. You thought she loved you.' Rudolf shrugged. It was a gesture of urbane regret for human fallibility. It was the action of a man of the world explaining the facts of life to an *ingénu*. 'I suppose you're thinking about shooting me now. There's no point, is there? It won't bring her back. It won't change history. It won't make her love you now, and it won't make her have loved you in the past. Any more than it will ensure the Russians don't come back and crush the lot of you. Can't you see the futility of it all? Can't you see that, Tamás?'

For a moment Thomas closed his eyes. Then he couldn't resist any longer. He was looking at the picture. He was in there. He had lost himself on the rocks. The black waters were lapping against the shore, and the angle of the precipice was as sheer as ever. The boat glided soundlessly towards its destination, and the white-robed figure turned back to confront him. Merciless, implacable. Perhaps he'd get away from Rudolf. One day, maybe, he'd get away from Greta. But he'd never get away from that figure in the boat. With his blown-out eye sockets, and his stench of death.

Suddenly he found he was crying. Tears were coursing down his cheeks. His hand was shaking as he tried to raise his aim once more in the direction of Rudolf. He could hear the mad birds crying. He could feel the cypresses blowing in the wind. He was vaguely aware that Rudolf was right up against the fireplace now, pressed against it. That his fingers were grasping out for something.

Then he heard the shot. For a moment he heard it as an observer, not a participant. Then it dawned on him: it was his gun. He'd managed to pull the trigger. Christ almighty, he'd

done it. He heard the scream, of anger and pain. Rudolf was
bent, his hands clasped round his calf. And then he realised
that because of his wayward aim he'd only hit him in the leg,
that it wasn't enough, that he must pull the trigger again. That
he must finish the job.

But before he could fire again, he registered that something
else was happening. Something extraordinary. Like an earth-
quake. The whole room was moving. Or more precisely the
fireplace where Rudolf had been standing clutching his lower
leg was revolving, like some sort of stage set. Rudolf was
being turned away from him. And so was the picture hanging
behind Rudolf. Together, inexorably, they were disappearing
from view.

He must act instantly, before it was too late. He raised
the gun again, determined to aim straight this time. Aim
for his head. Quick, before he's gone. With a gigantic effort
of concentration he lined up the rapidly diminishing target.
And squeezed the trigger.

Nothing. Oh, God. He should have reloaded.

The rotation was almost complete. Thomas sprang forward
to pull Rudolf back with his own bare hands. But he was too
slow. The whole mechanism clicked into place. Where the
fireplace had been, he was confronted with bare wooden wall.
He beat impotently on it with his fists.

No Rudolf. No picture. Together they had made their
escape. It was almost as if the one had melted irretriev-
ably into the other. As if the boatman had borne Rudolf
away too.

But he hadn't, had he? In his heart, Thomas knew that
Rudolf wasn't dead. You didn't die from being shot in the
calf. No, Rudolf had borne the boatman away rather than
the other way round. Rudolf had asserted his will even over
death itself.

Thomas ran out into the hall, trying other doors .which
led him into a series of empty rooms. Then he ran out into
the garden. Again there was no sign of his quarry. It was
impossible to see where Rudolf could have got to. Unless
the stories were true. Unless the system of underground
tunnels that he'd seen men feverishly trying to dig up in

Republic Square that afternoon also existed here. And the rotating fireplace had spilled Rudolf out into a subterranean escape route.

Defeated and exhausted, Thomas leant against one of the silver birch trees. The gun slipped from his hand and on to the frosty grass at his feet. He had failed. Failed to wipe out Rudolf. And in that failure he suddenly recognised with sickening and absolute clarity the inevitability of the failure of the whole revolution. Rudolf had been right. Rudolf was never wrong. Rudolf had won. The Russians would be back, as surely as winter followed autumn, just as Rudolf said they would.

Thomas was deluding himself. He was the ultimate self-deceiver, wasn't he? He'd persuaded himself that the Hungarian people could throw off the Soviet yoke by means of a succession of marches and a few street battles. He'd convinced himself that the woman they had sent to compromise him really loved him when all she had been doing was obeying orders. And he'd thought he could kill Rudolf. He was wrong every time. The futility of everything closed in on him and the tears came again. Hopeless tears. Tears dredged from depths profounder even than the black waters which lapped The Island of the Dead.

Minto reached out helplessly to the weeping man in the hospital bed. He saw the bony hand outstretched to him in grief, and he recognised it. This was the hand he should have held that other time when it was offered to him. This was the hand he'd turned away from then. This was his father's hand all over again. But this time, in desperation, he took it. This time he clutched it. As if the pressure might suppress the tears.

And miraculously after a time they began to subside.

'I am sorry,' whispered Donat, 'so very sorry.'

'You must rest now,' said Minto. 'Get some rest.'

Gently he withdrew his hand from the old man's. There was a limit, even now, to his compassion.

'No, wait.' Donat's voice was urgent again. 'There is one thing more. One thing I wish you to see before you go.'

'What do you want me to see?'

'I want to show her to you.'

'Her?' But he knew who Donat meant, immediately.

'She is in my wallet. There, in the cupboard by the bed. Get it out for me, please, I want you to see her.'

Minto knew exactly what he was looking for as he took the battered brown wallet from the locker and opened it up. He extracted the small, worn, grainy snapshot. The one that Thomas had taken that summer's day on the Danube Bend. The one Thomas had nearly thrown to the Atlantic waves from the boat taking him to Canada. And he saw her. Greta Kassák.

She was beautiful. That was undeniable, even in the fading brown tones of the photograph. Her hair was drawn back from her face and blew slightly in the breeze on the deck of the Danube steamer. She had clear, olive skin. And you could just see her teeth. The row of front teeth with the gap in the middle.

This was the woman who Thomas Donat believed had betrayed him. And the revelation of that betrayal had come to him in the painting. In *The Island of the Dead*.

'Thank you,' said Minto softly. 'Thank you for letting me see it.'

At last he got Isabella on the telephone that evening.

'I need to see you again,' he told her.

There was silence. A wavering silence. 'Oh my God, Minto. Why can't you leave me alone?'

'I'll come back to Munich. I've got to see you.'

'No, not Munich.' She was suddenly definite.

'You must come to London then.'

'No, I couldn't bear it. I hate it in London.'

'Do you want to see me again?'

'Christ, Minto. What are we doing? Are we crazy?' She paused, then it came in a rush: 'For God's sake, then, take me somewhere else. Somewhere away from all this. Somewhere different.'

'We'll go to Budapest.' He said it without thinking, but perhaps the idea had been there for some time in the back of his mind. Maybe it had been originally implanted by Betts. Betts was his paper's travel editor, and Betts had a closely guarded list of places available for selected staff to visit on freebies. These assignments were doled out as perks, to special friends and deserving cases. A weekend in Budapest was on that list, he'd seen it. And maybe what Donat had just told him precipitated it. After Donat's narrative, Minto needed to see the place. To get things straight. To understand. And for Isabella Budapest would be different. It would be anonymous. No one would know them there.

'Budapest?' She paused, then sighed. 'Why not?'

Later, after they'd made the arrangements, she seemed happier.

'My father always said that Hungary was the pits,' she mused, 'but what the hell? What did he know?'

What did he know? wondered Minto as he gently replaced the receiver.

17

A thin film of greasy cloud obscured the hot afternoon sun as Minto's flight from London landed at Budapest. The air was sultry and uncomfortable, and the place was alien, perceptibly rougher and wilder and more eastern than Bavaria. He stood for a moment in the arrivals hall, imagining Isabella coming through the gate from Munich in a few hours' time, marvelling suddenly at the miraculous fact that she was coming here for him. He decided to make his way into the city and wait for her at the hotel.

'No,' said the woman at the airport information desk, 'you no take taxi. Is much expensive, cost four thousand forints. You take airport bus, is like taxi, but only cost six hundred forints. No different, deliver you to front door of your hotel.' Minto, uncharacteristically unsure of himself, agreed and immediately regretted it as he was dragooned into a waiting area and told to sit with his luggage. Twenty minutes later the driver arrived, a feckless youth in dark glasses and a lurid green jacket, and Minto was piled into a passenger van with four middle-aged Americans. The interior smelt of fried onions. One of the American ladies pronounced herself 'nauseous'. Minto felt apprehensive, strangely tense. He knew he wouldn't relax until he was certain Isabella was coming. Until she'd actually arrived.

As they swayed along the dual carriageway through straggling suburbs and industrial wastelands, Minto looked out and observed the signs of Westernisation, the outward manifestations of Hungary's embrace of the capitalist dream: there were the advertisements for banks and credit cards and German automobiles; for clothes and computers. The same advertisements which decorated the approach roads to airports all over Europe. That was the market economy. It made everything look the same. Just once, when they paused briefly at traffic lights, he caught a glimpse of the rougher world behind the publicity hoardings. Behind a wall abutting the highway, a wall decorated with the neon image of a state-of-the-art video camera, there was an old man with a blue plastic bucket scavenging through a rubbish tip.

The hotel was modern, one of an American chain. Once inside he regretted this choice, too. The bedroom was comfortable enough, but there was nothing distinctive about the surroundings. Only when you went to the window and peered out at an angle did you catch a glimpse of the Danube and suspect you might not be in Manchester or Düsseldorf. Everything else was uniform. Thomas Donat would not have recognised this room as being in his birthplace, Minto reflected. And obscurely that depressed him.

Thomas Donat. Images from the man's story still haunted him, drifting in and out of his consciousness, their horror difficult to separate from the grim setting of the hospital in which Thomas lay. The images were of death. Like Tibor, dying in his arms. Like the children, puppets mown down by Soviet tank-fire. Like the figure in the boat in the picture. The skull with the mocking eyes.

Minto picked up the tourist magazine on the table and skimmed through it. Budapest, he read, was a city of free enterprise, capital of a country which had cast aside the shackles of restrictive Socialist practice. Business is booming, the magazine declared in bold type. As if by shouting something loud enough you could actually make it happen. Minto thought back to the old man with the plastic bucket scrabbling amongst the rotting vegetables.

He unpacked, showered, and put on a clean shirt. Then he lifted the telephone and dialled a number, as much out of curiosity as anything else.

It was a number he'd been given by his newspaper's Vienna bureau. Besides Austria, the correspondent there covered Czechoslovakia and Hungary, too. She was called Anna Schwarz and she was half Hungarian herself, so he'd figured she might know the direction in which to point him.

'What, the revolution?' she had said when he'd rung her

from London. 'You want an authority on the revolution of fifty-six? Half the population of Budapest that lived through it considers themselves authorities on the subject. Even the ones who were babes in arms at the time. But I do know someone who might help you. Try Toth, Dr László Toth. He used to teach at the university. Now he runs a bookshop where he's created a sort of historical archive of the revolution. He's got everything: newspaper cuttings, files, photographs. Even pieces of Russian tank. He's a bit of an obsessive. But you could try him. He probably knows as much as anyone.'

The voice that answered his call now was deep. And immediately enthusiastic. 'You are English, Mr Maitland? That is good, sir. Look, to speak English is for me always a pleasure, OK? I would be honoured to help you in your research. What exactly do you wish to know?'

'I'm trying to trace a woman who I think was an AVO agent in 1955. I know it's a very long shot, but her name was Kassák, Greta Kassák. Do you have any record of her?' And then he added as an afterthought, as a wild throw, as a piece of wishful thinking: 'It's just possible that she was married. It's just possible she could have had a husband called Peter.'

'Kassák.' Toth paused. Suddenly the line was very silent. For a moment Minto wondered if they'd been cut off. 'Kassák,' Toth repeated at last. Minto sensed him weighing the name up, as if it was an anagram or a puzzle of some sort.

'Yes. Greta Kassák.'

'It's an interesting question you ask me about this name Kassák. I have a feeling that it may not be entirely unfamiliar. I'm going to have to check my files, but ... No, it must wait till I have been through them. How long are you staying, Mr Maitland? You will still be here on Sunday?'

'Certainly.'

'Come to me on Sunday morning, then. Come at twelve. I will open the shop for you, and I will show you what I have found.'

Minto replaced the telephone thoughtfully. He was thinking of the man in the hospital bed, and his sad watery eyes. Of the feel of the weak hand in his own. He remembered the battered photograph of Greta. Maybe she had been simply an AVO agent, but there remained a lingering doubt. He wanted to help Thomas Donat. He wanted to give him peace.

At 8.15 that evening she arrived. The porter carrying her bag opened the door and Isabella came in before him. She ran appraising eyes around the room before allowing them briefly to rest on Minto. Suddenly he felt how little he knew her, how unfamiliar she was. He was unexpectedly shy of her. He approached and kissed her on the cheek.

'Give him something, will you?' she said. 'I've got no Hungarian money.'

He fumbled in his pocket and handed over too large a note.

When they were alone she sat down on the bed and stretched her legs. 'God, it's hot,' she sighed.

'Good journey?'

'So-so.'

'Did you come on that awful airport taxi? Or did you take a proper one?'

'Neither. I was given a lift.'

'Who by?'

She was offhand. 'Oh, someone I met on the plane who had a car meeting him.'

Minto felt a sick acid-swell of jealousy in his stomach. 'That was well arranged.'

She turned on him, angry. 'Look, you don't own me. OK?'

At dinner she was different, restrained. They talked politely, like acquaintances who have met by chance and decided to share a table. She kept her distance deftly, not rising to his compliments, retreating from his intimacies.

'Look at this,' she said as they drank their coffee. Open in her hand she had a small guidebook to Budapest. 'There are some really weird museums in this place.'

'Like what?'

'Well, it says here there's an elevator museum.'

'What, a museum of lifts?'

'That's what it sounds like.'

Minto laughed. 'A bit surreal, isn't it?'

'Oh, and this one's a must. Tomorrow we've got to visit the Meat-Processing Industry Museum.'

'Essential,' he agreed. But he felt uneasy with her in this mood, knowing her blandness was an act, but unable to identify its purpose.

He decided to smash it, this carapace of politeness. Better her passion than her indifference. The time had come to raise the subject of her father. When he told her he'd been making progress on the article, her eyes dropped, and she sighed. 'Is it nearly finished now?'

'Not quite, no. But I'd like to tell you about it. My investigations have thrown up something rather interesting concerning your father. Something you might not know.'

'Oh? What's that?' She spoke dully, but he could sense the tension in her again. The same ambivalence. The same simultaneous fascination and recoil.

'I met a woman who knew your father in the old days. She was his neighbour in the 1950s when he was living in north London with his mother, before your grandmother died in the car crash. I went to see her.'

'Did you?' she said.

'I did. And do you know what? She told me your father had a cousin. A cousin from Austria, who turned up to visit them and stayed with them a while.'

Her eyes blazed. 'What are you talking about? There was never any cousin.'

'Why do you say that? How are you so sure?'

'There was never any cousin,' she repeated. She said it very clearly, with emphasis. In order to close the conversation. Then she dropped her napkin on to her plate and got up. 'Look, I'm very tired. I'm going up.'

Minto followed her some minutes later. When he came into their room, she was already in bed, lying on her back chewing her thumb. She was wearing a peach-coloured silk nightdress, through which he could see her nipples. He undressed quickly and got into bed next to her. When he switched off the light she turned towards him and put her arms round him.

'Oh, Christ!' she murmured into his hair. 'This is serious now. You realise that, don't you?'

It was as if the darkness was a release, creating a temporary freeport for the emotions, a place where they could be declared without being taxed.

'It's serious,' he breathed.

'I don't know how I let it happen.'

'I'm glad you did.'

'No, no. You don't understand. It's out of control now.' There was a desperation to her tone. Almost a misery.

'How do you mean?'

'Each step, I thought I could control it. I thought when I agreed to see you again in Munich, it need go no further. I thought when I accepted to have dinner with you in Munich, I could leave it at that. I even thought when I slept with you that same night, I needn't see you again. Now here I am in a hotel in Budapest with you. Where's it going to end for God's sake?'

'Why can't you just be happy? Why can't you just enjoy it?'

She paused before answering, then said: 'Because I resent you, Minto.'

'Why?'

'I resent you because you're threatening my father's memory. I resent you because you're threatening my marriage. I resent you because I've fallen in love with you.'

He felt an enormous tenderness for her, so huge that it stifled him and he could hardly breathe. 'My darling, don't resent me. I love you too. You must know that.'

'Oh, that's easy for you to say.' She spoke from the bitter depths of her heart. 'You've got nothing to lose. It's so unfair. You've got nothing to lose but you've got the power to destroy everything. I can't forgive you that.'

She turned away from him and he reached out to her in the dark, trying to draw her back.

'No,' she said, 'leave me alone now.'

'Isabella.'

'No. I'm very tired. And I need to think. Dear God, I need to think.'

The next morning the weather changed. Thicker grey cloud

shrouded the city and there was sporadic rain. The concierge promised it would clear by the afternoon, but no one was inclined to believe him. Standing next to her under the awning of the hotel entrance, Minto listened to the sounds of an unfamiliar city: metal tram wheels resounding like tuning forks as they ground against the rails; people shouting at each other in an alien language. She shivered.

'Why didn't you take me to Venice?' she muttered.

'Why Venice?'

'Think of it: all those bells, and the constant lapping of the water.'

Uneasy, he said: 'Who took you to Venice?'

She did not answer immediately. When she spoke again it was in a softer voice: 'My father did. A long time ago.'

. He said: 'It rains in Venice too, you know.' And as he said it he began to wonder of whom he was the more jealous: her husband or her father.

She patted him on the arm. Consolingly. 'Don't worry,' she said. 'This morning I'm not going to be difficult. I am pleased to be here, and I want to see the city. Where shall we go first?'

A taxi drew up and he guided her in. 'Perhaps the Meat-Processing Industry Museum?'

'I think it can wait,' she said, smiling.

'Museum of Fine Art,' he said to the driver.

It had stopped raining when they emerged from the gallery, and they strolled a while over damp pavements. They reached a junction of roads where Minto paused and gazed down the long street which lay before him. And it was here that, without warning, the past overwhelmed him.

Suddenly he could see the barricades. The grey mist deadened the colours, subverting the crisp outlines of the elegant nineteenth-century façades into the quality of an old photograph, and suddenly he could imagine the derailed trams, the telegraph wires hanging loose, the sound of distant sniper fire, and the smell of burning. The shops that days before were selling cakes and sweets and women's dresses stood empty, their windows smashed. Families with children cowered behind locked doors and drawn curtains. Below, zig-zagging across the tramlines to seek better angles of fire from the deserted doorways, ran the street-fighters. Single-minded men. Patriots, madmen and murderers. Common criminals and heroes. Barely forty years ago, Soviet tanks had been ambushed in these thoroughfares, ambushed and destroyed. He reached out a hand and touched the brickwork of the building next to him. This wall had borne witness to the struggle. This wall had resounded to explosion and gunshot, to the cries of dying men. The violence had seeped into the stonework.

Minto looked up and saw the name: Andrassy Street. He caught a whiff of history. Saw past the advertisements for pop concerts, for perfumes, for Mercedes and all the paraphernalia of Western consumerism in the 1990s. Saw Andrassy Street grey and unyielding. As it must have looked to Thomas Donat when he'd been taken into custody, sockless and shivering in the depth of the night. As it must have looked to him numberless months later when he had been spilled out into it a broken man. As it must have looked later in 1956 with terrified pedestrians running in and out of doorways, sheltering from gunfire behind overturned trams. As it must have looked with Soviet tanks marauding up it like monstrous, vengeful insects.

He sensed Isabella at his side. Isabella, impatient now and annoyed.

'I'm going in here for a drink,' she said. 'I'm exhausted.'

He followed her into the café and they sat in the window watching the life of the street. She undid her jacket, let it sink down off her shoulders on to the back of the chair. There was a richness about her, an opulence to her movements.

'You're very quiet,' she said. 'What are you thinking about?' She had a way of lacing her tenderness with irritation.

He fingered the cuffs of his shirt. He spoke still staring out of the window up Andrassy Street. Not looking at her. 'I'm thinking about a man I met not long ago in London. A Hungarian.'

'Who was he?'

'I met him in connection with something I was writing. He

was ... he was rather an unhappy man, I think. He told me a lot of things about life here when times weren't so good. Under Communism. In 1956.'

'In 1956?' She ran graceful fingers through her short-cut hair, touching it back into place.

'The time of the revolution.'

'Oh, the revolution.' She paused. Her irritation was suddenly increasing. It was like a wall between them. 'Can't we order something? I've never known anyone as slow as you at getting a waiter's attention.'

He took his eyes from the view outside. For a moment he felt angry with her in return. But he called over the moustachioed figure from the bar and ordered two cups of coffee. The man had almost made it back to the bar again when she said: 'Actually, I'd rather have hot chocolate.'

'Christ almighty, Isabella,' he said through clenched teeth. He got the man back and changed the order.

She was doing it deliberately, of course. She enjoyed annoying him. She throve on friction. She had to create it. It was her stimulation. And her revenge.

'Something wrong?' she asked coolly.

'Nothing.' He stared out of the window again. In silence. He wouldn't give her the satisfaction of a reaction. Somewhere up that street, in a cell beneath the ground, a man had been imprisoned for weeks without end, for an immeasurable length of time, in a windowless little room lit by a single implacable light bulb. For a moment he also felt like a prisoner with this woman. She had him trapped, as surely as if the door was locked and bolted on him too.

Finally she said, 'Go on about your little man. The Hungarian.'

Your little man. He felt the jagged edge of anger. Patronising bitch. But he swallowed hard and continued: 'He told me a story. About how he fell in love with a woman here in 1955. It was just before the revolution. He was betrayed to the AVO, the secret police; he was tortured; and he was left with the awful nagging suspicion that it was she who betrayed him.'

'Why should it have been the woman?' Minto registered

that sudden clarity of tone that he'd heard before from her at moments when her attention or imagination was fully engaged. That sudden freedom from distortion. The way she'd been in front of the Tissot. The way she'd answered when he had first asked her out.

'He'd been in trouble with the authorities. He'd been part of a deputation of writers protesting at the government's curtailment of their freedom of speech. As a result he moved to a secret address. But she found out where he was staying and it seems she led them to him.'

'How did he know it was her?' She was intrigued. No, more than that, she was involved.

'She was the only person that could have told them. They came when she was in bed with him.'

'I don't call that very persuasive evidence. Maybe they just followed her without her knowing. Maybe she was in love with him too. Maybe she just couldn't keep away from him. Maybe she went to him against her better judgement. Because she couldn't help herself. Christ almighty, it happens you know.' She chewed angrily on her nail.

'Does it?'

She didn't reply at once. He sensed the resentment again. The fury that he'd made her compromise herself over him. Sensed the way that part of her was fighting against it.

'You bloody well know it does,' she whispered at last.

They sat in silence for a while before he went on: 'Well, my friend convinced himself that she'd betrayed him. The AVO men seemed to know too much about her. It seems she'd been working for them all along.'

'Men always want to believe the worst about women,' she said bitterly.

He was on the point of telling Isabella that according to the woman's story she'd already betrayed her own husband. But he stopped himself in time.

Isabella went on: 'I can see you do too. In your heart, you don't trust women. You probably don't trust me, do you? Go on, be honest.' This wasn't teasing. This was real. Suddenly she was spoiling for a fight. 'You don't trust me, do you?'

'I trust you, Isabella.'

'You say that now.'

'I trust you. Are you telling me I shouldn't?'

She didn't reply. She lit a cigarette and stared away from him. He looked out of the window again, up Andrassy Street. Into the misty distance. People with shopping bags were hurrying by. Confident, happy people. Preoccupied people. Bored, impatient people.

His eyes rested on the lamppost twenty metres beyond, and suddenly he saw with shocking clarity the image of the bloodied carcass of the AVO man hanging upside down. To be hated. To be spat upon.

'Do you think she's still alive?' Isabella was talking again.

'Who?'

'The wretched woman who you're so sure betrayed him.'

'I don't know. She could be.'

'Do you know her name at least?'

'She was called Greta. Greta Kassák.'

She paused. As if something very distant had stirred in her memory. 'You ought to find her. And ask her. Whether she betrayed your friend. God, 1956 isn't that long ago. She's probably only sixty or so. She could tell you once and for all now.'

'Come on,' he said, standing up. 'Let's go for a walk.'

For a moment he thought she was going to resist. Resist as she did so many of his suggestions. As a matter of principle. As a gesture of defiance. But for once she followed him without protest, pausing to pull the jacket back over her shoulders. She moved with a coltish grace, and he was struck once more by how beautiful she was. How agonisingly attractive he found her.

'OK,' she said. 'Where are we going?'

'Where would you like to go?'

'Let's go to the river. Let's go and look at the Danube.'

They meandered through the streets to Parliament Square and stood for a moment absorbing the gothic grandeur of the parliament building. Here, thought Minto; this must have been the place where Thomas Donat stood on that dark October night with thousands of his countrymen waiting for Nagy. He tried to envisage it, what it must have been like. The

smashed portraits of Stalin. The mood of anger, and of
expectation. And when Nagy didn't give them satisfaction,
the determination to move on. To the radio station. Thousands
of pairs of feet, trudging remorselessly out of this square to
their next goal. For some, like Tibor, it was the last journey
they would make.

She peered about her, frowning. Then, looking up across the
river to Buda, she caught sight of the rocky promontory rising
sheer from the embankment, crowned by the melodramatic
figure in black with arms raised to the skies.

'What's that?' Isabella demanded.

'I think it's called Gellért Hill.'

'And what's that statue?'

'It's the Hungarian statue of liberty.'

'It's rather magnificent in a vulgar sort of way.' She paused.
'Can we get up there? I bet there's a wonderful view from
the top.'

They caught a taxi which wound an interminable route
up behind the hill and deposited them on the stone rampart
at the summit. They waited a moment to allow a party of
earnest German tourists to pass. Some wore shorts; others
had pink plastic raincoats and batteries of camera equipment.
They had been rained on earlier in the day and they straggled
by morosely, shepherded towards their coach like remnants of
a defeated army. Then he led her to the railings and looked out
over the city. As the concierge had predicted, the cloud was
beginning to break. Beyond the suburban apartment blocks
Minto could just make out the misty woodlands which ran
down to the river to the north, towards the Danube Bend.
Nearer to, on the Buda side beyond the castle, he could see
Rózsadomb, an undulation of grand white houses. And there
was the parliament building again, further up on the Pest side;
seen from above it looked smaller, like a child's model.

'You were right,' he said. 'It's spectacular.'

'I like heights,' she said.

For a moment he was obliquely reminded of the view from
Elaine's office on the fourteenth floor. 'The illusion of power?'
he asked.

She thought for a moment and then said seriously: 'No, it's

not power. I'm not looking for power. It's something else.' She paused. 'Perhaps it's only distance.'

They turned away and looked up behind them. They were at the base of the gigantic black figure of Liberty holding an offering to the sky. There was something faintly absurd about the extravagance of the gesture, and she suddenly laughed. He recognised it as the signal of her change of mood. He was elated.

'And what about this chap?' he asked, pointing to the secondary statue on a pedestal next to them. The naked athlete struggling with a griffin. 'He's a bit of a monster.'

She giggled again. 'Well built, isn't he?'

They stood for a moment, inspecting it. Running their eyes over the exaggerated strength of the limbs. Then without warning she leant across and kissed him. Only on the cheek, but something in the action excited him. 'Seen enough?' he breathed.

She nodded. 'Let's get a taxi back to the hotel.'

In the back seat the current of attraction between them was suddenly charged. He put his hand gently on her thigh, then kissed her on the lips. When he drew his tongue across to her earlobe she arched her neck in an attitude of such physical abandon that he had to draw back from her, in order to restrain himself.

The concierge smiled benignly at them as he handed over the room key. 'You see it turned out well after all,' he said with satisfaction. Minto nodded at him as he drew her into the lift.

In the bedroom they eased each other out of their clothes with a suppressed urgency. When he had first seen her, standing against the wall in Courtney's, aloof, in black, he had imagined her body to be thin and spare. Now once again he was taken by surprise at her opulence, her undulations; the fullness of her breasts; the way her figure reminded him of a violin. Her hand closed over the back of his head, squeezing his hair, pulling it as he kissed her. Along the full length of their bodies, their skin touched.

He felt her grinding against him again, felt the anger in

her passion. But this time her aggression gradually turned in on itself, dissolved, and by the end she was clinging to him like a shipwrecked mariner to a life-raft, gasping for breath. He held her close for a long time, because he didn't want her to regret it.

'I've got a confession to make to you,' she breathed. She reached across the bed and brushed a strand of hair from Minto's eyes. Now she was looking at him unwaveringly. 'Last night I told you my father didn't have a cousin. But you were right. He did.'

There was silence for a moment while he assimilated the information, wondered how to react to it. He drew his finger slowly from her shoulder over the contour of her breast.

She shivered at his touch, then went on: 'Of course the cousin's dead. Long ago. He died in the same car crash, didn't he? My father began to tell me about him once. But . . .'

'But what?'

She laughed, bitterly. 'But I didn't want to hear about it. Not then. I suppose I was mixed up at the time. My mother had just died, you see. And my father came to me. I had this sense that he wanted to confide in me, tell me things, now that my mother was dead. Tell me things about the past, uncomfortable things. And I wasn't ready for him, I'd never seen him like that, never seen him not absolutely in control. It frightened me. I knew he wanted to unburden himself about something, but I couldn't cope with it, I didn't want the responsibility. I wanted my father always to be as he had been: strong, protective. In command. I didn't want to hear the things I sensed he wanted to tell me. I was cowardly, selfish. I said to myself, one day I'll let him tell me. Not yet. So I withdrew from him. In time I went to Paris, then on to Munich. And I never did come back to him and let him tell me. He died, and it was too late.'

'What did he say to you about this cousin?'

'Very little. Only that this cousin had come over to stay with them, from Austria I think, and that he'd died in the same accident as his mother.'

'Did he tell you the cousin's name?'

'I don't remember it if he did. You see, I was closing up to my father, trying to exclude what he was saying from my consciousness. It was irrational, but the whole thing disturbed me, this sudden need for me, this dependence on me. I shied away. I didn't give him the chance to go on.' She paused, then added tensely, with an effort of concentration, 'I do remember one thing, though. He started telling me about the funeral. How he'd had to bury this cousin next to my grandmother. In Highgate cemetery. There had been no point in sending his body back, apparently. He'd left no other relations behind him, in Austria or wherever.'

She shivered, as if a ripple of horror had passed through her.

Minto stroked her cheek, to calm her. But he mused on what she said. There was something strange about the story. Something disturbing. He tried to identify it. 'Your grandmother was buried in Highgate cemetery? But wasn't she Jewish?'

Isabella looked at him oddly. 'I think she was, originally. But not my grandfather. I guess she wasn't practising, anyway. I think they stopped all that when they came to England.'

'So your father would have been half Jewish himself?'

'Yes. But you wouldn't have known.'

I suppose you wouldn't, thought Minto. It didn't fit in with his image, did it? It wasn't an ancestry to emphasise, when you were reconstructing yourself as a being more English than the English. Even so, when you had Jewish blood, when you had an aunt who'd died in the place, it took something to make the sort of jokes he had made about Buchenwald. Something alarming and grotesque.

'Did you ever see the grave?'

'What, my grandmother's?'

'Yes. Or this cousin's?'

She shook her head, and shivered again. 'I never wanted to. I have a morbid horror of graveyards. Ever since I was a child.'

Of graveyards. Of tombs. Of islands where the dead are ferried to find their final resting place.

They lay there for a time in silence. In the distance there

was piano music, being played rather beautifully. Chopin perhaps. He thought about asking her if she recognised it, then rejected the idea. It was an unlikely enough sound to hear in this modern desert of a building. He watched the grey clouds massing again through the window.

He turned to her once more and asked, 'Do you think that after you rebuffed him your father might have turned to Max? To confide in, I mean.'

'I don't know.' She sighed, then added, unable to repress the residual note of pride: 'I would always have been his natural choice. But it's possible, I suppose.'

Possible. Possible that Max had been told something about his father. Possible that Winter knew it too. Something that had become a highly sensitive secret; so sensitive that it had to be suppressed rigorously. So rigorously that anyone who got close to it had to be silenced. One way or another. He thought of Theo Denton. He thought of Thomas Donat, lying broken on the hospital bed. What was the secret? Was it something to do with the cousin? Was it something to do with Hungary? Or was it something to do with *The Island of the Dead*?

Now he drew her head to him and kissed her hair.

'I'm sorry I went on about this cousin last night,' he said. 'I realise I made you very angry.'

'It's my fault in a way.' She looked up at him very seriously, frowning, analysing things as much for herself as for him. 'I don't know how to explain this to you, Minto. You have this strange effect on me, you see. You make me react in odd ways to things, in ways that frighten me. In ways I can't predict. When you started talking about this cousin, I panicked, tried to deny that he existed. You were getting too close.'

'Too close to what?'

'To my father. To me. I don't know.'

'And yet part of you still wants to find out about him, doesn't it? About your father, I mean?'

She nodded. 'I want to know. But I don't want to hurt him. And I refuse to let you hurt him, either.'

'But he's dead now, Isabella. You must accept that. His life is in the public domain.'

'I accept that he's dead. But I won't let anyone hurt him. I warn you, if you hurt him, I will not forgive you.'

At breakfast the next day she said she had to go home. He pleaded with her to stay, but she was adamant. It was Sunday, and she told him that she must be back in Munich by the evening.

'Why, for God's sake?'

'Because my husband will be there.'

He suddenly felt desperate. Why was she doing this to him?

'Don't go back to him.'

'But I must.'

'Stay with me.'

She was distant again. She had dressed in a skirt and a dark jacket and looked intimidatingly formal. 'What are you saying, Minto?'

'I'm saying that you should stay with me.'

'No.' She shook her head decisively. 'No. I have to go back.'

'Tell me something. Do you love your husband?'

For a moment she gave him that look again. Of venom. Of resentment. 'You've no right to ask me that question.'

'I think I have. Every right.'

'Well, I'm not going to answer it.' Her eyes were still blazing. Then without warning she subsided, and added in a low voice, 'But you know the bloody answer, anyway.'

'Then tell me why you're going back.'

'To prove to myself that I still can.'

'Why do you have to fight it?'

'Fight what?'

'Fight what we both know.' He paused, then felt her hand over his mouth.

'Don't say it,' she urged him. 'It's too dangerous to say it.'

'But I've got to say it. We love each other, Isabella. You know what that means? We can be happy, we can make each other happy, if we only let it happen ...'

'If we only let it happen,' she murmured.

'Don't you want me?'

She stared back at him, with that riven look. 'I want you so much that it frightens me,' she said.

Later he got up and put on his jacket. 'Look, I've got to go out. I've got an appointment at twelve.'

She looked up. 'Who with?'

'Some man who's going to help me with a little research I'm doing.'

She drummed her fingers on the tablecloth next to the remnants of her breakfast. 'How long will you be?'

'Not more than an hour or so. Then we can have lunch together.'

She was still drumming her fingers. 'What's this research you're doing, here in Budapest?'

'I'm seeing what I can find out about Greta Kassák.'

'Who?' She paused. 'Oh, yes. Greta Kassák. The woman you think betrayed your friend. So you are following her up. You really want to prove me wrong, don't you?'

He thought for a moment. Remembered Thomas Donat lying miserable in his hospital bed. 'No,' he said. 'I think I'd like to prove you right.'

Dr László Toth's bookshop was hidden down a forgotten side-street between Parliament Square and St Istvan's Boulevard. As Minto hurried along the pavements, past straggling groups of tourists, he felt a mounting urgency, and once again that underlying vulnerability, too. He was getting closer to something significant; and yet part of him recoiled from its discovery, as if the knowledge he might be acquiring would be dangerous. In some way destructive. The shop itself, when he found it, was several steps below street level, hollowed out of a basement. In descending the stairs to the doorway he had the illusion of being drawn down into some dark and mysterious nether region. Into the past, perhaps. Into a shadowy and alien area of the past.

László Toth shook him by the hand. He was a large, ungainly man with a baroque white moustache into which arched a rising semi-circle of yellow nicotine. 'Welcome, Mr

Maitland,' he said in his deep voice, closing the door behind him with a flourish. 'Welcome, sir, to my emporium. This is a pleasure. A pleasure and an honour, OK?'

He looked something between a bandit and an academic, a braggart and a preacher. Perhaps there was a strangeness to every inhabitant of that uneasy no-man's-land between scholarship and commerce. The walls were lined with books and files. In the centre of the room stood a desk, piled with more paperwork. The atmosphere was part shop, part private study. The air was heavy down here, even a little claustrophobic. For a moment Minto glimpsed the obsession which drove this man.

'It's good of you to see me,' said Minto.

'No, it is my pleasure.' Toth repeated, reaching into the pocket of his jacket for his pipe. 'It is an honour to make available to you this archive.'

'It looks as though you've gathered together an extraordinary amount of material.'

'But what you see here is just a part. Just a part, I tell you, Mr Maitland.' He struck a match and cupped his hands over the barrel of his pipe. Smoke wreathed him and he blinked back at Minto through rheumy eyes. 'There is more in other store-rooms. I had to consult in another place for the file on Peter Kassák.'

'My God! So he did exist? You have a file on him?'

Toth tapped the weather-beaten box in front of him. 'This is it.' He took his pipe from his mouth and became suddenly animated, passionate. 'Look, I know this Peter Kassák. I have done work on him in the past. When you mentioned his name, I thought it was familiar. He was a colonel in the AVO. He was a bad man. In fact his was a terrible case, one of the worst.'

'What sort of a case was it?'

'Let me explain something to you, something about what I have tried to do with my researches. Perhaps you look at me, and you think, what a crazy old man? I do not blame you. But there is a reason behind my madness. When I started this archive many years ago I had the intention that it should exist as a record of specific instances of AVO brutality. You must know that the secret police in the years leading up to 1956 were one of the most shameful features of my country's history. We none of us are proud of these things. I had the idea of amassing details of their crimes in order that the perpetrators might be brought to justice, at some future point. Now – well, I'm a realist – perhaps it is too late for justice. But what I am thinking is that at least my case histories can act as a warning to future generations. To prevent it happening again.'

Minto nodded.

'There were many instances to record, of course. Some were notorious and well documented, like the massacre by AVO men of the innocent inhabitants of Magyaróvár. Eighty-two people were gunned down there in cold blood on 26 October 1956. Some vengeance was taken at the time. But other cases were not so well known. Like the episode outlined here. In the Kassák file.'

Minto swallowed. The cold feeling of apprehension had returned.

'Can I see it?' he murmured.

Toth stood up to hand the file to him, but stopped, momentarily uncertain. 'Look, sir, I hope this material will not disturb you. It is no picnic, as you say in English. There are bad things recorded here.'

'I am a journalist,' offered Minto. Presenting his credentials. His passport to travel into prohibited areas.

'So, you are a journalist.' Toth sat down again and snapped open the file himself. 'Well, let me perhaps first give you a résumé of these contents. It is better, as you do not understand Hungarian, I think. So. This is Peter Kassák. He was a high officer in the AVO. He rose quickly, it seems. To be a colonel at twenty-nine, that is something out of the ordinary. Now, for this next part I am relying on the testimony of two freedom fighters who liberated an AVO gaol in the eastern suburbs of the city in the second week of the revolution. Yes, here we are: it was on 1 November 1956. In this gaol they found the bodies of nine prisoners. All shot, in cold blood. On Kassák's orders. It was the last thing he did, apparently, to give that order, before he ran for it, like a rat. Like a murderous rat. The freedom fighters went after him, even traced his home address. Needless to say, it was a very smart residence on Rózsadomb. But when they got there, he was gone. He was never caught. Who knows where he went? These AVO officers disguised themselves, threw away their uniforms; sometimes they even tried to pretend they were on the other side, to take the colours of the revolutionaries. Anyway, there is no more record of him. You know, I have not looked at this file for several years, but somehow I am not easily forgetting the name Peter Kassák.'

'No,' muttered Minto. Perplexed by the story. Wondering. 'I can understand that.'

'But wait. There is more. Something that will be interesting to you. There was a wife too, it seems.'

Minto caught his breath. 'Kassák's wife? Called Greta?'

'Let me see.' Toth turned over several pages of ancient typescript. 'Yes, you are right. Her name was Greta. You see, this is a completely separate file. From AVO records.'

'What does that file say?'

'According to these internal AVO papers, in December 1955 Kassák had his own wife arrested.'

It took a moment to register. 'He did what?'

'He had his own wife arrested.' Toth paused, blinking at him. 'It may sound strange to you, coming from England, with your Royal Family and your cricket and your famous "fair play". But in those days here in Hungary such things happened all the time. It doesn't say in this file precisely why she was arrested, but the explanation is probably that Kassák was up to the hokey-pokeys. With the other ladies. Probably he was tired of his wife and had her locked up on some trumped-up charge of anti-Socialist activity to get her out of the way. It's not unprecedented, I can assure you. These were bad men we are talking about. I can show you many other instances . . .'

Greta. So Greta had been arrested. In December 1955; just about the time that Thomas Donat had been taken into custody. Minto felt a simultaneous horror and elation.

He looked up. The lumbering form of László Toth was looming over him now. Looming over him, with a packet

of battered photographs in his hand. Pressing them on him.
Urgently. No more than small snapshots, really.

'You should see these, Mr Maitland. They would interest
you. As a journalist. They are powerful documents, OK?'

'What are they?'

'They are photographs made by the freedom fighters. One
had a camera, you see. When they saw what they found in
the AVO gaol they were both so sick, both so distressed that
they took photos of the corpses. It was a way, they said, of
relieving their feelings. Of purging themselves of the terrible
experience. And they hoped perhaps that it might be evidence
against Kassák in the future if they did this. I have kept them
here in the file ever since.'

Wordlessly he passed them across to Minto. One by one.
They were tiny, but they were horrible, black and white
records of death taken with a fortuitous precision of focus
which bordered on the macabre. Close-ups of faces. The first
three were men, their features contorted in a mixture of agony,
surprise and anger. The fourth was a middle-aged woman
with dried blood dribbling from her mouth. The fifth and
sixth were young men, hardly more than children.

And then came one of a strikingly beautiful blonde woman.
She lay there, facing the camera, her eyes staring sightlessly
ahead. But with her lips parted into a gentle smile. Parted to
reveal front teeth with a conspicuous gap between them.

Minto knew it then. He knew beyond doubt that he
was gazing at the features of Greta Kassák, just as he
had gazed at them in Thomas Donat's photograph in the
hospital. He saw her as Thomas Donat had seen her. He
saw her on the boat on that sweltering summer's day on
the Danube Bend. He imagined her windswept, in her scarf
and raincoat, on Gellért Hill. And now he was seeing her
as she died. Gunned down on the orders of a vengeful
husband.

He knew then, too, that Thomas was vindicated. That
what Rudolf had told him had been lies. That Greta had
not betrayed him. That if she had been an AVO agent she
would not have been imprisoned in December. She would
not have been shot in cold blood by AVO men in an AVO

gaol. Shot on her husband's orders. Her life taken because she loved another man.

He handed the group of photographs back to the waiting Dr László Toth. Greta's photograph lay on top. For a moment Toth paused, staring at it. Then he said, 'I am thinking this one had a notable beauty, did she not?'

Minto found it suddenly difficult to answer. Looking away from the other man, he said softly, 'I think she must have had.'

Toth nodded, and replaced the flimsy snapshots in the file. Regretfully. And with a certain gentleness.

A thought occurred to Minto as he was going. 'Tell me something, Dr Toth. I've never had the chance to ask this question of anyone who lived through it all. What was it like afterwards? After the Russians came back in the first week of November 1956?'

'It was the end of a dream,' murmured Toth, knocking his pipe out into the ashtray. 'The end of our illusion.'

'So it was just squashed? The uprising?'

For a moment the burly shoulders flinched. Minto sensed that there was something in the word he had just used which disturbed him. 'That's what they called it,' he explained at last. 'The uprising. That's how the new regime under Kádár viewed it. We knew it was a revolution, but they said it was an uprising. An outbreak of lawlessness that was successfully repressed with the help of our Soviet allies. A mass manifestation of criminality. Something like ...' Toth paused, frowning. 'Something like the Commune in Paris in 1871.'

Something like the Commune. For a moment the connection was there. With Tissot. AVO men had disguised themselves as insurgents; Tissot had been accused of donning the colours of the Communards. What was the significance of that historical echo?

'I must thank you,' said Minto, gathering up his things and handing over his card. 'I am very grateful for all the information you have given me. It seems to fit in with my own research.'

'Have you perhaps something in your own research which

might be of use to me? About what happened later to Colonel Kassák, for instance? I am still interested in these things.'

'I am afraid not,' said Minto quietly. But even then the idea was formulating. The suspicion. The need to check, at the very least.

As he walked back to the hotel he felt shaken, as if he'd just witnessed something harrowing. But he also felt exultant. On behalf of Thomas Donat he felt happy. The instinct of preserving her photograph all those years in his wallet had been correct. Greta had not betrayed him. He remembered that what he had just discovered vindicated Isabella, too. Why do men always think the worst of women? she had demanded. Maybe she just couldn't keep away from him. Maybe she went to him against her better judgement. Because she couldn't help herself. He looked forward to the moment of seeing her again. Of telling her that she had been right. Of telling her that he wasn't going to make the same mistake about her. Because he trusted her. Because he loved her.

But when he turned the key in the door of their room and came inside, he felt a sick feeling of desolation in his stomach. The bed was made and there was no sign of her things anywhere. The bathroom was void of her scents and bottles; the cupboard was empty of her clothes and suitcase. Feverishly he called down to reception. Yes, Miss Maurbach had left by taxi about forty minutes ago. She had booked on the early afternoon flight to Munich. No, she hadn't left any message.

He sat on the bed. Trying not to remember how she had lain here in his arms. Trying not to recall the way she'd told him she resented him for making her fall in love with him.

Trying not to think how Greta's sightless eyes reminded him of the mocking skull in *The Island of the Dead*.

Sister Mullins's father had been in the navy. The merchant navy, in fact, and if the truth were told he had not risen higher than the rank of chief petty officer. But she was fond of referring rather grandly to his naval career, and hinting at commands that he might once have held without ever committing herself to precise details. She liked to feel that there was a bit of salt-water running in her own veins as a result. That the sea was in her blood.

Sometimes, as she sat behind the glass in her observation post in the lonely hours of early morning, she saw herself as a captain on the bridge of a ship, guiding her vessel through the treacherous waters of the night. She would peer down the rows of beds in the ward to the windows at the far end and fancy that beyond lay the prow, cleaving the darkened waves. And as dawn broke she would congratulate herself on the imminent completion of another successful voyage to morning; that she had guided her sleeping complement through to a new day. One day nearer recovery for some. One day more of suffering for others. But no longer her responsibility at the end of her shift at six.

It was still dark outside now. An unreal greenish light insinuated itself through the blinds at the far end of the ward, casting strange patterns across the floor and wall, draping the two nearest beds in sharply slatted shadows. There were twelve iron-framed beds in all, six either side of the room, each occupied by a slumbering form. Some slept deeply, emitting wild and abandoned snores; others tossed in submerged anguish, raging, murmuring incoherent imprecations. Imprecations against the whole panoply of real or imagined forces arrayed to oppose them. Against the hospital, for shackling them; against fate, for visiting infirmity upon them; against their friends and loved ones, for deserting them. She ran her eye along the line, taking in the two young bricklayers who were in for observation after an accident on their building site had left them unconscious, on past the taciturn Indian gentleman who was in for tests on his pancreas, dwelling for a moment on the demented elderly man called Jefferies who had been there for weeks largely, she suspected, because he had nowhere else to go. Finally her gaze alighted upon the white-haired Mr Donat at the far end.

Mr Donat, with the sad eyes and the funny accent. A little bit transatlantic and a little bit of something else, too, that she couldn't quite identify. Not that he spoke much, not usually, anyway, but Sister Mullins was intrigued by him because she reckoned he was hiding something, that there was a story behind him. She guessed that because of the visitors he'd had, once he'd emerged into this ward out of intensive care. She'd been on the day shift last week, so she had noticed them: the neat middle-aged woman who was a relation of some sort. The good-looking young man. The young man who'd stayed for two and a half hours locked in conversation, his head bowed down close to Donat so as not to miss a word of what he was saying. After his departure she'd checked on Donat and found him crying, like a baby. Lying there wordlessly, with the tears streaming down his cheeks. Could she get him anything? He'd just shook his head. 'No,' he'd whispered. 'No. I'll be all right. I'll be all right in a minute.'

And then there had been the most recent visitor. The uniformed police officer. Checking with her on Donat's identity.

'Yes, he's Thomas Donat,' she'd confirmed, referring to her papers for his Christian name.

The policeman had been cradling his cap nervously, turning it round in his hands like a tambourine. 'Sustained injuries in a hit-and-run?'

She had nodded. 'Why are you asking?'

'Just routine, love. Checking on his whereabouts. He's on bail, you see. Failed to report yesterday. Just checking.'

'Bail? What's he meant to have done?'

'Don't ask me, because I don't know. I'm just the dogsbody that gets sent to corroborate information.' He'd thanked her and wheeled round to go.

'Well, he's in no condition to abscond from here,' she had called after him. Because she'd suddenly felt it was only fair that Mr Donat should have something said in his own defence. Because her instinct told her that whatever he was accused of, it couldn't be anything very bad.

But then again, it didn't do to get involved, did it? That was lesson one in the rulebook. Keep your emotional distance from the patient. You could indulge in the occasional bout of mild curiosity. And it was only human nature to have your soft spots, to find some of them more sympathetic than others. But there was a line beyond which you shouldn't go; a line so clearly defined in her mind that she was in no danger of transgressing it. She knew what happened on the other side. Once you started minding. So she had switched off from Thomas Donat and his problems. Hadn't dwelt on them. Instead she had given her mind over to the question of whether the hall in their flat needed redecorating.

Now she yawned. It was twenty-five past four. Sometimes she dozed herself a bit. It was hard not to. On night shift you never got normal sleep, did you? She'd go to bed at eight or nine in the morning, just as Ron was leaving for work himself, but it was unnatural, drawing the curtains on the daylight. She'd drop off for three or four hours, then a combination of sunshine and the noises of the city would disturb her, and she'd lie there, her eyes smarting and her limbs heavy, but knowing she would not sleep again.

Her head was falling forward for one of her periodic dozes when it happened. Suddenly. There was the flashing red light in the panel in front of her. She was roused instantly into lumbering action. It was mad old Jefferies who'd pressed the alarm bell. She swayed into the ward and between the beds; then she saw that it wasn't Jefferies who was in distress, it was his neighbour. Mad old Jefferies had had enough of his wits about him to raise the alarm. He was gesturing silently to Thomas Donat. To Thomas Donat writhing in the bed next door.

She'd seen enough coronaries in her time to recognise the symptoms at once. She knew the drill. Everything happened very quickly once she'd set it in motion. The emergency cardiac team was there within a minute. They arrived like ghosts in the night, three of them, steely grim-faced figures in green, carting their paraphernalia with them. Sister Mullins listened to the familiar sounds of the electrodes being clamped to the chest and the voltage wracking the patient's fragile frame. She busied herself with the screening off of the bed.

'You go back to sleep, Mr Jefferies,' she said.

'He's going to be all right, isn't he?' Jefferies looked at her with staring eyes, his sparse grey hair dishevelled.

'Terrible noise he was making. I called for help, you see. Did I do right?'

'You did quite right.'

'I wasn't sure. I wanted to do right.'

'You go back to sleep,' she repeated.

She put her head through the screens. The frantic movements of the green-coated team had subsided. Sister Mullins saw one of them look quizzically across at the other, and caught the answering shake of the head. So that was that, then. She ducked back out.

She glanced at her watch in the unreal green light. In not much more than an hour her shift would be over.

She wondered what she'd get herself for breakfast.

18

He found out almost as soon as he got back to his flat.

He'd stayed one more night in Budapest, then taken the first flight into London on Monday morning. He dropped his bag on the unmade bed. The familiarity of the place was depressing, the half-drawn curtains and the cups in the sink. So he checked his messages at once, in case Isabella had been in touch; in case she had arrived home in Munich and needed beyond anything to hear his voice, needed it as much as he needed to hear hers. But there was no message. Nothing. So he rang Leila Parsons. To check on Thomas, to make arrangements to see him. So he could tell him about Greta. The news he had discovered about her weighed heavily on him, like a piece of someone else's baggage that he had carried all the way home and could not wait to be rid of.

He heard the tension in Leila Parsons's voice even in the way she answered the telephone. He knew something was wrong.

'It's you, isn't it, Mr—'

'Minto.'

'Minto.' She sighed. It was the first time he had persuaded her into the use of the name. That in itself obliquely put him on his guard.

'I rang to check on Thomas. How is he? I've got news for him from Budapest.'

Her pause disturbed him. Then it came out in a rush. 'I'm so sorry,' she said. 'I'm so very sorry. Uncle Thomas died in the night on Saturday. It was a heart attack. A massive heart attack. All the pressure of . . . I mean, what with the accident and everything . . . I think it finally got to him, put an unbearable stress on his system. They rang us in the

night and then in the morning we had to go round to the
hospital to get his things . . .'

When he replaced the receiver, Minto sat for a while on
his bed with his head in his hands. Incredulous. And almost
unbearably sad. He saw her again, the same beautiful woman
whose photograph Thomas Donat had pushed into his hand
that last harrowing afternoon in the hospital ward. And then
he saw her once more in the other snapshot, with her sightless
eyes, and her lips half parted in a slow kiss of death. He would
now never be able to release Thomas's mind from the chains
which had bound it. He would never be able to let him know
the contents of Toth's file, to restore the old man's faith, to
re-establish the validity of his relationship with Greta, to give
it back to him intact. Peter Kassák had triumphed. Rudolf had
triumphed. The death's-head had gained a final victory.

And with Thomas's death, maybe Max and Winter were in
the clear. By accident or design, maybe the suppression which
they sought had been achieved. The suppression of the secret
about Alexander Courtney whose revelation might destroy
them. The secret which Minto still had not penetrated.

'You look all in, old boy,' said Ridley in the office later. 'Went
on one of those freebies this weekend, didn't you?'

Minto nodded.

'Where was it? Bucharest or something?'

'Budapest.'

'Same difference. Lived it up a bit, eh? I bet you did. Wine,
women and song, I suppose.' There was a touch of wistfulness
in his voice.

'You bet.' It was easier to roll out for Ridley the act that
he wanted, the responses he expected, than to allow him any
glimpse of what Minto was really feeling.

'How's the Courtney piece?' Ridley persisted. 'Coming
along?'

Minto nodded. 'Nearly finished,' he said mechanically.

Nearly finished.

But then it came to him: it wasn't, was it? Nothing was
finished. Nothing could be concluded yet about Courtney.
There were still questions to be answered about him,

uneasy, disturbing questions. He must continue to follow the interconnecting strands back into the past. And from their unravelling would emerge the truth. The story. The story that was going to rock them all.

Maybe it was then, with Ridley swaying unsteadily at his desk, with Ridley breathing whisky-scented breath over him, maybe it was then that a glimmer of the answer first came to him. Only an inkling, perhaps: but from that moment on Minto was driven by a new compulsion, a determination to settle it all one way or another. For the next seventy-two hours he was obsessed.

'Fancy a drink?' muttered Ridley.

'No, sorry. I can't.' Minto got up decisively.

'Going somewhere?'

Minto nodded. He was on his way to Highgate cemetery. To look at a gravestone.

There were fresh-mown swathes of grass either side of the path down which he hurried. It smelt rich as he walked, pausing occasionally to peer at the names cut into the stones now more clearly exposed by the scythe and the rotor-blade. Beyond, where the grass was less kempt, the tombs were overgrown with weed and ivy, metaphors of nature's reclamation of man's attempts to leave his monuments on this earth. Death was everywhere here. Its symbols multiplied in angels, urns and weeping women; in grotesque memorials; in extravagant mausoleums. Although it was hot, Minto shivered. He was thinking suddenly of the entrance to the tomb in *The Island of the Dead*. That opening of mysterious black emptiness. Of the birds screaming high up the rocky cliff-face.

It had all been very simple. He'd rung the cemetery. He'd given the name Frederica Courtney and the date of death, which he'd taken from the newspaper cutting. In a matter of minutes they had come back to him with a grave number and a location.

He strode on impatiently down deserted avenues. He had to see those gravestones with his own eyes. To be sure.

When he finally found them they were in a shadowy corner out of the sun. He was struck immediately by the simplicity of the message on the first: Frederica Courtney, he read. Beloved mother of Alexander. Born Vienna 1896. Died London 1957. *Requiescat in pace*. Nothing more. The bare facts of a life, defined by two random dates and places.

He turned to the smaller grave on the right. And suddenly he realised why he was there. Because this was the one he had really come to see.

He ran his eyes over the words incised into the stone. The name leapt out at him: Kassák, was all he registered. Kassák, it said. Born Budapest 1924. Died London 1957. It was him: the Courtneys' cousin was Kassák. Kassák, who had got out of Budapest in 1956. Kassák, who had finally made his way to London to seek refuge with his cousins. With his Austrian cousins in Strandwick Mansions. Not so unusual, perhaps, for there to be both an Austrian and a Hungarian branch of the same family. Not so unusual, either, for someone who had done what Kassák had done in Budapest to seek to cloak his Hungarian identity in the cover of the Austrian side of his family. This was the man who had given the order for the cold-blooded shooting of nine innocent prisoners in an AVO gaol. Including his own wife.

Only then did Minto look again at that second, smaller gravestone, in the lee of the memorial to Courtney's mother. Only then did he absorb the significance of the rest of the inscription. Of the other two names which followed the surname Kassák. Followed the surname in the Hungarian style. Kassák, he read; Kassák, Peter Rudolf.

Peter Rudolf? RUDOLF?

And suddenly it all began to hang together. What if Greta had called this man Peter, and Thomas had known him as Rudolf, but all along they were one and the same person? Then Rudolf had been Greta's husband: Thomas had been her lover. In vengeance, Rudolf had cold-bloodedly set about dismantling the balance of Thomas's mind. In vengeance he'd had Greta murdered in the gaol to which he'd consigned her. Then he had melted away in the confusion, side-stepping at the last Thomas's maladroit attempt to empty a gun into him. To re-emerge in London with the Courtneys as 'the cousin from Austria'. The cousin from Austria who had arrived bearing with him a picture. A picture called *The Island of the Dead*.

And the irony of it all was that the death he'd avoided in Rózsadomb had caught up with him not many months later on the English tarmac of the A1 near Hendon.

As Minto retraced his steps thoughtfully back through the cemetery, he marvelled at the precision with which he had succeeded in tracing the later provenance of the picture whose destruction Elaine McBride had originally commissioned him to investigate. Peter Rudolf Kassák had acquired it in Hungary, perhaps from the impoverished descendants of Count Barodi. Kassák had brought it to London on his flight from Budapest in 1956. And in 1957 Alexander Courtney had quietly laid claim to it after the death of its owner in the car in which he had himself been travelling. Laid claim to it, and sold it on to Marriott, from whose collection it had in turn passed to the Royal Gallery, where, three months after its first public exhibition it had been glimpsed by a Canadian visitor to London. Thomas Donat.

He reached the gates and stood for a moment looking for a taxi. What he had learned in this place had shaken him. It's not just pictures that have obscure provenances, he was thinking. People have them too. People like Kassák. And people like Alexander Courtney.

Later that evening, when he got back to the flat, he rang Isabella, but the Filipino maid told him she was out. Did he want to speak to Mr Maurbach? If so, she would see if she could interrupt him. He was in the drawing-room, playing. And as he listened, Minto realised that the piano music he could discern in the background was not a recording, but Maurbach's live practising. It was disturbingly beautiful.

'No,' he said. 'No, please don't do that.'

Then he turned back to the yellowed cutting from the *Highgate Times* which Miss Fulbrick had lent him. He laid it out on the table and stared at it for a long time. Gommersall. Harold Gommersall. That was the name of the lorry driver into whose path Mrs Courtney's car had veered. If anyone could shed light on the last moments of Peter Rudolf

Kassák, Gommersall was the man. And Minto suddenly felt a curiosity about that death on an English highway nearly forty years ago.

He made one more call that evening, to directory enquiries. 'Gommersalls,' he told the girl. 'Gommersalls of Doncaster.' She got the number for him almost at once.

19

The taxi left behind the last bleak row of terraced houses and ground on into a no-man's-land of straggling industry and unkempt fields. Where the landscape undulated, it was with slag-heaps rather than with hills; and where the countryside momentarily promised a moment of genuine wildness, it was immediately garlanded with pylons and ensnared. It was an area to hurry through, a mere route from one place to another. If you lingered here you became depressed. Or hard-skinned. Or both.

Sometimes, reflected Minto from the back seat, you did things by instinct. He could not quite define the moment when it had become imperative to make this journey, but he had woken up this morning with a mixture of apprehension and impatience and realised that the idea of going had solidified into decision. Perhaps what preyed on his mind was still only a theory. But it was a theory with a horrific plausibility. A theory that had to be tested against the memory of one man: the one man left living with the power to prove or disprove it.

Harold Gommersall was a Yorkshireman, and proud of it. He sat four-square in his chair, a loosened tie threaded round an unbuttoned collar, and stared belligerently at Minto. You could see him wondering what this fancy southerner was doing in his front room. Why he'd made the journey all the way from London just to ask him a few bloody daft questions. Gommersall's neck was so thick that you didn't register it. His head simply abutted on to the roundness of his body like the short squat spout on a kettle. His hands, as they clutched the armrests of his chair, were ingrained with the grime of decades of labour, stained by an infinity of engine oils.

'Aye, I've been retired these past six years,' he admitted in answer to Minto's enquiry. 'Put out to grass like. My two lads run the business now.' There was a profound regret to the statement; and such was the sense of frustrated energy still emanating from his bulky frame that Minto felt that its imprisonment here in this genteel sitting-room was inappropriate, indecent, like a rhinocerous caged in a suburban zoo.

'That's the haulage business, is it?'

'That's it. Gommersalls of Doncaster. Most likely you've seen our trucks up and down motorway.'

Minto said he thought he had.

'Fifty-four lorries we run now.' The figure was spoken with pride, the way some people enumerate grandchildren. 'Not bad, considering I leased my first vehicle in forty-seven with my demob money.'

He'd done well, clearly. The neat detached house with its acre of well-kept grounds was testament to that. The carpet in the sitting-room was of a deep and lustrous pile. The television in the corner boasted a screen of prodigious dimensions. Looking out through the french windows Minto could see a pond with an ornate splashing fountain set in the meticulously tended lawn.

Mrs Gommersall bustled in with a tray of tea. She was a red-faced, bovine woman with ankles so swollen that Minto moved forward immediately to relieve her of her burden.

'There you are, Mr Maitland,' she said, handing him a cup and saucer. 'Do you take sugar, love?'

'Thank you,' said Minto, noting that Harold Gommersall was presented with his tea in an uncompromising mug.

She stood there for a moment, wiping her hands on her apron. 'From the newspapers, are you?' she enquired.

'I am, yes,' agreed Minto.

'What is it you're writing about, then?'

'I'm doing a biographical piece on someone I think your husband may be able to help me with. Someone he may have met once.'

'Fancy,' she said without great interest, and stumped out. Her husband frowned thoughtfully as he sipped his tea.

'You know what young lads are, Mr Maitland. Stubborn buggers, they can be. Right stubborn. Think they know everything there is to know about the haulage game. Sometimes I have to drive myself into t'office and put 'em straight about certain matters. I can't say they always thank me for it at the time, though events generally prove me right in the end. Stands to reason, don't it? I've still got a thing or two to teach them after forty years in the business, and twenty-five of them spent on t'road.

'Take last week for a start. There were Tom, he'd set up one job from Grimsby down to Basingstoke on the Wednesday. Then he'd gone and got another lorry going down empty on the Wednesday night to pick up a load of kitchen equipment in Swindon on the Thursday morning. "Blood and sand," I said, "where's the sense in that? Basingstoke's only an hour from Swindon. Get first truck on to Swindon on Wednesday night and you've saved yourself a journey down." He hadn't seen it, had he? Him with his bloody computers and such like. He still hadn't seen it.' There was a note of triumph in his voice. Reasserting himself over the sons who had usurped his crown was one of the abiding pleasures of his retirement.

'You must have done the London run a good few times in your career,' suggested Minto.

'You can say that again. Knew bloody A1 like back of me hand.' He paused, preparing for his recitation. 'Twice a week, up and down, every year from forty-seven to sixty-one. Fifty weeks of the year, with one week off for Christmas and one week off when I took the kids to Bridlington.'

'That's quite a record.'

There was silence for a moment while Gommersall sat back in satisfaction and Minto reached into his file for Miss Fulbrick's cutting. Minto went on: 'Although you must have had a little time off after this, didn't you?'

'What's that you got there?'

Minto handed it over and Gommersall read it carefully, his lips moving involuntarily as his eyes passed over the words. When he'd done he folded the yellowed cutting and passed it back to Minto.

'Sounds like a nasty smash,' encouraged Minto.

Unexpectedly Gommersall rose to his feet. His muscular rotundity was as evident standing as it had been seated. He hitched up his trousers but they proved impossible to manoeuvre any higher than the underside of his considerable belly. Minto noticed two beads of sweat on his grizzled head.

'Come and look at t' runner beans,' he said, leading the way to the french windows. 'Runner beans are a bloody wonder this year. You won't see aught to match 'em this side of Pennines.'

Minto followed him out, round the corner of the lawn and past a greenhouse and hedge. They stood silently for a moment in front of the vegetable patch. There was a wind blowing from the east and it was suddenly cold.

'I don't like to talk about it in t' house in case Mrs Gommersall hears,' he explained at last. 'She were that cut up about it. She don't need reminding.'

'No, of course not.'

'It were the only accident I ever had in all me years on the road. Me only serious one, like.'

He stood there, defiant, with his hands in his pockets and his old bullet head set against the wind.

'I'm sorry. It must have been very unpleasant,' said Minto. He paused, running his eye along the neat rows of potato plants, savouring the geometry of the lines. 'You see the reason I've come to meet you is about Alexander Courtney. Does that name ring any bell to you?'

Gommersall swallowed. 'Alexander Courtney,' he repeated slowly.

'Yes. Do you remember? He was the survivor from the car. I'm writing a sort of study of his life. He became quite a famous figure in the art world afterwards, and a pretty rich one too. I came to you because I'd like to get an eye-witness account of what happened that time. In the accident.'

The other man shook his head. 'It were a rum do,' he declared.

Perplexed by the phrase, Minto opted to offer consolation: 'But clearly the accident was not your fault. When a car veers into your path like this one apparently did, there's absolutely nothing you can do, is there?'

Again he did not reply immediately. Instead he shuffled forward and bent to pull out two weeds from the line of potato plants. He tossed them into a wheelbarrow. He frowned, then said slowly, 'I just don't know, that I don't. It all happened that quickly, you see. But thinking about it afterwards, I used to wonder. It were a rum do all round.'

'A rum do? In what way?'

Gommersall peered into the distance. On the brow of the hill, beyond the select little green enclave where his house lay, you could see more chimneys against the horizon. Satanic mills, in England's green and pleasant land. Minto thought momentarily of Ridley and his suppressed tears. Of the memorial service to a man who might so easily have died nearly forty years before his time on the tarmac of the A1.

'It's that difficult to tell between what did and didn't happen,' said Gommersall at last. 'It's a good many years ago now, and then there was the concussion. You mustn't forget the concussion. Everything were bleary, like.'

'Of course. But tell me what you remember.'

'It were quite late in evening, seven o'clock or so, and light were beginning to go. I weren't more than a couple of miles from the depot where they were expecting my load. I looked across and suddenly t' car were all but underneath my wheels. It happened that quick. Morris Minor it were, God knows how it got there. When we hit, lorry jack-knifed across t' road and my head smashed against the top of the steering wheel.'

Minto was suddenly reminded of the German room. The German room in the Royal Gallery. What had she said, that security guard, the woman called Maureen? Like a car smash, wasn't it? she'd told him. One minute you're driving along thinking of nothing in particular and the next minute it's happened. There he was with the knife in his fist and the canvas in tatters.

'Did you lose consciousness?' he asked.

'No, I never lost consciousness, like, but some bits of what happened then are clearer than others. The whole do were like a nightmare. And when I think of it now I'm not that sure I didn't dream parts of it.'

'Were you able to get to anyone in the car?'

'I were that dazed it took me a little while to let myself out of the cab. The car was a mangled wreck. There was steam hissing from the radiator on t' lorry and smoke coming from what was left of t' car, as well as the smell of burning. I saw one man was free of the car, he must have crawled out, and he didn't look too bad. He was sitting there, on the roadside holding his head, a bit dazed like me. Then there was the other one. He must have been thrown through the window by the collision, because he were on the road, all spread-eagled like. He were a gonner, I reckoned. He just lay there, not moving. The first man called out something about getting help because there was a woman still trapped in the car. He said something like, "She's in there still!"'

'He said that to you?' Minto was there himself, suddenly absorbed in the scene, could almost hear the hissing of the radiator and smell the burning rubber.

'That were it, somat like. "She's in there still." It were the way he phrased it, because I remember thinking, aye-up, the lad's a foreigner.'

Minto nodded, picturing the scene, hearing the anguished cry. Alexander Courtney, embryonic Englishman, still not master of perfect idiom. Not in extremes like this, anyway.

'So he cried out – then what?' Minto prompted.

'I said – still a bit dazed like – "Who's in there?", and he said, "My aunt is in there." I remember that bit very clearly. That shows his concussion must have been quite bad, worse than it seemed, because as we later found out it was his mother in there, wasn't it? Anyway, by that time another motorist had pulled up and a local resident had called an ambulance. I went with the other motorist to see what could be done for the woman still in the car. But she looked a gonner too. Her head were smashed in and she were trapped, you couldn't move her. She weren't breathing, not even then.' Gommersall swallowed, and continued to look away from Minto, up towards the chimneys on the horizon. 'I'd seen them before you see, corpses. I were in Normandy in 1944, I'd seen 'em before in all shapes and sizes, so as you got not to care no more. Funny thing, you always knew when they were dead, though, you didn't have to check them. There was this stillness about them, you see.'

'Did Courtney come over to look at his mother, too, at that point?' Minto wanted to get it right. Every detail. Because he knew that if he didn't get these seemingly little things correct now, the big things would never follow. And there were big things hanging on this. Bigger than he'd ever imagined.

'No, not him. It were me and t'other motorist. Because when I turned round I saw another rum thing.'

'What was that?'

Gommersall had taken up a garden fork now and was leaning forward on it, swaying slightly. Minto noticed how hard his hand gripped the handle.

'Well, the first bloke, the one called Courtney, the one with concussion, he'd crawled over to his cousin, the one that was lying very still. I don't know if he knew what he were doing, or if he knew that I were watching him. He were leaning over him, and at first I thought he were feeling for t'other one's heartbeat. And then I thought, aye-up, he's taking somat out of his breast pocket. Why's he doing that? Then again, I thought, maybe he's putting something into the pocket, I couldn't be sure. Either way it didn't make sense. Anyway I went back to trying to release the woman, though it were bloody hopeless, and when I looked round again, the police had turned up and the first bloke, Courtney, he was telling them that he thought t'other one had had it, and the constable was telling him to sit down and take it easy till the ambulance came.'

Minto nodded, concentrating very hard. Courtney, at his dead or dying cousin's side. Courtney, reaching to feel his heartbeat. Or perhaps not. Perhaps instead he was reaching to find something in his breast pocket. Why, for God's sake? What had he been looking for? What in hell had been going on?

Because that was Kassák lying there, wasn't it? Peter Rudolf Kassák. The cousin, the mysterious cousin who had materialised out of the night nine months earlier with his three suitcases, lying broken in the road. And there was Courtney, struggling with concussion, still trying to get something from him at the last. Or leave something on him?

What had it meant, this last macabre act in the life of Peter Rudolf Kassák? Let's not forget what was going on here, Minto reminded himself: this was the death of Peter Rudolf Kassák, one-time AVO officer and fugitive from Hungary. Murderer of Greta. Torturer of Thomas Donat. This was the moment, one late summer's evening on a very English stretch of highway near Hendon, beneath the gaze of a line of irreproachably suburban villas drawn up along the roadside, when the death's-head had won. When it asserted its dominance even over Rudolf. The moment when the birds in the rocky cliff-top called out their final savage cries of triumph. The moment when the cypress trees whispered their ultimate enticements. The moment when the void of the open tomb loomed irresistible.

Or had it?

What had Courtney felt compelled to adjust in the breast pocket of this man in order to make everything right? What had he removed or placed there in order to set the record straight? In order to enable him to begin the rest of his own life.

'What happened then?' Minto pressed Gommersall.

'I think I came over a bit dizzy like, because the next thing I remember I were sat there on the roadside next to this Courtney bloke, waiting for ambulance.'

'Did he say anything to you then? Can you remember at all?'

Gommersall had brought out cigarette paper and tobacco. His face furrowed in concentration as his big fingers and thumbs moved with surprising dexterity to roll the thin white cylinder. Then he cupped his hands together to light it, and stood back a pace as he inhaled, the wind billowing the smoke away into the distance. He sighed thoughtfully. Narrowing his eyes to recall memories as elusive as the cigarette smoke.

'I think it were then that his mind began to wander a little, like. Delirious, he could have been. "He's dead," he said to me, all excited like, "he's dead, isn't he?" I told him not to worry himself, to calm it down. But he went on, almost laughing like, about entry permits and papers not being in order. About how it didn't matter any more now. Because he were dead, I suppose, this other bloke. I remember thinking at the time, it's an odd way of looking at it. Being pleased that a bloke's died because it gets that same bloke out of a bit of difficulty with the authorities. It didn't really make much sense. But it were the concussion, I suppose. And the delirium. They say it puts things out of proportion.'

Gommersall took another drag on his cigarette and stood there holding it between finger and thumb, turned in against his palm.

'And then?' persisted Minto.

'A lot of bloody fuss, as I recall. Suddenly there were several ambulances, all at the same time. I were carted off to hospital, given tests and that, then kept in for observation. But I were allowed out next day.'

'What happened to Courtney?'

Gommersall shrugged. 'I suppose he were carted off as well.'

'But you never saw him again?'

'Not hide nor hair of him. There weren't no call. There were no police prosecution, and the insurance paid out.'

There was a light rain falling now, blowing across in gusts on the wind. Autumn was on its way. Gommersall hunched his shoulders and turned towards the house. He dropped the fag end and trod it into the path. It was time to go in.

'He been showing you his vegetable patch, has he?' demanded Mrs Gommersall when they came back into the sitting-room. 'He bloody worships those vegetables, he does. Happen the Queen of England came to call, she'd be taken out there to admire them.'

'Hold your cheek, woman,' said Gommersall, not without tenderness.

But Minto hardly heard him. He knew he had to get out. The teeming particles of evidence which he had been amassing so assiduously had suddenly set miraculously into a pattern, a pattern at once so extraordinary and so appalling that he had to move on. Immediately. To shake the mosaic, to give the particles a chance to fall apart again, a chance to revert into random meaninglessness. Because if they didn't, then many things must happen. And happen fast. He realised he was on the verge of the biggest story of his life.

The taxi drove him back through the mutilated landscape to the station. He caught the London train with two minutes to spare. The first thing he did was to retreat to the first-class lavatory and ring Elaine. To ensure privacy. With something like this you didn't take any chances.

He could imagine her sitting there at her desk, with the sharpened pencils and the bottle of mineral water. He could feel her suddenly sitting up very straight once he spoke to her. Once he started telling her what he suspected. He spoke in short, clear, unemotional sentences, huddled in the tiny lavatory of the train with the mobile telephone clamped to his ear as the carriage swayed over the points.

'Shit, Minto.' You could hear her calculating the column inches, envisaging the spread on the front page of the review section. Working up the shout line. 'This could be the story of the year. One of the most incredible revelations of our times. You're made, if this comes off. But can you prove it?'

'I need to go to Munich to do that.'

'To Munich again?'

'Just once more. It won't take long.'

She paused. 'Get me this story, Minto. Go to Munich, if that's what it takes. But bring it back to me, OK?'

'OK, Elaine. I'll let you know.'

'Who are you going to see in Munich?'

'Various people.'

Elaine didn't forget. 'It's the daughter again, isn't it?'

'Got to go,' he said, deliberately turning the telephone fainter. 'We're just coming into a tunnel.'

The daughter again. Isabella. It was almost as if he had been repressing her from his consciousness because once he allowed her in she dominated everything, impaired his ability to concentrate on what he'd been striving to discover. But now he felt an aching longing for her, and he knew he had to see her very soon. The separation from her had gone on long enough.

He had to see her because he loved her.

He had to see her in order to lay before her what he'd found.

And he had to see her because she was the only person in the world who could now provide the story's final confirmation. He could not seek that confirmation from Max or Winter, even if they had it to give; the evidence of the cowed figure of Theo Denton was no longer relevant. And the time was past for persuading it out of Thomas Donat. No, it had to be found in Munich. In Grünwald. In one of the smartest apartments of that highly select suburb, in the room with the clinically clean fireplace and the immaculate white sofas and the silver-framed photographs on the grand piano.

20

That night he finally spoke to Isabella on the telephone. She answered the call herself, and Minto was taken by surprise, having anticipated the obstacle of a maid or even a husband. She sounded different. Not so much angry or resentful as tense; preoccupied, as if suppressing an enormous sadness only by a constant vigilance, by an unceasing act of will.

'What, you're coming here to Munich, tomorrow?'

'There are things I have to talk to you about. Important new things which I think you should hear.'

'What sort of things? About my father, I suppose?'

'About your father, yes.'

She sighed. 'Can't it wait, just a few days more? I need time to think, to sort myself out.'

'I have to see you again.'

There was a long pause, then she breathed, 'I know.' He drew measureless comfort from those two words; from the implication that she too acquiesced in the inevitability of their coming together.

'I love you, Isabella,' he told her.

'Don't say that. Don't say it on the telephone.' She was anguished, breathless. He suddenly realised that she was trying very hard not to cry.

That night he dreamed about the picture. He dreamed about *The Island of the Dead*. He dreamed about the rocky cliff-face and the strange green light. He dreamed about the picture emerging from a suitcase after a long journey. He had expected it to come out in tatters, as he had seen it lying on the slab in the conservation department. But to his horror it emerged intact, magically pristine, its power restored. And then he dreamed about the goldfish. The blackened ones, the flawed ones that had been consigned callously to their own private Buchenwald. They twitched feebly in the water. And somewhere in the distance he heard a man laughing. A cruel, macabre laugh.

And when he awoke early the next morning, before the taxi came to take him to Heathrow, he lay in bed thinking about Tissot. About Tissot and the Commune; about how he had fled a bloody insurrection and arrived in England with a question mark over his name; and how he had found a champion a hundred years later in Alexander Courtney. Such a fervent champion that you wondered what of himself Courtney had seen in Tissot. What private parallels he had needed to construct in order to preserve his self-respect. In the end, Minto supposed, all men deceive themselves. Even the richest and most powerful men.

She had told him not to come till two o'clock, because her husband was leaving at lunchtime, for a three-week tour of America. But somehow his own impatience was ungovernable, and the taxi deposited him at the familiar doorway a few minutes early. As the maid let Minto into the hall of the apartment, he did not immediately recognise the vaguely familiar dark man bending over his suitcases, adjusting a label. Maurbach stood up abruptly, disconcerted by the arrival.

'You are who, please?' He was taller than Minto expected.

'Dominic Maitland. From London.'

'And you have come to see me?'

'No. I have an appointment to see your wife.'

'My wife?' He spoke dully, abruptly losing interest. Minto diagnosed an acute case of self-absorption. Maurbach lifted both cases and added: 'I am sorry that you find me on my way out. So I cannot entertain you. It would have been a pleasure. Dora, where is the car?'

Minto was grateful that the man was unsympathetic. He had deep dark eyes and an arrogant manner, a whining timbre to his voice which endowed even his politenesses with an insulting ring of sarcasm. If you did not believe this man when he told you that he would have liked to give you his hospitality, how could you believe him when he said he loved you?

'Goodbye, Mr Maurbach. Have a good journey,' called Minto after him.

The Filipino shut the door on the departing figure. Excluding Maurbach from his own house. And in the same action drawing Minto in. Enclosing him. The symbolism was suddenly so conspicuous that Minto felt embarrassed in front of the maid.

'Mrs Maurbach in the drawing-room,' she murmured.

She was standing waiting for him, clutching the back of a chair. As he came in she closed her eyes momentarily, as if the sight of him was intolerable, as if looking at him would destroy her. He shut the door behind him and came over to her. She did not resist as he took her into his arms. But he sensed her tension. More than that, he felt something new in her. He sensed her fear.

'God almighty, Minto,' she said. 'What's going to happen to us?'

'It's going to be all right,' he said quietly into her hair.

But he felt her rigid against him. As if she were embracing her own executioner.

'Don't fight it,' he said. 'I love you.'

'You're such a bastard.' He felt it all surging back, her resentment on top of her apprehension.

'Trust me, my darling.'

'Why should I trust you when you'll only make me unhappy?'

'I won't make you unhappy.'

'Oh, Christ. Then I'll make you unhappy. I always do make people unhappy in the end. It's my talent.' She spoke bitterly.

'I won't let you.'

'I wish I could believe you. But I don't. I don't trust you, Minto, don't you understand that about me? I just don't trust you.'

'What do you mean?'

'Why are you here? You've come back here for something, haven't you? Something to do with my father.'

'I've come to see you. Nothing else is as important as that.'

But he felt her panic rising, welling up within her. 'You're looking at something,' she said desperately. 'I can feel it, over my shoulder.' She broke away from him and turned around. 'For God's sake what are you looking at?'

How had she divined it? Although he was barely aware of it himself, it was true. Ever since he had come into the room his gaze had been drawn there, only half-consciously, into the group of photographs on the top of the piano. Seeking one particular example out, drawn irresistibly to it. She followed the direction of his eyes and moved towards the piano in front of him as if to protect it.

'Tell me what you want?' She was almost screaming. 'What are you hoping to find?'

His pause betrayed him.

It was out now. That he was after something. He couldn't deny it. He had to do it now. Speechlessly he pushed past her to reach forward and pick up the photograph he had been trying to remember. The photograph showing Alexander Courtney with his children on the deck of the ship. The boy grinning contentedly in the company of his father. The girl distracted by something on a far horizon. And Alexander Courtney himself, exuding confidence, his lips half parted in a lazy smile.

She leant against his bare leg, the young Isabella Courtney. Against the side of her father's bare calf. When you knew what to look for, it was not hard to see it there, on the calf itself. The unmistakable weal in the flesh. The scar of a bullet wound.

'How did he do that, your father?' demanded Minto. 'How did he get that scar?'

'The scar on his leg?' She looked at him, frightened and uncomprehending. 'He said it was an accident with an air rifle. When he was younger. Why do you ask? Why, Minto? Why is it important?'

Minto sighed. It was almost a relief, now that he knew, now that he was sure. 'Come on,' he said, taking her by the hand and leading her to the sofa, 'you'd better sit down. There are things I have to tell you. Things I want you to know.'

Although it was still only early afternoon, he made her pour them both brandy. She agreed, bemused; and sat there with her elegant, nail-bitten fingers cupped round her glass.

He began with the accident. He judged it better to start there, because that was where the big lie of Alexander Courtney's life had its origin. In the wreckage of the Morris Minor, in the twisted metal and the broken glass. That was where the metamorphosis had taken place. The metamorphosis of Peter Rudolf Kassák, Hungarian refugee and former AVO officer, into Alexander Courtney, young British art dealer of Austrian extraction. Into Alexander Courtney, with an impeccable Jewish pre-war refugee provenance behind him; and a prodigiously successful career in the art world ahead. It was a perfect covering of the tracks, a complete obliteration of the past. And a remarkable piece of quick-thinking opportunism.

He tried to paint the picture for her: of Kassák, the refugee whose papers were not quite in order, the man with a dubious history, the man with something to hide, driving one summer's evening along the innocent north London highway. Driving with the cousin and aunt who had taken him in when he arrived in London in late 1956, an exile whose story was that he had come from Vienna; but an exile whose real origins were murkier, and further east. No doubt Rudolf Kassák, with his dynamism and charm, had by this time begun to dominate his cousin and his aunt. Certainly if the evidence of Miss Fulbrick was to be believed, the Alexander Courtney whom she knew had been a quiet, retiring sort of person; malleable in the hands of a force like Rudolf Kassák. But the Courtneys had one priceless thing which Kassak envied: their status as established British citizens. And one other point should be remembered, went on Minto, because it was to prove important: there was a certain physical family resemblance between the two cousins, between Kassák and Courtney. It was a resemblance noticed from the beginning by Miss Fulbrick and the other residents of Strandwick Mansions.

So when the crash came, when Mrs Courtney's outer tyre burst and the car lurched uncontrollably into the path of Gommersall's lorry, it was Kassák who picked himself up out of the wreckage. Not Courtney. It was Courtney who was lying spread-eagled on the roadway, dead or dying, having been thrown from the car. Kassák's perception of the potential of the situation wasn't quite instantaneous. He gave himself momentarily away to Gommersall by referring to the woman still trapped in the car as his aunt rather than his mother. But afterwards he could pass that slip off as concussion. Because almost at once the opportunity was clear to him. Here was his chance to establish himself at a stroke in England, by taking on the identity of his dying cousin. His cousin's mother would not live to blow the whistle on him. There would be no more trouble with documents. No need to wait seven anxious years for naturalisation which might never come. It was a chance pre-eminently worth taking. So he moved at once to substitute his own papers for those of his cousin Alexander's. And to remove from Alexander's body the proof of an identity which was from now on to be his own.

'What are you saying?' she murmured softly. There was a whiteness to her, a whiteness that extended even to her lips, giving her face a pinched and fearful quality. He poured her a little more brandy and held her hand for a moment.

'I'm saying that your father was a Hungarian refugee who took on the identity of Alexander Courtney.'

'But . . . but how could he get away with it? There must have been other people who would have noticed the change?'

'Maybe your father's greatest gift was his luck. His ability to take risks and get away with them. Circumstances conspired to help him. The Courtneys had just moved house, so their new neighbours didn't yet know them. Kassák – or Alexander Courtney as he now was – must have moved on instantly and started his new life in a different part of London. But he made sure that your aunt was given a decent burial. I've seen the gravestone. And he even put up a small monument to himself next door, although the body buried was that of the original Alexander Courtney. Just to tie up all the last loose ends.'

'How can you be so sure this was what happened?' She was chewing her lip, distraught. On the edge of tears.

'Everything else fits in now as well.'

'Like what? Like what, Minto?'

He'd been going to mention the goldfish. How the joke about Buchenwald would have been hard to credit if Courtney had been Jewish; how it would surely have stuck in his gullet if he had held any loyalty to his Jewish mother, which surely the original Courtney did. But coming from the lips of Kassák, it was plausible, because it was perfectly conceivable that neither of Kassák's parents had been Jewish. But he held back about the goldfish. Instead his eye ran round the room and came to rest on the little picture hanging in the shadow of the curtain. 'Like the Tissot business,' he said. 'That all makes sense now.'

'How do you mean?'

'Well, I've been thinking a lot about it. I think your father did first find out about Tissot from the book you showed me, the one up there with the inscription in it. But that book had originally been given to his cousin, to Alexander Courtney mark one, before Kassák appeared on the scene. Kassák inherited it in 1957 after the accident. And then began this strange process of your father's identification of himself with Tissot. They were both exiles appearing in London after . . . after harrowing experiences in their own countries. Foreigners making their way in English society. But there was a closer parallel once you realise it was Kassák. It explains the obsession with Tissot's behaviour in the Commune. In a way your father saw himself as Tissot; imagined himself falsely identified as one of the rebels. And it seems that just as Tissot was shattered by the experience of the Commune and felt it time to move on, to London, so Kassák felt it time to move on from Hungary. In a way he'd been shattered by his experience of the uprising. In justifying Tissot, he was obliquely justifying himself.' Minto caught himself up. He'd used the word uprising rather than revolution. That was the power of Rudolf. The power of the Alexander Courtney who frightened people. Even from beyond the grave.

She shook her head in wonder. 'But what was his experience of the uprising? What had he done in Hungary?' she asked quietly. 'Was it something terrible?'

Minto thought of Greta lying dead in the snapshot. He thought of Thomas Donat. He thought of *The Island of the*

Dead. 'I'm afraid you have to accept that he ... he was involved in some pretty bad things.'

'Is that where the bullet wound came from? In his leg?'

'Yes. He was shot as he was escaping.'

'And the woman you were talking about in Budapest, the one you think betrayed your friend. Was she something to do with it all?'

Greta. Greta could have been Isabella's mother. Greta was Isabella's father's first wife. He'd had her shot in cold blood.

'Indirectly,' was all Minto could bring himself to say.

'For Christ's sake, Minto, you bastard. You're talking about my father.'

He shrugged. He could not find the words to console her.

And then she turned on him, with narrowed eyes. The colour had returned virulently to her cheeks. 'I don't believe you,' she said loudly. 'I don't believe a word of all this. I refuse to.'

He held her by the wrists. 'You don't believe me because you don't want to believe me. But it's true, Isabella. You have to accept it.'

She wept then, out loud. First against the cushion of the sofa, turned away from him, her shoulders heaving in grief. And then he pulled her to him and she wept in his arms against his chest. Her misery was all-consuming, unbridled, gigantic. He felt impotent in the face of it, like a man who turns on the bathroom tap and is swept away by Niagara. All he could do was gently stroke her hair.

'I'm sorry,' he said at last. 'But it's better you should know.'

Some time later she took a deep breath. She pulled away from him and sat there, straightening her back. He watched her, and felt a surge of desire for her. The earlobes. The line of her neck. The way her nostrils flared. He had never known anyone like her. She was composing herself now. Taking herself in hand. For a moment he caught a glimpse of the enormous strength of will she could bring to bear when she wanted to achieve something. The strength of will she had inherited from her father. The strength of will that Minto suddenly feared, because he sensed it might ultimately break him.

'Listen to me, Minto,' she said. 'Listen very carefully, because this could be the most important thing I ever say to you. Do you remember what I once told you? That if you ever harmed my father's memory I would never forgive you? Do you remember that?'

He nodded.

'Well, it's as true now as it ever was then. I swear to you that if you publish a word of any of this, you're dead as far as I'm concerned. Do you understand that, Minto? Dead. As long as I live I will never see you again. I'll never speak to you again. And I'll never let you near me.'

They sat there for a moment in silence, and a succession of images passed through Minto's mind. Of Thomas Donat, weeping in the hospital bed. Of Greta Kassák's face in the photograph after she had been shot. Of Isabella, his Isabella, with that riven look in her eyes, telling him he was a bastard. Because she loved him. And she wanted him so much that it frightened her.

As he took her in his arms once more and they clung to each other, Minto realised that he had come to the end of a road. That he was entering territory he had never known before.

21

It was December, and the first really cold evening of the year. Minto hurried through the knots of frenzied late-night shoppers heading for Oxford Street, and ran up the steps to the Royal Gallery. It was warmer inside and he left his coat in the hall before being directed through to the German room by a security guard. 'The party's in there, sir. Quite a turn-out tonight.' The man's face was familiar; small and round and fat and a trifle unctuous.

The first person he met inside was Ridley.

'Hello, old boy. Didn't know you were coming.'

'I thought I'd look in.'

'Better get yourself a drink before it runs out. They're such stingy buggers, these public galleries.'

'Taxpayers' money, I guess.'

Ridley nodded thoughtfully. 'I suppose we should count ourselves lucky it isn't a pay bar.' He gave a little bitter laugh. He'd taken some trouble with his appearance tonight: he'd found a shirt with clean cuffs and a collar that wasn't frayed. On the whole he looked better than he had done in the summer. His face was less mottled. Perhaps winter suited him. Now he said: 'Seen much of the Gorgon of Glasgow recently?'

'The Gorgon of Glasgow?'

'Elaine McBride. The face that lunched a thousand shits. Our revered leader.'

'No, not so much. I'm keeping my head down these days.'

'That's the way, old boy. That's the way.'

Elaine McBride.

I got it all wrong, he'd told her. It was a complete misunderstanding. I put two and two together and made five. She'd looked at him oddly. 'Are you telling me that after all this there's no story?' All rumour, Elaine, it hadn't got the legs. Idle speculation. We'd have been in the shit if we'd run it, we'd have had the legal boys after us.

In the end it hadn't been so difficult to cobble together the article on Alexander Courtney. From the old material. It was the piece Ridley would have written, recycling the press releases. How Courtney had been the greatest dealer of his generation. About his charm. About his *coups*. About his heritage work. About the way he'd built up people's collections for them, collections like Leslie Marriott's. Too bad that Leslie Marriott had turned out to be a crook, but thanks to Courtney he'd still bought some wonderful pictures, including the Böcklin. The Böcklin which had been so tragically mutilated. It was simply a tragedy. And now, thanks to the sterling work of the Royal Gallery's conservation department, a tragedy with a happy ending.

'Look, Minto,' Winter had said one evening late that summer. Man to man, over a whisky and soda, in a conversation they could later both deny had ever happened. 'It wouldn't stand up. You know it, I know it. After all, what's the real evidence? A photograph of an old gunshot wound in a man's calf? The ramblings of a seventy-five-year-old lorry driver nearly forty years on? A lorry driver who on his own admission was concussed at the time? All the other witnesses are dead. It's utter hypothesis, sheer speculation. No one would believe it.'

'Maybe. But it happens to be true.'

'It happens to be true.' Winter had repeated the words slowly, carefully, giving each one due weight. Not so much in agreement with their message. More in its gentle valediction.

'You knew, though, didn't you?' Minto had persisted. 'You knew all along.'

Winter had sat there smiling at him, cradling his drink. Not denying it.

'And did Max know too?'

For a moment Winter had remained silent; then he said

softly: 'Max knows. But he'd rather not admit it to himself. That's the only way he can get by, you see.'

'What about Denton?'

'No. As it turned out, that alcoholic old pansy knew nothing. But it was better that he should be restrained from making wild accusations that he might later regret. I'm sure you'll understand the advisability of that, Minto.'

Then Winter had shrugged, given an abrupt little laugh, and stood up to go. To indicate the subject was exhausted. To signal the matter was closed.

'Remember old Courtney's memorial service?' mused Ridley now. 'In the summer?'

Minto nodded. Everything seemed to lead back there in the end.

'All this carry-on here tonight, it reminds me a bit of that memorial service.'

Minto scanned the people milling about the German room, talking and laughing. The art world at a party. He thought back to that stifling afternoon in St James's Piccadilly. 'Probably much the same guest list,' he suggested.

'On the other hand I suppose that what's being commemorated here is rather the reverse of what was going on then.'

'How do you mean?'

'Well, then someone had died. Now what's being celebrated is a rebirth. A bringing back to life.'

'Oh, the picture you mean?'

Ridley nodded reflectively. '*The Island of the Dead* being raised from the dead,' he declared. The conceit seemed to please him and he gave a throaty little cackle.

'Quite a triumph, don't you agree?' interrupted the corpulent figure who had just joined them. Minto looked up to see Michael Thornton-Bass beaming at him. He exuded self-satisfaction, as if the gathering were entirely in his own honour. 'An extraordinary feat of restoration, isn't it?'

'Amazing.'

'When you and I, Mr Maitland, stood in front of the wreckage of that picture, what, barely six months ago, I little expected ever again to see it looking the way it

does today. Have you had a chance to examine it carefully?'

Minto contemplated him. Thornton-Bass buoyant was even
less appealing than Thornton-Bass depressed. 'No,' he said,
'not yet.'

Thornton-Bass peered over in the direction of the wall
where the picture had been rehung. Several people were
clustered round it. 'It's miraculous. We thought a party of
celebration was in order. Hence this.'

Minto hadn't yet allowed his own eyes to dwell too long
on the reconstituted canvas. Now he was here, he was not
sure if he wanted to get too close to it. 'I'll take a look at
it later,' he said. 'When the crowds have thinned out.'

'You must,' declared Thornton-Bass. 'And have you thought
about doing a follow-up article? I read your first piece, you
know.' He made the pronouncement coyly, as if his mere
perusal of someone else's writing was a supreme accolade.

'Maybe.'

Thornton-Bass paused, apparently disturbed for a moment
by some distant echo from the past. Then he added, philo-
sophically: 'I suppose even in the best-ordered societies there
is no legislating for the occasional maniac. I wonder what's
happened to the attacker? Or didn't I hear somewhere that
he'd died, quite soon afterwards?'

'Did you hear that?' said Minto. 'I'm afraid I really don't
know any more about him. I lost touch with the story.'

Later, as he wandered round the room, he met Max Courtney.

'How are you, Minto? Doing OK?'

'Fine, thanks.' He nodded at the squat, smartly suited figure.
He wasn't so bad, old Max, once you got to know him.

It hadn't been so difficult to come to terms with Max. Not
after that day in August when an unknown motorist had
walked into Putney police station and given himself up to
the duty sergeant. Apparently the man hadn't been able to
live with himself any longer. He'd been the driver of the car
that had hit the old geezer early one Sunday evening four
weeks before. As God was his witness, he hadn't stood a
chance. The old boy was in a dream, completely out of it,

just stepped straight into the road in front of him without looking. But after smashing into him he'd panicked and driven off. He didn't know why he hadn't waited. He'd been in shock, he supposed. But now he couldn't go on. Not with that on his conscience.

This was no hit-man. Minto had checked. This was some poor weak-willed bastard suffering the protracted consequences of a moment's unthinking cowardice. The cowardice whose revelation made it possible for Minto tonight to shake Max's hand; if not with enthusiasm, then at least without distaste.

Max said now: 'Someone told me Isabella's in town for a few days. Seen anything of her?'

'I'm meeting her for dinner tonight.'

Max nodded benignly, touched his arm and moved on.

Minto looked at his watch. It was time to go. She would be waiting outside for him in the car, as they had arranged.

'Are you sure you don't want to come?' he had asked her.

'No, I hate that sort of party.'

'Not just for half an hour?'

'Absolutely not. But I'll pick you up afterwards. Eight forty-five. OK?'

Tonight was the night when he was going to broach it. About her finally leaving Munich and coming to live with him in London. Give it three months, she'd said. Let's see how we both feel then. Let's not rush it. We've been through a lot, we've got to have a chance to sort ourselves out. Well, it was five months now and he knew how he felt. Nothing had changed. He'd suffered no compulsion to test the uncoupling mechanism of their relationship. Quite the reverse, in fact: he still ached for her, still panicked at the thought of losing her. It was time for her to come to him.

She was easier now. More relaxed. Not so brittle, not so resentful. What had he once told her? The day you stop resenting me is the day I'll know you're going off me. A stupid thing to say, really.

He put his glass down on a tray and prepared to leave. But

for an instant he paused. He wavered, and was tempted. He had caught a glimpse of the picture out of the corner of his eye and suddenly he knew he must go back to it one more time. To test himself before it. A sad old man had died under its influence, but it was only paint on canvas, for God's sake. Only paint on canvas.

A sad old man. For a moment he felt Donat's hand in his own again. He saw him weeping inconsolably in the hospital bed. He remembered Greta's battered photograph, and Alexander Courtney's hard, unyielding eyes. For a moment the wave of revived grief threatened to sweep him away. But Minto braced himself. He had made his decision. His duty was to the living, not to the dead.

And then he was in front of the painting, staring at it, trying to break its spell. Trying to defuse it by dismantling it, separating off its various elements and thereby reducing their power. There were the cypresses. There was the rocky cliff. And up there the birds circled. His eyes lingered on the empty tomb, and then the boat with its white-shrouded passenger. Finally he sought out the skull. The death's-head that Thomas Donat's knife had inexplicably left intact.

'Not my favourite picture,' said the man standing next to him. Minto looked up and saw Theo Denton. Denton in the inevitable crew-neck jersey and denim jacket, with thin little spectacles on a cord about his neck. Denton pursing his lips in disapproval.

'But an amazing piece of restoration,' muttered Minto. As he spoke, he kept staring into the painting. He suddenly didn't want to meet Denton's eyes. In case they were mocking him. In case they demanded some silent acknowledgement of their mutual compromise.

'I don't know why they bothered, dear heart,' intoned Denton, massaging his neck and peering into his wineglass. 'Do you?'

Minto shrugged, smiled briefly in Denton's direction, and walked on to the door.